**She saw the man leaning in the doorway of the house next to hers, watching.**

Matt. Her heart fluttered, and her cheeks flushed. Hurt battled anger that he'd finally shown his face, after a full week of avoiding her like the plague.

Like a furry traitor, her dog Sadie leaped toward him. Matt bent to greet her, rubbing her neck as she bathed him in kisses, her tail a blur of excitement.

Well, at least someone was kissing him. Cara's face heated. Of all the men in the world, why did Matt have to be the one Sadie trusted?

He stood and faced her, then nodded toward the For Sale sign in her front yard. "Going somewhere?"

"Somewhere I can have dogs." She didn't even try to keep the bitterness from her tone.

His cocoa eyes fixed on hers again, steady and intent. Reluctantly, she closed the distance between them to pick up the end of Sadie's leash. Up close, she could smell his all-too-familiar scent: soap and sandalwood and man. Memories of their romp in the hot tub splashed unbidden through her mind. Bubbles and mind-blowing sex. The most wonderful night of her life. And he hadn't spoken to her since . . .

# UNLEASHED

## RACHEL LACEY

FOREVER

NEW YORK   BOSTON

Copyright © 2014 by Rachel Lacey
Excerpt from *For Keeps* copyright © 2014 by Rachel Lacey

Forever
Hachette Book Group
1290 Avenue of the Americas
New York, NY 10104

www.HachetteBookGroup.com

Printed in the United States of America

First Edition: October 2014

10 9 8 7 6 5 4 3 2 1

OPM

Forever is an imprint of Grand Central Publishing.
The Forever name and logo are trademarks of Hachette Book Group, Inc.

The publisher is not responsible for websites (or their content) that are not owned by the publisher.

The Hachette Speakers Bureau provides a wide range of authors for speaking events. To find out more, go to www.hachettespeakersbureau.com or call (866) 376-6591.

*In memory of my mom. This one's for you.*

# ACKNOWLEDGMENTS

I owe a huge debt to my family for their love and support while I chased what at times seemed an impossible dream. Endless thanks to my husband and son for supporting me on this journey. To my sister, Juliana, for being an amazing person, the best sister in the world, and a wealth of information on dog training. And to my own rescue boxer, Lacy, for inspiring me to write about Cara and her foster dogs.

Thank you to my amazing agent, Sarah Younger, for helping my dreams come true. You came into my life at a very crazy time and gave me so much to be thankful for. To my fabulous editor, Alex Logan, thank you for sharing your immeasurable knowledge with me. I feel incredibly lucky to have your guidance.

I'm nothing without my many friends in the writing community. To my "critters," Annie Rains, Nancy LaPonzina, and Eleanor Tatum, thank you for many late-night plotting sessions and your invaluable feedback and friendship. And to my "Romance Rookies," Joy McConnell, Peta Crake, and Monica Prejean, I couldn't have done it without you.

Thank you to Will Goodwin for answering my many medical questions. And a huge thank-you to all the friends who supported me along the way. You believed in me when I said I wanted to be an author, and that means everything to me. Love you all!

# UNLEASHED

# 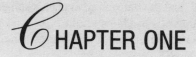HAPTER ONE

Cara Medlen felt the growl before she heard it, rumbling against her leg from the dog tensed at her side. She jiggled the leash to break his concentration. "Easy, Casper. You may not realize it yet, but today's your lucky day."

He looked up at her with dull eyes, one brown, one blue. A jagged scar creased his face. Ribs and hip bones jutted through his mangy white coat. And, oh boy, did he stink. Cara had yet to meet an ugly boxer, but Casper...well, he had the sort of face that made people cross to the other side of the street.

That same face grabbed at a tender spot in her heart.

"It's a blessing that Triangle Boxer Rescue can take him," the woman behind the desk, a volunteer named Helen, said. "Shelter life hasn't been good for him."

Cara nodded as she handed the signed paperwork to Helen. "I've worked with a lot of dogs like Casper. I'm sure we'll have him ready for adoption in no time."

But the warning she'd received from her homeowners' association over the summer weighed heavily on her mind: Keep her foster dogs in line or face disciplinary action by the board.

The door to the kennels opened, allowing raucous barking to spill into the lobby. Casper peered around her and fixed his gaze on the man who'd come through the door. His ears flattened, and the hair raised along his spine.

Yep, this dog was trouble all right.

Cara sidestepped to block his view. "Thanks, Helen. Happy New Year."

With a quick wave, she hustled Casper out the front door. He tucked his tail against the cold air, then raised his nose and sniffed the sweet scent of freedom. He slunk onto the brown patchy grass of the shelter's front lawn and raised his leg on a tree.

When he'd finished, she loaded him into the backseat of her little blue Mazda. She smoothed her hands over her black dress, wrinkled since the funeral by hours in the car and now covered in Casper's white fur. The ache in her chest rose up, squeezing her throat, and she shoved it back.

Later, she'd grieve. Now she needed to get Casper home.

She swung into the front seat and cranked the engine. "So, you've officially been sprung from doggy jail."

He gave her a wary look, then turned his head to stare out the window. She pulled onto High Street and took the ramp to Interstate 85, headed for her townhouse in Dogwood, a small town on the outskirts of Raleigh, North Carolina.

"But listen, no more shenanigans, okay?"

Casper cocked his head, his mismatched eyes somber.

"One of my fosters growled at my neighbor's dog, and she filed a complaint against me with the homeowners' association, so I need you to be on your best behavior."

With a dramatic sigh, he sprawled across the backseat and closed his eyes. Well, she'd take that as a yes. She'd put in a few extra hours of behavior training with him in the meantime, just to be sure. Casper slept for the next hour as Cara drove them home.

The latest Taylor Swift single strummed happily from inside her purse, and she shoved a hand inside to grab her cell phone. Merry Atwater's name showed on the display. "Hey, Merry."

"Hey. Just wanted to see how you're holding up," Merry said. "I've been thinking about you all day."

Cara tightened her grip on the steering wheel, blinking away the image of Gina's pale face inside the casket. "I'm okay, or I will be."

"Oh, sweetie, I'm so sorry. Let me know if there's anything I can do. Are you still planning to go out tonight?"

"Yeah, I'll be there, just maybe late. Casper and I have some acquainting to do."

"How is he?" Merry shifted into her professional voice. As the founder of Triangle Boxer Rescue, she had a vested interest in every dog they saved. Cara had no idea where she found the time to run a rescue on top of her day job as a pediatric nurse, but Merry somehow managed to juggle the two.

"Well, he's only growled twice so far." Cara glanced over her shoulder with a smile. Casper watched, his head on his front paws.

"What happened? The shelter didn't mention aggression."

Cara flipped on her blinker and exited the highway onto Fullers Church Road. "I think he's just stressed out. I'm not too worried about it. What time should I meet you at Red Heels?"

"Why don't I come over to your place and we can get ready together? I'll help you get Casper settled, and we can talk."

"Sounds great, Mer, thanks."

"You bet. See you around seven."

Cara shoved the phone back into her purse. Truthfully, the last thing she wanted to do tonight was go to a New

Year's Eve party, but she refused to sit home and feel sorry for herself. She'd go, and she'd even have fun, dammit.

It was what Gina would have wanted.

She pulled into the parking lot of Crestwood Gardens, her townhouse community, and guided her Mazda into its assigned spot, right next to her sexy next-door neighbor's shiny black Jeep Grand Cherokee. The man in question stood in his front yard, deep in conversation with a perky brunette in tight jeans and a low-cut sweater.

Cara felt a twinge of something like jealousy, which was ridiculous because she didn't even know his name. And she'd prefer to keep it that way. She shut off the engine and hurried to fetch Casper from the backseat. "Welcome home, dude."

He hopped down, tail tucked. It had been a long and difficult day for both of them. Time to get settled in and relax for a while.

One of her neighbors—Chuck Something-or-other—passed with a nod as Cara headed toward her townhouse. She offered a polite smile, her attention focused on Casper. The dog looked up at the older man. Their eyes met. The hair along Casper's spine raised, and he released a low, guttural growl that sent Chuck scrambling into the parking lot.

Cara swore under her breath as she shoved the key into the lock and pushed open her front door.

So much for making a good first impression on the neighbors.

* * *

Matt Dumont scrubbed a hand over his jaw as his Realtor snapped one last photo of the front of his townhouse. He watched peripherally as his elusive next-door neighbor scrambled through her front door with the mangy, miserable-looking dog who'd just growled at Chuck Sawyer.

It was a different damn dog than he'd seen in her yard last week.

In fact, from what he'd seen, there was a veritable parade of dogs in and out of her home, many of them looking rough, although this one had to be the worst. Matt didn't have much of an eye for dog breeds, but it looked like a pit bull from where he was standing.

He was starting to think something shady was going on next door.

"The listing will be live later tonight. It shows well, so I'm hopeful it will sell relatively quickly." Stephanie Powell pocketed her camera and pulled a red-and-white For Sale sign from her trunk.

He shifted his attention to the business at hand. "Mind if I do the honors?"

"Go ahead." She held it out.

Matt gripped the sign. With a grunt, he shoved the signpost through the grass and into the hard, red clay beneath. At least here in North Carolina the ground was still pliable at the end of December. Boston's frigid winters would be a readjustment.

But he could snowboard again. Yeah, he missed snowboarding, and skiing, and his mom's homemade meatballs. He was ready to go home.

He nudged the sign, then wiggled it a little farther into the earth. Satisfied it wasn't going anywhere, he turned to Stephanie. "All set, then."

She nodded. "I'll be in touch, and hopefully we'll have some showings scheduled for you in the next week."

"Great, Stephanie. Thanks." He shook her hand and headed for the front door of his townhouse, his thoughts again turning to the girl next door and her odd collection of dogs.

Matt knew most of his neighbors, was friendly with all of

them, yet she remained a mystery. He didn't even know her name. Perhaps that was why her face sometimes occupied his mind as he passed the long nights on surveillance.

His cell phone rang, and he swiped it from his back pocket. Felicity Prentiss. Shit.

"Mrs. Prentiss," he said as he strode toward his front door.

"I'm having second thoughts." Her voice was taut with nervous energy.

Matt held in a groan. He'd known when he met her yesterday that she was going to be a pain in the ass. Probably, he should have turned her down, but this job would bring in a lot of billable hours, extra cash to tide him over while he got things going up in Boston.

But honestly, Felicity Prentiss was one of the most uptight clients he'd ever worked with. Since she'd hired him yesterday, she'd already called five times, looking for updates, reassurances, and advice.

The woman needed someone to hold her hand. And that was not his job.

Not her husband's, either, since she had enlisted Matt's investigative services to secure evidence of his adultery for their divorce proceedings.

"I'll be honest with you, Mrs. Prentiss. I've never worked one of these cases where it turned out the spouse wasn't cheating. You want proof, I'll get it for you. You want to call it off, tell me now before there's no going back."

On the other end of the line, she sucked in a shaky breath. "I do want to know—I *need* to know. But what if he sees you? He'd kill me if he knew I'd had him followed."

Matt closed and locked the front door behind him. "He won't see me. Is your husband violent, Mrs. Prentiss?"

"No." A long pause, then a sigh. "No, he's a sweet and gentle man, or at least I thought he was until I caught him sneaking into the house in the middle of the night smelling of another woman's perfume."

"All right, then. Let me do my job. I'll get what you need for the lawsuit, and your husband will be none the wiser. Don't worry."

"It's just... with the New Year and all, I'm ready to get on with my life, you know?"

Did he ever. Matt flipped on the overhead light and sank into his leather recliner. "I do, and you will. Since you'll be with him tonight, I plan to start surveillance tomorrow. Shouldn't take more than a week, maybe two."

Felicity Prentiss hoped to file an "alienation of affection" lawsuit, taking advantage of an outdated law in North Carolina that allowed a wife to sue her husband's lover. The problem was that Felicity couldn't file for divorce from her philandering husband until the necessary evidence had been gathered.

Matt planned to get the evidence she needed for her lawsuit and her divorce proceedings as quickly as possible. Because once he closed this case, he was going home.

He headed upstairs to log some background information on the Prentisses in his office. It always paid to know whose closets you were poking around in before you brought out the high-powered lens. A loud bark drew him toward the window in the hall, from which he had a decent view of his next-door neighbor's backyard.

Enough to see her outside with the white dog and another larger brown dog. She'd changed from her black dress and pumps into an ice-blue jacket and dark-colored jeans that hugged a shapely figure. Her hair was the color of his fantasies, somewhere between blond and red, a delicious apricot that shone in the sun with soft waves that brushed her shoulders.

As he watched, the white dog snarled. The brown dog

hesitated a moment, then they were on each other like a couple of wild animals, growling and snapping. The sound made the hair on the back of his neck rise.

Blood streaked the white dog's fur.

Holy shit. Was his pretty golden-haired neighbor training fighting dogs?

With a grunt of disgust, Matt stepped away from the window. It was time for them to finally meet, because there was no way in hell he was going to look the other way if she was mistreating those dogs.

* * *

The dogs were fighting.

"Hey!" Cara clapped her hands and shouted, making as much noise as she could. Casper slunk off to hide behind a bush. Mojo trotted over, looking sheepish.

Cara knelt and ran her hands over him, checking for injury. She suspected the skirmish had been more bark than bite, but with Mojo's dark fur, it was hard to be sure, and she'd seen blood on Casper.

Mojo sat, tongue lolling, tail wagging, as she checked him out. Blood oozed from the gum behind his left incisor. With any luck, that was the source of the blood she'd seen on Casper. She shooed Mojo inside, then coaxed the frightened white boxer from behind the bush.

"Easy, Casper." She dabbed at the blood streaking his fur, and it came off on her fingers. He watched her with those unnervingly solemn, mismatched eyes. Other than Mojo's bloody slobber, he was unharmed.

*Thank God.* Cara plopped down on the grass at Casper's side, her legs rubbery, heart pounding. "You are not good for my adrenaline levels, you know that?"

Casper was going to take some work. He'd come into the

shelter as a stray, and he would need time to feel comfortable again as part of a family, if he ever had been. He wasn't a mean dog, just frightened and defensive. He lay beside Cara now, head between his front paws, weary eyes glazed.

In retrospect, she shouldn't have offered treats in front of both dogs so soon. Mojo had sniffed at Casper's cookie, and Casper had defended what was his. Resource guarding wasn't unusual for a dog like Casper, who'd been on his own for a while. Cara had made a rookie mistake. She was distracted today, but that was no excuse.

Mojo whined from the other side of the door. Casper watched, his posture relaxed.

She stood and opened the back door, keeping a close eye on her troublemaking canines. Mojo trotted out, nuzzled Cara's hand, and took off across the yard in search of a ball. After a moment, Casper got to his feet and followed him. Mojo spun around him, his front legs pressed to the earth, tail up, as he invited Casper to play.

*That's more like it.* Cara breathed a sigh of relief. She shoved her hands into the pockets of her jeans to ward off the cold breeze as she watched them.

Mojo was a funny-looking dog with brown brindle stripes that darkened to black along his back. He had a sturdy body, full tail, and a face thicker than a full-blooded boxer. No one knew what he was mixed with, but something in his coloration and stance suggested German shepherd to Cara. No matter his heritage, he was all fun, the most laid-back, well-mannered foster she'd ever had.

After watching Mojo try in vain for several minutes to get Casper to play, she headed for the house, chilled from too long outside in only a thin jacket. The dogs bounded ahead and waited for her at the sliding glass door.

"Lead the way, Mojo," she told the brown dog. His tail beat the vinyl siding as she opened the door, then he scrambled across the kitchen to check his bowl, as if the dog food fairy might have filled it while they were playing outside. "In a little while. Let's get Casper settled in first."

Despite his emaciated appearance, Casper had been well fed at the shelter for the past three days, and she didn't want him to get sick from eating before his nervous stomach settled. Cara flipped on the gas fireplace, then led the way upstairs.

Casper tucked his tail as he followed her into the master bedroom.

"It'll be a while before we make it up here tonight, I'm afraid. It's New Year's Eve, and I'm going out. But I wanted you to see it first in the daylight. You can join Mojo and me in the big bed." She eyed his soiled fur, then grabbed an old sheet and spread it over her pink-flowered comforter. Before she went out tonight, he definitely needed a bath.

She kept talking, knowing that her calm voice and demeanor, as well as Mojo's, would put Casper more quickly at ease. She sat on the bed and patted it, inviting them up. Mojo leaped up and made himself at home, while Casper stood anxiously at her feet. She told him all about tonight's party while stroking his chin until, with a shy wag of his nub, he hopped up on her other side.

"That's a good boy." She lay back and closed her eyes, a dog on each side.

What was better than that? Maybe she'd take a quick nap before Merry arrived. Gina's funeral had left her drained.

The chiming of the doorbell sent Casper into fits of hysterical barking. He launched himself off the bed and ran a lap around the bedroom. Mojo jumped down and headed for the hall, his bark mixing with Casper's as both dogs raced downstairs.

Cara glanced at her watch as she hurried after them. Merry wasn't due for another two hours. Whoever it was had lousy timing.

She sprinted into the kitchen and grabbed a handful of peanut-butter dog biscuits from the counter.

"Come, Casper." She used the biscuits as a lure, and the dog crept into his crate, still eyeing the front door with suspicion. She rewarded him with a handful of peanut-butter yummies, then draped the crate with a thick blanket, hoping the darkness would help calm him.

The doorbell pealed again. Casper's booming bark filled the room, accompanied by the sound of his body slamming into the metal bars of the crate. So much for calm.

"Shhh," Cara whispered, then hurried toward the front door. "Coming."

Mojo stood in the hallway, tail wagging in anticipation of their visitor.

Without pausing to check the peephole, she yanked the door open, then gaped at the man standing there. He filled her doorway, tall and solid in worn jeans and a black leather jacket. Dark brown hair was pushed back from his forehead with a slight wave. His brown eyes settled on hers, and a little ping of warmth traveled through her.

"Matt Dumont. I live next door." He jerked his head toward the townhouse to the left of hers.

Cara nodded. Oh yeah, she knew who he was, and she'd been doing her best to avoid him for the past year. Well, now she had a name to put with the face formerly known as "Mr. FMH," a term she and her friend Olivia had coined back in college for a guy that was "fuck me hot." Matt sure was, not that she had any intention of acting on it.

She glanced down at herself, painfully aware of the streak of bloody slobber on her shirtsleeve and the way she was panting for breath after wrangling an uncooperative sixty-pound boxer into his crate. Of course, if they had to meet after all this time, she'd be a mess.

She pasted on the sweetest smile she could muster as

Casper growled from the kitchen. "Nice to meet you. I'm Cara Medlen."

"'Bout time I knew your name, don't you think?" The corner of his mouth hitched in amusement as those cocoa eyes searched hers. He was even more handsome up close, staring at her like that, so intense she almost forgot to breathe.

"I guess so."

"So, what's the story with your dogs, Cara?"

She sucked in a breath. "What story?"

His eyes narrowed, less warm now. "You tell me."

She crossed her arms over her chest. What was it with her neighbors and their closed-mindedness about her foster dogs? "We haven't broken any rules, Mr. Dumont, so if you don't mind…"

She moved to close the front door, but he stepped forward, blocking her. "Actually, I do mind."

Cara felt the force of his stare right down to her coral-painted toenails.

"The white dog—is he receiving some kind of medical treatment?"

He was so close now she could smell the faint scent of his aftershave. Too close, but she refused to give him the satisfaction of backing away. She straightened her spine, wishing for a few more inches so she could glare at him without having to look up. "What exactly are you suggesting?"

"I can see into your backyard from my upstairs hallway." He tilted his head. "I think I know what's going on here."

Cara scrunched her nose. What in the world was he accusing her of, mowing her lawn in the wrong direction? Crap, had he been watching last week when she tripped over Mojo and fell in a pile of dog poop? She'd stripped out of her jeans right there in the backyard and run inside half naked. Her cheeks burned. "Perhaps you should be more specific."

He glanced down at the dog at her feet. Mojo sat, ears

back, his shoulder against Cara's left leg. A crash echoed from the kitchen as Casper thrashed in his crate. "You fighting these dogs, Ms. Medlen?"

She couldn't help it; she snorted with laughter at the absolute absurdity of his accusation. "Are you serious?"

Matt pinned her in his laser-like gaze, looking deadly serious. "That a pit bull?"

"A boxer. Thank you for your concern, Mr. Dumont, but maybe next time you should mind your own business."

And with that, she slammed the door in his face.

# 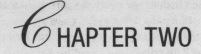HAPTER TWO

$\mathcal{T}$he heel of Cara's brand-new silver Vera Wang pump sank deep into a wad of gum and stuck. That's what she got for splurging on designer shoes.

"Ack!" She grabbed Merry's elbow as she jerked her heel free. She lifted the shoe for inspection and frowned at the gooey coating left behind.

Merry looked down at Cara's heel and shook her head. "First stop, the ladies' room. We'll get you cleaned up."

"It better come off. I never should have let you talk me into buying these shoes." She felt frivolous wearing them now, on the day her friend was laid to rest.

"But they're sparkly and adorable, and you never splurge on yourself. And how awesome would it be if we met a couple of hot guys tonight to help us ring in the New Year?"

Maybe Merry had a point. Cara dressed up and went out about as often as—okay, she hadn't since last New Year's Eve. As for hot guys, well, Matt Dumont came to mind, but she sure as hell wouldn't be kissing *him* at midnight. She scuffed her sticky heel against the pavement.

Anyway, despite a lousy start to the day, she was determined to end the year on a positive note. Red Heels was her favorite restaurant, and she was ready to toss back a pomegranate martini, or three.

They stepped inside, taking in the soft, pink lighting and bluesy music thumping. Oh, yeah. Cara's shoulders loosened, and her toe tapped to the beat.

"I'm starved." She glanced around for the buffet tables as they made their way toward the hostess desk.

The girl behind the desk looked up, her eyes wide with apology. "I'm so sorry. We stopped serving food at nine. There was an electrical problem in the kitchen. We'll refund your ticket price, whether or not you decide to stay. There are light hors d'oeuvres, and the bar's open until two."

Merry tucked a strand of curly brown hair behind her ear. "Well, damn."

"Blame it on Casper," Cara said. She and her friend had spent the past hours sitting in her living room with the dog while he adjusted to his newfound freedom.

Merry tapped a finger against her lips. "We could go over to Finnegan's and grab a burger, then come back for martinis before midnight?"

Cara nodded. "Deal. Because light hors d'oeuvres aren't going to cut it."

They turned around and walked back out into the night. Cara wrapped her arms around herself. Her wool peacoat was warm enough, but it left her bare legs exposed to the biting wind from the knees down.

Country music bled into the night from Finnegan's Pub two doors down. Merry pushed through the door ahead of Cara and straight into the throng of people inside.

Cara gazed longingly at the packed tables as they made their way toward the bar. "It's ten-thirty on New Year's Eve and we're trying to get a burger? This is hopeless."

"We'll order them to go. If we can't find a spot to eat,

we'll carry them back to Red Heels. They can't complain if they're not feeding us themselves, right?" Merry, as usual, refused to let anything step on her good time.

She shoved her way up to the bar and ordered two bacon cheeseburgers with fries. Cara shrugged out of her coat and draped it over her arm, then glanced around for a spot for them to stand or, better yet, sit.

The bar was packed. Off to the left were several pool tables, all occupied, and rather loudly at that. Her gaze settled on a familiar profile at the first table. He wore a long-sleeved, navy blue Henley shirt tucked into what might be the same worn jeans he'd had on earlier, when he'd shown up at her front door.

As he leaned forward to line up a shot, Cara was treated to a view of his shapely buns. She scowled.

"Merry." She poked her friend to get her attention. "That's him."

"Him? Who?" Merry turned from the bar, her hazel eyes following Cara's to the pool table in the corner.

"Matt Dumont."

"FMH guy?"

"Yeah. FMH guy who accused me of fighting my dogs."

Merry snickered. "I wish I could have seen that."

They watched Matt for a moment as he shot a red ball into the side pocket.

"But damn if he isn't hot," Merry said.

*No kidding.* "I saw a For Sale sign in front of his place this afternoon, so I guess he won't be my problem for long." Cara stepped back and felt her left shoe stick to the polished wood floor. "I forgot I had gum on my shoe. I'll be right back."

Merry nodded. "I'll try to snag us a few inches at the bar to eat our burgers."

Cara made her way toward the back, jostled by boisterous partygoers. Someone's beer splashed her right foot, cold and sticky.

"You've got to be kidding me," she muttered. She was never again spending more than forty bucks on a pair of shoes.

"Not trying to sneak out the back, are you?" A familiar voice spoke behind her as a warm male hand settled on her elbow, guiding her through the crowd.

Cara glanced over her shoulder and into Matt's brown eyes. Her spine stiffened. "And risk missing another enlightening conversation with you? Not a chance."

"Yeah? At least there's not a door for you to slam in my face this time." He pinned her in his gaze with an unnerving intensity, and her silly heart pounded with more enthusiasm than it had any reason to.

"Actually, there is." She smiled brightly as they reached the restrooms, and she closed the door to the ladies' room behind her.

* * *

Matt glared at the second door Cara Medlen had slammed in his face today. She was infuriating, irritatingly cute, and he really wanted to like her. He'd had a chance to think it over and was open to the possibility that he had jumped to the wrong conclusion when he'd confronted her earlier.

She'd pretty much laughed in his face when he accused her of fighting her dogs, which suggested innocence, but she'd been deliberately cagey in answering his questions. And that, in his experience, pointed to guilt. If there was a reasonable explanation for what he'd observed in her backyard, why didn't she just tell him?

Determined to find out, he planted himself in the hall across from the restrooms, arms crossed over his chest.

Several minutes later, the door opened and she stepped out, her eyes widening when she saw him there waiting for her. She looked good enough to eat in a slinky green dress that favored her strawberry-blond curls and revealed plenty of smooth, pale skin. His gaze slid down to her silver heels.

Sexy.

"A little overdressed for Finnegan's, aren't you?" He grinned, crossing one foot over the other as she frowned up at him.

"Yeah, well, I won't be staying long." She attempted to brush past him.

Matt shoved off the wall, putting himself directly in her way. "In a hurry?"

"As a matter of fact. Do you mind?"

"Need to get back to your friend, or afraid of being alone with me?" He stepped closer, deliberately crowding her. She smelled sweet, like honeysuckle. Her blue eyes locked on his, and desire curled in his belly.

She lifted her chin. "Afraid? Hardly."

Matt stared down at her, using his full six feet two inches to tower over her approximate five foot four. "So what's the deal with your dogs, Cara?"

Cara's freckles stood out as her cheeks darkened. "What is it with you and my dogs? If you're so concerned, call animal control."

She pushed past him and marched toward the crowded bar, her back to him.

Matt watched her go. He didn't like her attitude one bit. Hell, he'd never been face-to-face with an animal abuser. Maybe they came in middle-class, really cute packages these days.

One way or another, he intended to find out. If she didn't want to talk, he'd just do a little investigating of his own.

The bar floor shook with some country tune about spilled beer and a girl in cowboy boots. He'd been in Dogwood for five years, and country music still made his ears bleed. That was his only complaint about Finnegan's, though. The place was always packed, plenty of local beer on tap, and pool tables to cut loose with some of his buddies at the end of a long day.

Not a bad way to see in the New Year.

He glanced one last time at Cara. She'd wedged herself in next to her friend at the bar. If looks could kill, he'd be greasing the floor about now. He shrugged and walked back to his table.

"She's cute," Jack commented as he smoothed chalk over his cue. "Who is she?"

As a fellow private investigator, it didn't surprise Matt that he'd noticed her. They got paid to notice every detail.

"My next-door neighbor."

Jack grinned. "Doesn't look like she likes you much."

"Nope." Matt reached into his pocket to check his cell phone, out of habit. He doubted any of his clients would need to reach him tonight of all nights, but in his line of work, you never knew.

The phone showed two missed calls from his mom. It was past eleven now, but she'd be sitting on the couch with a bag of popcorn and a flute of champagne, watching the ball drop in Times Square.

He stepped outside into the frosty night to be able to hear her. "Hey, Mom."

"Matthew, what are you up to tonight? Not working, are you?" Brenda Dumont asked.

"Nope, I'm out shooting pool with the guys."

"Just the guys? No special girl you'll be kissing at midnight?"

He shook his head. "Not this year, Mom."

"I'm not getting any younger, you know. I'd like some grandkids before I'm too old to play with them."

"Yeah, well, someday. I put the house on the market today."

She sighed into the phone. "You act as if I have one foot in the grave."

"No part of you is anywhere near a grave. It's just time for me to come home, is all. And I know you're not complaining about me going into business with Jason."

That was mostly true, anyway. His mother's recent bypass surgery had been a shock and a wakeup call to both Matt and his younger brother, Jason. But especially Matt. He'd had his reasons for leaving Boston, but they seemed long ago and far away now.

The opportunity to go into business with his brother was prime. Jason's skills with the computer would pair nicely with Matt's investigative expertise to make a solid agency. Matt would just have to get used to the fact that his business was no longer solely his own. That his decisions affected someone else, and vice versa. That part wasn't going to be easy.

He'd been a one-man show for a long time. Too long, maybe.

His mother laughed. "You know you can stay here until the townhouse sells."

"Planning on it, Mom. Thanks. Listen, I'm freezing my butt off out here talking to you. I'll call you this weekend, okay?"

"Happy New Year, honey."

"Same to you, Mom."

He turned around just in time to bump into Cara Medlen and her friend.

* * *

Cara let out a whoosh of relief as she stepped back into Red Heels, with its soft lighting and bluesy music. She'd barely avoided another confrontation with Matt Dumont outside Finnegan's, but as he seemed to prefer beer to martinis, she shouldn't have to worry about seeing him again tonight.

She headed straight to the bar for a pomegranate martini, with Merry at her heels.

Drink in hand, she toasted her best friend. "Here's to the New Year. And forty-five minutes left to find a couple of cute guys to kiss at midnight."

Merry cast a glance around the room. "Not seeing any eligible bachelors. But I know where to find a man willing to kiss *you* at midnight." She winked.

"I'm certain I have no idea what you're talking about."

"No? You're not even remotely attracted to Matt Dumont?"

Cara swirled her drink. "Hardly."

"Then why didn't you just tell him you foster for Triangle Boxer Rescue? Why let him think you're abusing your dogs?"

*Because it was safer this way.* "Because it's none of his business."

"And what if he calls animal control?"

"So what? I haven't done anything wrong. They'll take one look at my papers and curse him for wasting their time."

Merry leaned against the bar and took a long sip of her Sex on the Beach martini. "Given the things I've seen over the years, it's nice to know there are still people out there who're willing to say something when they see a dog who looks abused."

Cara downed her drink and turned around to order another.

Merry wasn't finished. "So tell me, how long have you two been neighbors, and why is it you've never exchanged words until today?"

"A year, and I don't know. I guess we're not very sociable neighbors."

"Or maybe you've been avoiding him because you're attracted to him."

"I told you I'm not."

"So you call him Mr. Fuck Me Hot just for fun?"

She shrugged. "Just because I think he's hot doesn't necessarily mean I'm attracted to him."

"And this doesn't have anything to do with the fact that the friend you went through chemo with just died?"

Cara stared into the pink depths of her drink. "Like I've always said, I'll start living my life when it's safe."

"I'll tell you what I think. I think you're deliberately pissing Matt off because you'd rather have him angry at you than risk a relationship with him. And don't even get me started on the dog thing."

Cara bristled. "What dog thing? And what's with the lecture?"

"You know, you're our only foster home that doesn't have a forever dog in it. Keep one. Keep Mojo—he's a gem."

"But the HOA covenants only allow two pets, and I'd rather keep two fosters. I can save more dogs that way."

Merry gave her the side eye. "Uh-huh. But you're right, no lecture. It's almost midnight. Let's go find a couple of guys to kiss."

Cara glanced around the room. It was crowded with groups of women laughing over martinis and couples leaning in close to each other. At the far end of the bar, she spotted two well-dressed men who were clearly a couple themselves. "That might be a problem."

"Hmmm, our chances probably would have been better if we'd stayed at Finnegan's." Merry looked down at her rose-colored dress, as if disappointed no one of the opposite sex would get to admire it. Maybe because she spent so much time in scrubs, she always put extra effort into looking cute in her off time.

Cara wished she had half of her friend's fashion sense. "Kissing random strangers is overrated anyway."

Merry gave her a look that said she disagreed. "Well, I do have one bit of news worth celebrating tonight. Remember that little girl I told you about, the one who was in a car accident on Thanksgiving?"

"Of course." The girl had been in the hospital ever since. At one point they hadn't expected her to survive. Cara shuddered at the thought.

"She went home today." Merry's face glowed the way it always did when one of her tiny patients went home to their family. As a pediatric nurse, she dealt with life and death on a daily basis. Today, for this little girl, life had won.

As the final countdown to midnight began, Cara and Merry donned sparkling party hats, blew on noisemakers, and shouted along with the crowd. When the clock struck twelve, the room erupted with confetti and cheers. "Happy New Year!"

Merry clinked her champagne flute against Cara's. "To the New Year."

"To the New Year."

"May it bring good health, many adopted foster dogs, and a steamy new romance for Cara."

Cara already had a mouthful of champagne by the time Merry finished her toast. She choked on it. "What? No. Good health and many adoptions. That's it."

Because only luck had put Gina in that casket this morning and not Cara. They'd been seventeen when they'd met, both cancer patients at Duke Children's Hospital, and they'd kept in touch over the years. Cara had gone to Gina's wedding, her baby shower.

Part of her had envied Gina's ability to live without fear, to embrace life to the fullest. And then last year, she'd called. *It's back*, she'd said. And now her friend was gone.

So Cara could be patient for a few more years, until she got the "all-clear." Then she could start living the rest of her life. And not a moment before.

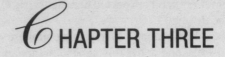

# CHAPTER THREE

The problem, Cara decided, was that it had been a very long time since she'd been kissed. Nearly a year since she'd even gone on a date. And a heck of a lot longer than that since she'd felt anything like the awareness tingling through her body when Matt Dumont had crowded her against the wall in Finnegan's Pub. Her hormones were still recovering.

Maybe she'd throw caution to the wind and put romance on her New Year's resolution list after all. The sizzling kind, not the boring kind she usually settled for. Maybe she'd pick up a random guy in a bar and have her way with him.

And maybe pigs would sprout wings.

Cara's sneakers squeaked across the linoleum as she approached the metal gate leading to the dog pens. A heavy feeling settled over her, as it always did here, pressing harder against her chest the closer she came.

"Morning, Cara." Darlene's cheerful voice pulled a reluctant smile onto Cara's lips.

"Morning, Darlene. How many today?"

"Eleven. Here are their names and pen numbers." She held a small paper ripped from a notepad toward Cara.

"Thanks. Anyone to watch out for?"

"Nah, they're okay. Duncan, the Pom in Thirty-Six, will growl at you, but he's a lover in disguise."

"Okay." Cara took the paper, adjusted the camera strap on her shoulder, and pushed through the gate into the dog kennel. A crescendo of barking echoed up and down the hall as the gate clicked shut behind her. Dozens of dogs sprang to life, begging for her attention in a variety of voices: loud, soft, high-pitched, and low. Metal clanged as paws were thrust into the fencing at the front of their pens.

The sound jarred her soul, but the quiet ones bothered her more. The ones who stared at her with silent, begging eyes. And, worse, the ones who didn't even acknowledge her presence. They just lay staring at the wall, too depressed to move.

Cara had visited the Dogwood County Animal Shelter dozens of times, maybe hundreds, and she left each time with tears in her eyes.

She looked down at the paper in her hands. First on the list was Nina in Kennel Seven. Cara's heart pinched as she caught sight of the dog. Nina was a brindle pit mix, her coloration similar to Mojo's. She lay curled in a tiny ball in the middle of her pen, despair clinging to her like a shroud.

Cara crouched down in front of her kennel. "Morning, Nina. Want some fresh air?"

The dog raised her head to stare at Cara. Hope flickered in her eyes.

Cara unfurled a black nylon leash from the wall opposite the kennels, opened Nina's door, and clipped the lead onto her collar. "Come on, let's go outside."

She led Nina down the hall past the other dogs, many still barking and lunging for her attention. Nina shuffled at her side, tail tucked and head down as she realized they were headed toward the exercise pen in back and not the true freedom that waited on the other side of the metal gate.

The vise over Cara's heart squeezed. If she could take home every one, she would. She remembered Merry's words on New Year's Eve. How could she justify keeping one forever, when she could save so many more by passing them on?

She unclipped Nina and watched as the dog did her business on the sparse, dry grass. Cara gave her a few minutes of peace to walk around, sniff the scents of the great outdoors, and feel fresh air against her fur.

She tried to engage Nina with a ball, then a tug toy, but she only stood, staring at the trees in the distance. This was a dog who understood the implications of her surroundings. There was no misplaced hope. No blind expectation that the next person to walk through the door would take her home.

Cara removed the lens cap and turned on her camera. She centered Nina in the shot, then adjusted the aperture to soften the patchy grass behind her.

"Nina," Cara called, and the dog turned her head, her eyes the color of hot mocha on this cold, crisp morning.

Click.

She took several shots, then crouched down and took a few more. She reached into her pocket for a couple of peanut-butter bites, and Nina's tail gave a shy wag.

"Here you go." She tossed one, and Nina caught it with a snap of her jaw, swallowed, then looked up expectantly for more.

Click.

Cara repeated the action, then tried again with the ball. No dice. Nina's rump hit the earth with a thump.

"Wanna chase me? You need some exercise before you go back inside, girl." Cara set the camera on a white plastic chair. She bent and patted the ground in front of Nina in an invitation to play, then took off running toward the other side of the enclosure.

Nina watched for a moment, then sprinted after her. They ran, dodged, wrestled, and even tugged on a rope together for a solid ten minutes. By the time they'd finished, Nina stood with her mouth open, tongue lolling out the side as she panted.

Click.

Cara spent another five minutes with her, lavishing her with ear rubs and kisses. If she spent this long with all of them, she'd be here all morning. Well, who was she kidding? She had two and a half hours until she had to pick up Dylan, the little boy she nannied for, and she'd be coming straight from the shelter. Just as she did every Monday.

Reluctantly, Cara returned Nina to her pen, then turned to the next name on her list. It had become her unofficial second job, photographing all the new dogs for their online listing. Photography, and animal photography in particular, was Cara's passion. It turned out she had a knack for capturing their personality, their spirit, with her lens.

Since she had begun photographing them, adoptions from the Dogwood Shelter had increased nearly thirty percent. For a small county shelter, that was a big deal. A big enough deal that Cara spent every Monday here photographing the week's new canine arrivals.

She'd be back on Wednesday for the cats.

By the time she'd worked her way through the list—and been growled at by the diminutive Pomeranian in Kennel Thirty-Six—she had just enough time to wash up and drive to the preschool to pick up Dylan.

"Cara, I'm so glad I caught you." Marilyn Branch, the shelter's director, hurried across the lobby as Cara emerged from the bathroom, scrubbed clean and purse in hand.

"Hi, Marilyn. What's up?"

"Do you have a minute?"

"Sure." Cara followed her down the hall to her office,

which was little more than an oversized closet and overflowing with photos of the many animals saved.

Marilyn turned toward her, hands clasped, eyes bright. "Remember that photo of Margo, the hound mix we entered in the SPCA's Shelter Tails contest?"

"Of course." She'd taken it one ridiculously hot summer morning as Margo bounded through the wading pool in the exercise pen, her tail up, mouth open to catch the stream of water from the hose held by another volunteer.

"You won."

Cara pressed a hand against her chest. "No kidding. Really?"

"Really. We're getting a ten-thousand-dollar grant to renovate the clinic, and your photo will be featured on the cover of their next magazine."

"Wow, Marilyn. That's fantastic."

"It is, and we can't thank you enough. This grant, the clinic renovation, it's an amazing gift. We're naming you our Volunteer of the Year, and we'll be honoring you at our Starry Paws Gala next month. Mark it on your calendar."

"Marilyn, I don't know what to say. Thank you."

"You're welcome. Now I know you're late to get Dylan, so run along. We'll see you on Wednesday. And really... thank you." Tears shone in the older woman's gray eyes.

A lump rose in Cara's throat. With the grant, they could save even more lives this year. And to be honored as Volunteer of the Year. Wow. She'd been invited to the Starry Paws Gala in previous years, but couldn't afford the cost of the ticket. It was a black-tie event and a huge fund-raiser for the shelter. She was still smiling as she pushed through the door to the parking lot where her little blue car waited.

Margo's photo—*her* photo—on the cover of the SPCA magazine.

The streets passed in a blur as she drove to the Hopeful Kids Preschool on Magnolia Street. Dylan's family paid her while he was in school, since she was still on duty in case anything came up, but they allowed her to spend those hours volunteering at the shelter, as long as she kept her cell phone handy in case of a call from his school.

Truly, she couldn't work for a better family. She'd been Dylan's nanny since he was eight weeks old. He'd taken his first steps with her. She'd changed his diapers, kissed his boo-boos, and planned to be his caretaker until he started kindergarten.

She walked in, signed him out at the computer in the lobby, and approached the wooden door decorated in monkeys that housed the Twos class. The teacher, Miss Angela, smiled at Cara, then ushered her blond-haired charge toward the door.

Dylan looked up, his pink-stained cheeks strained with an oversized grin.

"Cawa, Cawa!" He rushed toward the door, tripped over his sneakers, and landed in a heap on the colorful rug. Unfazed, he picked himself up and kept coming. "Look, blue dog!"

He held up a picture with a large blue blob in the middle, his face lit with pride.

"Wow, Dylan, that's fantastic. Is that for Mommy and Daddy?" Cara crouched down for a better look.

"Uh-huh, fij?"

"You bet. We'll go home and put it right on the fridge so Mommy sees it when she gets home. You ready?"

He nodded. Cara brushed back a lock of blond hair from his eyes, then stood.

"See you Wednesday," his teacher called. Dylan waved, then followed Cara across the lobby into the parking lot, babbling the whole time in a language that Cara, had she not been his nanny since he was an infant, would have been convinced was not English.

She spent a happy afternoon with the little boy, then drove home. Her agenda for tonight included heating up a pizza and editing the photos she'd taken that morning. Oh—and calling her mother. She'd left messages yesterday and today and might just show up unannounced on Cara's doorstep if she didn't call her back soon.

Jean Medlen had been known to do just that when she was worrying about her daughter, and with Gina's death still fresh in their minds, she was definitely worried. Cara loved her mom and was grateful they lived only forty-five minutes from each other, but, this week especially, the last thing she needed was another dose of her mother's paranoia about Cara's health.

She parked next to Matt's Jeep. Thankfully, there was no sign of him, angry or otherwise, as she jogged up the front steps of her townhouse. Inside, she was greeted by a chorus of barks from her dogs. She shooed them out the back door and turned to check her answering machine.

The light was blinking. Cara punched it, while keeping one eye on the dogs roaming her backyard. It was time for another leash lesson with Casper tonight. She'd need to walk him before supper or it would be too dark. No need to walk a nervous dog after dark.

"Hi, Cara. My name is Betsy Tarleton. I adopted a beagle mix, Molly, from the Dogwood Shelter a few months ago. Marilyn told me you do their photography and that you also take bookings, so I was calling to inquire about a session. Some portraits of Molly, and some family portraits as well. You can reach me at 555-5720."

Cara flattened her palms against the counter. A photography session. Yes, she did them. Not very often, but often enough that she had a Web site to host client photos.

Enough to give her a taste of the dream.

She thought of the award from the SPCA. If someone

asked Cara what she wanted to be when she grew up, she would say a photographer. It was what she had always wanted.

She'd just been waiting—well, waiting until her life came off hold. Until she knew there would be enough years left to build a career and live it.

And that didn't start for two more years.

* * *

Matt sat in a beige Nissan Versa, an unread newspaper spread across his lap. In his right hand, he held his trusty Nikon D5100 outfitted with a 55-300mm telephoto lens.

His legs were stiff from several hours of sitting. Ken Prentiss was discreet, Matt would give him that, but he was definitely up to no good. Yesterday, he'd gone to lunch with a well-dressed blonde when his secretary had said he was in a budget meeting. Unfortunately, he'd kept his hands to himself the whole time; not even a peck on the cheek as they said good-bye.

He'd been nervous as hell, though, his leg tapping a jig below the table while they ate. It was just a matter of time before Matt nailed him to the wall.

It gave him great satisfaction every time he brought closure to a husband or wife whose spouse was cheating. If only someone had been there to do the same for Matt. He'd forever feel a fool for believing Holly would stay faithful while he served overseas. For keeping her photo by his bed all those long nights in Iraq while she was screwing around on him at home.

No one deserved that. And Matt would catch Ken Prentiss soon enough.

Felicity deserved closure too.

Matt flexed his shoulders and shifted in his seat. He glanced at his watch to see if he had time for a quick pit stop at the coffee shop across the street before tailing Ken home. Probably not.

Five minutes later, Ken exited the law offices of Fletcher, Smith & Prentiss, hustling toward the silver Lexus parked beneath a tree at the back of the lot. Matt leaned forward.

Ken stepped into the car, cranked the engine, then pressed his cell phone to his ear. He sat back, talking rapidly, his expression taut with worry. He sat there for almost twenty minutes, carrying on a heated conversation before finally shoving the cell phone back into his pocket.

Matt watched from his parking spot on Lenoir Street, the street behind Ken's building. Something about this case had his neck prickling with misgivings. He couldn't put his finger on it yet, but he would.

He watched Ken leave, alone, then tailed him home. Nothing to see.

He glimpsed Felicity's gold Mercedes in the garage before the door closed behind Ken's Lexus. No point in hanging around now, but he'd be back later, after dark.

He drove home and found Cara out front with the white dog. He supposed it was the same white dog. Only now, a week later, its sides had filled in and its coat appeared to be clean and less mangy.

He pulled past his assigned spot, occupied by the Grand Cherokee, and parked in one of the visitor spaces near the end of the parking lot. The Versa was a rental he'd return tomorrow. Sometimes when he sat surveillance on one person for an extended time, he liked to mix things up with different vehicles to keep anyone from getting suspicious.

Cara stood with her back to him, giving the dog commands. Sit. Lie down. Stay. He couldn't hear the words, but he saw the dog obey. Saw the way she lavished him with praise and treats for each successful response.

Not at all what he'd expect from a woman abusing her

dog. But he knew as well as anyone that appearances could be deceiving.

Over the past few days, he'd spoken to several of their neighbors, hoping to find out more about Cara and her dogs. Few of them even knew her name. No one knew what was going on with her mangy canine companion.

Matt was ready to solve this little problem before his conscience forced him to put a call in to animal control.

He spotted Betty Albright shuffling toward the mailboxes, a toy poodle under each arm. Betty glanced over her shoulder at Cara and her dog as if the devil were at her heels. Betty lived in the townhouse on the other side of Matt. A petite woman in her late seventies, she might be the only person who knew more about the residents of Crestwood Gardens than Matt did. If anyone knew what Cara was up to, it was Betty.

Matt stepped from the car. "Hey there, Betty. How's that new shower treating you?"

Last month, Betty had fallen in the shower and bruised her hip. Afterward, Matt and his buddy Jack had installed one of those new shower stalls with a seat and a rail for her.

Betty's wrinkled face brightened as she saw Matt, and her step quickened. "Oh, Matt, you dear, it's been splendid. I still owe you a pot roast dinner."

Matt shoved his hands into his pockets and smiled. "That's right, ma'am, you do."

The woman cooked like Julia Child. Matt would be happy to eat in her kitchen for the rest of his life—not to knock his own mother's cooking, of course.

"Tell you what. I'll pick up a roast tomorrow at the market. Are you free for supper?"

He winked. "For you, I'm free any night."

Betty chuckled with appreciation. With a furtive glance

over her shoulder, she set the dogs on the ground. Both of them promptly trotted over to Matt and sniffed his boots.

"You afraid of that dog, Betty?" He nodded his head toward the white dog, who now sat watching Cara intently as she stepped backward away from it.

Betty leaned forward, her eyes narrowed. "Between you and me, those dogs are a menace. One of them growled at Princess last summer. I thought it was going to maul her."

"That dog? The white one?"

"Oh no, dear. She just brought that one home last week. This was a different dog. She gets them at the shelter, you know."

Matt clucked his tongue against the roof of his mouth. Nope, he hadn't known that. "And then what does she do with them?"

"She works with them until they find homes. Fostering, I think she calls it."

*Fostering.* Well, that certainly put a new spin on things.

He wished Betty a good evening and strode toward Cara and her foster dog.

* * *

*Here comes trouble.*

Cara's breath caught as Matt sauntered up, looking all dark and dangerous. Her gaze locked on his mouth, then slid down. God, the man was sexy in jeans.

He stopped a few feet away, looking from Casper to Cara. "So you rescue dogs from the shelter."

She couldn't hold back the smile. "You've been talking to Nosy Betty."

He returned her smile, and well, if he was sexy while scowling, his smiles were practically orgasm-inducing. "Betty owes me a home-cooked meal."

"You don't cook?"

He raised an eyebrow. "Actually, I cook quite well. Just don't find much use for it when it's only me at the dinner table."

Cara glanced down at Casper, to make sure he wasn't feeling uncomfortable enough to growl again. The last thing she needed was more ill will toward her foster dogs from the townhouse community.

The dog sat at her feet, watching their conversation closely. Alert, but not tense. He'd made terrific strides in the week he'd been with her. Not only was he filling out physically, but he was more relaxed as well. And anyway, Matt oozed that calm confidence that put dogs at ease.

"Why didn't you tell me, Cara?" Matt's voice was quieter, almost intimate. She didn't dare look up into those intense brown eyes, afraid of what she might see.

She let out a sigh, still watching Casper. "You caught me on a bad day, okay?"

"In my line of work, people usually keep secrets because they have something to hide."

"And what is your line of work?" She risked a glance up, then wished she hadn't. His eyes burned into hers.

"I'm a private investigator."

She nibbled her bottom lip. "Hmm, not a very good one, I guess, if you thought I was training fighting dogs."

A muscle in his cheek twitched. "No, you're right. I shouldn't have jumped to conclusions. For the record, though, I'm a damn good investigator, and I know plenty about you, Cara Medlen."

"Oh yeah?" She wasn't sure she liked the sound of that.

"I know when you're not rescuing dogs, you're a nanny. You go for a jog most mornings around six, and despite living here over a year, you don't know your neighbors very well."

Cara stepped back. "Well, that's . . . interesting. And how did you come to this enlightening conclusion?"

"I happen to know our neighbors quite well, so I did some asking around this week, since you weren't willing to talk to me. Most of them don't know much more than your name. As far as I can tell, only Betty knows your dogs are fosters."

"So?"

Matt shrugged. "Just an observation."

"Great. Glad we cleared that up." She turned on her heel and marched toward her front door, Casper trotting briskly at her side. Why was she so out of breath? And why had Matt noticed when she went for morning jogs?

Nope, she wasn't even going to attempt to answer either of those questions.

The phone was ringing as Cara closed the door behind her. She lunged over the kitchen counter to grab it. "Hello?"

"Hey." Merry's cheerful voice greeted her. "Guess what?"

"What?" She unclipped Casper's leash and watched as he scampered off after Mojo.

"I've got a family interested in Mojo. Two kids, five and seven. Mom works from home. Big fenced-in backyard. Trista did the home visit, said any dog there would be spoiled rotten."

Happiness flared in Cara's chest. "Oh, that's perfect. He loves kids."

"I gave them your information, so you should be hearing from them soon."

A loud crash echoed down the hall. "I gotta go—the boys are getting into trouble—but this is awesome news. Start looking for a new foster for me, okay?"

"Will do."

Cara hung up the phone and ran down the hall to find Casper knee-deep in dirty laundry with a pair of her underwear slung across his ears.

* * *

Matt stared after Cara, frustrated that he no longer had a reason to deny the attraction he felt for her. She wasn't an animal abuser, or even an irresponsible dog owner. On the contrary, she was pretty damn exceptional.

Shaking it off, he went inside. Nothing greeted him but the hum of hot air whooshing from the vents. He thought of Cara next door, the dogs always there to welcome her home.

Maybe, once he was settled in Boston, he'd get a dog.

He walked upstairs to the office and settled into the cracked leather chair that had been his father's. Sometimes, if he leaned back and closed his eyes, he could still smell the sweet aroma of his cigars. He'd spent many an evening on Dad's knee, listening to tales from the trenches, tales no doubt well tailored to suit a little boy's ears.

John Dumont's service in Vietnam had ultimately inspired Matt's decision to join the marines as a cocky teenager looking to take on the world, a decision that served him well. He'd learned self-discipline, honor, integrity—the ideals he'd admired most about his dad put into practice. He'd learned to depend on others, and to have them depend on him.

With a frown, Matt reached down and ran his palm over the scar on his right thigh. He could barely feel its raised edges through his jeans, though it ached viciously whenever he thought of that night in Iraq.

The pain of betrayal. It clogged his throat, dry and coarse as desert sand.

He shook the memories away and opened his email. Three new messages from Felicity Prentiss waited in his inbox. That woman could single-handedly drive him out of North Carolina. No wonder her husband was fooling around on her. She made a beauty queen look low maintenance.

There was also a message from his brother. Matt read through it, then dialed Jason's cell phone.

"What's this about trouble with the insurance paper-work?"

"Just a technicality. Don't worry about it." The click of Jason's fingers on a keyboard carried through the receiver.

"Tell me anyway." Matt raked a hand through his hair. Jason might be a genius at cyber-sleuthing, but he'd fucked up his first business venture, something Matt couldn't afford to see happen twice.

"They said the deductibles weren't high enough. No worries, bro, I'll get it sorted out."

"Well let me know when you do, okay?"

"Will do. Have you talked to Mom lately?"

Matt was clicking through emails as they spoke, but now he paused. "Not since Saturday. Why?"

"She just seemed a little...confused the last time I saw her."

"Confused?" Matt leaned back in the chair and frowned.

"Mmm, I went over for dinner, and she had forgotten I was coming. Then she left one of the burners on while we ate and burnt up her favorite pan. It might not sound like much, but you know Mom."

Matt did. His mother was sharp as a tack.

"It's probably nothing, but I'll try to keep a closer eye on her. Be glad when you're home to help me out."

"Yeah, me too."

"Any bites on the townhouse yet?"

"Not yet, but it's only been on the market a week. As soon as the Prentiss case and a couple of other things are wrapped up, I'll be on my way. It'll show better without my crap junking it up, anyway."

Jason chuckled. "True, true. Well, that's good. I've got a few office spaces lined up for us to go look at."

"Perfect. And I'll be staying with Mom for a while, so I can keep an eye on her."

"Great. Okay, gotta run. I'll check in about the insurance thing."

"Thanks, Jason."

Matt hung up the phone, then turned to the emails from Felicity Prentiss. Time to ease her worries before she did something stupid and jeopardized the case.

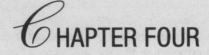

# CHAPTER FOUR

Cara wiped away a happy tear as the Sinclairs loaded Mojo into their minivan.

"Everything okay?"

She whirled in surprise at the familiar voice behind her and offered Matt a watery smile. "Sorry, I always cry a little when one of them goes home."

He stood there in jeans and the same black leather jacket he'd worn the day they met. His cocoa eyes stirred a restless desire inside her. "I don't know how you do that."

"Do what?"

"Love them, care for them, then pass them on to someone else."

"Oh, well, that's the best part, really. Knowing they might not have made it out of the shelter otherwise. And this was a perfect match. I just love when that happens."

He studied her with an intensity that zigged along her spine. "So the brown one got adopted?"

"Yes, Mojo. He's going to be so happy." She leaned back against the door of her car, unable to wipe the silly smile off her face. When she looked up, Matt had stepped closer.

He stood over her with a new glint in his dark eyes. Heat. Desire.

Cara straightened and tried to step backward, but found herself trapped against the car. Her heart pounded and heat pooled in her belly as his eyes traced the outline of her breasts beneath her thin yellow sweater. She fingered the zipper of her jacket, torn between an urge to zip it to her neck or yank it the rest of the way down. In the end, she did neither.

He leaned closer, until she could smell the warm, masculine scent of his aftershave. Soap and sandalwood. "You are something else, Cara Medlen."

Oh God, he was going to kiss her. This was such a bad idea. The worst. Her lips parted in anticipation.

But he stepped back, shot her a sultry smile, and sauntered off toward his front door.

Cara stared after him, breathing like she'd just finished a five-mile run.

She was in big trouble. And since she apparently had no self-control where he was concerned, she'd better make it a priority to stay far away from Matt Dumont.

* * *

"Morning, Cara."

"Morning, Darlene. How many this week?" Cara asked as she approached the metal gate to the dog kennel.

"Nine." Darlene handed her the paper with their names and kennel numbers, and Cara walked inside. As always, she flinched against the sudden onslaught of sound: barks, howls, and the rattling of metal.

Before she fetched the first dog on her list, Cara walked to Kennel Seven. A white poodle mix stared up at her with a hopeful expression, tail swooshing back and forth against the cement like an automatic duster.

Cara stopped short in surprise. Nina, the brindle pit mix who'd tugged at her heartstrings the week before, was gone. She clapped a hand to her chest, imagining Nina at home with her own family, those sad eyes shining with life.

"Hey, Darlene," she called back to the reception desk.

"Yeah?"

"Did Nina get adopted?"

There was a long pause, then Darlene appeared in the hallway. "No, hon. She came down with a respiratory infection on Wednesday. We didn't have anywhere to quarantine her. Once we have the new clinic..."

Darlene's voice trailed off, and Cara followed her gaze toward the door at the end of the hall. The euthanasia room.

Cara staggered back against the wall, the air knocked from her lungs as if one of the dogs had just leaped onto her chest. *Oh, Nina.* She swallowed hard and nodded. "Thanks, Darlene."

Darlene retreated to her desk.

This was the part that broke Cara to pieces. If she didn't know her photographs would help save more lives, she'd never be able to force herself to come back. But she had nine dogs waiting for her, waiting to have their photos added to Petfinder.com, waiting for their chance to find a family and live a happy life.

Cara drew a deep breath and started with the first name on her list.

By the time she made it home that night, she felt like an old dishrag, limp and threadbare. For some reason, Nina's death had really punched the spirit out of her. Maybe it was because of the empty dog bed in her own house. She was painfully aware that somewhere out there, a boxer waited, time ticking to make it out of the shelter alive.

Merry had sent her a bulletin last night for a senior female named Marigold, dumped at the shelter by her family when they moved out of state. Tomorrow, Cara would call and arrange to pick her up.

Her spirits lifted at the thought of bringing Marigold home. It had been a little while since she'd fostered a senior, and she looked forward to the opportunity. Marigold deserved a warm bed and happy home for her last years.

A white envelope had been shoved beneath her front door. Cara bent to retrieve it, then hurried through the living room to the kitchen, where Casper barked restlessly in his crate.

He missed Mojo. So did Cara.

"Lonely by yourself all day, huh?" She opened the crate, and Casper bounded out, leaping and twirling and howling his pleasure. Cara didn't bother to unzip her jacket. Instead, she ushered him out the back door into the yard to burn some energy.

While he ran, Cara pushed her finger under the flap and ripped the envelope open. She pulled out a piece of paper: Crestwood Gardens stationery. Her homeowners' association.

They'd better not be raising the HOA dues again, because—

*Due to a recent complaint, you hereby have thirty days to remove all dogs from the property...*

The words floated up at her, but at first they didn't fully register.

Oh no. No, no, no.

Cara sank onto the yellowed grass beneath her.

*Until further notice, you are asked not to keep pets of any kind or risk further action by the Homeowners' Association.*

This had to be a mistake. She and her dogs hadn't broken any rules. She'd been very careful to follow all of them.

Cara sprang to her feet and rushed inside. She dialed the phone number listed on the letter, praying that someone was still in the office.

"Crestwood Gardens, Lenore speaking."

Cara quickly explained the letter she had received. It had to be a mistake. Lenore would clear it up for her.

"Oh, Miss Medlen. I'm sorry, but we've received another complaint about your dogs. Per the HOA covenants..."

Cara felt like heavy towels had been wrapped around her, smothering her, muffling the words Lenore spoke. This was the third complaint filed against Cara and her foster dogs. Action needed to be taken. She could file an appeal, collect signatures, but in the meantime she had thirty days to get rid of her dogs.

One month.

Not enough time to guarantee a home for Casper.

And not nearly enough time to prepare herself to live alone. To quit fostering. To stop saving lives.

Oh God, what was she going to do?

* * *

Matt lurched from his desk chair at the sound of someone pounding on his front door. He jogged downstairs and peered through the peephole.

Brow furrowed, he yanked the door open.

Cara Medlen stood there, her sunny blue eyes gray with fury. "You bastard."

"Excuse me?" He stepped back, and she stormed into his living room. He hadn't seen her in days, so he had no idea why she was here now, looking at him like he'd just run over one of her dogs with his Jeep.

"They're making me get rid of my dogs!" Her voice shook, and her fists flailed. "You filed a complaint, and they're making me get rid of my dogs."

Her war cry faded to a whisper, and she looked like she might crumple into one of his leather chairs and cry. Well, hell, he hated to see a woman cry. "Slow down, Cara. Who's making you get rid of your dogs?"

Her throat bobbed, and she crossed her arms across her chest. "Crestwood Gardens—the HOA board. Because you filed a complaint."

"Hold on, there. I didn't file a complaint, with Crestwood or anyone else."

She jerked her eyes up to his. "Of course you did. You accused me of animal cruelty and I slammed the door in your face. It's my fault, I guess, really." A weary sigh escaped her lips. "I should have just told you the truth."

Matt reached out and pushed a strand of hair back from her face. "Cara, I didn't file a complaint. I'm a private investigator. When something doesn't add up, I investigate. I didn't like what I saw when you brought home that white dog, so I did a little asking around and found out you foster for Dogwood Shelter."

"Triangle Boxer Rescue," she whispered. "I foster for Triangle Boxer Rescue. I got a letter...someone filed a complaint, and I have thirty days to get rid of my dogs."

He took her shoulders and guided her to the couch. "What kind of complaint?"

She stared at him with wide, watery eyes. "I don't know. I—I'm sorry for accusing you, Matt. I just assumed..."

He nodded. "A logical assumption."

Cara stood abruptly. "I should go."

He came around the couch and cut her off. "I'm sorry they're doing this. For what it's worth, I think you have grounds to fight it. I mean, you haven't violated any of the HOA covenants, have you?"

Cara shook her head, and another apricot-colored curl fell over her face. He resisted the urge to touch her again, because right now he really wanted to kiss her, and that would be a bad idea. Cara Medlen wasn't the type of girl he could take to bed without a committed relationship, something he was in no position to offer at the moment.

"No," she said. "I mean, I've had a dozen or so dogs since I've been here. Some of them were lacking social skills, but they'd never hurt anyone."

"Hmm." Matt shoved his hands into his pockets. Dammit. Why didn't she fix that curl? "Well, I'm not sure it'll help anything, but I'll ask around. I'm sure I can find out who made the complaint, at least. Might've been Betty. She told me one of your dogs tried to maul her poodle a few months ago."

Cara blew a puff of air that lifted the wayward curl back into place. "Nosy Betty. That was Taz, and she just growled at Precious... Princess, whatever her name is."

"Princess, I think. Princess and Duchess."

Cara wrinkled her nose.

He chuckled. "Why, Miss Animal Rescue, you got something against poodles?"

"No, I just prefer my dogs big enough to go for a jog. And with actual names."

"And what is your dog's name?"

"Well, Casper. But I didn't name him."

"Ah, Casper the white dog. So you don't have one of your own, only fosters?"

"Only fosters. Which makes it easy to comply with the board, technically. I just have to find a home for Casper." She bit her lip, and her shoulders sagged.

"Hey, don't give up, Princess. Fight it. I think you'll win."

She narrowed her eyes at him. "Did you just call me Princess?"

He shrugged and scraped a hand over his chin to hide a smile as temper sparked in those sunny blue eyes.

She glared at him. "Real cute."

Yep, that she was, all right. Electricity crackled in the air between them.

She stared at him for a long moment. "I should go. Sorry again for accusing you. I shouldn't have jumped to conclusions."

"Neither should I, on New Year's Eve. I'd say we're even."

"Right. Bye, Matt." She slipped out his front door.

Matt stood there for a moment, then headed upstairs to finish running a background check on a new employee for one of his corporate clients. But damned if he didn't spend the next half hour staring into space, thinking about Cara and her apricot curls.

* * *

Cara leaned into the couch and closed her eyes. "I am so screwed."

"Well, did you call and talk to them about it?" Merry asked.

She shifted the phone to her other ear. "Yeah, and apparently, since this was the third complaint, I have to get all the other owners to sign a release to get the order lifted. What if they won't sign?"

"You'll just have to be really persuasive. Explain what you're doing, show before-and-after photos, bring some Happy Tails stories from your fosters in their forever homes."

"That's a good idea. And Matt said he'd ask around and find out who filed the complaint."

"Matt, huh?" Merry's tone changed. "Things heating up with Mr. FMH?"

*Sort of.* "Hardly."

"Hey, you said he's a PI, right?"

"Yeah."

"Remember those dogs in Trista's neighbor's backyard, the ones without shelter? The temperature's supposed to drop again at the end of the week, and we still don't have enough evidence to convince animal control to seize them. Could you run it by him? He might have some suggestions for us."

"Yeah, that's a good idea. I'll ask him." Even if she didn't really want to. Or she did—and that was the real problem, because every time she saw him, she wanted him to kiss her.

"Awesome. Listen, I've got to go, I'm being paged. Talk to you later?"

"Yep. Bye." Cara set her phone on the coffee table and glanced at the dog sprawled beside her. She might as well take advantage of this last day of mild weather and go for a jog to burn off some frustration.

Her cell phone rang again before she got the chance. She glanced at the screen and flopped back onto the couch. "Hi, Mom."

"Hi, sweetie. How are you? I was just looking through some old photos of you and Gina and, before I knew it, I was bawling like a baby."

Cara pressed a hand over her eyes. "Oh, Mom…"

Jean sniffled. "Her poor family. I just can't imagine what they're going through this week."

Cara was trying very hard not to think about that, but she couldn't forget the agonized look on Gina's husband's face at the funeral. The tearful confusion when Ben, her three-year-old, asked when Mommy was coming home. "I'm sure it's been hard on everyone."

"Well, I brought over a couple of casseroles."

"That was nice of you, Mom."

They chatted for a few more minutes, and Cara changed the subject to vent about the ultimatum from the homeowners' association. Then Jean's call-waiting beeped, and Cara begged off to go for a much-needed run with her dog.

She went upstairs to change into running clothes, then dangled Casper's leash. "Come on, dude. Let's go for a run."

They headed down the street to the paved jogging trail that ran around the outskirts of town. Cara pulled up the hood of her sweatshirt to ward off the cool air whistling in her ears.

Casper glided along at her side, head down, nose up, relaxed and peaceful in motion. It was amazing what a good jog could do for an anxious dog. Or an anxious girl.

The inability to run had been one of the harshest side effects of her illness. Chemo had left her so sick, and so weak, that she hadn't exercised for over a year. She'd watched her muscles atrophy and felt her soul wither right along with them. Running cleared her head, helped her think.

One foot in front of the other. A great metaphor for life.

The sting of Gina's death would fade. They hadn't been best friends, not even close friends these last few years. But once upon a time, they'd huddled together on a hospital bed, their heads swathed in bandanas, whispering the hopes and fears of teenage girls faced with their own mortality.

Now Gina was gone, and Cara felt all over again how fragile her life had been. How fragile it could be again, if cancer recurred.

A timely reminder to keep things in perspective.

Her photo shoot with Molly the beagle mix had been fantastic. The little dog was brimming with personality from her long brown ears to the tips of her white toes. The family seemed as thrilled with their photos as Cara had been with taking them. They'd placed a sizable order for prints and promised to recommend her to any friends looking for family or pet portraits.

She'd always meant to make a career in photography. In two years, when Dylan started kindergarten and no longer needed a full-time nanny, she planned to have a portfolio and client base sufficiently built to make it her full-time job.

A little part of her yearned to snatch at this opportunity

and try for it now, but she tamped it out with the pounding of her feet against the pavement. Not yet. Because the first milestone she'd set for herself was to make it ten years in remission.

Then she could plan her future. And not a moment before. Losing that battle would be hard enough, without dragging anything more complicated like a career, a family, even a dog, down with her.

The chilly air made her lungs ache. Winded after a solid five miles, Cara and Casper ambled home, relaxed and rejuvenated.

Tomorrow, she'd begin collecting signatures.

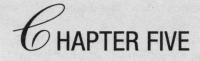

# CHAPTER FIVE

$\mathcal{F}$elicity Prentiss stood at the dining room window, glancing furtively up and down the street. Matt frowned and set aside his binoculars. She'd asked him to give her a heads-up whenever he planned to do surveillance, saying it would freak her out to think of someone watching without her knowledge.

Now she was risking his investigation by acting like a damn fugitive. From his darkened Jeep at the end of the street, neither she or Ken could see Matt, but Ken could easily walk in on his wife spying out the front window. He needed to have a little chat with Mrs. Prentiss tomorrow. Maybe he'd even come by unannounced one night. After all, she was paying him to catch her husband in the act, not run a charade.

He leaned back in his seat and rolled his neck. She'd left the window, no doubt frustrated that she hadn't seen him lurking outside. Maybe that was what it was about. She wanted to make sure he was doing his job, that she wasn't paying him big bucks and he was actually at home sleeping in his warm bed.

Matt wished that were the case. In fact, he wished someone was in his bed with him, someone with honey-scented apricot curls and a sassy mouth he couldn't stop thinking about. He wanted to taste that mouth, and a whole lot more of her.

To pass the time, he imagined what she might taste like, all sweet and hot for him. How soft those curls would feel between his fingers. Her smooth, freckled skin. He imagined those freckles dipping down her chest, a light smattering between her breasts. Her breasts would be small and firm, just enough to fill his hands. A perfect fit.

Going lower, he pictured her firm, rounded ass. He'd seen it enough times through the thin material of her jogging pants to know it met with his approval. He suspected every inch of her was trim and toned. Soft, but firm.

He imagined flattening his palms against her butt and yanking her up against him. He suspected they'd be a perfect fit there as well.

Ah, hell. Matt scraped a hand over his face and shifted in the seat. Suddenly, his jeans felt about two sizes too small. He was pathetic, sitting here on this darkened suburban street fantasizing about the girl next door.

All was quiet in the Prentiss house. He'd wait until the lights were out for the night, then head home. Felicity said her husband sometimes stayed up "working" on his computer, then went out for a late-night rendezvous after she was in bed. When she awoke to an empty house and later asked him where he'd been, he naturally claimed to have been handling an emergency at work.

If booty calls were considered an emergency.

Now, if Cara Medlen called, that might qualify as an emergency.

Matt had been so caught up in work lately and planning for the move that it had been a while since he'd dated. He really, really needed to get laid. He needed someone to cook for, to take out. Yeah, he needed a woman.

He'd take care of it in Boston.

It was two in the morning, and Matt was exhausted and sexually frustrated by the time the light in the office went out and Ken Prentiss joined his wife in bed. This case was really starting to piss him off.

He drove straight home, stripped to his boxers, and fell into bed. Several restless hours of sleep later, he got up, dressed, and spent the day sleuthing on the Internet. There had to be something he was missing with Ken Prentiss. That prickling sensation along the back of his neck was still there, nagging him that he'd missed something important.

The sun was nothing but a purple stain in the western sky by the time he left his home office, tired, irritable, and hungry enough to eat rocks. He had no patience to cook so he stepped into a quick shower to make himself presentable, dressed in jeans and an old UMass sweatshirt, and headed for the Jeep.

Cara's blue Mazda had just turned into the lot. Matt dawdled by the Jeep for a chance to say hello. He did have some news for her, though, or at least that was his excuse for lingering.

She stepped out of her car and gave him a shy smile. Matt felt his eyes drawn toward her chest, to see if the freckles of his fantasy really existed, but she was all buttoned up in a brown corduroy jacket.

"Betty did make a complaint, but it was last year. Phil Durgin did too. Lucky number three is Chuck Sawyer," he said.

Cara closed the door, and her blinkers flashed as she clicked the button to lock it. "Well, I guess that shouldn't surprise me. He's never been fond of my dogs either."

"And Casper did growl at him the other day."

She grimaced. "Yeah, he did. Thank you for looking into it."

"You're welcome." Matt turned toward the Jeep, keys in hand. It was a little cold to be dressed in only a sweatshirt, and he was seriously starving.

"Hey, Matt?"

Cara's voice stopped him in his tracks.

"Yeah?"

"Do you think, sometime, I could ask you a couple of questions about an animal cruelty case our rescue is working on? Nothing official, just to get some advice."

"Sure. You hungry?"

"Oh, well, yeah. Where're you headed?"

"Jimmy's. You like wings?"

She nodded.

"Hop in." He pointed toward the passenger door of the Jeep.

"Can you give me ten minutes? Casper's been in there all day, and I'm sure he's heard me out here talking to you by now."

Matt nodded, despite an urge to start gnawing on his own hand if didn't get hold of some spicy wings in the next five minutes. "Sure. Take care of Casper, but make it snappy. I'm starving."

"Okay. Come in. I'll be quick." She motioned him in after her as she opened the door to her townhouse.

They were greeted by a series of loud barks and the sound of a metal cage banging into the wall. Cara rushed into the kitchen to fetch Casper. Matt lingered in the living room, hands in his pockets as he surveyed her home.

The walls were painted traditional beige with a warm undertone, more pink than yellow. A red couch and matching loveseat were covered with several worn throw blankets. For the dogs, he presumed. Several large landscape photographs of the Dogwood area were framed on the wall leading from the living room into the dining room.

Casper bounded in, still barking, but his stub of a tail wagged enthusiastically. He'd filled in completely now, and his hair was growing back too. He was still funny looking, though, with those mismatched eyes and a pink scar splitting his face.

He planted his front feet on Matt's chest and let out a powerful bark right in his face.

"Off, Casper," Cara commanded, and the dog obeyed. "Bad dog. Go on outside."

She ushered him out the back door, then turned to Matt apologetically. "Sorry about that. He's still learning his manners."

"No problem. He looks great."

Her eyes sparkled. "He does, doesn't he? He's come a long way."

"You start collecting signatures yet?"

She looked down at her sneakers. "I got five yesterday, but I've already had two people refuse to sign."

"I imagine you could be persuasive if you wanted to be."

"Yeah, Merry said I should take pictures of some of the dogs, like before-and-afters."

He nodded. "That's a good idea. Who's Merry?"

"My best friend, and also the director of Triangle Boxer Rescue."

Matt wandered over to admire the photos on her wall. He recognized one as a lookout in Umstead State Park, where he sometimes hiked on the weekends. "Nice pictures. Local photographer?"

Cara blushed. "Yeah, me."

He raised his eyebrows. "You took these?"

She nodded.

"These are really amazing, Cara. You have talent."

She ducked her head and turned toward the kitchen to check on Casper. "Thanks."

Matt followed the photos along the wall. She'd captured

the old Methodist church on the far side of town, its brick steeple reaching toward a perfect sky. A red hawk soaring over the treetops, wings spread wide. Two boxers racing across a field, ears flapping in the breeze, mouths wide and tongues lolling. "Have you thought about a career in photography?"

"I take clients now, just a few. Pet portraits mostly, some families. I'm building a portfolio so that I can make a go of it in a few years."

"That's great." He moved over to the mantel above the fireplace. These were more personal. A couple he presumed to be her parents. Lots of boxers. On the end, he found a photo of two girls with their arms around each other and grinning at the camera, one strawberry blond, the other golden haired. "You and your sister?" he guessed.

"Susie," Cara said. "I was eleven; she was nine, or somewhere around that."

Interesting that this was the only photo of Cara in the room.

"Cute," he said. "Does she live around here?"

She glanced out into the yard, checking on Casper. "Yep, Susie lives in Cary."

"And your parents?"

"My mom lives in Raleigh. Dad's in Maryland. They split up when we were teenagers."

"You guys keep in touch?"

She shrugged. "I see my mom and sister fairly often, my dad mainly on holidays."

He picked up the photo of the smiling girls. "Your hair was straight."

She turned to face him. "You're very observant. It grew in wavy after the chemo. I guess I like it this way now."

Matt rocked back on his heels. *Chemo. Damn.* "I've heard of that happening. What did you have chemo for, Cara?"

"Hodgkin's lymphoma. Here comes Casper." She opened

the back door, and the dog bounded inside, tail still wagging
frantically. "You're going to hate me," Cara told him. "I have
to feed you and put you back in the crate."

Matt was still processing all the information he'd learned
about Cara Medlen in the last five minutes. He watched as
she poured kibble into a bowl. Casper devoured it as if one
of them might snatch it and finish it for him if he paused for
breath. He wasn't too far off. Matt was about hungry enough
to eat dog food.

He did feel a little bad for the creature as Cara lured him
back into his crate with murmured promises of making it up
to him later. Matt wondered exactly what that entailed. He
doubted Casper's demands resembled any of the ideas tumbling through his own mind.

"Okay, let's go." She grabbed her purse from the table
and led the way outside.

They drove in silence half a mile down the street to Jimmy's Wing Hut, which served, as far as he was concerned,
the best wings in the state. The scents wafting out the door
had him salivating like a dog.

"You been here before?" he asked as they slid into opposite sides of a green vinyl booth.

"Many times. Wanna share Jimmy's Kickin' Sampler?"

"Hell, yeah." Well, shit, how was he supposed to resist
her when she kept surprising him, and all in good ways?

Ten minutes later, Matt was a much happier man with a
platter of wings in front of him, a lager in his hand, and a
gorgeous woman on the other side of the booth. A gorgeous
woman sucking wing sauce off her fingers. Christ.

"So tell me about this case." He dragged his eyes from
her mouth, set down his beer, and snagged another wing
from the pile.

"Okay. So one of our foster families, Trista Benford, has a
neighbor who keeps these two boxer mixes in the backyard.

They bark all day long. They're a neighborhood nuisance, not to mention boxers aren't really meant to live outdoors. They have low tolerance for heat or cold."

"Really? I would think they'd be well suited for heat with the short coat."

She sipped her beer and nodded. "You would think. But it's the short snout. They can't vent enough heat through panting. Boxers are actually at high risk for heat exhaustion around here if you leave them out during the summer."

"Interesting. So these two are left outside..."

"And the whole neighborhood's complaining about it. Trista called animal control, but there are a lot of hoops to jump through to get the dogs seized so we can take them into rescue. That's where I wanted your advice."

"Okay." Matt selected another wing and bit in as Cara continued.

"There's no overt abuse. The dogs are fed and have water. But there's no shelter. They put them in the crawl space under the house at night. Can you imagine?" She shuddered. "It must be like a dungeon down there, dark and cold and probably piled with dog crap."

Cara nibbled on another wing as she told him everything they'd learned from animal control. It was an interesting dilemma they were in. The law didn't make it easy to seize dogs from an owner who still wanted them, even if Matt couldn't imagine why someone would keep dogs like that. What was the point?

He mulled it over as he devoured another wing. "Honestly, it sounds like your best bet is to catch them left outside when the weather's dipped below freezing. Clear violation of the law and grounds for seizure."

She nodded. "That makes sense. We have another cold snap coming so Trista said she'd sneak over one night and see if she can get a look."

"That's trespassing. I don't like the idea of any of you sneaking around over there after dark. Is the yard visible from the street?"

"Sort of. There are a lot of trees. That's been the tricky part. Sometimes we can hear them but we can't see them. And just hearing them isn't enough to get them seized. We've already tried that."

"I have equipment for this sort of thing. Let me handle it."

Cara shook her head. "We can't afford to pay you. I just wanted your advice on the best way to handle it."

"It's okay. I have a light caseload right now, with the move coming up. Give me a heads-up on a night they've been left out, and I'll go over and get the documentation you need."

"Are you sure?"

"No problem. Like you said, we have some cold nights coming. Should be simple enough. Will you be able to adopt out dogs like that?"

"I don't know yet. Hopefully we can work with them, maybe find them a home where they can be someone's farm dogs or something."

"I hope so." Matt didn't know much about dogs, but he did know socialization was important, something these dogs probably hadn't had. He wasn't particularly convinced they'd make good pets, but anything had to be better than the way they were living now.

She looked up, her blue eyes vivid in the soft light of the bar. "Well, thank you. Seriously. If you can do this for us, I'll owe you big time."

"Not a problem."

"So where are you moving?" Cara licked another spot of buffalo sauce from her index finger, and Matt's mind went straight down the drain.

"Massachusetts."

"Change of scenery?"

"Going home. Mom's had some health problems this year."

"Ah." She nodded. "Do you have siblings?"

"A brother, Jason. He's a computer geek. We're going to set up shop together. Dumont Investigative Services."

Cara took a long drink of her beer, and Matt's eyes were drawn to her throat. He watched her swallow. Oh man, he had it bad for this girl, and he'd just agreed to help her on a case. A better idea would be to stay the hell away from her until he left town.

"I'm sure they'll enjoy having you back home," she said.

"Sure they will."

They haggled over the check, although Matt eventually prevailed. His mother hadn't raised him to let a woman pay the tab, no matter the circumstances.

The temperature had indeed begun to fall as they drove home. Matt was glad for the jacket he kept tucked behind the backseat. He shrugged into it, then walked Cara to her front door.

"Thanks for dinner, and for helping us out. Really, if you get us the evidence to get those dogs seized, I won't even know how to thank you." Her warm eyes shone up at him as they stood on her front porch.

Matt gave her a devilish grin. Seriously, did she say these things just to drive him crazy?

Cara licked her lips and took a step back toward her front door.

"No problem." His gaze slid to her neck, soft skin gleaming white as marble in the silvery light of the moon.

He saw her pulse pounding there. Her chest rose and fell with rapid breaths. Her eyes met his and held on like a magnet drawing him in.

Matt tried to resist. He really did.

And then her lips parted, and his blood turned to steam, and the only thing he could hear was his own pulse hammering away in his ears.

He leaned forward and brushed his lips against hers. Cara let out a whimper that caught in his chest and tugged at his restraint. Her lips were soft and warm, tentative as they pressed against his. Her eyes slid shut.

Matt gave her one more gentle kiss. Just a little good night kiss, nothing either of them would regret in the morning. He ran his fingers through her curls, and they were as soft as he'd imagined. Softer.

She was kissing him back now, her lips pushing against his, asking for more.

His tongue swept into her mouth. She tasted spicy, like wing sauce and the promise of hot, sweaty sex. The next thing he knew, she was pressed against her front door, Matt's body crushed against hers. Cara's arms were around his neck, her tongue tangling with his, her soft moans driving him right out of his mind.

After a minute, she ripped her mouth from his, gasping for breath. "Damn, what did they put in those wings?"

All he could do was smile.

Cara leaned in and brushed her lips against his. Then she winked. "Good night, Matt."

She slipped inside and shut the door in his face.

Matt swore under his breath. He was really starting to develop a love-hate relationship with Cara Medlen's front door.

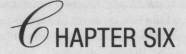

# CHAPTER SIX

*Oh. My. God.*

Cara leaned against the wall, heart flipping in her chest, silly grin on her face. She couldn't quite believe she'd just been wedged up against her own front door with Matt's big, hard body pressed against hers while he kissed her like she was a friggin' Playboy model.

Okay, now she got the fuss about kissing. With other guys she'd enjoyed it, but it was nothing she couldn't live without. She was always worried about where she should put her hands and how quickly he was going to start unbuttoning her blouse.

She'd have unbuttoned her own blouse if Matt had asked. Good lord. His kiss had heated her blood and curled her toes, all those clichés she'd heard but not experienced. *Phew.*

That kind of combustion made Matt Dumont a very dangerous man. If she wasn't careful, she could get swept in way over her head. Lucky he was leaving town. She'd known he was selling his townhouse, but not that he'd be moving to Massachusetts by the end of the month. So there wasn't too much risk of things getting out of hand. She could behave herself for a few more weeks.

Probably.

With a sigh, she dropped her purse onto the end table and walked toward the kitchen where Casper was whining and banging around in his crate. She let him out, and he nearly knocked her down in his excitement.

"I know, I know." She steered him out the back door. Time to spend some quality time with her dog. Something she knew and understood. They played tug with an old rope toy until she was shivering, the last heat from Matt's touch dissipated from her body.

Then they went inside to snuggle together on the couch. Cara slid the memory card from her camera and loaded the latest batch of shelter photos onto her laptop.

Thirteen new dogs today. She opened Photoshop and ran her usual batch to adjust levels and balance. Then she opened the twenty-plus photos she'd taken of the first dog, a yellow Lab named Taffy with wonderfully expressive eyes. She easily narrowed the field to seven.

With these, she took her time, cropping and adjusting color and white balance to best show off the dog's soft, honey-colored coat and warm, chocolate eyes. She selected three: a close-up that captured the happy, loyal expression on Taffy's face, an action shot of the dog running across the outdoor enclosure, and one of her gazing at a ball Cara held, ears perked as she prepared to fetch her prize.

That was Taffy. Happy, loyal, playful.

She spent the next two hours editing the rest. When she'd finished, she emailed them to Darlene to be added to the shelter's Web site and each dog's Petfinder.com page.

The house felt lonely with only one dog in it, although Casper didn't seem to mind too much. He'd sprawled across every inch of couch Cara wasn't occupying, head against her thigh and snoring contentedly. She reached over and rubbed his belly. He rolled to his back, presenting it for further petting, eyes still closed and tail wiggling approval.

He'd come so far in his short time with her. It might take time to find the right match, but he would get his forever family. She felt sure of it. The thought of him being adopted made Cara a little sad. She'd grown pretty fond of his patchy white butt and snarly face.

She thought of Marigold, the abandoned senior she'd been about to take in before the homeowners' association issued its decree. What had happened to her? Cara hadn't seen her mentioned as a new foster in Triangle Boxer Rescue. That didn't necessarily mean she hadn't been pulled by a different rescue, or even adopted from the shelter.

But still, a knot formed in Cara's gut as she tapped off a quick message to Merry asking about her. Merry replied right back, her message short. "We didn't get her out in time. Don't worry, you'll get this mess sorted out and save the next one."

So Marigold died because Cara hadn't been able to take her in. Okay, Marigold died because her jackass family abandoned her at an already overcrowded shelter. Cara knew that, but it did nothing to ease the pain in her chest or the feeling that she'd failed her.

Tomorrow she'd visit Chuck Sawyer, Phil Durgin, and Nosy Betty with some foster success stories and see if she could sway their opinion.

* * *

"It's not that I don't appreciate what you're trying to do for these dogs. It's just that this is a townhouse community, not an animal shelter. We've had several complaints of growling and other aggressive behavior. Someone could get hurt."

Phil Durgin squinted at Cara through the ultra-thick lenses of his glasses.

He'd been halfway up his front steps when she'd approached him, which gave him the effect now of towering over her where she stood on the sidewalk. Somehow, she'd failed to realize he was the president of the homeowners' association. Matt was right; she really didn't know her neighbors. And without Phil's signature, she was dead in the water.

She looked up at him. "I understand, Mr. Durgin, but I assure you no one's going to get hurt. I keep my dogs on leash or in my fenced-in yard at all times. These aren't aggressive dogs, just dogs who need a little TLC while they wait for their forever homes."

"Like I said, I do sympathize. I don't like to see an animal mistreated any more than you, but the HOA covenants were designed for people's pets, not as a halfway house for shelter dogs. We have a number of units on the market right now, one right next to yours, as a matter of fact. Frankly speaking, some of the dogs you bring around here might scare off potential buyers."

Cara felt her chest deflate. "Maybe you'd like to meet Casper, my current foster? He looked pretty bad when I brought him home, but he's doing great now. He's really sweet. He won't scare anyone away, Mr. Durgin."

"Maybe not, but what about the next dog? And the next? This is not the right setting for what you're doing."

"But—"

"I'm sorry, I really am. Now if you'll excuse me." He opened the door to his townhouse, putting an end to the conversation.

She forced a smile. "Thank you for your time."

Cara stood on the sidewalk, unsigned petition clutched in her hands, blinking back tears. Dammit, she was not going to cry about this. Maybe if she got everyone else to sign and went back to him at the end, he'd realize he was overreacting and agree to add his name as well.

It was worth a shot.

Otherwise, she might as well put her townhouse on the market too, because she couldn't live without dogs. It was unthinkable.

A tear broke free, and she dashed it with the back of her hand. She was twenty-eight years old, for crying out loud. Phil Durgin would not make her cry.

The real kicker was that maybe, if she'd taken the time to get to know her neighbors better instead of keeping herself so closed off while she waited for her life to come off hold— well, maybe this wouldn't be happening. If they knew her and liked her, they might be more forgiving. They'd understand why she needed to keep fostering.

Maybe no one would have complained in the first place.

She couldn't go back and change things now, but she could make an effort to be friendlier with her neighbors in the meantime. It couldn't hurt.

Cara huffed a deep breath, then spun on her heels to walk to the next door. She slammed straight into a tall wall of man, smelling of sandalwood and Ivory soap, her two new favorite scents.

"Well, hello." Matt's low voice rumbled through her.

She removed her face from his chest and took a step back. "Hi."

"Any luck?" He jerked his head toward Phil Durgin's front door.

Cara stared at him blankly. He was asking about her petition? Because at that moment, the only thing in her head was the memory of Matt kissing her, his mouth doing amazing things to hers while he pressed his incredibly hard body against her. Her cheeks flushed hot.

A slow grin spread across his face, and his eyes got that

hungry gleam again, although it boggled her mind why a man like Matt Dumont would be attracted to plain, boring Cara. The thrill of the chase, maybe?

She cleared her throat. "Uh, no. He says a townhouse community is no place for what I'm doing. My dogs might hurt someone, or, worse, scare away potential buyers."

"Hmm." He hooked his thumbs through the belt loops of his jeans. "That doesn't sound promising. Temperature's supposed to drop down to the teens tonight. Any word on those dogs?"

"No, but I'll call and find out."

"All right." He pulled his wallet from the back pocket of his jeans, slid a business card from it, and passed it to her. "Give me a call. I can ride over there tonight."

"Okay. Thank you."

He nodded, gave her a smile that made her heart go pitter-pat, then strolled off toward his front door.

She watched him go, disappointment mingling with relief. Matt stirred her up like no man ever had. And it wasn't just that she wanted to leap into his arms and pick up where they'd left off last night, although her body was begging to do exactly that. Everything about him drew her in: his calm professionalism, his love for his mom, his willingness to help her out on this case without getting paid.

He was everything she wanted in a man, which was precisely why she couldn't have him. Not even for a quick fling before he left town. Her heart could never handle it.

Cara pressed a hand to her chest, then hurried to her own door. She'd make that phone call before she forgot, then try to collect a few more signatures before supper. Besides, it was freezing, and she could use a few minutes to warm her fingers.

She didn't have Trista's number so she dialed Merry, who promised to call her right back with the information.

Cara microwaved herself a cup of hot chocolate while she waited. Merry called before she'd had a chance to take her first sip.

"Okay, if you need it, Trista's number is 555-3854. She says the dogs are out now. She can hear them barking. Usually, they bring them in around eleven, before they go to bed."

"Thanks, Merry. Cross your fingers Matt gets what we need tonight."

"Let me know how it goes."

"Will do."

She took a long sip of her hot chocolate while Casper watched with hopeful eyes. "Haven't you heard chocolate is bad for dogs? Go play, dude."

She took another sip. It was ridiculous that the very thought of calling Matt set butterflies flapping in her stomach. She grabbed the phone and dialed.

He answered on the second ring. "Hello."

Damn, he sounded even sexier on the phone, all low and serious.

"Hey, Matt, it's Cara."

"That was quick."

"The dogs are out. The owner usually brings them in around eleven."

"Let's see." There was a thump, then the clicking of a keyboard. "Okay, looks like we should be around twenty-nine degrees by eleven. That'll work."

"Great. So what will you do?"

"Take a few photos with a time stamp. We can match it with the weather report later. I've got lenses with the zoom and night capability we need, presuming I can see into their yard well enough. We could shoot video too, if you want to document the barking."

"Wow, that's great. Yeah, you can see patches of the yard

through the trees. Let's hope the dogs cooperate. Would it be wrong to bribe them with treats or something?"

Matt chuckled. "Yes, that would be trespassing. I can't set foot on their property."

"Right. Sorry, I've probably watched too much TV."

"It's not as exciting in real life. We have to abide by the law. You want to ride along?"

"What?" A real stakeout? When else would she get that chance? "Well, yeah."

"Meet me out front at nine thirty. And wear dark clothes."

"Okay." Cara hung up, her heart thumping in her chest. Dark clothes? Dark car. Matt. She swallowed hard.

Casper cocked his head to the side, his gaze flicking from her mouth to the mug of hot chocolate in her hand.

"Dogs, chocolate, bad. I'm serious." She shooed him off.

She didn't want to crate him again while she collected more signatures if she was going out later. And for all her talk to Phil Durgin, Casper wasn't well socialized enough yet to go door to door and be trusted to mind his manners. She might as well heat up her supper now and work on updating the gallery on her photography site until it was time to meet Matt.

This morning, she'd gotten a call for another booking. Friends of the Tarletons who'd seen the photos she took of Molly last week. And yesterday, at Marilyn's request, she'd dropped off a stack of business cards for her to place next to the SPCA magazine in the lobby.

Excitement sparked in her blood. She was a long way from earning a living through photography, but things were definitely picking up. Maybe she'd give it a little more attention, try to keep the momentum going. She wasn't violating her ten-year plan by starting to build a portfolio now. A photography business took years to grow.

By the time she looked up from her laptop, it was just past nine. She set it aside and took Casper out, then went upstairs to change. She tied her hair back in a ponytail. For some reason, that seemed stealthier than curls tumbling over her shoulders.

Time for a stakeout.

* * *

Matt fought a grin as Cara came out, dressed in a navy shirt and black jeans. "I was kidding about the dark clothes, Nancy Drew."

Her eyes rounded. "Oh."

He pointed to the Jeep. "Tinted windows. Come on— temp just hit thirty-two. Should be below freezing by the time we're in place and I get the shot lined up."

She nodded and climbed into the passenger seat.

Matt slid behind the wheel. He twisted the key, and the engine purred to life. He noticed that Cara kept her eyes straight ahead while her hands fidgeted in her lap. Yeah, he couldn't quit thinking about that kiss either.

"Had my first showing today," he commented to get some conversation going.

"Really?"

"Young couple, I'm told. Sounded interested."

"That's good." Cara watched the houses passing by outside her window. "Will you move as soon as you get an offer?"

"I'll move as soon as I close my last case. Doesn't matter when the townhouse sells, but I could easily have things wrapped up before a closing if they made an offer."

He swung a right onto Keeney Street. "This it?"

She pointed. "The brown one there."

Matt cruised down the street, taking in the house and its yard. It was located on a corner lot, which gave decent access to the backyard except for the trees Cara had mentioned. He pulled over near the back of the property and killed the

engine, then turned toward her. First things first. "I like you,
Cara. A lot. If I wasn't leaving town in a few weeks, I'd be
courting you so hard right now your head would spin."

She gulped, her eyes locked on his.

"But I don't start things I can't finish. I don't regret kissing you, and God knows if the situation was different, I'd be
angling for a chance to do it again. Hell, I'd like to do a lot
more than kiss you, Cara."

She licked her lips, and Matt fought a groan. She was
about the sexiest thing he'd ever laid eyes on, and she didn't
even know it. Somehow that made her even sexier.

"So I just wanted you to understand why I'm not going to
kiss you again. Because it sure as hell isn't because I don't
want to. I have to get to Boston, for my mom, and the business I've set up with my brother. You ever decide to visit
New England, give me a call, okay?"

She nodded.

"Okay, let's get to business. Give me the lay of the land."

Cara swallowed. "What?"

A smile tugged at his lips. "The case." He pointed toward
the shadowy backyard beside them. "The dogs."

"Oh." She swallowed again. "Right."

He leaned back. The Grand Cherokee suddenly seemed
far too small for the two of them.

Cara cleared her throat and looked away. "So, I don't hear
them barking right now, which probably means they're lying
on the back deck. You said we couldn't trespass, but if we
rolled down a window and let them hear us talking, they
might start barking and come over to investigate."

"Let's see what we can see before we start making any
noise." Matt reached into the backseat and pulled out his binoculars. He scanned the backyard, but saw no sign of the dogs.

Cara looked skeptical. "Can you actually see anything
through those at night?"

He grinned at her. "Oh, honey, these aren't the same binoculars you took to the Backstreet Boys concert when you were a teenager. Want a look?"

"I never saw the Backstreet Boys, and yes, please." She held out her left hand, and he passed them to her.

"Be careful with them."

"Yeah, yeah. Oh!" Her mouth fell open as she looked through the viewfinder and discovered the world lit through night vision.

"You should see all my spy tools; they're impressive."

Cara turned and looked at him with one eyebrow raised. "Your spy tools, huh?"

"That's what I said, isn't it?"

"Mm-hmm." Her eyes strayed briefly to his lap, then back to his face.

Matt felt her gaze in the sudden pressure against his fly. "So did you see them?"

"See what?" She glanced at his crotch again.

"You may look sweet and innocent, Cara Medlen, but your mind is in the gutter. The dogs. Did you see the dogs?"

Even in the near darkness, he saw her cheeks flush pink. "No, I didn't see them."

"So did they go in early tonight, or what?" He checked the thermometer on the dash. It read thirty-one degrees. If they located the dogs, it was showtime.

Before he could stop her, Cara rolled down the passenger window and made a series of clicking sounds, like a person makes when calling a dog. The cold, still night air was immediately shattered by ear-splitting barks.

"Guess not," she said with a shrug.

Matt glared at her. "Next time, ask first."

Her eyes widened. "What?"

"This is a surveillance operation, not a 'look at the two Peeping Toms in the car with night-vision binoculars,' okay?" Ordinarily, he notified local PD before setting up surveillance, but tonight, since he didn't expect to be here long and with Cara riding along, he hadn't.

"Okay."

Matt raised the binoculars and panned the backyard again. "I'm still not seeing anything. Where are they?"

Cara frowned, squinting into the darkness. "I don't know. Usually they'd be over here jumping against the fence."

"Are they under the house already?"

"I don't think so. I mean, Trista's heard them more than I have, but I don't think they'd be this loud if they were already in the crawl space."

"I agree. They'd sound more muffled."

"So, Mr. Hot Shot, if I were you I'd make more noise. Get them *really* riled up."

"This isn't really riled up?"

She shook her head.

Matt swept the binoculars across the surrounding houses. Lights off. No faces visible in any of the windows. No movement on the street. With a hard look at Cara, he tapped the horn.

The dogs went nuts. Barking. Snarling. The sounds made the hair on the back of his neck stand at attention. He would not want to be in that yard right now. And yet, still no sign of the creatures putting up all that racket.

"I don't like this." Cara voiced his own concern.

"I don't either." Matt rolled down the window and listened carefully to the commotion invading this otherwise peaceful neighborhood. Behind the barking and growling was something else. A clink of metal.

Beside him, Cara stiffened. "Chains," she said.

"Could be. Would explain why they're not rushing the fence."

"That's illegal in Durham County. There's a proposal on

the ballot to outlaw it here in Dogwood too. It won't be voted on until next year." Her hands clenched into fists.

"Then it doesn't help our case, even if it's true. On the contrary, now we can't see the dogs to prove they're outside."

Cara stared into the darkness. "It's inhumane."

"I agree."

She took the binoculars from him and panned across the yard. "They must be over there behind the deck. It's wooded on the far side of the lot. The dogs wouldn't be visible from the street."

"Sounds likely."

"Could we go around through the trees and try to get them from the other side?"

"No. The photos are only admissible if they were taken from a public location where someone could reasonably expect to be seen, like the sidewalk or the street. No snooping around in the woods behind their house."

"I don't like this, Matt. Not only are they stuck outside in freezing conditions with no shelter, but now they're tethered as well. The owners are decreasing their freedom, the level of care. How long until they quit bringing them under the house at all? Do they have access to food and water? This is bad."

Yep, it was bad, all right. He'd planned to wrap this up tonight. The last thing he needed right now was another open case hanging over his head, let alone one that put him in close quarters with Cara.

He placed a hand over hers. "I'll look into it tomorrow, okay? Let me poke around and see what I can find out."

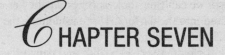

# CHAPTER SEVEN

*C*ara sank back against the couch and took a long sip of wine. At her feet, Casper tugged on one end of a rope toy while Merry's boxer, Ralph, pulled from the other end.

"Chains. Are you sure?" Merry frowned into her wine.

"Pretty sure. What a mess."

"Tell me about it." Merry pushed a wayward brown curl from her eyes. "It's been a lousy week for boxers. Two were euthanized because we didn't find rescue in time, not including Marigold. I've got seven more on our urgent list right now. We need more foster homes. I'm going to put out a plea on Facebook."

Cara's fingers tightened on her wineglass. "It's killing me not to take in another one, Mer. It's so unfair."

"I know."

She let out a long sigh. "I'm not going to get the signatures. I've talked to all but two people. Five have refused to sign. And I told you what Phil Durgin said."

"What are you going to do?"

"Keep fighting. In this economy, I don't want to have to

sell. Especially with the unit next door for sale too. But I will, if I can't get this fixed."

"It sucks, Cara. Plain and simple."

"Yeah, it does." She took another sip of her wine and nudged Casper with her foot. He turned from the rope and gnawed playfully on her leg.

"He looks great." Merry looked down at him proudly. "I just approved a family that might be a good match. Young couple, active, experienced with boxers. I'm going to recommend him."

"That would be great." Cara smiled, but it fell flat. She wanted Casper to go on to his forever home. He deserved it, but when he was gone, she'd be all alone. No dogs.

She loved the ritual of it all. Bringing them home. Loving them, watching them blossom. Then seeing them go home with their family. It was a wonderful cycle, as long as it meant a new dog would soon follow.

Merry slanted a look in her direction. "You need a stand-alone house. No one to mess with your business."

"On my salary? In my dreams. Not to mention how long it will take to sell this place. And I can't afford to even look until it's sold."

Merry frowned, as if Cara's reality had truly sunk in for her. "Man, this really does suck. You're one of my best foster homes. What if I go talk to the HOA people?"

"Be my guest. I don't think it can hurt."

"I will. Maybe Thursday morning before my shift—"

The doorbell pealed, and both boxers leaped to their feet and rushed the front door, barking madly. Cara followed, wineglass still in hand.

"Ralph, sit," she told the brown dog, and he sat. "Stay. Casper, quiet." She hooked two fingers through his collar and held him at her side. His front-door manners had improved somewhat, but she hadn't worked on it that much yet, since she didn't get many visitors.

She peeked through the peephole, and her heart gave an embarrassingly childish leap in her chest. Matt stood there, looking way too handsome for his own good.

She pulled the door open, her fingers tightening on Casper's collar.

"Hey, I just came by to..." His voice drifted off as he looked down, then back at her. "Did you get a new dog?"

"What? Oh, no, Ralph is Merry's."

Matt nodded. "Merry, founder of the boxer rescue."

"Right. Come in." She motioned him inside. He walked past her into the living room where Merry sat, wide-eyed behind her wineglass.

"Matt Dumont." He extended his right hand.

Merry took it with an appreciative smile. "Merry Atwater."

"I live next door. Cara probably told you about our trip to the Rogers house last night."

"She did."

Matt bent to greet the dogs, and Merry's eyes locked on Cara's. She mouthed "FMH" with a naughty grin. Cara felt her cheeks grow warm. She did not want to think about how "fuck me hot" or not he was looking right now. No way.

Matt straightened. His eyes darted between Cara and Merry, and his left eyebrow lifted ever so slightly. The man missed nothing. Probably a good thing, considering his line of work. "So, I did some poking around today on the case."

"Find anything good?" Cara took another sip of wine, to give herself something to do with her hands—and lips.

"Plenty."

"Would you like something to drink, by the way?" She suddenly remembered her manners. "I've got beer, wine, iced tea...."

"No, thanks." His eyes twinkled. "I won't stay long—don't want to interrupt your girls' night."

"You aren't interrupting," Merry told him.

Matt leaned a hip against the side of the couch. "Anyway, the Rogerses rent that house."

"Really?" Merry leaned forward, resting her elbows on her knees.

"Yep. In the last six months, there have been over three dozen complaints made about the barking. The police have spoken with them about it twice. No charges filed."

Merry nodded. "That we knew. Thanks for checking into it for us, though."

He held up a finger. "I'm not finished yet. They've lived at the Keeney Street address for just over a year. Previously, they rented a house in Durham. Similar pattern of complaints. Animal control eventually decided to seize the dogs, but when they showed up, the Rogerses had skipped town, no forwarding address."

"Whoa," Cara and Merry said in unison.

"I spoke to Durham PD. They've washed their hands of it. Too much time has passed, no longer their jurisdiction, yada yada. But the animal control officer did say that he'd be willing to forward the paperwork he has to Dogwood AC, so I passed along the info. Maybe that'll help put a bee in their bonnet."

"Wow, Matt, that . . . that's fantastic," Cara said.

Damn, she was in trouble. Not only was he sexier than any man had a reason to be, he was apparently pretty good at his job too.

Merry looked similarly awed. "Seriously. It's really awesome that you've done this for us."

He shrugged. "Like I told Cara, my caseload's pretty light right now. Anyway, I'll swing by and see if I can get some photos for you, but in the meantime, thought this might help."

"I hope it will. Thank you."

"Okay, I'll let you two get back to whatever it is you were

doing." Matt smiled the smile of a man who had no desire to know what women gossiped about over wine. "I'll talk to you tomorrow, Cara."

"Okay." She stood and walked with him to the front door. "Thanks again."

His eyes hovered on hers, and her insides heated up.

"You're welcome," he said.

"Good night." She closed the door behind him.

"Liar, liar. Cara's pants are on fire." Merry wagged a finger at her when she returned to the living room.

"What?"

"You and Matt?" She gestured toward the front door with her wineglass.

"Nothing's going on with me and Matt."

"Yeah, sure. I saw the way you two looked at each other. Tell me you haven't kissed him."

Cara shrugged. "Okay, I kissed him. Just once."

"Why just once? That man is gorgeous, and he's obviously into you." Merry's eyes narrowed. "Don't even tell me you gave him some lame excuse why you couldn't get involved right now."

"No, *he* told me he wasn't going to kiss me again."

"Oh." Merry sat back. "Why?"

"Because he's about to leave town and didn't want to start something he couldn't finish."

"Well, damn. He's honorable too. He's the perfect man. Can't you convince him to stay here in Dogwood?"

She shook her head. "His mom's not well. He's going home to Boston to be closer to her."

"And he loves his mother. Oh, my God. There's a catch, right? Why isn't he married?"

Cara rolled her eyes. "I don't know. I've only known him a couple of weeks. He's hotheaded, independent. Maybe he's not looking to settle down."

"My advice? Take whatever he's offering until he leaves town. Seriously, Cara, a hot fling would be good for you. You need some passion in your life."

"Just because you like to try a new flavor each month doesn't mean that works for everyone."

"No, but a few orgasms wouldn't hurt you either."

Cara covered her eyes with her hand.

"You are such a prude. Maybe you need a man like Matt to show you what the fuss is all about."

"I get what the fuss is about. Can we change the subject now?"

Merry smirked. "Have sex with Matt, then come talk to me about what the fuss is all about. So, I'll stop by Crestwood Gardens office on Thursday before work and see if I can put in a good word for you."

"That would be great. And cross everything you have two of that it works."

Merry crossed her eyes, then raised her glass toward Cara. "Here's to you, girl. I hope it all works out."

* * *

Matt turned onto Keeney Street just past nine o'clock the next morning. According to the information he'd gathered, George Rogers was an accountant, Stacy a dental receptionist. Both should be at work by now.

He cruised to the end of the block and turned onto Loblolly Lane, a cross street that ran behind their house. He pulled over and cut the engine. From here he could see most of the yard, with the exception of that far corner behind the deck where he and Cara had heard the dogs barking night before last.

He didn't see the dogs today either, leading him to believe they were still chained. Why have a fenced-in backyard, then keep your dogs chained? For that matter, why keep dogs in the backyard without human contact?

It was beyond Matt's comprehension why they'd go to such trouble to keep these two dogs when they clearly didn't want them. Then again, he'd learned long ago not to try to figure out why people did the things they did. In his line of work, he'd seen it all.

He peered through his binoculars, scanning the backyard. It was a good forty-five degrees right now, so he wasn't here to collect evidence. He needed to get the lay of the land in daylight. Assess the dogs' condition, if he could, their range of movement, and their access to food and water.

The back of the yard, where he had parked, was shrouded by several tall pines, with what looked to be an oak tree in the corner. Matt was a poor judge of tree species in the winter when there were no leaves on the branches. The center of the yard had some scraggly grass. Much of it had been worn down from the dogs' constant running and pacing, revealing the red clay beneath. Deep holes lined the perimeter of the fence.

On the deck, a rusted grill stood next to a worn, white plastic patio set. Two of the chairs lay on their sides, unused. He wondered if they ever used their backyard at all. Were the dogs even tame?

Through the binoculars, he spotted movement below the deck. Bingo.

He sharpened the focus. Four brown legs moved about below the wooden beams, and there—yes, he saw the chain. It was medium grade, two-inch links perhaps. Just heavy enough to do the job. The dog stepped out into the sunshine.

It was dark brown, striped like the other dog Cara had when he first met her, with the stocky body of a boxer, but taller. The snout was longer. Some kind of mixed breed. The dog stared straight at him with uncanny accuracy, despite the fact that Matt would be next to invisible to him through the trees on the far side of the yard.

As he stared into those brown eyes, Matt's interest in the case went from casual to ferocious. The poor creature sat and scratched at the chain with its hind leg, trying to rid itself of the cumbersome weight.

No animal deserved to live that way.

Matt took careful notes of the layout of the backyard. He maneuvered the Grand Cherokee along the fence line until he located the clearest line of sight and noted that too.

He'd be back after dark, when the temperature dropped.

\* \* \*

Cara stared at the photo on her screen. The pretty little fawn boxer named Sadie crouched against a cinder-block wall with chipped blue paint. She wore the glazed expression of doom Cara had come to know so well, a combination of fear and despair. Her back hunched; her eyes were cast downward at the cement floor.

The email wasn't unusual. Cara got several like it each week: "Urgent, Boxer needs immediate rescue." Sadie's owners surrendered her to the shelter following her diagnosis of a mast cell tumor on her right front leg, saying they could no longer afford to care for her.

Abandoned. Alone. With cancer. Cara felt her heart ripping right out of her chest.

She'd already failed Marigold. She couldn't let Sadie die too.

The dog had until Friday to find rescue. This was Monday. Due to her cancer diagnosis and an overcrowded shelter, she had been bumped to the top of the euthanasia list.

Cara would watch over her until then. And if Friday came without rescue for Sadie? Well, she couldn't be held accountable for her actions. Homeowners' associations and their stupid rules be damned.

She sighed. It was late, and she should have been in bed an hour ago. Dylan wasn't exactly likely to tone down his toddler exuberance because his nanny hadn't gotten a good night's sleep.

The knock on her front door was so quiet she almost missed it. Casper didn't. He leaped to his feet, hackles raised. Ear-splitting barks ripped from his throat. Cara lunged for his collar, shushing him. The last thing she needed was a noise complaint about her dog barking at—she glanced at the clock—ten 'til midnight.

Who in the world was knocking on her door at this hour? Feeling a bit uneasy, she approached the front door, one hand still gripping Casper's collar, and pressed her eye to the peephole.

Matt.

She smoothed her hair back from her face and drew a deep breath, then pulled the door open.

"Hey." His dark eyes landed on hers and stuck there. "I didn't want to wake you, but I saw the light on downstairs."

She nodded, motioning him inside. "Should be in bed, but I'm still up."

Cara glanced down at herself and held in a groan. She wore a pink, long-sleeved T-shirt and pink flannel pajama pants with little sleeping puppies all over them. And no bra. She released Casper and crossed her arms over her chest.

Matt's eyes drifted down, lingered for a moment on her chest, then made their way back up to her face, looking a shade darker than they had moments before. Underneath his usual clean soapy scent, she smelled something meaty, like—bacon?

Casper practically tackled him, sniffing up and down his jeans and shoving his snout into Matt's hands as if to check for yummy treats.

She chewed her bottom lip and watched him. Why was Matt Dumont paying house calls at midnight? And why was she so damn happy to see him?

No good answer to either question.

"I staked out the Rogers place again tonight. Went over and got a feel for it in the daylight. The dogs are definitely on chains. I had a visual on one of them this morning. Anyway, got something for you." He held out a thumb drive and gestured to her laptop. "May I?"

"Sure."

He sat on the couch and slid the portable drive into one of the USB slots on her laptop, then turned toward her. "What's this?"

Sadie's heartbreaking photo filled the screen.

Cara sat next to him and clasped her hands in her lap. "Just a dog I'm torturing myself over because I can't go pull her from the shelter."

"I'm sorry. Will someone else take her?"

"I hope so. She has cancer. She only has until Friday to find rescue."

"Cancer." He had a way of looking at her that made her feel like he was seeing right through her skin. It was at the same time intimate and unsettling. "Is that why she ended up at the shelter?"

Cara nodded. "Owners didn't want to pay for treatment."

"And now she's gotten under your skin."

She nodded again, her throat uncomfortably tight.

"What will you do if she doesn't find rescue?"

She looked down at her hands. "I don't know yet, Matt, but I can't let her die like that."

He placed a hand on her knee. "Will she die? From the cancer?"

"Probably not. It's a slow-growing tumor, but she needs surgery as soon as possible."

"And you guys take in dogs like that, dogs that will need a lot of medical treatment?"

"Oh, well, yeah. A lot of them do. I mean, Triangle Boxer Rescue's spent hundreds on Casper already, between his mange and his heartworms. It might take time to raise the funds, but we would never turn Sadie away because of her cancer diagnosis."

"I'm sure someone will take her. You're not the only foster home out there."

"No, but there's a wait list right now to get into rescue. There aren't enough foster homes, and, without me, it's one less."

His eyes were heavy on hers. "She's not your responsibility. You can't save them all. Think of all the dogs you've helped. Just look at Casper."

Cara looked down at the white dog curled over her feet. "I know. Anyway, you said you had something to show me."

"Right." Matt minimized the photo of Sadie and pulled up the photos on his thumb drive.

Cara squinted at the image before her. It was a grainy black-and-white image of the Rogerses' backyard with two sets of glowing eyes shining out of the darkness.

"I'm not sure if these will do the job for you. It was right at thirty-two degrees while I was over there so it's on the bubble, I guess, but maybe with Durham PD's report, it will be enough."

"It's worth a try." Cara clicked through the photos. There were close-ups of each dog, visible mainly in outline, but clear enough to be identifiable. A slender chain drooped from each neck. The dogs stared straight into the camera in almost every shot. "How did you get these? We couldn't see them at all the other night."

"That's my job, sweetheart," Matt said smugly. "Like I said, I went over during the day to scout out the area and find the best location to photograph them. Then tonight I brought a big slab of hot greasy bacon with me to lure them where I wanted them."

Cara's eyes widened. "Isn't that trespassing?"

"Who says I got out of the car? Dogs have a keen sense of smell, I'm told."

She couldn't help it. She grinned up at him. "So what happened to the bacon?"

"I ate it."

"You didn't even save a piece for poor, hungry Casper? No wonder he was about to lick your hands off when you got here."

"I think I should invite him over for breakfast before he can eat my bacon." His voice sounded lower, more intimate.

Cara realized she was sitting way too close, her hip against his, leaning over him as she tabbed through photos on the laptop. She glanced up and froze. Matt's eyes were hungry, and not for bacon.

The air between them warmed. Tingles of awareness glided over her skin, stirring a yearning deep inside her. Oh man, but she really wished he hadn't promised not to kiss her again. His eyes blazed into hers, then slid lower. A faint groan escaped his lips.

Cara looked down and saw that her nipples had hardened beneath the thin cotton of her shirt, revealing her lusty thoughts. She sat back, pulling at the fabric as her cheeks burned. God, this might be more embarrassing than when he'd caught her staring at his crotch the other night in the car.

"Don't hide them on my account." Matt offered a lopsided grin. His eyes raked over her with an intensity that made her squirm. He leaned closer, until she felt the heat radiating off him. "Remind me again why I can't kiss you?"

"Because you're moving to Boston?" Her voice sounded breathless, which was probably because she couldn't breathe.

"That's a damn shame." He leaned back, retrieved his thumb drive, and stood.

She clutched at the edge of the couch to keep from reaching for him. Desire throbbed inside her, an aching need she had a feeling Matt could satisfy in completely mind-boggling ways.

"I copied those photos onto your hard drive. Let me know how it goes." He was walking toward the door.

She stood and tucked her arms around herself.

"Good night, Cara." He gave her a slow smile that melted her from the inside out, then let himself out into the night, leaving behind only a blast of cold air and the faint scent of bacon.

# 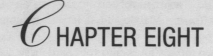CHAPTER EIGHT

*J*'m just—I'm in shock." Felicity Prentiss leaned back in her chair and pressed a palm to her pale forehead. Her husband's December Visa bill lay on the desk in front of her. On it were charges for an L-shaped diamond pendant and two nights at the Atlanta Marriott.

"I can see why this is upsetting," Matt said. "Obviously, it confirms your suspicions about his affair. Unfortunately, you didn't hire me until the end of December, so I wasn't there to photograph them together, but we're closing in, Mrs. Prentiss. It's only a matter of time."

She leaned forward and smashed her fist against the credit card statement, her brown eyes gone hard as stone. "I want to meet this 'L' bitch and rip that diamond right off her neck."

Matt didn't flinch. "That's not advisable, but don't worry, you'll make up for it in the settlement."

Felicity released a sigh and slumped in her chair. "I have to say, I really am disappointed the investigation is taking so long."

"Yes, ma'am. I understand your frustration." Matt was

pretty damn frustrated himself. He'd been on this case for two weeks, and despite her recent discovery on the Visa bill, he was no closer to catching Ken Prentiss in the act than he had been when she hired him.

Matt drummed his fingers against the worn laminate desktop. He came into the office space he rented on Porter Street only a couple times a week. Usually, he preferred the comfort and convenience of his home office, but business like this couldn't be conducted at home.

This morning, the eight-by-ten office space wasn't nearly big enough.

Felicity turned her doe eyes on him as two fat tears spilled over her lids and dripped down her cheeks. "It's just—I still have to live with him, you know? I'm ready to file for divorce and get on with my life."

"We've discussed before the pros and cons of installing a GPS device in his Lexus. I think this is the time to use that option. I've followed him from work. I've sat outside your home and waited for him to sneak out after you're in bed. Whatever he's doing, it's very discreet. With the GPS unit, I'll know where he is and where he's been. We'll find his love nest and get the photos we need."

She patted back a flyaway strand of blond hair that had escaped the elegant twist at the nape of her neck. "Well, if you think it's best. I was hoping to avoid the extra expense. I'm only doing this to make sure I get the money I deserve for all the emotional pain he's put me through, you know?"

"Absolutely. And I'll make sure you get the evidence you need. I promised you that up front."

He figured her for a gold digger, more or less. They'd only been married a little over a year, and from what he'd gathered, Felicity had married the lifestyle, not the man. He doubted her heart was actually broken; although, who knew? He'd been wrong before.

Either way, Ken Prentiss deserved what he had coming for cheating on her, and Matt didn't feel guilty in the least that this man was going to lose a sizable chunk of his savings to Felicity. He had no tolerance for men, or women, who messed around on the person they had sworn to love.

He'd felt that betrayal firsthand, and while the pain had gone out of the wound, he suspected that his disgust for those who cheated would last a lifetime.

"Thank you, Matt." Felicity wiped the tears away and straightened in her chair. "So how quickly will we see results with this GPS thing?"

"It depends on which model you decide to go with. There's the FastTrak, which sends real-time tracking updates to my laptop every ten seconds. I can see where he is and go catch him in the act. That one's going to run you close to four hundred dollars. Then you have the Power Tracker, which stores all the information for me to download once I've retrieved it from his car. That one's less than two hundred. Either one will get the job done. It's a matter of how quickly you want the results and how much money you're willing to invest."

She tapped her index finger against her lips and eyed Matt with suspicion. "That's a lot of money just to help you do your job."

"It's an investment, Mrs. Prentiss. Either you can pay me to sit on your husband's tail twenty-four/seven, which will cost you significantly more than four hundred bucks, or you can spring for the GPS and save us both a lot of time and hassle."

"Well, all right, then. I guess there's no guarantee of the cheaper one helping us, since you can't see where he's been until after the fact. How frequently will you be monitoring him if you had the one with live updates?"

"I'll keep tabs on him at all times. I can set it up to notify me on my cell phone of any movement on the vehicle, even if that's at three in the morning. If he's out there, I'll catch him."

She nodded more decisively this time. "Okay, then. Get that one. Do you need me to sign something?"

Matt slid the paperwork across the desk to her, feeling relief loosen in his chest. She'd given him a retainer up front to cover half of the estimated cost of the case, but they'd already exceeded that amount in man-hours. Disgruntled clients sometimes skipped out without paying. Felicity Prentiss had become worrisome. She was nervous, agitated, and eager to have this over and done with.

He didn't blame her a bit, but he still needed to get paid. And he was ready to get this show on the road.

After Felicity left, Matt straightened up his desk and packed his satchel. He'd spend the afternoon in the comfort of his home office. His cell phone beeped.

He glanced at the caller ID and answered with a smile. "Hey, Mom."

"Jason? Where are you? You were supposed to be here an hour ago."

His smile faded. "Mom, it's Matt. Where are you? Is everything okay?"

"Matt! Oh my goodness, how embarrassing. I pushed the wrong number. I was looking for Jason. He said he'd be over this morning to fix a clogged drain."

"Well, you know Jason. He's probably lost track of time. Want me to track him down for you?"

"Oh goodness, no. I'll call him. How are you? I heard you met a girl." He could hear the smile in her voice.

Matt straightened in his chair. Damn Jason and his big mouth. "It's not like that, Mom. I'm just helping her on a case."

"Uh-huh. Don't you go and fall for some sweet southern belle now that you've finally made plans to come home."

"I'm coming home. You can go ahead and get my room ready."

"Oh sweetie, I can't wait." Her voice grew wistful.

Neither could Matt.

\* \* \*

"Eight, nine, ten…ready or not, here I come." Cara tiptoed around the door and peered into Dylan's bedroom. "Hmm, where could Dylan be?"

Giggles burst from the back corner of the room. Cara grinned. "Oh I know, he must be behind the chair."

She made a production of looking behind the overstuffed glider as the giggling intensified. "Nope, not there. He must be in bed, then."

She pulled back the Curious George bedspread and looked underneath it. Dylan's giggling had reached near hysteria. Any moment now, he would roll out of the corner in a fit of uncontrollable happiness.

"Hmmm." She ambled toward the back corner and peeked around the bookcase. "Oh, there you are!"

Dylan sat doubled over, clutching his belly as he laughed himself silly. It was the same place he had hidden the last four times, and yet it never got any less entertaining.

Cara ruffled his feathery blond hair. "You got me. Whose turn next?"

"Me again!"

"Okay, okay. But my turn after that?"

He nodded vigorously and scampered off toward the bookcase before Cara even made it out the door. She had leaned against the railing to begin counting again when she heard the squeak of the garage door below them.

"Hey, Dylan, someone's home early. Let's go see who."

"Mommy!" He burst through the doorway, eyes bright.

"Probably. Here, hold my hand." She gripped his chubby fingers in hers as they walked down the stairs.

"Mommy!" he screamed again as Robin Smythe stepped through the door.

"Dylan, hey, baby." She bent down and held her arms out. He slammed into her chest and nearly sent her sprawling.

It warmed Cara's heart, the love of a little boy for his mother. Just the sight of her made his whole day. And from the look on her face, the feeling was mutual. Cara hoped she would be lucky enough to experience that bond someday.

Robin stood with Dylan wrapped in her arms and deposited her purse on the kitchen counter. It was only a few minutes past three, two hours earlier than she usually came home. She looked at Cara, her eyes watery and red.

*Uh-oh.*

"What a nice surprise," Cara said. "I'll go start tidying up the playroom. Dylan, would you like to help me while your mom takes off her coat?"

"Okay." He slid to the ground and ran ahead of Cara into the playroom.

"Thank you, Cara," Robin said.

Cara nodded. She followed Dylan into the playroom and pretended to gobble his hands with the bag as he dropped his building blocks inside. In a few minutes, the floor was clean, and Dylan was running laps around the train table.

He stopped and picked up a section of wooden track. "Buildin', Mommy, look!"

Robin stood in the doorway, watching her son with a warm smile. "Why don't you build me something extra special, Dylan, while I talk to Cara for a few minutes. Then you can show it to both of us."

"Big hill. Biiiig." He waved the track dramatically.

"Sounds cool, Dylan. I'll be right back." Cara followed Robin to the kitchen table.

They sat across from each other, and Robin raked a hand through her blond hair. Cara felt a twinge of unease.

"I was let go today," Robin said.

"Oh... wow. I'm so sorry. What happened?"

"Internal shenanigans. They were consolidating departments, and my position was cut. This isn't the way I wanted to tell you, but I'm expecting our second child in August."

"Oh, my God, congratulations. On the baby, I mean."

"Thank you." Robin looked up, her expression heavy with apology.

Cara's stomach fell as the ramifications sank in. *Oh no.*

"I'd been tossing around the idea of staying home after the baby comes, and then this happened." She shrugged. "I'm so sorry, Cara. I hate to leave you in the lurch, but with me being home, we won't need a nanny. We'll give you three weeks' severance pay. That should be enough time to get something else lined up, shouldn't it?"

Cara gulped and nodded. "That's very generous of you. Yeah, you know, things move pretty quickly with nanny positions. I'm sure I can find something...."

Tears stung her eyes.

Robin reached across the table and grabbed her hand. "We'll have you over to dinner one night so that you can say good-bye to Dylan. Maybe we'll go out. I'm still working this whole thing through my head. We're going to miss you so much, Cara. You've been so wonderful with Dylan."

Cara nodded, her throat too swollen to speak.

Robin stood and walked with her to the front door. "List me at the top of your references. I'll sing your praises."

\* \* \*

"Impromptu girls' night at Red Heels. Please come, I haven't seen you in ages. You can even crash at my place tonight."

"But Cara, I told you I'm not drinking alcohol right now. It's part of my new cleanse."

Cara rolled her eyes and shifted the phone to her left ear. Her sister, Susie, was always on some random crusade. "Well, you don't have to drink. Just come."

"Did you know alcohol is a neurotoxin that causes your brain cells to swell?"

Cara sighed. "No."

"It's also a depressant. Not what you should be drinking right after losing your job. You should let me make you one of my pomegranate-almond shakes and come with me to a yoga class. Get in touch with your inner chi."

"Okay, you know what—never mind. I'll call you this weekend, okay?"

"Well, I'll come." Susie sounded offended. "I just wanted you to be informed."

"Okay, Sus, I'm informed. We're meeting at Red Heels at seven, but you can come here earlier if you want to ride together."

"I'll probably be over around five. I just have to get this week's column submitted." Susie wrote an alternative health column for *Southern Health & Fitness*, a local magazine.

"See you then."

Cara hung up the phone and resisted the urge to pound it against the table. She adored her little sister, really, but Susie could be as infuriating as she was endearing.

Cara changed into her running clothes and took Casper for a long run, until the cold air made her lungs burn. Then she stepped inside a hot shower and shed a few tears into the steam. Just a few, because it was only a job and she'd find something new.

She had just finished blow-drying her hair when the door-bell rang.

Casper's frantic barks filled the house, accompanied by

the scrape of toenails across the hardwood floors in the foyer. Cara bounded down the stairs, hooked two fingers through his collar, and pulled the door open.

Susie stood silhouetted in the doorway, her blond hair glistening in the sun. She wore a purple jacket and a brightly colored peasant skirt that swirled around her ankles. "Oh, you have a new one! What's his name?" She bent down, and Casper lunged forward to kiss her face.

Everyone loved Susie. She was bright, colorful, vivacious. Energy shimmered around her in a tangible aura.

"Casper."

"The Friendly Ghost." Susie rubbed his chin, then stood and thrust an orange thermos at Cara. "I brought you that shake. Drink it. Where's Mojo? Did he get adopted?"

"Thanks." Cara took the thermos, unscrewed the lid, and sniffed at the contents. "He did; he found a really great family. What did you say is in this?"

"Pomegranate-almond. It's good for you. Flush out some junk before you go drinking tonight."

Cara sipped. Sweet, tangy, with a nutty aftertaste. "It's pretty good. Thanks. So when did you give up alcohol?"

Cara led the way into the living room and settled on the couch next to her sister. The last she'd known, Susie was focused on the healing powers of incense.

"About two months ago. I met this amazing guy, Marco. You met him that night at Mom's." Susie looked at her, and Cara nodded. Of course, because everything with Susie involved a man.

"That's right." Cara remembered him. Marco was a little different from Susie's usual type, with long hair and cowboy boots.

"Anyway, he's opened me up to a lot of new stuff. My last two columns have been inspired. I've gotten so much great fan mail."

"That's awesome. I liked the one you did about the hidden dangers of canned food. I had no idea there was BPA in my tomato sauce." Cara took another long sip of the shake.

"Thanks. So what's up with the Smythes firing you?"

"They didn't fire me. Robin got let go, and she's decided to stay home for a while, so they don't need a nanny anymore. They're giving me severance pay, which is nice. It just makes me sick, though, to think I'm not going back."

"I bet." Susie's eyes were sympathetic.

"I miss Dylan already. And I doubt I'll get lucky enough to find a family that great twice in a row. Ugh, I dread the job search. I'll start tomorrow. Tonight, I'm just not thinking about it."

"You know, maybe it's time to quit nannying and start focusing on your photography. You're so talented, Cara, and you're wasting it." Susie's gaze roamed over the framed photographs on the walls.

"I'm working on it. I've taken three new bookings this month, but it's not enough to live on. That takes time."

"And commitment." Susie's blue eyes locked on Cara's. "Something you've lived for eight years without."

"Yeah, well, you know why." Cara swallowed more pomegranate-almond shake and hoped her sister hadn't put anything weird in it. She'd done one of Susie's cleanses before, and it was not an experience she was eager to repeat.

"Have you been talking to Mom again? Those numbers are meaningless. You could reduce your risk of cancer just as much by changing your diet and cleansing the toxins from your body than waiting around for some doctor's statistical chart to declare you cured."

"Not cured." Cara shook her head. "Just a ninety-five percent chance of staying in remission."

A ninety-five percent chance of not winding up like Gina.

And a guarantee she wouldn't leave behind a heartbroken husband and child if the worst were to happen.

Susie shrugged. "Whatever. It's just a number. Anyway, if you're going out tonight, we need to get you all dolled up. Come on, let's go explore your closet."

* * *

An hour later, they stepped into Red Heels, and Cara's spirits immediately lifted. This place always put her in a good mood, even if her sister was the one drawing looks from every man in the place.

Susie swept toward the bar in her long skirt, swirling aqua and purple from her slim hips. She wore a form-fitting teal blouse, which complemented her skirt as well as her complexion, and set her ample breasts on display. Susie radiated confidence, vitality, and sensuality.

Cara smoothed her hands over her own lavender skirt as she followed Susie to the bar. Next to her sister, she felt very pastel. Olivia Bennett and Beth Ruben, Cara's former college roommates turned good friends, already sat on velvet stools, pink drinks in hand.

Olivia stood to give Cara a hug. "Sorry about your job, Car."

"Yeah, really sorry," Beth said.

"Thanks. At least I can get hammered tonight and I don't have to get up for work in the morning." She shrugged. "And Susie's not drinking, so I have a designated driver."

"That's the spirit." Olivia slapped her a high five. "We'll all buy you a round for good luck."

Merry pushed through the door then, her cheeks rosy from the winter air. She hurried to the bar and slung her jacket over Cara's on the extra bar stool, then slid onto a seat and ordered a strawberry martini. "I can't stay too long tonight, girls. I've got a sick dog at home."

"Oh no. Which one?" Cara pushed her empty martini glass toward the bartender and nodded for another.

"Piper, the new one. She'll be okay, just needs some TLC. This is some serious shit you're in, Cara—first with the dog thing and now your job."

"What dog thing?" Beth spun on her stool, and suddenly all eyes were on Cara.

She filled them in on the complaint from the homeowners' association, then Merry gleefully took over with tales of Matt.

"I'm telling you, ladies, the man is delicious. And Cara's kissed him." Merry's eyes sparkled impishly.

"Wait a minute." Olivia pointed a finger at Cara, her eyes wide. "Is this the infamous Mr. FMH?"

"Yeah, yeah." Cara sipped her new martini.

"Oh my God. She's blushing." Beth clapped her hands with delight.

Susie quit flirting with the bartender and tuned into their conversation. "And when's the last time we saw Cara blush about a guy?"

Merry nodded. "Exactly."

"Oh, please." Cara's cheeks grew even hotter. "Okay, he's hot, and he's a great kisser, but he's leaving town. The end."

Susie rolled her eyes. "Which gives you a convenient excuse."

Merry hooked an arm through Susie's. "Girl, you nailed it."

"Yep, you're totally busted," Olivia said. "And speaking of guys, I happen to be dating my own FMH guy right now."

Cara gave her a grateful smile as all eyes and ears turned to Olivia as she told them about the construction worker who was keeping her warm at night. Cara leaned an elbow against the bar and relaxed. This was exactly what she'd needed tonight: fabulous drinks in her favorite bar surrounded by her closest friends and family. Damn, she was lucky.

The martinis flowed, along with the laughter. They shared appetizers and brownie sundaes, and Cara felt the room beginning to soften and spin around her. It was definitely a good thing she didn't have to drive herself home or get up for work in the morning.

Olivia regaled them with tales of her social-media battle against Halverson Foods, a local chicken-processing company that had recently come under fire when workers had been videotaped kicking helpless birds before they were slaughtered.

Merry listened, wide-eyed. "I never knew this side of you, Olivia."

Cara nodded. "She used to paper the halls of our dorm with photos of slaughtered pigs."

Her former roommate might look harmless with her waterfall of blond hair and sweet smile, but she was all fire and vinegar when it came to animal rights. She'd almost lost her job at the Main Street Café last year when she'd left pamphlets on the counter protesting the treatment of dairy cows.

"Have you ever thought about fostering?" Merry asked.

Olivia scrunched her nose. "No way. I live in an apartment, and I work full time."

Cara laughed inwardly. Merry was equally hardheaded when it came to her beloved Triangle Boxer Rescue. Olivia didn't stand a chance.

Around ten, Merry stood from her bar stool. After promising to call Olivia to arrange for her first foster, she gave Cara a hug and a kiss and headed home. Susie had become infatuated with the bartender, so Cara spent the next hour gossiping and catching up with Olivia and Beth. By the time they called it a night, Cara was ready to do the same.

"You need a ride, Cara?" Olivia asked as she gathered her coat.

"No, thanks. I came with Susie."

"Okay, then. Great seeing you tonight. Good luck with the job search."

Cara hugged them both, then slid in next to Susie at the bar. Her sister was bent forward, deep in conversation, honey-blond hair sweeping over the laminate bar top.

She looked over at Cara and grinned. "Hey, sis. Sorry for neglecting you."

Cara eyed the twenty-something, dark-haired, and well-muscled bartender, then whispered in her sister's ear. "What about Marco?"

Susie laughed. "Oh, please. We're just talking."

Cara didn't bother to point out that Susie's definition of talking was actually flirting. And, if she was perfectly honest, it was the reason she'd found herself hoping they didn't run into Matt as they left her townhouse earlier. When Susie was around, men didn't notice Cara.

Case in point, the bartender still stared at Susie in rapt attention. Not that Cara cared if the bartender checked her out.

Nor should she care if Matt noticed her. But okay, even if she couldn't date him, she really didn't mind knowing that he wanted her. Okay, she sort of secretly loved it. She'd never played this kind of game with a man before, and the sexual tension between them was hotter than anything she'd ever experienced. Maybe it was knowing he was off-limits that made him so much more desirable.

Or maybe she would have desired him no matter the circumstance. She let out a dreamy sigh and slurped from her martini.

Susie was giggling at something the bartender said, and Cara sobered. There were only a handful of other people at the bar, so his attention was largely undivided. But that wasn't what gave Cara's stomach an uncomfortable squeeze.

It was Susie's giggle. Her drunk giggle.

"Susie, are you drinking?" Cara focused on the sparkly pink drink in her sister's hand, which somehow, in her own tipsy haze, she hadn't previously noticed.

"Shhh, don't tell." Susie giggled again.

"You were supposed to drive us home."

"Oops. You're not drunk, are you?" Susie looked her up and down.

"Not sober enough to drive."

"Oh, well. I'm sure Olivia or Beth can drive us." Susie turned and swept her eyes around the room.

"They've gone home. It's okay. We'll call a cab."

The bartender looked at Cara and shook his head. "Dogwood Taxi stops running at midnight."

Cara looked down at her watch. It was twelve fifteen. "Well, crap."

Susie's eyes twinkled. "Let's call Matt. I want to meet your FMH guy."

"No way." Cara shook her head. She tried to weigh her options, which was difficult considering the foggy state of her brain. Calling a cab in from Raleigh or Durham would cost a fortune. She could call one of her friends back, but they were all home by now. It was late, and she and Susie were the only ones who didn't have to get up for work in the morning.

"If you wanna hang around until two, I'll drive you home." The bartender gave Susie a promising smile.

Cara glanced between them. *Hell, no.*

"Okay, let's call Matt." She pulled out her phone and sent him a quick text. *You awake?*

Thirty seconds later, her phone rang.

"What's up?" His voice was low and rough, and, dammit, her heart started beating a little faster just at the sound of it.

"This is embarrassing." She glared at Susie, who raised her eyebrows in wide-eyed innocence. "My designated driver forgot to stay sober, and we need a ride home. Would you mind picking us up?"

Matt chuckled. "Who's 'we'?"

"My sister and me. We're at Red Heels over on Main Street."

"I'll be there in ten."

Cara hung up the phone and looked at Susie, who was so gorgeous men practically lined up to flirt with her. And now Matt was on his way over. Her stomach flopped.

She should have called a cab from Raleigh.

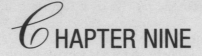

# CHAPTER NINE

$\mathcal{M}$att strolled into the martini bar. His eyes, like heat-seeking missiles, panned the mostly empty room and locked on the golden-haired beauty at the bar. The blonde next to her would be her sister, Susie.

He watched them for a moment, unobserved. Cara's sister was bold, flashy. The bartender was practically drooling in her lap. Beside her, Cara sat in a pale purple skirt and sweater a shade darker. She sipped from a pink drink, looking so damned beautiful she took his breath away.

He sauntered over and slid onto the bar stool next to her. She turned, her soft blue eyes stirring restless yearnings in his chest. "Hey."

She smiled, a sweet smile that turned restless yearnings into flat-out dishonorable intentions. "Thanks for coming."

"Not a problem."

Her sister turned around then, fixing him with bright blue eyes and a man-eating smile. "Susie Medlen." She thrust her hand toward him.

He took it and shook. "Matt Dumont. So what are you

two lovely ladies doing out past midnight on a Tuesday, both too drunk to drive yourselves home?"

Cara drained her glass. "I lost my job today."

"I'm sorry."

"Thanks." Her voice wavered just the tiniest bit.

Matt steeled himself against the urge to pull her into his arms. It was endearing, the way she wore her heart on her sleeve. And telling of her personality that after losing the job she loved, she'd rallied her friends around and gone out for a night on the town.

"And thank you for coming to get us," she said.

Susie leaned in. "Yes, thank you. I totally forgot I was supposed to stay sober enough to drive us home, although I think this turned out even better."

Matt decided not to mention that he'd already been in bed when Cara's text came through. This seemed like a worthwhile loss of sleep.

"Cara was just telling us about you, and here you are." Susie gave Cara's shoulders a squeeze, and Cara's cheeks flushed pink.

"Is that so?" This outing was getting more worthwhile all the time.

"No, it's not so. You guys all need to get a life. Let's go home." Cara pushed off the stool in a huff and stumbled right into his chest.

Matt slipped a hand around her waist to steady her. "I'd say you made the right call in not driving home."

"Yeah, well, everyone kept buying me drinks." She rested her head on his shoulder and leaned into him. Her left hand drifted down to his butt. Oh yeah, she was definitely drunk. He was stone cold sober, which meant he had no excuse for keeping his arm around her, encouraging her behavior.

She looked up at him, and the lust in her eyes almost brought him to his knees. With a sigh, she tugged free and leaned over to grab her jacket, giving Matt a nice view of her ass.

Susie gave the bartender a kiss on the cheek, grabbed her jacket, and walked with them out the front door.

Matt clicked the locks on the Grand Cherokee, then opened the front passenger door for Cara and the rear for Susie. By the time he'd walked around to the driver's side, they were both seated and arguing in hushed tones around the headrest. Matt caught the letters FMH, something he'd overheard from Merry as well. He suspected it referred to him in some way.

Susie sank back with a giggle and a satisfied grin. Cara scowled.

Matt glanced between them and decided to be grateful for what he didn't know. He started the engine.

"Where do you live, Susie?" he asked as he pulled onto Main Street.

"Oh, I'm crashing at Cara's tonight, thanks."

He nodded and signaled to turn right on Joplin Road. That was a blessing in disguise because if he'd wound up escorting Cara home alone, he probably couldn't be held accountable for his actions. She was drunk, her guard was down, and he had no business being anywhere near her.

Three minutes later, he pulled into his spot in Crestwood Gardens.

Cara and Susie slipped out into the darkness. He came around and found them headed for Cara's front door, Susie's arm draped over Cara's shoulders.

Cara turned and gave him one last smile. "Thanks, Matt. I owe you one."

He nodded and watched until they were safely inside with the front door locked. Then he let himself inside his own townhouse. Now completely awake, he walked to his laptop and tapped the screen to life.

Earlier tonight, he'd successfully placed the GPS locater under Ken Prentiss's silver Lexus GS while he was at dinner with his wife at Le Brasserie. The blinker on his screen showed Ken was now at home, presumably asleep in bed.

Tomorrow, the real fun would begin.

* * *

"Drink up." Susie slid a tall glass of something resembling pond slime across the kitchen counter toward Cara.

She grimaced and rubbed her forehead. "Um, I think I'll start with coffee, thanks."

"Coffee dehydrates, and dehydration is why you feel like crap already."

Cara glared at her. Susie looked fresh faced and happy, which was so unfair. Cara had a pounding headache, and just looking at the glass of green goo made her gag.

"I'm serious. Close your eyes and drink it. You'll feel so much better. You just need to flush all the toxins from the alcohol out of your body and rehydrate."

"No way."

"It tastes like lemons. Trust me. Go on." Susie pushed the offending glass closer.

Cara lifted it gingerly and sniffed. It did smell like lemons. "I don't have any lemons in my kitchen. What is it really?"

"It's my special hangover cure, complete with real lemons. I went down the street to Harris Teeter while you were still asleep."

Cara gave her sister a meaningful look and sipped. "Okay; it doesn't taste as bad as it looks."

"See? Go on, now. Drink it all, then take a shower. You'll be good as new."

Cara managed to drink the whole thing, then showered

and dried her hair. By the time she'd finished, she did feel tons better, and she hadn't even taken anything for her headache.

Susie was waiting for her in the kitchen, thumbing through messages on her phone. "Hey, sis, I have to get going, but I didn't want to leave while you were in the shower."

"I'm glad you came. We need to do this more often."

"Definitely. And by the way, you totally need to hook up with Matt."

"Not you too." Cara reached for an apple and took a big bite.

Susie grinned as she stood and slid the phone into her purse. "Not only is he freakin' hot, but he's hot *for you*. So what if he's leaving town? Give it a try, see what happens. Then, you know, if he moves, figure out what to do about it."

Cara took another bite of the apple and chewed through her thoughts. She hadn't been drunk enough last night to miss the fact that Matt's attention never strayed, not even with Susie standing right there giving off all her "men love me" vibes.

She shrugged. "It's fun flirting with him. Probably best to leave it at that."

"But why? He's leaving town, so he doesn't even threaten your whole 'no commitment' thing. Go live a little, for once."

"Because . . ." She shook her head. "Just because."

Susie stared at her for a long moment in uncharacteristic silence. "Wow, you've got it bad for him, don't you? You're afraid he'll break your heart?"

*Something like that.* "Don't be ridiculous. I'm not in love with him. I'm just not a casual-fling kind of girl, that's all."

"Mm-hmm." Susie pulled her in for a hug. "Well, let me know if you change your mind. I'll take you lingerie shopping. Anyway, I'll check in later this week to see how the job search is going, okay?"

"Thanks, Sus. And thanks for the . . . whatever that was I drank for breakfast."

"Welcome." Susie flashed another bright smile and breezed out the front door.

Cara stood there for a moment, in the void left behind. Her sister radiated some kind of crazy energy that made everything a little more colorful in her presence, and a little bit barren once she'd left.

Casper trotted into the kitchen and nosed around Cara's feet. She had an interested family scheduled to meet him on Friday.

If they decided to adopt him, she'd be left with an empty house.

And no job.

Hopelessness welled inside her, rising up until it stung her eyes.

Okay, time to get on that. She marched into the living room and booted up her laptop. She needed to update her resume and reactivate her profile on nannycare.com, the Web site she'd used to get her job with the Smythes.

First, she stole a quick peek at Sadie, the beautiful fawn boxer in the Shelton County Animal Shelter. She was still there, awaiting rescue, with two days left until her execution date.

Cara buried her face in her hands for a long moment, then closed the browser and opened her resume. First things first.

She was totally engrossed in her work when her cell phone chirped from its perch on the coffee table. She shifted her laptop to the side and nudged the phone with her left foot until she could reach it.

The text message was from Matt. *Feeling ok this morning?*

She grinned like a schoolgirl with a crush. *Susie detoxed me with something green and slimy. Much better now.*

Matt chimed right back. *I don't wanna know. U free for supper?*

Cara's heart beat double time. *No plans.*

*Stop by around 6. Bring Casper.*

Stop by? As in dinner at Matt's house? Cara lurched from the couch and stared at her living room wall, imagining him on the other side, holding his cell phone with that devilish smile on his face. *That sounds like a date.*

*Just dinner. Friends can have dinner, right?*

Not with chemistry like theirs, but then again, he seemed to be taking his promise not to kiss her again pretty seriously. *You're cooking?*

*Told you I cook. Don't bake though.*

Cara stole another glance at the wall, then texted him back. *I bake. Don't cook.*

*Together we've got a whole meal.*

Dammit, now she had to go to the grocery store.

\* \* \*

Cara rang Matt's doorbell promptly at six.

He opened the door wearing jeans, a long-sleeved Red Sox shirt, and the kind of smile that made her knees shake and something funny tingle deep in her belly. His gaze traveled over her pink sweater and jeans, then back up to her face. "Hey."

"I made a fruit tart." She shifted Casper's leash to her right hand and held the covered dish toward Matt. He'd said this wasn't a date, but it sure as hell felt like one. She felt half seduced already just by the idea of him cooking for her.

"Thanks." He took a step back and motioned her inside.

She followed him in, closed the door behind her, and unclipped Casper's leash from his collar. He trotted off to greet Matt, tail wiggling in delight. Cara surveyed the room,

taking in black leather furniture, white walls, and an enor-
mous flat-screen TV mounted to the wall. Typical guy stuff.

It was clean, though, well kept. Lots of family photos on
the mantel. And the aroma of something delicious wafted
from the kitchen.

She'd been here once before, the afternoon she accused
him of filing a complaint with the homeowners' association,
but she'd been too upset then to notice her surroundings.

"Dogs like you," she said, as Matt knelt to rub Casper
behind his ears.

"And I like them. We always had dogs when I was growing up. Maybe I'll get one once I'm settled in Massachusetts."

"Make sure you adopt."

He straightened. "Sure thing. I've got no interest in potty
training a puppy anyway. You hungry?"

She nodded. "Whatever you've got cooking in there
smells amazing."

"Chicken breasts with a white wine, mushroom, and shal-
lot sauce, baby potatoes, and grilled asparagus."

Cara's eyes widened. "Wow. You really do cook."

"My mom raised us both to know our way around the
kitchen. I'd offer you a glass of wine, but guessing you might
not be in the mood after last night?" He gave her a crooked
grin.

She winced. "Yeah, water might be better." And safer
too. The last thing she needed was to make this dinner more
romantic, or lower her inhibitions around Matt.

"Water it is." He walked to the cupboard and pulled out
two glasses. "So how did you spend your first day as a member of the unemployed?"

"Recovering from my hangover, then working on getting
myself employed, then baking. Went by pretty fast, actually."

He set a glass of water on the counter in front of her.
"There must be a lot of nanny positions out there."

She nodded. "There are. It's just a matter of finding the right fit. I doubt I'll find another family who lets me volunteer at the shelter two mornings a week."

"Yeah, that was a sweet thing you had going. Any word on the dogs over on Keeney Street?"

"Merry met with animal control yesterday and gave them your photos. They were going to ride over today, have a talk with the owners. I haven't heard yet how that went."

"Keep me posted."

"I will."

"Temps are going to drop again. I heard maybe even snow this weekend. I could probably get some better pictures for you if you need them."

Cara watched as he arranged chicken, potatoes, and asparagus onto two plates. "You're a softie under that tough exterior, aren't you?"

He turned his head and offered her a slow smile. "Shh, don't tell."

Her insides melted like the butter he was currently drizzling over their asparagus. "Your secret is safe with me."

"Hungry?"

She nodded and followed him to the table. Casper trailed behind them, his toenails clicking against the linoleum.

"How's your mom?" she asked as they sat.

Matt's warm eyes clouded. "She says she's okay, but she's not quite herself. I'll feel so much better when I'm there to keep an eye on her."

"Is she sick?"

"She was diagnosed last year with heart disease and high blood pressure and had surgery to bypass a blocked artery. Caught us off guard. Maybe Jason and I are worrying too much about her now."

"It's good that you guys are looking out for her. She's lucky." Cara took a bite of her chicken. "This is delicious."

"Thanks. One of Mom's recipes."

They chewed in silence. She studied the curve of his jaw, the thick column of his neck, the swirl of dark hair visible at the collar of his shirt. Flirting with Matt was fun, but this was a little too close, too intimate. The truth was, she liked everything about him, way too much for her own good.

"How did you become a PI? Was it something you'd always wanted to do?"

He shook his head. "Nah, I wanted to be a marine. Fell into PI work by accident about five years ago."

"Did you join the marines first?"

"Yeah. Served two tours in Iraq. You learn a lot about yourself when you're in the middle of the desert, trusting that the guy behind you has your back, knowing that the guy in front of you is trusting you with his life."

"I bet." Cara watched him with new admiration. Of course he was a soldier. She was surprised she hadn't noticed it before. Growing up near Camp Lejeune, she'd known her share of marines. The simple, clean, orderly lifestyle. Honor. Integrity.

"Just couldn't sit in an office after that."

"Why'd you leave the corps?"

Matt looked down at his plate. "Our convoy got hit by a roadside bomb. I was sent home on the DL. Couldn't reenlist. Anyway, PI work seemed to fit the bill."

Cara took a bite of asparagus. She knew him well enough to sense there was more to that story. But it wasn't her place to pry. "Is Jason a PI as well?"

"More of a computer geek, but he just got his license. We should make a good team. He's a cyber genius. I'm into more of the dirtier stuff. Surveillance, good old-fashioned sleuthing at the courthouse."

"Together you've got it all."

"More or less."

"Well, that's exciting. I bet your mom's over the moon about her boys going into business together."

"Pretty much."

They ate for a few minutes in silence, until a loud beeping interrupted from somewhere in the living room. Casper leaped from his resting place beside Cara's chair, his head cocked to the side as he stared through the doorway.

"My subject's on the move. Check this out." Matt led her to his laptop on the coffee table. A map filled the screen. On it, a red blob blinked and beeped as it inched its way down Fuller Street.

Cara peeked over his shoulder. "What in the world is that?"

"Tracking a philandering husband. Last night I placed a GPS locator under his car. Now I know wherever he goes."

"That's a little stalkerish, isn't it?"

He turned to her with a sly smile. "Yet perfectly legal. This guy's sneaky. I'm ready to nail his ass."

"So that you can get out of town."

His smile faded. "Yeah."

They were standing too close again. His scent filled her lungs, and his warmth touched her skin.

"Although I've got to say, you're taking all the enjoyment out of it for me, Cara."

She laughed a little, not sure what to say. He reached out and brushed a thumb over her lips. The sensation of his rough skin made her heart pound and her body tingle with anticipation.

Matt's hand cupped her jaw, his eyes hot and heavy on hers. So what if it was a bad idea? She leaned forward.

With a sound like she'd just punched the wind out of him, he dropped his hand from her face and took a step back. "Ready for dessert?"

He turned and walked back to the kitchen.

"Huh?" She licked her lips and swallowed. Her throat felt like sandpaper.

"There you go with your mind in the gutter again. You are really driving me crazy here—you know that?"

"I, uh..." She shook her head. "What about the guy?" She pointed to the blinking dot on the screen.

"Looks like he's headed home from work. If I get lucky, he'll try to sneak out and meet his mistress later tonight after the wife's in bed. Best part, I can keep tabs on him from the comfort of my couch." He came around the counter with two slices of Cara's fruit tart. "This looks delicious."

She accepted the plate he held toward her. "Thanks."

Thirty minutes later, she stepped outside into the cool night air. With Matt at her side, she walked across the parking lot to let Casper pee, then headed for her front door. The whole evening had been lovely—and unsettling.

"Thanks for dinner." She stared at her door, remembering the toe-curling kiss they'd shared there.

"You're welcome. I'd walk you to your door, but then I'd only be thinking about pushing you into it and kissing you again."

Well, at least they were on the same wavelength.

Cara sucked in a breath, then blew it out. "Right now, I wish you would."

Matt took a step toward her, his eyes heavy with desire. In his face, she saw the promise of everything he wanted to do with her, a promise of something heartbreakingly fantastic.

He groaned and shoved his hands into his pockets. "Go inside, Cara, before I take you up on that offer."

And, like a coward, she did.

# CHAPTER TEN

*C*ara stared at the pitiful little tabby cat in front of her and sighed. She loved animals, all animals, big or small, furry or feathered, but she'd never been much of a cat person. Usually she would have spent Wednesday morning here at the shelter photographing all the new cats, but what with her hangover and visiting with Susie, she hadn't made it.

So here she was, a day late and filled with all sorts of regret. None of which had anything to do with the tabby cat named Jewel. More to do with the fact that she hadn't had sex in over a year, and Matt Dumont was driving her ten kinds of crazy.

To be fair, he really needed some kind of flaw to make her dislike him. Like if he hated dogs. Then he could be as gorgeous and irresistible as he wanted, and she wouldn't feel like flinging herself on her knees and begging him not to move to Boston.

"Here, Jewel." Cara rolled a ball across the floor, trying to entice the little cat to jump out of her cage for some exercise and her photo shoot. The cat eyed her warily, ears pinned back. She remained crouched in the back of the cage.

Cara reached in to pet her. Jewel hissed.

"Okay, then." Cara sat on the floor and stared at her hands. Stubborn little cat. Before she knew it, tears pooled in her eyes.

Well, that was just pathetic. She brushed them away and leaned against the wall of cages. From behind her head, she heard purring. Then soft fur brushed against her hair. Cara turned her head to see golden eyes staring into hers. A black-and-white cat pressed himself against the metal bars, desperate for her affection.

Cara looked at his name tag. "Hi, Charlie."

The tag said he'd been here at the Dogwood Shelter since September. Four months in this cage. And still he could purr like her very presence in the room had made his day.

She reached back and opened his door. Charlie leaped into her lap, his front paws kneading contentedly until her thigh felt like ground beef. "Why hasn't anyone taken you home, Charlie?"

He gazed up, amber eyes narrowed in contentment. Blissfully happy to have her affection, even if just for a few minutes. Could she do that with Matt?

Not likely. Why couldn't people be more like animals? Why did they have to carry around so much baggage instead of living for the moment?

Cara heard a light thump to her right and turned to see Jewel beside her. Charlie leaned over and sniffed her, then returned to purring and kneading in Cara's lap.

Jewel took a tentative step closer, then climbed onto Cara's calves, curled into a little ball with her head against Cara's left sneaker, and closed her eyes.

Cara reached for her camera and snapped a photo. The click of the shutter caused Jewel to raise her head.

Click.

Cara sharpened the focus, bringing out the cat's amber eyes, the delicate swirl of gray fur around them.

If Crestwood Gardens wouldn't let her have dogs, what about cats?

Ah, hell. No offense to the two souls resting on her legs, but she had to have dogs. Maybe, someday, a cat too. But definitely dogs. If she couldn't fix the problem at Crestwood Gardens, she'd have to sell and move. What other choice did she have?

Cara reached down and stroked Jewel under her chin. She was rewarded by a thin purr. "Okay, you're kind of cute. If the situation were different, maybe I'd bring you home."

Jewel's purr was all but drowned out as Charlie cranked his up, eager to recapture Cara's full attention.

"Sorry, kids. As much as I'd like to keep sitting here, I've got to take some more pictures if I'm going to make it through all the new arrivals by lunchtime." The words were no sooner out of her mouth than she realized she didn't need to be finished by lunchtime.

The privilege of unemployment.

Too bad she couldn't just work here at the shelter, but playing with the homeless dogs and cats didn't pay money. Besides, she wasn't sure her spirit could handle working here, seeing these cats and dogs day after day, waiting for someone to take them home.

Let alone the ones who didn't make it out.

Yeah, two mornings a week was plenty. When she was finished here, she'd go straight home to browse for new job postings on nannycare.com.

The happy strumming of a guitar drew Cara's attention to the cell phone ringing in her purse. She shifted Charlie and grabbed it. "Hey, Merry."

"Where are you?"

"At the shelter. Why?"

"Because I'm on your front porch. You forgot I was coming over, didn't you?"

Cara sighed. "Completely. Did you already talk to the homeowners' association?"

"I did, and I'm afraid it was a bust. I left a letter vouching for you and your dogs, as well as some information about the rescue, but I didn't get a good vibe from the lady in there. I pretty much felt like she was just humoring me."

Cara lifted Charlie and set him back in his cage. With a final rub, she closed the door behind him. "Thanks for trying. I'm still planning another round of visits with my neighbors, see if I can win them over."

"That's the spirit. Are you almost done? I'm covering Charlene's shift starting at one, and I was hoping we could do lunch before."

"Yeah, how about I meet you at the Main Street Café in half an hour?"

"Cool. See you then."

Cara rubbed Jewel for another minute, then placed her back in her cage and moved on to the next cat. She had five left on her list. Three were kittens. They made her job easy with their abundant cuteness.

She photographed them all, then made her way out to the lobby to wash up and meet Merry for lunch. Marilyn came out of her office to greet her.

"Cara, next time you're here, bring another stack of business cards. We've given out so many; everyone is loving your photo." She pointed to the stack of SPCA magazines on the display table, with Cara's nearly depleted stack of business cards beside it.

"Wow, that's great, Marilyn. I've had a lot of calls this week too. Thanks so much for the opportunity."

"It's the least I could do. Your photos have helped us so much."

Cara smiled, but she didn't feel it inside. Chances were, she wouldn't have two mornings a week to spend here with her next job. She'd have to volunteer on her own time, probably on the weekends, and weekends were her photography time.

That meant a hard decision was coming, with all the increased bookings she was getting from the shelter's referrals. Help the animals or work toward her career?

\* \* \*

Matt felt like punching a fist through the wall. He'd slept like hell last night, after Cara had left him out in the cold. He really had it bad for the girl with the apricot curls.

Why the hell had he lived next door to her for over a year and not met her until he had one foot back in Boston already? Life had a really lame sense of irony sometimes.

The only thing he could do was hurry up and get the hell out of town, saving himself the misery of having to see Cara every morning. Which led him to the real reason he wanted to punch his fist through the wall. Why hadn't Ken Prentiss hooked up with his mistress yet?

If the man was half as horny for his girlfriend as Matt was for Cara right now, he'd be in the nearest motel, screwing her brains out. But Ken Prentiss remained, annoyingly, at work. Leaving Matt bored and irritable. If he never ran another criminal background check, it would be too soon.

He was banking on this weekend. Ken Prentiss was a workaholic, so he must get his jollies on his own time. Maybe he'd even head to Atlanta to meet "L" again. If Matt didn't nail him by Monday, he was going to be a seriously miserable son of a bitch.

The doorbell rang. He stood and ran a hand through his hair, then tossed on a Henley over his ratty UMass T-shirt.

He yanked the door open to find Merry, Cara's curly-haired friend, standing on his doorstep.

She looked up with a smile. "Hi, Matt."

"Hey, Merry. What can I do for you?"

"Well, I came to see Cara, but she stood me up, so I figured I'd stop by to give you an update about the dogs on Keeney Street. Got a minute?"

"Sure do. I was wondering how that panned out." He motioned her inside.

Merry stepped into his living room, hands shoved into her pockets. There was something untamed about Merry. She looked conventional enough, in her burgundy corduroy jacket, with pink scrubs underneath. She was tall and slim, attractive.

Yet he had the unexplained image of her galloping across open fields bareback with her hair blowing in the wind. Maybe it was just the knowledge that she'd founded an animal rescue that put the notion in his head.

"I heard I missed you the other night at Red Heels." Merry gave him a sly grin.

Matt chuckled. "Yes, I rescued the damsels in distress."

She stared at him a long moment as if she wanted to ask him something else, then gave her head a slight shake. "So, I met with animal control, and they went and had a talk with the Rogerses. They filed a formal complaint against them and fined them a hundred bucks for failing to provide shelter."

"That's it?"

"Yeah, that's it. Not quite what we were hoping for, but more than we had. Maybe it'll be a wake-up call to them. . . ." She drifted off and shrugged.

"But probably not."

"Probably not. Especially now that they've started keeping them chained. Doesn't bode well in my book."

"Mine either." Matt tapped his fingers against his chin. "Would more photos help?"

"I think yes, especially now that they've been warned. I

don't want to impose, since I know you're trying to move, but, well, I run a non-profit. It's my job to grovel and beg for favors." Merry tipped her head and batted her lashes.

"I saw those dogs, and I don't like it either. If I can help you get them out of there, I will. Weather's supposed to be nasty this weekend. Let me see what I can do."

"Thanks, Matt. I really appreciate it. Those dogs deserve a better life. We can't pay you, but if you keep track of the time you spend working on this, I can get you the paperwork so that you can at least use it as a tax write-off."

"I'd appreciate that. But as long as I'm in town, I'm happy to help you guys out."

"So how long are you in town?"

"Probably another week or so. Maybe less. Honestly, I might wrap everything up this weekend if things go my way."

"Hmm." Merry's brow scrunched. "Bummer, you know."

"Yeah, I know. Send her to Boston for me."

"Oh! But no, I need her here. She's one of my best foster homes, and my best friend."

"So you see my dilemma."

She sighed. "I do. I worry about her, though—this whole ten-year plan she has going on. She never dates guys with long-term potential. Trust me, if you weren't about to move out of state, she'd probably never have given you the time of day."

Matt lifted an eyebrow. And here he'd thought Cara Medlen was an open book. "Why's that?"

"She had cancer as a teenager. You knew that, right?"

He nodded.

"So her doctor told her that if she made it a decade in remission, her chances of long-term survival would go up to ninety-five percent. She won't start living her life until she hits that ten-year mark."

Matt rocked back on his heels as his view of Cara came into sudden, startling focus. "Nannying instead of photography."

Merry nodded.

"Fostering with no dog of her own."

"You're a quick study. And she only dates guys with zero chemistry."

"No comment."

Merry giggled. "Right."

"So how long has it been?"

Her eyes widened. "Since she had a boyfriend?"

He winced. "No, you said the doctor told her ten years. How long has it been?"

"Eight."

"Interesting." He thought of Cara's home, with no photos of herself. The neighbors who didn't know her. She'd built a whole temporary life for herself.

"Yes, it is. And should you decide to stay here in Dogwood, you have my blessing to go sweep Cara off her feet."

"Sorry I can't make that happen."

"Me too." She shrugged. "But I have to be going. Thanks again for your help with the Rogerses. Really, we appreciate it so much."

"You're welcome."

Matt watched her leave, wishing like hell there was a way for him to stay in Dogwood.

* * *

Cara slid into the booth across from her friend. "I almost adopted a cat today."

Merry sat serenely, managing somehow to look professional in pink scrubs embroidered with tiny cupcakes. She sipped her coffee and scrunched her nose. "What?"

"I know, I'm totally losing it." Cara tossed her purse beside her and rubbed at the bridge of her nose. "What am I going to do?"

"Get a new job and fight the jerks at the homeowners' association."

"Working on it. Tell me Sadie's been pulled."

Merry narrowed her eyes. "No, and she's not going to be. It sucks. I hate it for her. Most shelters try to work with us, but some just don't care, and, unfortunately, Shelton is one of them."

Cara's eye twitched. "That's bullshit."

"It's bullshit that happens. Dogs are put down every day. Hundreds of them. It breaks my heart, but we can only do what we can do."

Marigold's sweet face filled Cara's vision. "And sometimes that's not good enough."

"Hon, don't take this one so personally. I know it's killing you, when you only have Casper right now. There will be other dogs."

Cara felt tears gathering in her eyes. "I can't do this anymore."

Merry straightened. "Yes, you can. You're feeling a little emotional right now because you lost your job, and you've got this bullshit with the homeowners' association, and you've got the hots for Matt, and apparently something happened with a cat this morning at the shelter, but you'll get it all sorted out. Take a deep breath and order a milkshake with your lunch."

Cara laughed through her tears. "A milkshake will solve my problems?"

"Well, no, but it might help you feel better, right?"

"It certainly can't hurt."

"Did someone say milkshake?" Olivia Bennett, their waitress and Cara's former college roommate, leaned a hip against their booth and tapped her pen in Merry's direction. "None for you, because you are an evil, evil woman."

Merry's eyes rounded. "Cut it out. They're adorable."

Cara looked between them. "What?"

"She stuck me with a litter of puppies. Nine of them!" Olivia extended her arms in Cara's direction, mottled with red scratches. "I've been mauled, I've barely slept in days, and my entire apartment smells like pee."

Cara gave Merry a playful swat. "You were supposed to break her in easy. How do you expect to keep foster homes if you're starting them off with a whole litter of puppies?"

"Because what's cuter than a pile of puppies? She's just mad because her boyfriend won't visit until they're gone."

"Having your shoe pooped in tends to have that effect on a man." Olivia's brown eyes widened. "I should box up all their accidents and mail it to Halverson. Can you imagine the looks on their faces when they opened it?"

Cara snorted with laughter. That chicken-processing plant wasn't going to see a moment of peace until Olivia had her say.

"Anyway, who needs a milkshake?" She pulled out her order pad.

Cara ordered a chocolate–peanut butter explosion to go with her BLT and was well on the way to an emotional rebound when her mother called.

"I just came from my yoga class, but somehow I got on the highway going west instead of east, and when I saw Dogwood on the sign, I thought maybe we could do lunch. It feels like I haven't seen you in forever. I was thinking we could try that new place—"

Cara cleared her throat loudly. Across the table, Merry snickered. Jean Medlen never paused for breath, not even to let her daughter answer a question. "Actually, I've already eaten, Mom."

"Really? Oh." She sounded so disappointed that Cara actually winced. "Well, it's just been so long, and I'm never up this way. I was hoping we could see each other, and..."

Merry leaned forward with a smile, making sure her voice would carry. "Why don't you have your mom meet us here?"

"Who was that? Is that Merry? I'd love to join you girls if you don't mind an old lady crashing your party."

Cara rolled her eyes. "We're at the Main Street Café, Mom. Come on over."

"Perfect! I'll be there in about five minutes." The line clicked and went dead.

*Well played, Mom.* This was payback for avoiding her phone calls since Monday.

Cara shoved the phone back into her purse, then took a fortifying gulp from her chocolate–peanut butter explosion. Olivia swung by with a wink and a refill.

Consequently, Cara was already feeling a little sick to her stomach by the time her mom strolled in, her graying hair pulled into a tight bun, wearing blue yoga pants and a matching hoodie. She pulled Cara into a bear hug, then slid into the booth next to Merry.

"I'm so glad this worked out! Have I missed any good gossip?" Her mother looked between them expectantly. "What have you girls been up to?"

Merry wagged an eyebrow, and Cara glared her into submission. No way, *no way*, her mom needed to know anything about Matt. "Nothing too exciting, Mom. How about you?"

"Well, I saw Dr. Price again last week about that pain in my back. He can't seem to find anything wrong, but I'm telling you, every day it gets a little worse. I'm concerned." Jean's gray eyes clouded. "Merry, you're a nurse. Do you think it's odd he hasn't ordered an MRI?"

And here they went. Cara gave herself a mental slap on the forehead for inquiring after her mom's health instead of steering the conversation elsewhere. Anywhere. Even the weather was preferable.

Merry tapped her lips in exaggerated thought. "Well, I'd probably look closer to home first. How old is your mattress?"

"Well, I don't know. I guess I've been sleeping on it since Tom and I got divorced."

"And that was what, ten years ago?"

"Eleven."

Merry nodded wisely. "My advice would be to get a new mattress. They make some really nice ones these days with that memory foam on top. Great for sore backs. Might be the answer to your problem."

Jean pursed her lips. "So you don't think I have a ruptured disk? Or spinal stenosis?"

Cara cringed. The Internet was a dangerous place for someone like her mother. The woman had never suffered anything worse than a bout with the flu, yet she constantly obsessed about every ache and pain, convinced that something terrible was wrong with her.

Merry patted her knee. "If you just came from yoga class, then no."

Jean beamed. "Okay, then. Well, a new mattress never hurt anyone. Maybe I'll go shopping this afternoon. In fact, I think I heard Mattress Warehouse was having a sale—"

"Go for it." Merry cut her off seamlessly. "Well, unfortunately I've got to get to work. It was great seeing you, Jean."

Cara felt a flicker of panic. Merry handled her mother's worries with ease. Cara, not so much. Her friend slid out of the booth and, with a wave, she was gone.

Cara gulped from her half-melted milkshake.

Her mother leaned forward and placed a hand on hers. "You've been quiet this morning, sweetie. Everything okay?"

She forced a smile and nodded. "Yeah, it's just been stressful with this ultimatum from the homeowners' association and looking for a new job."

Jean's brow furrowed. "I can only imagine. Have you been taking care of yourself? You look a little pale."

"I'm fair-skinned, Mom. I'm always pale."

"Well, you look tired. I worry about you, you know. Especially after what happened to Gina. Such a tragedy."

Cara sighed. "I know, and I appreciate it. Don't worry; nanny jobs aren't hard to find. I'll be fine."

"Well, I don't like to see you looking so worn-out. When is your next checkup? Maybe you should call and see if they can fit you in any sooner. I mean, I'm sure—"

"Mom!" Cara's fingers clenched around the frosty glass containing the remnants of her milkshake. "There's nothing wrong with me. Stop it."

A dull ache settled between her eyes, and she pinched at it. If her mother made one more comment about how tired or crappy she looked this morning . . .

"Well, I can't help worrying about you. To think that cancer could come back at any time, after everything you've been through . . ." Tears welled in her mother's eyes.

"It's not going to come back, Mom." But her words lacked conviction.

After all, wasn't that her greatest fear?

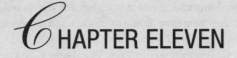

# CHAPTER ELEVEN

*I* don't know, honey. What do you think?"

Cara watched as Dan and Tina Swanson evaluated Casper. The dog sat with his back to her, tail tucked, ears back. Behind them, people strolled in and out of McDonald's, unaware of the doggy-life-altering event taking place in the parking lot.

"I like him. You said he's good with other dogs, right?"

"Yes. He just needs slow introductions sometimes. More so with people than dogs. He's still a little socially awkward, but he's made so much progress, and he's so young."

"Has he been to the dog park?"

"Not yet, but I'm sure he could enjoy it once he's more settled."

They'd been quizzing her for almost ten minutes, without making much of an effort to get to know the dog himself. Casper pressed against Cara's right leg, uncomfortable with the situation.

"Well, I think he'll be great." Tina bent down at last, and Casper licked her face with enthusiasm. "We'll take him."

Cara exhaled slowly. Casper had done it. He'd found his

new home. Happiness mixed with a bitter sadness in her chest as she wondered when and if she'd get to do this again. The Swansons were great people, an energetic young couple who were longtime boxer lovers, but she didn't quite get the warm and fuzzy vibe from them that made her heart do a happy dance.

Sometimes dogs went to fantastic homes, and sometimes they went to good homes. This was a good home. Maybe great. Who knew? Her impression could be totally wrong.

Cara led them through the paperwork. She gave Casper a kiss and a pat, keeping her own emotions firmly in check so as not to upset him. He gazed adoringly at her over his shoulder as the Swansons led him to their pickup truck and loaded him inside.

She watched stone-faced as they pulled out of the parking lot. Then she cranked the radio and drove dry-eyed all the way home from Wilson, North Carolina, an hour outside Dogwood.

The first tear fell as she closed the door to her empty house.

* * *

Matt watched from his living room window as Cara loaded her car. First a black duffel bag, then a dog bed, a cooler, and other odds and ends. Leaning against her rear bumper, she had a heated conversation on her phone, gesturing wildly with her hands and stubbing the toe of her right sneaker repeatedly against the asphalt.

Clearly, she was up to no good.

Once the phone was back in her pocket, he strolled outside. "Going somewhere?"

"Yeah, I'm pulling a dog, and don't even talk to me about all the reasons it's a bad idea. I don't care." She tossed her purse onto the front seat of her Mazda and glared at him.

"The one you showed me Monday night. The one with cancer."

"Yeah, she's a lost cause. Whatever. I'm pulling her, and I'll deal with the consequences tomorrow."

Matt thought on that for a moment. Cara obviously understood that bringing home a new foster dog right now would be a hit against her chances of winning the approval of the homeowners' association. From a logical standpoint, she was making a very stupid decision.

One look in her eyes told him Cara wasn't feeling very logical right now.

He gestured toward her bags. "Where are you headed?"

"Shelton. I'm hoping to be back tonight, but who knows with the weather? I thought it was better to be prepared."

Shelton, North Carolina, was a small town in the Smoky Mountains, near the Tennessee border. Easily a four-hour drive from Dogwood, not counting the snow they were expecting later tonight.

He eyed Cara's little Mazda, with its semi-bald tires and front wheel drive. "That's a foolish drive today, in that car, with the weather we're expecting."

She tossed her head. "Yeah, well, Sadie's got until six o'clock before she gets the needle, and apparently I'm the only one who cares, so..."

Tears glistened in her eyes and tugged at his heart. Dammit, he really, really hated it when a woman cried, and Cara either knew this or teared up easily. He suspected the latter.

It was already past one. A close call, even without the weather to contend with. He groaned. Goddamn, he really was a fool. "Get your stuff out of that car. You'll never make it."

She stiffened, glaring at him. She opened her mouth, no doubt to tell him off, but he put out a hand to stop her. He opened the trunk of the Grand Cherokee. "Hell, put your stuff in there and give me five minutes."

"What? No way. Thanks, but no."

"Did you check the weather report? Freezing rain, turning to snow later tonight. And that's around here. I imagine the mountains are expecting worse. Look at your tires!"

"Well, I meant to get new ones, but—"

"Jesus, Cara. Let's argue about this on the road, okay? Put your damn bags in the Jeep."

He turned and strode back into his house. He packed up his laptop, an extra battery pack, and a few other supplies. Luckily, he kept an overnight bag and survival essentials stored in the Jeep in case of an impromptu excursion like this one.

When he walked back outside, the trunk was closed, and Cara sat in the passenger seat, her jaw set, eyes blazing.

She turned on him as soon as he climbed inside. "This is *so* not a good idea."

"You're telling me," he grumbled as he started the engine.

"That's it." She reached for the door handle, and he closed a hand over hers.

"Settle down. If it's humanly possible, I'll get you there by six. Okay?"

She leaned back into her seat, and Matt swung the Jeep out of the parking lot before either of them had a chance to have second thoughts.

He tapped the GPS on the dash. "Tell it where we're going."

Cara gave him another uncertain look, then reached forward and began tapping the address of the animal shelter into his navigation system. A few moments later, the automated voice gave them an estimated arrival time of four fifty-six.

"Cutting it close," he said.

Cara nodded. "I've already called and told them I'm on

my way. They're expecting me before closing, so Sadie's safe for now."

"Good."

"You don't—don't you have work you should be doing?"

Matt kept his eyes on the road. "Sure do. Wouldn't get a bit of it done worrying about you plunging off an icy mountain road in your little death trap of a car."

She gave him a long look but said nothing.

The thought of anything happening to her twisted uncomfortably in his gut, along with Merry's words from yesterday. Eight years in remission. He'd never really considered that she might not be healthy. That it could come back.

That Cara could still die.

Cara lived her life every day with that knowledge.

His palms had grown slick against the steering wheel. He lifted them one at a time and rubbed them against his jeans. "So, I heard the Rogerses got a complaint and a fine."

"How did you hear that?"

"Merry stopped by yesterday."

Her eyes widened. "She did?"

"Said you stood her up, so she came over to give me an update."

"Oh yeah. That makes sense, I guess. She just didn't mention it."

"Nervous?"

She nibbled on her bottom lip. "About what?"

"Bringing Sadie home. You're shooting yourself in the foot."

"Well, yeah, I know, but life's been bossing me around all week, and I'm sick of it. I'm saving her—to hell with the consequences."

Matt's hands tightened on the steering wheel. He couldn't help but admire her for that kind of logic. "What about Casper?"

She looked at her hands. "He was adopted this morning."

"That's great."

"Yeah."

"And Merry's on board with your plan?"

"Well, no. She thinks I'm having an unemployment-induced lapse of judgment."

"Hmm." Matt bit back a smile. That might be true, partly. But it didn't stop him from admiring the hell out of Cara for heading out to save this poor, cancer-stricken dog when it was really the stupidest thing she could do, for many reasons. The least of which being the snowstorm bearing down on them.

He looked up at the sky. Still and gray. Clouds pressed over them with the heaviness that preceded snow. Having grown up in Massachusetts, driving in it didn't bother him. The Grand Cherokee would handle well with four-wheel drive and new all-weather tires. But out there on the twisty mountain roads, untreated with salt or sand, conditions could get bad pretty quick.

He estimated he could have them home by midnight if the weather held out.

Five minutes later, the first fat flake hit the windshield.

* * *

Snow swirled outside the Jeep like a snow globe that had been shaken. Cara watched with white knuckles as Matt guided them through the storm. Snow wasn't exactly unusual in North Carolina, but a snowstorm like this happened rarely enough to make her wish she was safely at home. Ordinarily, the sight of it would make her want to stick her tongue out to taste it and flop on her back to make snow angels.

Not tonight.

In the driver's seat, Matt's face was set in a frown. "I

don't like this. These roads haven't been treated. We're starting to lose traction."

"Should we look for somewhere to pull over until it lets up?"

He nodded. "I have been."

They were way out in the mountains now, far from suburbia. A half hour ago, when the flurries that had plagued most of their drive turned into near-whiteout conditions, Cara realized they might not make it to the shelter by six. She'd called and been told the shelter staff was heading out soon themselves. Sadie would be safe there until morning.

She could only hope that they would stumble on a hotel somewhere out here, and soon. Much as she hated to admit defeat, they needed to get off the road before they became a storm statistic. Matt had just better not have any ideas about them sharing a hotel room.

"So, how soon are you leaving for Boston?" she asked, to keep her mind occupied by something other than thoughts of Matt next to her in bed.

"Next week, I hope. This last case I'm working on has taken a little longer than I anticipated, but I—" Matt's voice cut off abruptly. Headlights slashed across the windshield.

The Jeep lurched beneath her, and then they were falling. Branches slashed the windows. Snow came at them from all directions. The seat bucked under her legs like a horse gone mad. Her stomach somersaulted into her throat.

There was a horrible crunch, then silence. Cara released the edges of the seat she hadn't realized she'd been gripping and looked out. White-coated pine needles pressed against her window. Behind them, darkness.

"Fuck." Matt thumped his fist against the steering wheel. "You okay?"

She nodded. "Peachy. What happened?"

"Some idiot in a pickup truck ran us off the road."

She looked over her shoulder toward the darkened road. "And they didn't stop?"

"Doesn't look like it. Might not have even realized what happened. I'm going to go have a look." He unclipped his seat belt, opened the door, and stepped outside to survey the damage.

Cara stayed where she was, waiting for the post-adrenaline jitters to wear off. She craned her head but couldn't see anything past the twin beams of snowy trees illuminated by the Jeep's headlights. It was as if they'd been swallowed by the darkened forest.

She shivered.

A few minutes later, Matt opened the back of the Jeep, then he was gone again. Finally, the driver's-side door opened, and he climbed back inside. He shut off the headlights, then turned to face her. "We may be stuck here for the night."

She stared at him blankly. "What?"

"We're a good ten feet off the road, down an embankment. The snow's drifted deeper down here. This Jeep's not coming out without a tow, and that's not likely to happen before morning, given the weather. Check your cell phone. Mine doesn't have coverage."

Cara held her phone up, illuminating a screen blinking "No Service."

Matt nodded. "We've got two options. We can try to walk out of here and hope we find a house nearby or some other signs of life. Or we bunk here for the night."

"Bunk here for the night?" Her voice was embarrassingly close to a squeak.

"That'd be my recommendation." Matt looked her up and down. "You're not dressed for a hike in this weather, and that road's treacherous. I'd just as soon not wander down it in the dark during a snowstorm."

"Oh." Cara glanced over her shoulder at the backseat of the Grand Cherokee. And she'd thought sharing a hotel room with him would be bad. "Well, what if the people who ran us off the road called for help?"

"It's possible. I left some emergency cones out by the road to draw attention if anyone comes looking, but I think it's safe to say we're stuck here for the night."

She stared at him. Oh God, this was really happening. She was going to spend the night here, with him, in the Jeep.

"I'm pretty well stocked for emergencies. I've got a sleeping bag, blanket, heavy duty flashlight, bottles of water, power bars, all the essentials. The seats let down in back. I've slept in here before. It's not that bad."

"Hmm." She fidgeted in her seat. Of course, now that she would be spending the next twelve hours trapped in the car with Matt, she had to pee. "Yes, you're a hell of a lot better prepared than I would have been in my Mazda."

Matt switched the key, shutting off the ignition. "I'll get things set up in the back. We'll need to keep the engine off most of the night to conserve gas, so we'll want to use the blanket and sleeping bag to keep warm."

"Okay." She watched as he laid the backseats flat and pulled out various supplies from a hatch in the floor.

"This dog bed clean?" he asked as he unfurled the blue plaid bundle she'd wedged behind the backseats.

"Yeah."

He rolled it out, then tested it with his hands. "That's pretty soft."

Matt looked up, those cocoa eyes locked on hers. "Two ways we can do this. I can give you the sleeping bag and use the blanket myself. Or we can conserve body heat and lay under both together. It's going to be pretty cold tonight."

She cleared her throat. "Um, your call. I guess, probably the second option sounds a lot warmer."

A wicked smile curled his lips. "Sounds a hell of a lot warmer to me. And I'll be a gentleman, I promise."

Her cheeks burned. "Right."

"Well, come on back, sweetheart." He patted the carpet next to him.

Cara fought a groan. It was only six o'clock. This was going to be the longest night in history. "Thank goodness we stopped for burgers back in Asheville."

"Yep. I was thinking the same thing." He spread a navy blue sleeping bag across the dog bed. "This is five-star accommodations, as far as sleeping in the car goes."

"Great." She climbed over the center console and sat next to him, her back against the door.

Matt handed her jacket to her and pulled a red plaid blanket over their legs.

"So." She looked over at him.

His eyes twinkled. "So."

Ah, crap. The air in the Jeep was still warm, and the snow swirling outside the windows was damn romantic. All she could really think about was how much she wanted him to lean over and kiss her. From the glint in his eyes, she suspected Matt was thinking the same thing.

He was leaving town next week, for good. Was there really any harm in her indulging in a little hot and steamy sex before he left? There was the small matter of her heart, which was already dangerously entangled with his.

She sighed. "Tell me more about your family. Your mom. And your dad—where's he?"

"He died about ten years ago; car accident."

"Oh, I'm sorry."

"It's just been my mom and us boys for a while. We take good care of her. "

"I bet."

Matt chuckled softly. "'Course, now she rants about how

she must have one foot in the grave the way we're carrying on over her."

Cara smiled. It warmed her heart to hear the affection in his voice when he spoke about his mom. "Will you stay with her after you move back?"

"Yeah. She offered to let me stay there while I look for a place. I think I'll take my time."

She patted his knee. "You're a good son, Matt Dumont."

"She's a hell of a mom. What about you? Are you close with your parents?"

"Yes and no. Our house was very strained when Susie and I were growing up. A lot of tension. My parents didn't get along, but didn't have the courage to go their separate ways. They finally split when I was in high school. It was a really hard time."

Matt watched her closely. "Is that when you got sick?"

She sucked in a breath. "Yeah. My sophomore year of high school. Everyone was fighting, my parents weren't speaking, and I felt awful, physically and emotionally. I was so wrapped up in my family's misery, I waited too long to see the doctor."

"It spread?"

"I was in stage three by the time it was diagnosed. I had radiation on the largest tumors, and chemo. It was tough. Really tough."

"How did your family take it?"

"More fighting. God, there was so much fighting." She closed her eyes and swallowed over the lump in her throat. The emotional toll had at times been even more grueling than the physical pain of the cancer.

"I'm sorry." Matt took her hand in the darkened Jeep. His skin was warm and rough against hers. "I can't imagine how hard that was for you."

"We had a family dog, a boxer. His name was Ziggy. He

stayed by my side while I puked my guts out. He lay with me on the couch when I was too weak to get up. He was my rock."

"And that's how you got into animal rescue. He saved you, now you save them."

She stared into Matt's warm eyes. "Something like that."

The air around them seemed suddenly warmer. Heavier. Pressing in on them, pushing them together. Cara scrambled back against the seat, breaking the spell. "Um, this is embarrassing, but I really have to pee."

Matt grinned. "Gonna happen sooner or later. I have a box of tissues in the dash."

Her cheeks burned again. "Thanks."

She climbed back into her seat, realizing for the first time that the air in the Jeep really had chilled. It was freezing outside their cozy cocoon. She opened the glove compartment, grabbed a tissue, and plunged into the snowy wilderness.

Her sneakers crunched into thick snow up to her ankles. *Yikes.*

Quickly, she trudged behind a large tree and took care of business. The bottom of her jeans was soaked by the time she made it back inside the Jeep.

Matt had stretched out on the floor, hands behind his head, staring at the ceiling. Cara paused to admire his profile, the hard jaw already bristling with dark stubble, and those eyes that saw right through her. He turned toward her with a smile, and her insides gave a nervous flip-flop.

"How is it out there?"

"Cold," she said, "and wet." She toed out of her sneakers and rolled up her pant legs, trying to get the wet fabric away from her skin.

Matt frowned at her soggy jeans. "Wet clothes are no good." When he looked back up, his expression had taken on a wicked gleam again. "You know, it's better to conserve body heat when you're skin to skin."

She gasped. "You said you'd be a gentleman."

"And I will be." He patted the sleeping bag beside him. "If that's what you want."

# 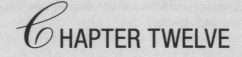CHAPTER TWELVE

*M*att was in big trouble. Cara's blue eyes widened, her rosy lips parted in surprise, and he knew this was going to be the longest night of his life.

Cautiously, she slid onto the sleeping bag beside him, careful to keep several inches of space between their bodies. She watched him with moonlight dancing in her eyes.

"Keep talking, Cara, before my mind starts to wander." Matt allowed his gaze to roam over her.

She sucked in a breath. "That's not fair."

"Just being honest." Not entirely. No amount of talking could change the truth. He wanted her. Bad. And here they were, trapped in his Jeep. If she decided to spoon him at any point tonight to conserve warmth, she was going to feel just how much he wanted her.

"Okay." She bit her lower lip.

He slid closer and pulled the blanket over her. "You're not talking."

Her breath warmed his cheek and stoked the fire raging inside him.

"I can't think of anything to say." A shy smile played across her lips, and Matt knew he was a goner.

He groaned. "Oh hell, Cara."

She shifted beneath the blanket, and her foot bumped his shin. Their hands touched.

He lowered his mouth to hers and whispered against her lips. "You know I promised not to kiss you. I never break my promises."

And in this case, he didn't have to. Cara rose up and pressed her lips to his. He tugged her closer, deepening the kiss. His tongue slid against hers, and her fingers clenched around his. Oh, God, she tasted good. A soft moan escaped her lips, and he was lost.

This was every teenaged boy's dream. The girl he'd fantasized about, trapped in the car with him for the next twelve hours or so. A soft bed beneath them, a warm blanket over them. Snow swirling outside the windows.

There was one limitation on this grown-up version of the fantasy: Matt would not be getting Cara naked in the back of his car tonight, no matter how desperately he wanted to. But this was a damn fine way to pass some of the cold hours of the night ahead.

Cara scooted closer, her body pressed to his. Matt shrugged out of his coat and tossed it aside. She did the same. He slid his left thigh between her legs, feeling her heat through the denim of her jeans.

"Matt," she gasped. Her thighs tightened around him.

Matt hissed out a breath. He pushed a hand beneath her sweater, unfastened the clasp of her bra, and cupped her breast in his palm. A perfect fit.

Hell, yeah. He brushed a thumb over her nipple, and Cara gasped again. He pushed her sweater up and brought his mouth to her breast, nipping and teasing until she made another of those little moans that drove him wild.

Goddamn, he could only imagine how she sounded when she came.

"Don't stop," she whispered. Her hips thrust against his.

His cock jumped in response. He was so hard he expected to see the button from his jeans fly off and ping against one of the windows at any moment.

They kissed until the windows steamed and Cara writhed beneath him, her body plastered to his like a second skin. Matt drew a deep breath and held it. He had to slow down before he lost control.

"If we keep this up, we won't need to turn on the engine at all," he whispered against her neck. Sweat dampened his brow and ran between his shoulder blades.

"You mean it's cold in here?" She slid a hand beneath his shirt. Her fingers felt like heaven against his skin. "Because you feel pretty hot."

"Baby, you have no idea." He kissed his way across her jaw and down her neck. When she shivered, he doubted it had anything to do with the temperature in the Jeep.

She shifted beneath him and looked away, sucking in deep breaths. Matt could practically hear her brain spinning as it caught up to speed.

"Don't worry, honey, I'm not going to do anything but kiss you."

Her eyes widened. "Really?"

"Really. For one thing, I don't have protection. And anyway, our long-term situation hasn't changed. I'm not going to take advantage of you just because we're stuck here in the Jeep together."

Cara's lips puckered. "I'm hardly sweet and innocent."

He groaned. Maybe not, but something about her was exactly that. It was a damned good thing he didn't have a condom, because that might be the only thing that kept him from breaking his promise to her during the long hours that lay ahead.

She sighed and pulled herself to a sitting position. "But you're right. It's better to keep our clothes on tonight."

"Doesn't mean we can't have a little fun in the meantime."

Cara looked at her watch and frowned. "It's only eight thirty. We're going to need a distraction if we're going to make it through the night fully clothed."

Okay, she had a point.

Matt's eyes were drawn to the still-wet ankles of her jeans. "Don't take this the wrong way, but we need to get you out of those jeans."

Her eyes narrowed. "Excuse me?"

"They're wet. You brought a change of clothes, right? Put them on. I'll turn on the engine for a little while, and we'll dry them on the heat vent."

"Oh. Um, okay."

Now that they were no longer lighting fires with their bodies, it was uncomfortably cold in the Jeep. He watched Cara rummage through her duffel bag to produce a pair of black knit pants. She crawled into the front seat and gave him a measured look, reminding him to mind his own business.

With a rueful smile, he turned toward the under-seat storage in back. He poked through it until he found the small snow shovel he kept in case of emergency, then risked a glance over his shoulder. Cara was in the process of shimmying the black pants up her legs, offering him a glimpse of creamy skin and blue lace panties.

Matt dropped the shovel with a thump. He busied himself retrieving it, minding his business until Cara called to him from the front seat. "Done."

"I'm going to have a quick look around outside and make sure the exhaust pipe's clear before I turn on the engine. Then we'll get some heat going in here."

Cara mumbled something under her breath about how they

already had some heat going, then tossed him a naughty smile, and he almost dropped the shovel again. He pushed open the rear driver's-side door and bent down to shovel away the snow that had drifted against the side of the Jeep.

No sense getting their clothes any wetter than necessary when nature called. The snow had all but stopped; only a few stray flakes drifted in the breeze. Through the snow-covered branches above, the moon was a hazy blob glowing through what remained of the storm clouds.

A solid six inches of heavy, wet snow covered the ground. Matt cleared the side of the Jeep, then stepped out and closed the door. He cleared a quick path behind the nearest tree for Cara's benefit, then checked around the rear. The exhaust pipe cleared the snow by several inches, but he shoveled it away just in case any new snow fell during the night or the wind blew a drift their way. Better safe than sorry.

With that accomplished, he answered nature's call himself, then shook off his boots and climbed back into the Jeep. Cara sat in the front seat, arms hooked around her knees, teeth chattering.

Matt cranked the key, and the engine rumbled to life. "Snow's stopped."

She looked over at him. "That's good, but this still sucks."

"Not a fan of camping out?"

"Oh, I love camping. My friends and I go every year. Just not in the winter or, you know, in the middle of a snowstorm."

Matt adjusted the vents, now that warm air blew from them. "Don't like the cold weather?"

"Nope, sorry. I'm a southern girl through and through."

Yes, that she was. He loved the subtle twang in her voice and the idea of her camping out under the stars. He liked the idea of himself there with her even more.

He retrieved his cell phone from the center console and plugged it into the charger. Service or not, he'd need as much battery power as he could get when they walked out of here tomorrow morning. "Let me see your phone."

Cara held up a Samsung similar to his own.

"Great. I'll put yours on for a charge after mine."

She nodded and handed it to him. "How'd you wind up here in North Carolina, anyway?"

"Needed a change of scenery."

She studied his face for a long moment. "And that's code for...what? A girl broke your heart?"

He chuckled. "You chicks have a sixth sense, don't you?"

"Really? You got your heart broken?"

"Something like that. Holly and I had been together four years. Thought I might marry her, except it turned out she was screwing around on me while I was serving overseas." The burning sense of betrayal had faded now, leaving behind only a bitter indifference.

"Oh, Matt." She touched his shoulder. "That's terrible."

He shrugged. "So I came to North Carolina. Didn't mean to stay this long—just got comfortable, I guess."

She nodded, staring out into the snow.

"While we're answering personal questions, what the hell is FMH?"

Cara lurched forward with a sound like she was choking. "What?"

Yep, it definitely referred to him. "You heard me."

She buried her face in her hands, still spluttering. "You really don't want to know."

"Oh, but I really do."

She peeked at him between her fingers. "Promise you won't laugh?"

Oh, this was going to be good. "Honey, I don't make promises I can't keep."

She sighed and mumbled something under her breath.

"What?"

"It means . . . fuck me hot." She spoke into her hands.

Matt would have laughed, if his jaw wasn't hanging open from hearing those words come out of Cara's mouth. "Fuck me hot," he repeated.

"It's so stupid. My friend Olivia and I made it up in college. When we saw a hot guy we liked, we'd say he was FMH."

"And?"

She sighed again. "And it's what I called you before I knew your name."

"Because you thought I was . . . fuck me hot?" His dick jumped to attention.

"Yes, I thought you were hot. Happy now?" She finally looked at him, and the air between them began to sizzle.

"Be a lot happier if I had a condom."

She gave him another look, then surprised the hell out of him by slithering over the console and into his lap. "You didn't laugh," she whispered, then kissed him senseless.

Hadn't he? He thought he had, but Cara was short-circuiting his brain with her sweet scent, those soft lips, her warm body fitted so closely against his.

"You wanted to fuck me?" He yanked her against his erection.

She gasped. "In theory."

Matt grabbed her ass and ground her against him. He was so turned on he could barely think. Kissing Cara had gone from bliss to an exquisite form of torture. She moaned, and the sound almost undid him.

She never dated men she had chemistry with, Merry had said. Guess that explained why she'd been avoiding him like the plague for the last year, because they were positively combustible together. How long since she'd been driven wild by a man's touch, since a man had made her lose control, made her scream with pleasure? Ever? The urge to give her that pleasure grew stronger than his own need.

He couldn't have her, but he could do this for her, give her release from the need that had her rocking restlessly in his lap. He bent his head and kissed her while his right hand traced down her belly and slid inside the waistband of her black knit pants.

He could feel her, hot and wet, through the cotton of her panties.

She gasped at his touch.

"Cara." His voice was low and rough as he pushed her panties to the side and slid two fingers inside her.

"Matt, what—" She let out a squeak of pleasure, her body arching against him. Goddamn, it was almost as good as being inside her. Almost.

"Let me do this for you, Cara." He held her against him as his fingers did the job his cock was dying for. "Let me hear you come."

Her hips rocked against his, and he took pleasure from the rhythm of their bodies and the soft cries she made as his fingers drove her wild.

She gripped his shoulders, her body tense. "Oh—"

He stroked his thumb across her flesh, and she surged in his lap. The look of wonder on her face was the most beautiful thing he'd ever seen.

She came apart in his arms with a wild cry, and Matt damn near came himself from the sound of her orgasm. He gritted his teeth and swore under his breath. Her hips pressed into his, and his cock throbbed painfully. He held himself against her until she collapsed in a boneless heap in his arms.

"Holy shit," she whispered. Her breath tickled his neck as she panted against him. He held her close until she'd regained her senses, then pulled back. There were limits to his control, and she was testing them.

Big time.

"Matt, I...but you..." She looked down, eyeing the front of his jeans.

"Don't worry about it." He'd suffered worse, although at the moment he was having trouble remembering when. For her, he'd do it again. His only regret was that he hadn't gotten the chance to hear her scream his name.

Cara stared at him, still glowing with pleasure, her blue eyes crinkled with concern.

He leaned forward and kissed her, then lifted her back into her seat. The cabin had grown uncomfortably warm, or maybe that was just the steam still hissing in his veins. "We should probably turn off the engine soon and turn in for the night. Why don't you go ahead and get settled."

She scooted into the back and pulled the blanket over her.

"I'm going to take one last look around outside." He stepped out into the blissfully frigid air and stood there, sucking in deep breaths until he'd cooled off enough to think clearly.

He took one last look around the Jeep, then climbed back into the front seat, turned off the ignition, and joined Cara under the blanket.

He lay on his back, staring at the ceiling. She lay facing him, her eyes touching him like a physical presence in the dark. Without the whooshing of the vents, the night hung heavy and silent around them.

Already, he felt the chill seeping back into the air.

"We could have had the Rogerses dead to rights tonight, you know," he said.

"You're right. It's below freezing, probably snowing at home too. That totally sucks."

He shrugged. "That's the way it goes."

Much as he wanted to be pissed about being stuck here like this, unable to track Ken Prentiss on his GPS or help Cara with her case, he just couldn't. He'd nab the cheater tomorrow, and enjoy this night with Cara.

Beside him, she shivered.

"We're probably going to need to get inside the sleeping bag together," he said after a minute.

"Probably."

He sat up and zipped it closed. "Ladies first."

He was glad for the darkness as Cara slipped inside. No way his hunger for her wasn't written all over his face. Once she was situated, he shucked his jeans and eased himself in beside her.

It was a tight fit. She lay on her side, facing away from him, which left him no choice but to lie facing her, his body fitted to hers, his right hand resting on her stomach.

Nope, they wouldn't be cold now.

Cara shifted restlessly within the confines of the sleeping bag. Matt closed his eyes and did his best to ignore his body's response to her, the aching need to flip her over and kiss her senseless. To bury himself deep inside her and pound them both into sweet oblivion.

"Matt…" Cara wiggled again, and her butt landed against his erection.

His arm tightened reflexively around her.

"Shh. Let's try to get some sleep, okay? We have a long day tomorrow."

And it was going to be a long, painful night.

* * *

Cara woke, disoriented to find herself in Matt's arms. The sky above was just beginning to streak with reds and purples. A beautiful winter morning.

The interior of the Jeep was frigid against her exposed nose and cheeks, but inside the sleeping bag it was toasty warm. Behind her, Matt slept, his breathing steady against her neck.

It had taken several restless hours for either of them to crash. After all, how could she sleep with his erection poking her in the back? Just thinking about it got her hot all over again. What he'd done for her last night, giving her pleasure without taking his own—no man had ever done anything like that for her before.

As if he could feel her thoughts, Matt shifted behind her, and there it was again, pressing against her like a sinful invitation.

She spun to face him, the close confines of the sleeping bag pushing her up against every hard inch of his body.

Matt's eyes gleamed in the gentle light of dawn, their rich espresso color appearing almost black. "Morning."

"Good morning." She leaned forward and gave him a quick kiss. Why not? She'd probably never get the chance again.

Need burned through her at the simple touch of her lips to his. She mourned the thought of what might have been, because there was little doubt in her mind that sex with Matt would have been mind blowing. Maybe even life altering for someone like her, who really hadn't experienced great sex.

His arms circled her, then he kissed her back, slow and gentle until she thought the sleeping bag might melt right off them. They both seemed to understand that once they left its zippered confinement, the spell would be broken.

Cara closed her eyes and surrendered to the feel of his lips, the slide of his tongue against hers. In the depths of the sleeping bag, her toes curled.

"God, you're beautiful." His voice sounded low, raspy.

She opened her eyes. He traced a finger over her lips, his eyes heavy with desire. She felt the truth of his words deep in her soul, even if what rose to her lips was an automatic dismissal of his claim. That a man like Matt found her so desirable was one of life's greater mysteries.

He kissed her again, then brushed his fingers through her hair. "We should probably get moving, try to get ourselves rescued."

Rescued. Right. The whole Jeep-stuck-in-a-snowdrift situation.

She sighed. "Yeah."

"Brace yourself," Matt said, then unzipped the sleeping bag.

Cold air hit her, swift and brutal. She curled her arms around herself.

"Stay there," he said, and zipped her back up. He pulled on his jeans and climbed into the front seat. Seconds later, the engine grumbled to life. "Should feel some heat in a minute."

She looked up at the frost-covered windows surrounding her. The prospect of hiking out of here in search of help didn't sound nearly as appealing as the idea of staying warm inside the sleeping bag with Matt.

He laced up his boots and shrugged into his coat. "Gonna have a look around. You stay put until the car warms up."

Well, if he insisted. Cara snuggled into the warm flannel. She'd have to get up sooner or later, though; rescue or not, she had to pee. And then...Sadie was waiting for her at the shelter.

That thought galvanized her into leaving the warm cocoon of the sleeping bag. She pulled herself to a sitting position and reached for her coat. It felt like ice against her skin as she zipped it over the thin knit shirt she wore.

Through the spider webs of frost on the windows, she saw Matt poking around outside. He walked off toward the road, no doubt planning their escape.

Cara reluctantly pushed the sleeping bag from her legs. She crawled into the front seat and grabbed her jeans, thankful he'd thought to put them over the heat vent the night before. They were ice cold now, but dry, and would be a lot better to hike out of here in than her cotton knit pants.

She changed into her jeans, put on her sneakers, and decided to venture outside to pee before Matt returned. The air outside the Jeep wasn't much colder than inside, so there was no great insult when she opened the door and stepped out. A stiff breeze blew over her, ruffling her hair and raising goose bumps on her skin. She glanced up, through snow-covered branches, at the sky beginning to lighten with the coming day.

A thinly shoveled path led behind one of the larger trees. Obviously, Matt had had her in mind when he'd been out last night. She hurried behind the tree to take care of business, then walked back to the Jeep.

It felt positively balmy inside after a few minutes in the gusty woods. Matt followed her in and closed the door behind them.

"Breakfast," he said, handing her a protein bar and a bottle of water.

"Thanks." She ripped open the wrapper. "So what's the plan?"

Matt adjusted the vents to blow more warm air over them. "I don't think we're too far from Poole. We'll start walking that way, until we reach cell service or we flag someone down to call for a tow."

Cara bit into the chocolate-flavored protein bar. She was hungry enough that it tasted like heaven. The clock on the dashboard told her it was not quite seven o'clock. She wasn't sure what that meant for their chances of another motorist passing by.

By the time they'd finished eating, the Jeep was cozy, and she dreaded leaving its relative comfort. Matt had juiced up both of their cell phones while the engine ran to give them enough battery power to last the journey ahead.

"Okay, let's do a clothing check. It's cold out there. You got a hat? Gloves? Scarf?"

She nodded.

Matt looked her up and down. "What about those black cotton pants you had on last night? You should wear those under your jeans. It'll keep you warmer."

Cara straightened in her seat. "Why? You think we're going to be walking awhile?"

He shrugged. "Could be. Hopefully not, but better to be prepared."

"Okay." She grabbed her black pants and an extra long-sleeved tee from her overnight bag and crawled into the back to layer up. When she peeked over her shoulder, Matt was adding a blue thermal over his own gray, long-sleeved T-shirt.

Five minutes later, layered and bundled with all they had, they stepped out into the cold, still morning. The sky had finally brightened to blue, illuminating the way to the road. Matt wore a backpack containing dry socks and the remainder of the power bars and bottled water.

"Ready?" His breath crystallized in the air between them.

Cara nodded, then fell into step behind him as they crunched away from the Jeep.

It was easy to follow the indent of their tire tracks from the night before up the incline toward Route 441. She tried to step in Matt's footprints to keep her sneakers dry, but by the time they reached the paved road, her feet were soaked through regardless.

She spared one last glance over her shoulder for Matt's Jeep, barely visible through the trees. They were so lucky they hadn't hit anything bigger than a sapling on their wild ride last night. Her stomach clenched at the thought.

They trudged on in silence, picking their way through various wheel ruts on the unplowed pavement to keep their feet from getting any wetter. It hadn't been fifteen minutes since they'd left the Jeep, and already Cara was losing feeling in her toes.

She shivered again, then again. Her teeth started to chatter.

Matt looked over, his lips compressed with concern. "How wet are your feet?"

"Pretty wet."

"That's no good. Those sneakers are terrible for walking in this mess."

"I'll be fine. Hopefully someone will come along soon, anyway."

They kept walking, both of them holding up their cell phones every few minutes, checking for a signal. If help didn't come on its own, with any luck they could summon it to them.

The sun rose above the treetops, bathing the eastern sky in a pink glow. It glistened on the white-coated tree branches, making them sparkle like so many jewels. The air around them was silent but for the crunching of their footsteps.

"You have to admit, it's beautiful." Her words hung in glistening puffs in the air.

Matt nodded. "Like a postcard. If I could get a signal on my phone, I'd stop and just take it all in."

"You're probably wishing you'd minded your own business yesterday when you saw me loading up my car."

"Not if it meant you out here doing this by yourself."

"I'd have been fine." She took another step. "But I'm glad you're here."

He looked back. "Me too."

An hour later, Cara felt like she'd been chipped out of a block of ice. Her feet were numb, her nose probably had frostbite, and her entire body shook until she ached with the effort. She'd never been so cold in her life.

The snow-covered trees stretched on endlessly.

Down the road, a vehicle rumbled into view.

"Oh, thank God." She stopped for a moment to rest her hands on her knees. Matt put his arm out to wave down the SUV sloshing down the road toward them.

Cara stood beside him, imagining how warm it would be inside that SUV. Her toes tingled in anticipation.

She could see the driver now, a middle-aged woman, gripping the wheel and staring at the road as if she might lose control and spin out at any moment. She never even glanced at Cara and Matt as she drove right past them, sending a deluge of sludge in their direction.

Icy water rained over them.

"Fuck." Matt swiped his face and turned toward her. He brushed slush from Cara's jacket and jeans while she shook herself like a dog.

She swiped a muddy droplet from the end of his nose. Now they were filthy and wet, on top of being cold. Without warning, she doubled over in laughter.

"You think this is funny?"

"No," she gasped. "But . . ."

Matt grimaced, then managed a smile.

Cara's laughter bordered on hysteria. She blinked back tears and sucked in a deep breath. "I can't believe she didn't stop."

"How are you holding up?" Matt wrapped an arm around her and drew her against the warmth of his body. She might have cried on his shoulder if the tears wouldn't have turned to ice on her cheeks.

"Cold," she admitted.

He rubbed his hands up and down her arms. "If someone doesn't pick us up soon, we're going to have to find somewhere to stop for a few minutes and try to get you warmed up."

"I'll be okay."

"Worst case, according to the sign over there, we're only three miles from Poole. We can walk there in another hour or so. Think warm thoughts."

Cara slanted a gaze in his direction.

Matt threw his head back and laughed. "There you go with that dirty mind again. Whatever keeps you warm, sweetheart."

She scowled. This really sucked. She was well and truly miserable now, but what choice did she have? She had to keep walking.

"Well, what do you know." Matt looked down at his cell phone and held it toward her. It showed nearly a full signal.

Relief left her weak kneed. She pulled her own phone from her pocket and discovered a similar result. "Oh, thank God."

"All right, time to get us rescued." Matt dialed directory assistance to arrange a tow truck.

Cara thought of Sadie, still waiting at the shelter. It was past nine now. Someone should be there. She pulled up her call history and dialed the shelter's main line.

"Shelton County Animal Shelter," a woman's voice said.

"Hi, this is Cara Medlen." Cara's voice sounded a little strange due to the numbness in her lips. "I'm picking up Sadie for Triangle Boxer Rescue this morning."

"Sadie? The fawn boxer? Oh, I think she got pulled by the attending for a health check this morning. Hang on."

There was a click, then static-filled silence. Cara glanced at Matt, heard him giving their location to someone on the other end of the line. God, please let the tow truck come quickly. Her bones were starting to shake loose beneath her skin.

"Miss Medlen?"

Cara turned her attention back to the phone. "Yes."

"When will you be here to pick her up?"

"A few hours; that's why I was calling. My car went off the road in the snowstorm last night. We're just now getting a tow truck, and then we'll be on our way to Shelton."

"Well, here's the thing. Sadie's showing symptoms of an upper respiratory infection this morning. Green nasal discharge. Cough. We don't have an area to quarantine contagious dogs. Our policy is to euthanize once symptoms are documented."

Fear slammed Cara backward. She stumbled in the snow, grabbing Matt's arm before she went down in a heap. No way. Not after she'd come this far. "Don't euthanize her. I'm on my way, I swear. Just give me a couple of hours."

"We're trying to wait for you. That's why we didn't put her down first thing this morning. But like I said, we don't have a quarantine area. I've got someone sitting out back with her."

"I'll be there as soon as I can."

"Well," the woman drawled, "our trainer, the one who's sitting with Sadie—she goes home at noon. I can't promise anything after that."

Cara's fingers clenched on the phone. "Don't euthanize her. Wait for me. Please."

"Ma'am, we're doing our best, but we're on a limited staff today, and we can't risk infecting other dogs. Like I said, get here by noon."

Cara hung up the phone and glanced wildly at Matt.

"Tow truck should be out here in a half an hour or so," he said with an apologetic shrug.

"Half an hour?" Cara looked at her watch and ran the math through her head. "We have a problem."

# CHAPTER THIRTEEN

Matt looked at Cara. "What kind of problem?"

His biggest problem at that moment was getting her warm. She'd stumbled a few times, and he suspected her feet were completely numb, thanks to her soaking wet sneakers. Now her jacket and jeans were splashed as well, courtesy of the idiot in the Explorer.

Her eyes had gone wide and glassy. "Sadie's sick. They can only hold her until noon."

"What happens at noon?" he asked, although he had a feeling he knew the answer.

Cara threw her arms into the air. "She gets the needle. Or maybe they still use the gas chamber out here, I don't know. We've got to hurry!"

Matt considered this. He didn't like the idea of the poor dog being euthanized any more than the next person, but Cara remained his primary concern. "Don't panic. Tow truck should be here by ten. Figure thirty minutes to get the Jeep back on the road. I don't think we're more than thirty, forty minutes from Shelton. It's doable."

Cara took a deep breath and puffed steam into the

cold morning air. "Okay. So what do we do until it gets
here?"

"Keep moving. We'll be colder if we stand still. Truck's
coming from Poole, so we'll keep walking this way. I know
your feet are bad. How's the rest of you?"

"Better than my feet."

That wasn't saying much. He rubbed his hands up and
down her sleeves, hoping to generate a little warmth for her.
Cara'd been shivering for over an hour now, and he was anxious to get her inside and warmed up. She wasn't dressed for
the weather, despite her layers.

Her winter coat was more of a jacket, something to be
worn as she crossed the parking lot from the car to the store,
not for prolonged hiking in below-freezing temperatures.
But his main concern was her feet.

His own feet were cold enough. Despite his rugged winter boots, some moisture had seeped inside, dampening his
socks and chilling his skin until he could no longer feel his
pinky toes. Uncomfortable, but not dangerous.

Cara trudged along beside him, her jaw set with determination. He sure hoped the dog made it until they arrived and
was worthy of the hype she'd worked up over saving her.

What if Sadie was mean-spirited? Or too far gone to be
saved?

The sun had risen high and warm in the sky, beginning
to melt some of the snow off the roads. Here and there, a car
crawled through, but Cara insisted they wait for the tow truck.

Matt heaved a sigh of relief as the big, red flatbed truck
rumbled into view. He waved at it, and the rig slowed and
pulled over beside them.

"You the folks whose car went off the road?"

"That's us," Matt said.

"Climb on in," said the driver, a heavyset man in worn
jeans and a patched, red athletic jacket.

Cara looked up and smiled. "Gladly."

Matt placed a steadying hand on her waist as she hauled herself into the cab, then slid in beside her. The warmth inside wrapped around them. Cara leaned back and closed her eyes with an appreciative groan.

"Name's Larry. Y'all from out of town?"

"Matt Dumont, and this is Cara Medlen. We're from Dogwood, outside Raleigh. Appreciate you coming out in this weather."

Larry nodded. "That's the job."

"Jeep's about three miles back this way." Matt gestured out the window.

"Y'all spent the night in the car?" He put the truck in gear and pulled back onto the road.

Cara nodded. "It was pretty cold."

"Speaking of cold..." Matt tapped her right leg and gestured for her to put her feet on his lap.

She rolled her eyes as she complied. "I'm fine."

"We need to get your feet dry." He peeled off her soggy sneakers and socks, revealing feet that were bone white and ice cold. He rubbed them briskly until she grimaced, letting him know that the pins and needles had set in, then he pulled a pair of dry socks out of the backpack.

Matt slid her feet into the socks and positioned them on his lap so that the heat vent on the dash blew directly onto them. Cara's eyes slid shut, and he felt her shivers stop for the first time since they'd left the Jeep.

"Right up here," Matt told the driver as they rounded the bend and the Jeep became visible through the trees.

"Alrighty, let's go have us a look." Larry shifted the truck into Park and stepped out into the snow.

Cara glanced at the clock, then gripped Matt's shirt-sleeve. "Hurry."

\* \* \*

Cara watched through the window, feeling half drunk with the warmth of the truck. She hadn't fully appreciated just how cold she'd been until she was warm. Now she sagged against the worn upholstery in boneless relief.

Outside, Matt and the tow truck driver tromped down the slope into the woods to attach a cable to the Jeep's rear bumper. They went around to the back of the truck, where she couldn't see them, and a motor churned to life. The Jeep began inching its way up the incline toward the road.

Thank goodness. Just a few minutes and they'd finally be back on the road, on the way to Shelton. And Sadie.

Larry pointed at a dark stain in the snow where the Jeep had been. Matt frowned, then scraped a hand over his jaw. He glanced up at Cara with worry written all over his face.

She looked at the clock. Ten thirty. An hour and a half to get to the shelter. Fear knotted in the pit of her stomach. No way was she going to lose Sadie when they were this close. She'd put her wet sneakers back on and walk to Shelton first.

Matt rapped on the glass. Cara fumbled around on the door until she located the button to lower the window.

"Problem," he said. "Looks like we've got a puncture in the oil pan. It's been leaking slow and steady all night."

"What does that mean?"

"Means we can't drive it out of here. Larry's going to tow it back to his shop."

"Matt—"

"I know, Cara. Don't worry, honey. I'll get you there in time."

She narrowed her eyes. Had he just called her *honey*? "How, exactly, without a car?"

"I'm working on that part. Let me talk to Larry and see what we can work out." He walked off toward Larry.

She closed the window and leaned back into the seat to watch as the Jeep crept toward the road. Then they were out of sight, maneuvering it onto the flatbed behind her.

Cara closed her eyes. Exhaustion slithered over her and squeezed energy from her limbs. The back of the Jeep had actually made a fine bed, but she'd barely slept thanks to the man in the sleeping bag behind her. She suspected he had suffered the same consequence.

Men didn't get erections like that in their sleep—did they?

Warmth crept into her cheeks. Good thing they'd be home by suppertime. Another night with Matt might drive them both into delirium.

Both doors burst open without warning, blasting Cara with cold air.

"Scoot over." Matt nudged her as he climbed into the passenger side, while Larry swung into the driver's seat.

Cara found herself sandwiched between them. She chose to lean on Matt, putting a little breathing room between her and Larry. No offense to Larry.

"I've got good news and bad news," Larry offered with a friendly smile.

Cara eyed him for a moment, then turned to Matt. His lips were set in a grim line.

*Uh-oh.*

"Good news first, I guess," she said.

"Good news is I've got a loaner for you. She's kind of a clunker, but she'll get you by. I'll even let you take her to Shelton to pick up the dog." Larry threw the truck in gear and began inching forward, careful not to spin his tires on the icy pavement.

She exhaled in relief. That was *great* news. "That's

awesome, Larry. I really appreciate it. What's the bad news?"

"Bad news is it's going to take a few days to get in the parts I need, this being the weekend and all."

"Okay." She glanced between Larry and Matt, not yet grasping why this was bad news.

"He means we've got to wait around until the part comes in, Cara. We'll be spending a couple of days out here in the mountains."

Her mouth fell open, but she quickly snapped it closed. "What? Why? Can't we just go home and come back?"

Matt shook his head. "It's a four-hour drive, and the roads out here are still a mess. Larry's loaner might not make it all the way to Dogwood so we'd have to find a proper rental, which would probably mean driving all the way back to Asheville. Then we've got to drive Larry's car back to Poole. By then, it would be too late to get home today. Why spend half the day tomorrow driving home, only to come back Monday morning to pick up my Jeep?"

Cara straightened, wishing for a little room between her and Matt that wouldn't put her in Larry's lap. "But what about Sadie?"

"I reckon you can find a motel that takes dogs," Larry said.

Matt shrugged, but he wasn't smiling. "Looks like we're spending the weekend together."

* * *

Matt beheld the battered blue Chevy Larry pointed out and held in a groan. The Jeep was his palace. This was a heap.

Beside him, Cara was practically frothing at the mouth. "How far did you say we are from Shelton?"

" 'Bout thirty minutes," Larry told her.

Matt glanced at his watch. Eleven forty-three. Towing the Jeep, plus completing all the necessary paperwork, had taken longer than expected. Cara had been on the phone with the shelter at least twice in the last hour, but they refused to make any promises past noon.

He seriously doubted they'd euthanize a dog at twelve o'clock if they knew rescue would be there in the next half hour, but he'd sure as hell hate the result for Cara if he were wrong. "All right, then, let's get going. Thanks, Larry—appreciate all your help. Give me a call if anything unexpected comes up."

The other man tipped his cap. "Will do."

Cara was already in the process of shoving the dog bed and her duffel bag into the backseat of the Chevy. Matt slung his bag in next to hers.

He opened the driver's door and slouched into the well-worn bucket seat.

Cara slid in next to him. "Hurry."

"I am." He put the car in gear and backed out of the parking lot.

"I'm going to let them know we're on our way." Cara pressed her cell phone to her ear.

She was nothing if not dedicated to her cause. Even rumpled and mud-splashed from their early-morning hike, she was about the sweetest thing he'd ever seen.

And he was stuck here in the mountains with her until Monday. He'd better ask for hotel rooms on opposite ends of the building.

Beside him, Cara pleaded with whoever was on the other end of the line, explaining yet again that they were on their way and would be at the shelter in the next thirty minutes. She held the phone clenched in her left hand, her right fisted into the denim of her jeans.

Well, hell. He nudged the gas pedal and gave the Chevy

a little more juice. Couldn't take it too fast out here—the roads were still a mess—but Cara's desperation was getting to him.

The wheels spun as he turned onto Pleasant Street, headed for Shelton—and Sadie.

Cara tossed the phone into her purse. "That woman is such a bitch."

"No luck?"

"They've got someone sitting outside with Sadie, but she goes home at noon, and they can't let Sadie back in the building without risk of infecting the other dogs."

He frowned. "Infecting them? What's wrong with her, exactly?"

"Upper respiratory infection. Cough. Snot. It's very contagious among shelter dogs."

"I bet."

"Can't you drive any faster?"

"Not unless you want to end up in a ditch for the second time in twenty-four hours."

She sighed and tapped her fingers against her thighs. "Sorry."

"It's okay. We'll get there." And then they'd figure out what the hell they were going to do for the rest of the weekend. But first things first.

He fought the urge to glance over his shoulder at the laptop bag stowed on the backseat. It was killing him that he hadn't checked the GPS logs on Ken Prentiss's car since lunchtime yesterday. Matt could see real-time updates on his phone, but until he booted up his laptop, he wouldn't know where Ken had been last night while he and Cara were stranded without cell service. He hoped the snowstorm had kept the man home with his wife.

He didn't want to consider the alternative.

Cara fidgeted in her seat as Matt carefully navigated the

snow-covered roads to Shelton. Fortunately, the animal shelter was on the near side of town, just off the main road. He pulled into its mostly empty parking lot and studied the one-story brick structure with interest.

He'd never visited an animal shelter before. Curiosity propelled him after Cara as she flung open the car door and sloshed across the parking lot.

She pushed through the glass door into a dingy lobby with gray-painted, cement-block walls and scuffed linoleum floors. The sound of dogs barking closed around them at head-pounding levels. The place smelled like a urinal that hadn't been cleaned in years.

Cara glanced around and grimaced. "I was afraid it would be like this."

"Is this average or sub-par?"

"This is crap. Let's see if we made it in time."

Matt stood back and watched Cara stride up to the reception desk, all fire and determination despite her soggy and bedraggled appearance. He took in the bulletin board papered with various ads and notices and another with photos of what he presumed to be adoptable animals here in the shelter.

In the corner, a young couple sat with a black dog, looking as if they'd just met their new best friend. They wore wide smiles, and the dog's tail swooshed against the linoleum with enthusiasm. So at least someone was having a happy ending today.

"I'm Cara Medlen. I've been in touch about picking up Sadie." Cara rested her palms on the desk and fixed her eyes on the middle-aged woman behind it.

"Oh, Miss Medlen, finally. We weren't sure if you were going to make it. Be a shame to have to put down a nice dog like Sadie with someone out there wanting to take her."

Cara drew a visible breath at the news that she'd made it

in time. "Yeah, it would. Like I told you on the phone, the snowstorm derailed us. We spent the night on the side of the road. Do you have the paperwork for me? I'm pulling her for Triangle Boxer Rescue."

"Ready and waiting," the woman said, with a hint of bite to her words.

Cara shot her a withering look. Matt turned away to hide his grin.

"How will you be paying today?"

"Cash," Cara said as she accepted the clipboard of papers the receptionist pushed toward her.

"That'll be twenty-five dollars for the pull fee."

Cara scribbled her way down the page, one foot tapping impatiently against the linoleum.

Yeah, he was ready to get on with things too. They'd pick up the dog, find a place to stay for the next two nights, and then he was more than ready for a hearty meal and a hot shower.

After all the anticipation, he sure hoped Cara and Sadie hit it off.

Cara reached into her wallet and placed several crisp green bills on top of the clipboard, then shoved it across the counter.

"Thank you, Miss Medlen. She's out back with J. J. Goodwin, our trainer. You'll find her in the blue station wagon."

"Let's go." Cara looked up at him, her eyes ablaze with excitement.

"You get this excited for every new foster?"

"No," she admitted.

They walked out the front door and sloshed through several inches of slush toward the row of employee cars parked in back. The blue station wagon sat on the end.

Visible inside was a woman holding a scrawny, brown dog.

# CHAPTER FOURTEEN

Cara's gaze landed on Sadie and stuck there. Something warm swelled in her chest as the dog lifted her head and stared back. Wide, brown eyes met Cara's.

*This.* Moments like this were what drove her when nothing else seemed to make sense. Another life saved. And, really, what could top that?

The driver's door opened, and a tall, slender woman stepped out. She wore a brightly colored patchwork jacket and bell-bottom jeans over brown leather work boots, with a thick braid of red hair over each shoulder. "J. J. Goodwin. You must be Cara."

"I am." Cara returned her smile, then felt her gaze drawn again to the dog on the front seat, still watching her with somber eyes. "Thank you for staying with her."

"Oh, please." J.J. shrugged and ruffled Sadie's head. "Don't let Virginia give you any hell on my behalf. I would have stayed as long as it took for you to get here."

"Do you work here?" Cara stepped forward and stroked Sadie's chin. The dog's tail wiggled, then a hacking cough wracked her frail body.

"I'm a dog trainer. I offer an obedience class here on the weekend to people who've adopted from the shelter. No one showed up today, on account of the weather, so I spent some time with Sadie instead."

"I really appreciate it. Do you know of a place around here we can stay? Our car's out of commission until Monday."

"Hmm." J.J. tapped a finger to her lips. "Well, the only place in town's Barbara's Bed & Breakfast over on Main Street. I'm not sure if she'd take a dog, but doesn't hurt to ask, given the situation. There's a Travelers Inn and a Super 8 back in Poole, but I don't think either of them allow pets. Try Barbara's first. She's a sweet lady—tell her I sent you."

"Will do, thank you."

"You might want to get this girl to a vet." J.J. stroked Sadie's head. "Doc Wattley's open until four today. I think she could use some antibiotics for that cough."

"I was thinking the same thing."

"He's on Main Street too. Not much else around. Here's my card if you need anything while you're in town." J.J. handed her a blue-patterned business card.

"Thank you so much." Cara accepted the card and the red leash J.J. held toward her.

Sadie hopped obediently from the front seat and splashed into the messy parking lot, her nub of a tail tucked tightly against her rump.

Cara crouched in front of her. "Hey, there. Feel like coming for a ride with us?"

Sadie stared straight ahead, looking uncertain and frightened. She shivered against the cold and let out another hacking cough. Being ankle deep in slush was no good for her weakened immune system.

"Come on, sweetie. Let's get you warm and dry. Thanks again, J.J."

"Anytime. Good luck with her."

Matt led the way to the Chevy. He opened the back door for Sadie and cleared a spot for her among their bags. Cara flattened a section of the dog bed across the seat and patted it to motion her up.

The dog hopped up and curled herself into a tiny ball. Cara gave her a quick once-over. She was a petite girl, probably not much over forty pounds, with a fawn coat and white socks on each paw. Ribs protruded from her sides and heaved with each coughing breath she took. She stank with the pungent smell of an unwashed shelter dog.

That, at least, could be fixed with a quick bath.

"To the bed-and-breakfast?" Matt asked as he slid behind the wheel. He didn't look any more enthusiastic about that option than she felt.

"I guess." Cara closed the back door and climbed into the seat in front of Sadie. The dog tracked her with watchful brown eyes.

Cara really just wanted to go home, although the thought of another four hours in the car did indeed sound torturous. A soft, warm bed and a hot meal might cheer her up. And a shower.

Just the thought of it made her skin feel scummy. Yeah, a shower. Food. Bed.

Not with Matt.

She glanced over at him. He grinned, as if he'd read her thoughts.

Matt turned the car onto Pleasant Street. Outside, the streets sloshed around their tires. Behind her, Sadie watched, so quiet, so serious. Cara suspected the dog knew, on some level anyway, the close call she'd had. They had a sense about these things.

A few minutes later, Matt turned right onto Main Street. Sprawling ranch houses gave way to a quaint downtown area with little shops and chrome-posted street lamps. They drove past Sammy's BBQ, the Downtown Diner, Speedy

Mart, an antique store called A Time Remembered, and a handful of other local businesses.

At the end of the block, a large, yellow ranch house boasted a flowery sign announcing "Barbara's Bed & Breakfast. Come for the view, stay for the food."

Cara wasn't sure yet what the view was like, but she sure hoped Barbara had a room.

Make that two.

* * *

"Oh dear, what a time you've had!" Barbara glanced from Matt to Cara and pushed the glasses higher up the bridge of her nose. "Well, this snowstorm has really hit us hard. Stranded a whole group of students passing through on a field trip to Knoxville. They've taken up most of my rooms, but I do have one left in back."

"Just one?" Cara's voice sounded a little more high-pitched than normal.

Matt thought he knew why. The thought of spending two nights in a cozy bed-and-breakfast with her had him feeling a bit strangled as well.

Barbara nodded. "It's the two of you, right? It will be perfect. The Bennington Suite—it's our unofficial honeymoon suite, very romantic. That's why I didn't assign it to the high-schoolers. King-sized bed, Jacuzzi tub, it's even got a fireplace. And it looks right over the lake. Not that there's much to see on the lake today . . ."

Barbara rambled on, but Matt's hearing had gone fuzzy somewhere around mention of the Jacuzzi tub.

"I don't normally allow pets, but I'm a dog lover myself, and I admire what you've done to save this one, so she can stay—long as you promise to clean up after her and keep her out of trouble."

"I will, and thank you so much, Barbara." Cara smiled warmly at her, studiously avoiding looking at Matt.

She kept her eyes straight ahead as they walked out to the car, then fussed over Sadie as he drove them around back to the spot Barbara had indicated.

The Bennington Suite had its own private entrance, which would come in handy for walking the dog. Overlooking the back of the property, several snow-covered acres sloped toward what was probably a nice-looking pond during most of the year. Today it was a slushy indent in the snow-covered landscape.

He shoved the key into the door and turned.

"This is . . . interesting." Cara kept her back to him as she surveyed their room.

It was nicer than what Matt had imagined a bed-and-breakfast to be, which was good for what he was paying for the damn thing. A cream-colored quilt topped the king-sized bed, with a floral blanket folded neatly across the end. Plush carpeting squished beneath their feet.

He'd expected perhaps an overload of flowers and doilies, but this was tasteful. The bed featured a solid wood head- and footboard, intricately carved with a natural finish. The walls were a warm beige with paintings of what he presumed to be local scenery. A large wood carving of a deer sat on the end table.

Across from the bed, a gas fireplace beckoned. Matt crossed to it and switched it on, certain that Cara and Sadie could use the extra heat. Then his eyes fell on the Jacuzzi tub, not tucked away in the bathroom, but positioned in a nook by the window, overlooking the rolling hills beyond.

*Shit.* He'd rather sleep in the car than try to share this room with Cara for the next two nights and keep his hands to himself.

Matt cleared his throat and forced away images of Cara

in the tub with bubbles sliding between her breasts. "I'm starved. How about I go get us some lunch while you get her settled?"

Cara looked up from where she'd kneeled by the bed, examining Sadie. "Oh yeah, I'm hungry too. Whatever you want is good with me."

"You got it." Matt grabbed his keys and headed for the door.

Half an hour later, they were seated at the table in the corner, devouring hot meatball subs from the Corner Deli as Sadie napped in the dog bed. While he was out, Cara had showered and changed back into her black knit pants and a pink sweater. Her sneakers were propped in front of the fireplace to finish drying out.

"I called the vet and made an appointment for her at three. I guess we need to find someplace to buy dog food too."

Matt nodded. "I'll go on a supply run before we go to the vet."

"Thanks." Cara walked to the fireplace and stood, rubbing her hands up and down her arms.

He joined her and pulled her in for a hug. "Hell of a day so far."

"Yeah." Cara's arms came up to encircle his neck. She stared deep into his eyes. "This room is romantic."

"Sure is. But the same rules apply as last night." And yet, try as he might, he couldn't force himself to let her go.

"That's the thing..." Cara went up on her tiptoes and pressed a kiss to his lips.

Heat flared inside him, quick and powerful like the flames in the fireplace when he'd flicked the switch. His arms tightened around her, but he didn't kiss her back. "No 'thing.' We're not doing anything you're going to regret later. I'll sleep on the floor, and you take the bed."

She shook her head, and a curl fell across her face. He reached up instinctively to brush it back.

Cara bit her bottom lip and looked up again. "The thing is, I think I'd regret it more if I didn't."

Well, *shit*. "Be careful what you ask for, Cara Medlen."

Those wide, blue eyes never wavered. "I am. You're not sleeping on the floor. And unless you want to spend another night pretending to sleep while we fantasize about ripping each other's clothes off, I'd suggest you pick up a few extra supplies while you're out."

Matt lowered his head and claimed her mouth with an intensity that almost robbed him of the ability to breathe. Cara kissed him back, matching his enthusiasm with her own, her body pressed tight against his.

"You're sure?" The thought of having her in his bed tonight left him weak at the knees.

Cara nodded, breathless. "If we don't, I'll always wonder what it would have been like. No regrets."

"What happens in Shelton stays in Shelton?"

She nodded. "Exactly."

"Oh hell, Cara." He stepped her backward against the wall and flattened her against him. "I want you so bad."

Cara wrapped her legs around his hips and settled herself so that his erection rested between her legs. He devoured her mouth as her hips moved restlessly against him until he wasn't sure he had the strength to let go of her long enough to go out and buy condoms.

He'd never wanted a woman as badly as he wanted Cara. And for this weekend, she was his.

"Oh, no." Suddenly she was shoving him away, her voice tight with fear. Matt opened his eyes, still hazy with lust. Cara slid to the floor and dashed from his arms. "Sadie."

He turned. The dog lay with her eyes closed, panting rapidly with white foam around her mouth.

Cara took her head in her hands. "Sadie…oh, no."

Sadie's head rolled limply into her lap.

* * *

Cara paced the exam room until she was dizzy. Matt stood by the door, arms folded over his chest, his expression serious. Nearly thirty minutes had passed since the veterinarian had rushed Sadie out of the room for emergency treatment.

She could only hope the little dog had enough fight left in her, because to lose her now, well, that felt an awful lot like defeat.

The door opened, and Dr. Wattley entered, carrying a clipboard.

Cara stopped and stared at him. His lips were pressed together in a thin line, but his eyes were bright.

He tapped a pen against the clipboard. "Sadie's stable."

Cara's breath whooshed out, and her knees sagged. "Thank God."

"She's suffering from acute respiratory distress, brought on by the respiratory infection which has begun to develop into pneumonia. It's not surprising, given her overall health and background. We've started her on antibiotics, steroids to reduce inflammation in her airways, and oxygen treatments. So far, she's responding well."

Cara sucked in a deep breath. "That's great news."

"We'd like to keep her overnight to continue oxygen treatment until her lung function has improved. By morning, I expect she'll be feeling much better."

"But she's going to be okay?"

Dr. Wattley smiled. "I expect her to make a full recovery. Are you aware of the growth on her right front leg? That looks worrisome."

She nodded. "It is. She has a mast cell tumor. I'm planning to have it removed as soon as she's up for the surgery."

"Great. Well, I'll walk you out to reception. We'll be in

touch if there's any change in her condition, but otherwise you can pick her up tomorrow morning after nine."

"Thank you so much."

She grimaced at the paperwork he handed her. Merry would have a fit if she saw the medical bills Sadie had racked up in her first hours of rescue. There weren't enough funds in the rescue's bank account to cover it. Cara had taken it on herself to save Sadie, so she'd cover her bills for now.

She'd make up for it with a few extra photography bookings.

"You okay?" Matt's warm hand rested on her shoulder.

"Yeah." She felt good about Sadie spending the night under a veterinarian's care. It would save her from endless worry tonight.

She handed over her credit card, then signed on the dotted line.

Matt led her toward the parking lot where the Chevy sat. "I'll drop you back at the room, then go get those supplies we talked about."

"Okay." She didn't ask why he didn't just bring her along on his errands. The truth was, she'd just hit a wall, numb with fatigue.

So she didn't complain as she shuffled into their room at Barbara's Bed & Breakfast and the Chevy pulled back out onto Main Street. Cara staggered to the big, soft bed and collapsed onto it.

She woke to the sound of Matt's fingers clicking on his laptop. He sat at the table in the corner, brow furrowed in concentration. Across from her, a warm fire crackled in the fireplace. Pretty close to the perfect view. She lay on her side, on top of the covers. She'd been too tired to even crawl inside before she passed out.

Matt had showered and shaved. Gone was the slightly disreputable growth of beard on his cheeks she'd found so irrationally sexy. His hair was damp and wavy, and he wore a crisp black polo and clean jeans.

"Goddammit." He slammed a fist into his thigh, then glanced in her direction.

She shrugged up on her elbow. "Everything okay?"

He frowned. "I'm sorry. Did I wake you?"

She shook her head. "Work?"

"Goddamn sneaky bastard. Of course he'd choose today to shack up in a hotel."

"Talking about yourself in the third person?"

The corner of his mouth turned up in an almost-smile. "Client. I've been tailing this guy for weeks, waiting to catch him in the act. Now I'm stuck way out here in the middle of nowhere, and he's checked into a hotel with his mistress, safe from my lens."

"Sorry. That really sucks."

He shrugged, his shoulders stiff. "Nothing I can do about it. You feeling better after a nap?"

She nodded. "What time is it?"

"Almost six. You looked like you might pass out on your feet by the time we left the vet." A soft smile curved his lips.

"Wow, yeah, I guess I was tired." And she felt much, much better now.

"Hungry?"

"Yeah, a little." She sat up and rubbed her eyes.

"Our options are pretty limited, given the roads, but there's an Italian place around the corner looks pretty good."

"Sure." She got up and walked into the bathroom.

Nerves filled her stomach and choked her lungs. A date. With Matt. Probably the only one they'd ever have, unless she counted the time he'd cooked dinner for her at his place. And all she had to wear was this sweater and cotton pants, or the jeans she'd had on yesterday. No makeup but some tinted lip gloss.

At least she was wearing clean underwear.

Cara groaned. Her hair was flat on one side from sleeping. She fluffed it with her fingers and applied a fresh coat of lip gloss. Not much else she could do.

When she stepped back into the bedroom, Matt was once again frowning at his laptop, frustration etched in sharp lines across his face. She knew how long and hard he'd worked to catch this guy. It had to be killing him that he was stuck out here in the mountains with her right now.

He looked up, and a slow sexy smile spread across his face. He stood and pulled her against him for a kiss that stole her breath, and probably the lip gloss too. "Ready for dinner?"

Cara nodded, feeling not the least bit hungry with Matt's hands on her butt. In fact, she was probably going to be too nervous to eat a thing.

"The vet's office called while you were asleep. Sadie's off the oxygen and resting comfortably."

"Really? That's good news."

"It is."

"Sorry you're stuck here with me instead of busting that cheating husband."

Matt pulled her closer for another kiss. "I'm sorry I'm not busting him, but not sorry about being stuck here with you."

She slid her fingers across his chest, feeling the hard contour of muscle through his shirt. Heat radiated from him, warming her fingers. His eyes took on that predatory gleam she'd come to recognize right before he kissed the daylights out of her.

When he pulled back, they were both gasping for breath. "Come on, let's go eat before we get distracted."

Distracted? Cara was well past that point. She meant what she'd told Matt earlier: she might regret hooking up with him this weekend, but she'd regret it more if she didn't.

She'd never been with a man who brought out such a strong response in her, who could drive her so crazy with nothing but a kiss.

This was about more than chemistry, though, for her, anyway. Matt Dumont was a man she could fall in love with. He was honorable, strong, intelligent. He made her laugh. He'd given up his whole weekend to help her rescue Sadie without a single complaint, and not even expecting to get laid.

No, she didn't regret her decision, but what with rushing Sadie to the vet and now dinner, the anticipation was starting to get to her. She had no idea how she was supposed to concentrate on eating knowing what would happen afterward.

They were seated in a burgundy upholstered booth near the back of the restaurant. Cara fiddled with her menu while Matt ordered a bottle of Merlot.

"You're allowed to change your mind, you know."

She did know, and that made her want him even more. "I don't want to."

"Then don't be nervous." He placed a big, warm hand over hers.

He looked incredibly handsome sitting across from her in his black shirt and jeans, his dark hair tousled, those chocolate eyes so warm on hers.

And so Cara muddled her way through a glass of wine and a plate of lobster ravioli without tasting much of it. It was probably excellent, but her attention was devoted to the man on the other side of the table.

He drove them back to their room, taking care on the slippery roads. Much of today's snow had melted, but temperatures in the mountains had once again dipped below freezing, turning the afternoon's slush into an icy mess.

"I have a prediction," Matt said as he turned into the parking lot behind the bed-and-breakfast.

"Oh yeah?" She blushed in anticipation of whatever it

might be. Goodness, did he like to make bets about it ahead of time?

"Sadie's going to be the one you keep."

"What?" That was so completely off track from what she'd been thinking about that her mouth fell open in surprise.

Matt chuckled. His eyes met hers briefly in the dim light of the car. "You and that dirty mind. You drive me absolutely crazy—you know that."

"I didn't—" But that was exactly what she'd been thinking. As far as keeping Sadie, Cara didn't know what to say. Certainly there was a bond between them, even though they'd scarcely met, but keeping her? No. That wouldn't happen.

Then they were stepping through the door of their room, and Matt was taking a bottle of champagne out of a mini-fridge Cara hadn't even noticed, and she quit thinking altogether.

# CHAPTER FIFTEEN

The champagne tickled her mouth and warmed her belly. Cara took another sip, then set the glass aside. Matt took her wrist and tugged her up against him. She lifted her right hand to his chest and felt his heart pounding, the heat of his skin through that layer of cotton.

He brushed his lips against hers then pulled back. "I just wanted you to know I'm crazy about you, Cara. If the situation were different, I'd be hoping this was just the beginning for us."

Her heart clenched. "Really?"

Unless she had completely misjudged him, Matt wasn't the type of guy to feed her a line. As far as she could tell, he spoke exactly what was on his mind, no more and no less. And no man had ever looked at her the way Matt was right now. As if it pained him they wouldn't get that chance.

Which made her glad, no matter how much it already hurt, that this would go no further than Barbara's Bed & Breakfast. It wouldn't be fair to either of them for her to get tangled up with Matt before her health was clear.

His eyes held hers, steady, honest, and burning with desire. "Really. I know this has the potential to get messy after we go home, but I hope we can both look back on this weekend as something wonderful."

"I want that."

His arms tightened around her, and he gave her another teasing kiss. "I want you so much. I've fantasized about this moment."

Cara blinked. "Me too."

She gasped as he kissed his way across her jaw and down her neck. She had a feeling he was going to fulfill every one of her fantasies tonight, and then some. Hell, he'd already given her a mind-bending orgasm in his Jeep without even taking her clothes off.

What began tender and slow soon exploded into a frantic fire. Matt's mouth was on hers now, doing all sorts of wonderful things with his tongue that made her knees tremble and desire pool between her legs.

His hands slid beneath her sweater. With practiced ease, he popped the clasp of her bra and cupped her breasts in the heat of his hands.

He teased her nipples until she moaned with pleasure. She ripped his shirt from the waistband of his jeans, desperate to feel his bare skin beneath her fingers, drunk with the knowledge that he was hers. Tonight. Tomorrow.

His skin was hot and firm beneath her touch, and his abs bunched as her fingers slid across them. Cara lifted the shirt over his head. A smattering of dark hair covered his chest, thickening in a happy trail that led to the waistband of his jeans. A black military tattoo circled his upper right bicep, with a bulldog in the center, looking ferocious. A bulldog, because he was a marine.

She traced her fingers over it. Something about him having a dog tattooed on his skin, no matter the meaning behind it, felt . . . right. She looked up and saw the desire on his face. The heat, the yearning. For her.

"Like what you see?" His voice was low, rough.

"Oh yeah."

He yanked her sweater off. Her unclasped bra went with it, tumbling to the floor. His eyes swept over her, darkening as they went. "Me too."

He stepped her backward toward the bed, pausing to grab their champagne glasses from the table by the door. He held her glass to her lips, and she took a long sip, the liquid sweet and bubbly on her tongue.

In one fluid movement, Matt set the glasses on the bed-side table and lifted her into his arms. He laid her across the cream-colored bedspread, then lowered himself next to her. His right thigh slid between her legs, pressing into the parts of her that begged for his touch.

Then he was kissing her again, as if they had all the time in the world, which she supposed they did, but she was more accustomed to men who got straight to business. Matt treated her as if she were a fine wine to be savored, not gulped.

He raked his eyes over her with a satisfied smile. "My God, you are beautiful."

Her cheeks flushed hot.

He reached beside them for one of the champagne glasses and drizzled the frothy liquid across her breasts. She gasped at the splash of cold against her overheated skin, then gasped again as he lowered his head and sucked it from her chest with sensual swirls of his tongue.

Her hips lifted from the bed, arching into him, seeking and finding the hard bulge in the front of his jeans. "Matt . . ."

He kissed his way across her chest, one breast, then the other, until she panted beneath his touch. His fingers traced across her stomach and lingered at the waistband of her pants. She whimpered.

Matt lifted his head and smiled at her, his eyes all hot and dark, his chest heaving for breath. Cara was certain no man had ever looked sexier.

He tugged at her pants, those hot fingers blazing a fiery trail across her bare skin. He brushed a hand across the front of her panties, teasing her. She gasped, her hips moving restlessly against him.

Matt groaned in response.

Cara leaned forward and tugged at his jeans, but she fumbled the button as he slid her pants down her legs. She kicked them to the floor. Thank goodness she'd always indulged herself in girly underwear, because, when she'd left the house yesterday, she'd had no idea Matt would be coming with her, let alone that she'd wind up in bed with him.

Apparently her pink lace panties met with his approval. He let out something similar to a growl as he traced a finger over the lacy fringe. No way was she going to lie there in nothing but her panties while he still had his jeans on. She fumbled with the button again, the front of his pants strained tight by his erection.

This time it came free. She tugged the zipper down, and Matt helped her slide him out of his jeans and navy blue boxers.

She drank in the sight of his lean, muscled body, and in particular, the rather impressive sight of his penis pointed right at her.

*Wow.*

Matt chuckled as he slid beside her on the bed. "Wow?"

Cara scrunched her face. Had she actually said that out loud? But yeah, wow. She could stare at him all night, if she wasn't completely preoccupied with other things she could be doing with his naked body.

He leaned down and kissed a spot right above her panties. "What's this?"

"A dumb idea I had in college." She knew without looking

that his interest had been attracted by the little pink heart she'd had tattooed there when she was nineteen.

"It's sexy." He traced it with his tongue, then slid her out of her panties.

He was kissing his way down her belly, and she knew exactly where he was headed. Cara was generally uncomfortable with any man kissing her below the waist. She tensed to protest, but then his tongue reached her most intimate parts.

*Oh, God.*

Pleasure exploded inside her, so strong it stole her breath. Her fingers gripped the comforter as his tongue performed magic on her body. Pressure built inside her, her breath coming in shallow pants. Before she could even think about what was happening, she shattered, ecstasy rolling over her in waves while Matt urged her on to still-greater heights.

She cried out at the sheer wonder of it. *Wow.* She'd never let a man do that for her before. Now that he was kissing his way back up her belly, she felt a tiny bit embarrassed about it.

And a little disappointed. She'd never come twice in one night and would have rather waited until he was inside her.

Matt nibbled a sensitive spot below her ear, his body big and hot and hard against hers. The last shimmers of pleasure still pulsed inside her as he reached into the nightstand and pulled out a little foil packet.

"Let me," she said, surprising herself. She'd never put on a man's condom, either, but tonight promised to be full of firsts, and she couldn't resist the opportunity to touch him as he'd already touched her.

He handed it to her, his eyes hot and heavy. She slid her thumb over the head of his penis. He jerked in her hands, and his eyes closed. Feeling empowered, she traced the length of him, then gripped him hard and squeezed. Matt groaned deep in his chest. His hips moved against her as he thrust himself into her hand.

She brought her head down and took him in her mouth. Matt shuddered with pleasure. This big strong man, this soldier turned PI, trembled in her hands. She continued to stroke him with her hand as her mouth gave him pleasure, until he closed his hand over hers.

"Oh God, that's good, Cara, but I want to be inside you when I come." His voice was low and rough, strained with the tension she felt pulsing through every inch of his body.

Her own body tightened in response. She lifted her face to his and kissed him as his erection pressed hot and hard into her belly. Then she ripped open the foil packet and rolled the condom down the length of him.

Matt rolled over, positioning himself above her, and then with one long stroke, he slid inside. Cara gasped, and her body tightened around him. She wrapped her legs around his hips, drawing him in deeper.

Matt groaned. Sweat beaded on his brow. He stroked slowly at first, drawing out her pleasure, then faster and harder as he finally allowed himself to lose control. And she was right there with him, riding the wave until ecstasy poured over her again. The orgasm ripped through her, even more powerful and intense than the first.

Cara's world exploded. She bucked beneath him, out of control, wild, unleashed. She needed more, and he gave it to her. He thrust into her again and again, pushing her higher until stars danced before her eyes and she screamed his name. "Matt! Oh, God, Matt!"

With a final thrust, his body clenched, and his eyes closed. He held himself inside her with a deep groan as he found his own release. Cara was still flying, still riding the waves of pleasure he'd given her, as he collapsed against her, chest heaving.

"Holy shit." She flung her head back against the pillow, completely undone.

Matt rolled to his side with a satisfied grin. "That good, huh?"

She nodded, breathless.

"Yeah, for me too."

He kissed her, then disappeared into the bathroom to get rid of the condom. The toilet flushed, then he slid back in next to her. Had it really been as incredible for him as it had been for her? She wasn't that experienced, but surely he'd been with other women who were.

Then he stared into her eyes, and she saw the truth there. He looked as awestruck as she felt.

"Wow." That time she knew she'd said it out loud. Her heart gave a funny little flutter in her chest, and she knew something else too.

She'd just fallen in love with Matt Dumont.

* * *

"You okay?" He stroked a finger across Cara's cheek.

She gulped a breath and tried to calm her racing heart. "Oh yeah."

Better than okay. Much better.

So she was a tiny bit in love with a man she couldn't have. She was a big girl. She could handle it. Even if he wasn't leaving town, the outcome would have been the same. She was in no position to offer a man her heart. Not yet. Not for two more years.

Until then, she would enjoy this weekend. No regrets.

Cara traced the bulldog on Matt's shoulder while he watched with eyes still glazed with satisfaction. She ran her fingers through the coarse hair on his chest, over the firm outline of his abs, and onto the sculpted expanse of his thigh. The man was seriously built.

And sexy. *Oh my.*

She paused when she encountered the jagged edge of a scar cutting through his skin. Her gaze followed her fingers, settling on a shiny patch of scar tissue, sunken and snarled into his flesh. His muscles tensed beneath her touch.

"War injury?"

He nodded. "IED. A roadside bomb. I got off lucky."

But he didn't look like he felt lucky. Pain haunted the corners of his eyes and tugged his lips into a frown.

"This is why you were sent home?"

Matt nodded again.

"Would you still be a marine, if you hadn't been injured?"

He shrugged. "Maybe, maybe not. I joined fresh out of high school, didn't really have my life all planned out yet."

Cara watched him for a moment. There was something else causing his pain. "And the rest of your convoy—were they as lucky?"

He rolled to his back and folded his arms over his chest. "I lost seven men that day."

"I'm sorry." She placed a hand on his arm. "Were you close?"

"Yeah." His voice grew husky, his eyes glossy.

Cara's heart ached. There was nothing more humbling than to see a man cry, especially over the loss of a buddy. "What happened?"

His face hardened. "You've seen that video on YouTube of marines urinating on corpses of Taliban members?"

That was not at all what she'd expected him to say. "I've heard about it."

"Wasn't my unit, but it put an ugly light on the corps. It was disgraceful, to show that kind of disrespect for the dead, not to mention a violation of the Geneva Convention." His body was taut with anger.

She rested a hand on his bicep.

"I heard some mutterings of support in my squad. There

was this kid, Brent, just a cherry, fresh out of boot camp. So cocky, ready to take on the world. I pulled him aside, had a chat about honor, respect. He said he understood, gave me his word." In his voice, she heard the frustration, the anger, but also the responsibility.

She ran her fingers down his arm and over his tightly clenched fist. "You were in charge of these men?"

He nodded. "Squad leader, Third Battalion, Fourth Marines, Company K."

A leader. Of course he'd been a leader. And he carried the responsibility of these men's lives, their deaths, on his shoulders.

"A few weeks later, Brent made a lewd gesture over an Iraqi girl's body, in full view of the remaining insurgents. She'd been an intended suicide bomber, but a sniper got her before she could detonate the vest."

"He broke his word," she said.

Matt turned his head, his eyes fierce. "He was nineteen. Just a kid, a cocky, ignorant kid. I should have spent more time with him."

"You can't make someone honorable, Matt. They have it, or they don't." And Matt had it in spades.

He shook his head, his lips compressed as if she didn't understand. "Iraqi retaliation against our squad was fierce. We lost three men to gunfire, four more to the IED. Seven good men lost their lives that night, under my command."

"Brent?"

His head jerked a quick affirmation. "He made a bad decision. He didn't deserve to pay for it with his life."

*Oh, Matt.* Her heart broke for him, for the weight he carried. For him, their deaths were a personal failure. She ached to tell him it wasn't his fault, that he was only human, but knew it wasn't her absolution to give. Instead, she wrapped her arms around him and kissed him. "I'm sorry."

Matt kissed her back with animal-like ferocity, his hard body covering hers as he poured his pain into passion. Cara held on for the ride, and as they both floated back down to the bed after another mind-bending orgasm, he pressed his head against her chest. "Thank you."

"For what?" She stroked her fingers through his hair.

"For not offering meaningless condolences or pity."

*No, thank you for trusting me with your pain.* She had a feeling it wasn't something he shared with just anyone. "You're an honorable man, Matt Dumont, and I'd trust you with my life any day."

* * *

Matt sat on the edge of the bed, watching Cara and Sadie sleep. They'd picked the dog up first thing this morning, and Cara, apparently exhausted after last night, had curled up on the bed with her and promptly passed out.

Now he was left to watch them, battling all sorts of unwanted and mushy emotions. Cara lay on her side, those apricot curls spread across the pillow. Sadie curled into the curve of her body, her head nestled against Cara's leg, an oversized towel beneath her to protect Barbara's bedspread from her shelter filth. A blue bandage around her left front leg was the only visual reminder of her night at the vet.

Matt liked the sight of them in his bed, wouldn't mind waking up to this picture every morning. Maybe he should extend an invitation for Cara to visit him in Boston, see what happened. Except he'd be living with his mom, caring for her, and in no position to nurture a relationship.

He sighed, then bent to place a kiss on her forehead. He slid from the bed and padded to the table by the window, where his laptop blinked on Ken Prentiss's GPS location.

Naturally, the bastard had checked out of the Atlanta

Marriott and gone home to his wife. Who was this mysterious "L"? Traveling to another state to shack up hinted at something more than a casual affair. How long had it been going on?

Felicity would be furious when she found out Matt had blown this opportunity to nail him.

He was pretty pissed about it himself. Not that the circumstances could have been helped. And he certainly couldn't complain about his current company or the way he'd spent last night. His body hummed with satisfaction, and he felt oddly at peace with Cara knowing the humiliating reason for his discharge from the marines.

She'd taken the information in stride, without a hint of judgment or pity. Then, without blinking, she'd told him she trusted him with her life.

And his world hadn't been the same since.

Matt pushed back his chair, grabbed the car keys, and stepped out into the chilly January morning. It was almost noon, and they'd need lunch when Cara woke. The snow here in Shelton had nearly melted, and he'd been told that what little they got back in Dogwood had been gone by midday yesterday. If his Jeep was ready tomorrow morning as promised, they could go home.

He drove to the deli down the street and collected turkey sandwiches, chips, and sodas. When he let himself back into the room, Cara and Sadie were just stirring from their nap. Sadie stretched, lifted her head, and let out a hollow cough. Cara sat up and rubbed her back.

"She sounds a lot better."

Cara nodded. "Sure does. I'm glad we didn't try to drive home yesterday. It might have been too much for her."

"I'm glad we didn't drive home yesterday, for other reasons." He gave her a devilish grin, which she returned.

"Yeah, that too."

Sadie hopped from the bed. She looked up at Matt with those solemn eyes that had seen too much, then wiggled her nub of a tail at him.

"Beats doggy jail, doesn't it?" He bent and rubbed behind her ears. Sadie placed an appreciative kiss on his cheek, leaving behind the fetid urinal smell of the shelter. "You really stink, you know that?"

Cara laughed. "She does. I think a bath's in order for her as soon as we get home."

Matt straightened. "I'll take her out."

He clipped a leash to the little dog's collar and walked with her into the soggy grass behind the bed-and-breakfast. Sadie did her thing while Matt admired the small lake at the bottom of the hill, visible now that the snow had melted. Behind it, the Blue Ridge Mountains smudged the horizon in majestic silhouette.

They spent the rest of the afternoon curled in bed together watching a *Law & Order* marathon on TV, with Sadie sandwiched comfortably between them. Every so often, Cara would lift her head and peer over Sadie to smile at him. She snuck in questions during the commercials about his mom, his brother, his plans for the future.

"I guess I'll get married someday, have a couple of kids. You?" He bent to adjust the towel beneath Sadie, making sure her smelly butt stayed off Barbara's bedspread.

Cara nodded, her expression wistful. "Yeah. Someday."

After she'd made it ten years in remission. The thought irked him. He wanted her to have those things. Wanted to give her those things. A future. A family. Damn, but he wished they never had to leave Barbara's Bed & Breakfast.

They ate dinner in front of the fireplace, takeout from the Italian place down the street, then Cara fussed over Sadie as she gave her her evening medication and checked on her breathing.

Matt was developing breathing problems of his own. He liked the dog, but she'd been between him and Cara all day. This was his last night with her, and he didn't want to spend it reaching over forty pounds of smelly, coughing canine.

"So, I was thinking about a bubble bath." Cara's voice intruded on his thoughts.

He clicked off the TV and turned to find her by the fireplace, one hip against the wall, arms folded over her chest. She'd laid the dog bed in front of the fireplace, and Sadie had curled herself onto it in cozy slumber.

Cara cocked her head to the side. "Care to join me?"

He'd been in a state of semi-arousal all afternoon, which turned to full-fledged desire in the time it took to cross the room and pull her into his arms.

"I take that as a yes?" She gasped as he bent his head and kissed her neck, his fingers already tugging at her sweater.

"More of an 'I thought you'd never ask.'" He yanked her sweater over her head and traced his fingers over the contour of her bra. "Don't move."

He went to the tub and started the hot water. A bottle of raspberry-scented bubble bath had been left on the ledge beside it for their convenience. He poured some into the tub, then went to the mini-fridge and opened a bottle of Chardonnay. He poured two glasses.

Cara stepped up behind him, wearing nothing but a beige towel. She bent down and pressed the button to start the jets. The water churned, frothing with fruity-smelling bubbles.

Before he could do the honors, she dropped the towel and slid into the tub. Matt scrambled to follow, fumbling the button on his jeans in his hurry. Then he sank into the hot, frothy depths of the tub, his legs entwined with Cara's.

"To being snowed in in the mountains?" She lifted her wineglass.

He grabbed his glass and clinked it against hers. "Hell of a way to spend the weekend."

Cara took a sip, then shifted to place her glass back on the ledge. Her foot brushed against his erection. He'd never been so thankful for close quarters.

She scooped her hands through the mountain of bubbles between them and blew a puff in his direction. "Just out of curiosity, how much bubble bath did you put in?"

"I don't know, a couple squirts, why?"

She giggled. "A capful is usually enough, especially with these jets. We may float away here in a minute."

"Really?" But his eyes had been drawn to the bubbles clinging to her breasts, the way they glistened with the light of the fireplace, the steady rise and fall of her chest.

He reached out and took her hands, then tugged her close. Bubbles whooshed up between them and splatted Cara in the face.

"Pah!" She swiped a hand over her nose and mouth.

"Sorry." He wiped her face clean and slid her into his lap.

Cara leaned forward to brush a glob of bubbles from his cheek. His hands tangled in her hair, guiding her lips to his.

He wanted to drink her up until he'd had his fill, only the more he had, the more he seemed to want. She was an insatiable thirst.

He kissed her with abandon, sliding his tongue against hers, tasting her, touching her, absorbing everything about her. Cara pressed forward, unleashing another explosion of bubbles. Her hips met his through the hot, swirling water, driving him nearly wild with the need to thrust himself deep inside her.

A blob of bubbles landed on top of her head, like she'd been pegged with a snowball. Matt brushed it away. He settled her more comfortably into his lap, only to have a geyser of fruity-scented foam burst up between them.

Okay, she might have a point about the bubbles. This was getting ridiculous. In fact, there were now at least six inches of fluffy white stuff floating in the tub, coating them and sloshing dangerously with every move of their bodies.

Her fingers trailed through the hair on his chest, then traveled down to wrap around his cock. He groaned deep in his chest. His hips thrust against her hand. She stroked him with a leisurely rhythm that nearly broke him to pieces.

"Oh God, Cara." He grabbed her ass and pulled her closer, so that their bodies pressed together with every stroke of her hand. Cara's pupils dilated and her head fell forward. Her hips rocked against him.

Bubbles sloshed onto the floor.

He groaned. Bubbles squirted between them like froth in the ocean whipped by a hurricane. He felt as wild as nature's most primitive force. He yanked Cara closer still, and she moved her hands, wrapping them around his back.

Nothing separated them now. They moved together, their bodies as hot as the water swirling around them. A cloud of bubbles rained over their heads. Matt devoured her with his mouth, desperate to sink himself inside her but savoring the exquisite torture of waiting.

"Now, Matt. Please."

He fumbled behind his head for the condom he'd placed on the ledge. He ripped it open, then attempted to clear enough bubbles out of the way to see what the hell he was doing.

The bubble situation had gotten completely out of hand. A capful next time. Right. Cara's fingers bumped his beneath the surface of the water. Bubbles rose everywhere, covering them until he could see nothing but her face and the top of her hair.

"Hurry up." She traced her fingers down his cock. The condom slipped from his fingers, lost in the churning depths of the tub.

"Dammit." He made a grab for it, sloshing more bubbles over the side of the tub.

She took one look at him, then burst out laughing.

"What's so funny?" Because that was the only condom he'd brought to the tub.

"This." She squished her hand against the top of his head, squashing the glob of bubbles he hadn't known landed there.

"And this?" He scooped another pile onto her head.

Then they were smearing each other with bubbles, an erotic, indoor version of a snowball fight. Bubbles flew, splattering like snow through the air.

She pegged him with a big splat to the chest. He smeared bubbles through her hair and kissed them from her lips. Laughter mixed with kisses. Bubbles mixed with passion.

He kissed her until he thought he might explode, then pulled back. He'd just carry her to the bed to save time because he needed to be inside her. *Now*. Cara bent forward. Her fingers brushed against his cock.

He hissed in a ragged breath and tried to push her away. There was no way he could withstand another assault from her deliciously talented fingers. But then he felt something else. She was rolling the missing condom down his length.

*Oh, hell yeah.*

Matt lifted her hips so that the head of his penis rested against her. Her eyes slid shut. She let out a little sound of pleasure, then sank onto him, taking him deep inside her.

He thrust into her, unable to hold back, overcome with need, drunk with his feelings for Cara, completely out of control. Bubbles sprayed, coating them and bursting up with each thrust of his body into hers.

She threw her head back, gasping with pleasure, her hands gripping his shoulders. Matt looked at her, saw the passion, the sweetness, everything that made Cara the most damn amazing woman in the world. Around her, the room swirled with glistening bursts of bubbles.

It was beautiful. Breathtaking. He held her tightly in his lap and poured himself into her until his world came apart. Cara screamed his name as she found her own release, and the sweet sound of her pleasure carried him even higher, to a place no woman had ever taken him.

A place he never wanted to leave.

# CHAPTER SIXTEEN

Cara stood straight and tall as she climbed the front steps to her townhouse. She even managed a casual wave to Nosy Betty before jamming the key into the lock and giving it a good twist. The door swung open. Sadie peered around her leg, then looked up at Cara as if asking permission to come inside.

"Home sweet home," Cara told her. For now, anyway.

"Cara, wait." Matt followed her up the steps, dog bed under one arm, duffel bag on the other.

"Thanks."

He stepped through the doorway and set her things down. They stood for a moment, facing each other. *And this is where things get awkward.*

"Cara..." His dark eyes were troubled.

"No regrets. I mean it." She took a step backward.

Matt stepped forward, closing the distance between them. He settled his hands on her shoulders and pressed a kiss to her lips before she could protest. "Thank you."

She didn't ask for what. Instead, she nodded and pulled free. Matt opened his mouth as if he had more to say, then shook his head and walked out the front door. It closed with a solid thunk. Heavy. Final.

The breath left her in a whoosh. Sadie looked up and whined.

"It's okay, hon. Vacation's over, that's all. Let's get you settled." Cara led her to the back door, grateful for the distraction.

The house felt empty without Casper to welcome her home. How would it feel in another two weeks without any dogs inside? And who would take Sadie?

Not an option, Cara decided. She'd meant to spend the weekend working on it, but she still had until Friday to finish putting together her appeals packet for the homeowners' association. She just couldn't mess it up, that's all.

Sadie scampered across the backyard, looking small and frail against the expanse of yellowed winter grass. Cara would get her healthy soon enough, but Sadie would always be small. Just a runt of a boxer, with a face that belonged on a poster.

Maybe the perfect ambassador for Cara's cause. If only there was a way to introduce her to the homeowners' association without rubbing their faces in the fact that she'd gone behind their backs and brought home another shelter dog.

Hmmm.

What were the chances any of them knew for sure what dog she'd had when the notice was received? Would anyone notice she had a brown dog now, instead of a white one?

It wasn't a risk she was willing to take. She'd play it safe with Sadie, try to fly her under the radar. If the HOA board got wind of her, that she was new, Cara could kiss her appeal good-bye.

Sadie trotted over and plopped at Cara's feet, panting heavily. Her lung function was still impaired, but she was definitely on the road to recovery. Cara opened the door and let them back inside. She set down a bowl of water for Sadie, then punched the red button blinking on her answering machine. It showed five new messages.

"Wow, I was popular this weekend." Cara settled onto a bar stool at the kitchen counter as the machine began to play. Somehow, it never quite seemed like she was talking to herself if one of her dogs was there with her.

The first two messages were people inquiring about booking photography sessions. Cara felt excitement over the first one, trepidation at the second. This photography thing was taking off faster than she could handle.

The third message was Marilyn at the Dogwood County Animal Shelter. "Hi, Cara. I just wanted to remind you about our Starry Paws Gala coming up next Saturday. You and a guest are invited as our guests in appreciation for everything you've done for the shelter this year. We'll be honoring you as our Volunteer of the Year. It's black tie. Great food, lots of fun. See you there."

Cara jotted notes as Marilyn spoke. She had indeed forgotten all about it. Fancy galas weren't really her style, but this one was for a good cause, and she couldn't really see any way out of going, since she was being honored as Volunteer of the Year. She hoped they didn't expect her to make a speech or anything.

She'd have to buy a new dress to wear, not that she needed to be spending any extra money right now. Maybe Merry would go with her—to find a dress and to the ball. No one would enjoy a party to benefit animal rescue more than Merry.

The fourth call was another interested client, looking for a session with the dog she'd adopted from Triangle Boxer Rescue last year. Cara tapped her knuckles against the counter. When was she going to fit in all these photography sessions around her work at the shelter and going back to work full time?

"Hey, lady, it's me." Merry's voice signaled the start of the final message. "You must not be home yet, so call me when you get this. I've got major news about the dogs on Keeney Street, and also I want to hear all about your weekend. Snow, mountains, Sadie . . . Matt. Call me."

Cara smiled. She was lucky to have such a good friend. She picked up the phone and punched in Merry's number.

Her friend answered on the second ring. "Hey! How was the drive home?"

"Uneventful." And awkward. When they'd packed up and gotten in the car this morning, Matt had pressed her against the window and kissed the daylights out of her. But the closer they got to home, the more stilted the conversation became. By the time they reached Crestwood Gardens, she'd been more than ready to jump out of the car and put some distance between them.

Merry giggled. "I bet. We've got to schedule a girls' night so you can share all the juicy details. I'm off work tomorrow at seven. Want to grab dinner after?"

"Sure, but who says there are juicy details?" Cara wasn't even remotely ready to dish about her weekend with Matt, not when the emotions were still so fresh.

"You and Matt spent a weekend together in the mountains. Whichever way that went, I want to hear about it."

Cara cleared her throat. "So, what happened with the dogs on Keeney Street?"

"Word is, the Rogerses skipped town. No one's seen them since Friday, before the snowstorm. But get this: they left the dogs behind."

"What?"

"Yup. Trista chucked some food over the fence last night, but I need to get over there and check it out. Thought you might want to come with me or run it past Matt to see what he says."

"Oh, um, yeah. Maybe we can do that before dinner tomorrow?"

"Sure. Listen, I've gotta run. I'm being paged. I'll call you tomorrow, okay?"

"Sounds good. Bye, Merry."

Cara hung up and bent to give Sadie an ear rub. "How do you feel about a nap?" She sniffed the dog's head. "And maybe after that, a bath."

Sadie closed her eyes and wiggled her nub in appreciation. She had to be exhausted after their trip, and it was important for her to rest up and get healthy as quickly as possible so that Cara could schedule surgery for that tumor on her leg.

Cara knew better than anyone what happened when you waited too long to treat cancer.

She started across the living room to lead the way upstairs to her bed for a nice afternoon nap, and that was when she saw the envelope on the floor inside her front door.

The return address read Crestwood Gardens.

* * *

Cara pressed the button to lower the passenger-side window, then stared across soggy grass at the brown-paneled house they'd parked in front of. She squinted her eyes to peer through the bay window to the living room inside. "Are you sure? I still see furniture in there."

"No one's seen them since Friday." Merry unclipped her seat belt and leaned over Cara for a better look.

Cara shrugged. "Maybe they're on vacation."

"Yeah, but I keep thinking about what Matt said, about how they skipped town in Durham last year, when animal control was closing in on them."

"True. So why didn't they take the dogs with them this

time?" Cara looked at the house again. Her heart broke for the poor dogs left behind, chained in the backyard during that snowstorm.

"Good question."

"So what's the plan?" Cara asked.

"Make sure no one's home, then sneak around back to check on the dogs and see if it looks like anyone's been feeding them." She opened her door and stepped out.

Cara followed, her sneakers squishing on the wet pavement.

Merry marched straight up the walkway and punched the doorbell. Chimes rang inside the house. The air shattered with the snarling barks they had both come to know so well.

They waited a full minute, then rang the bell again. Still no response from inside the house. It was past seven o'clock, and the sun had already set. Around the neighborhood, lights glowed from windows as families went about their business. Inside the Rogers house, all was dark.

"No one's home, and it's getting too dark to see." Merry led the way across the front lawn and around the right side of the house. A six-foot wooden privacy fence surrounded the back of the property and hid the dogs from view.

Cara pressed her face against it and peeked through a crack between boards. The two dogs stood beside the back deck, heads up, hackles raised along their backs, staring straight back at her. One growled, then they both resumed barking their heads off.

This was the best look she'd ever had at them. They were bigger than purebred boxers. Trista said she thought they were boxer-mastiff mixes. They were tall and dark-coated, with long, slender tails, big, jowled heads, and thick, muscular bodies.

Cara wouldn't want to tangle with one off-leash. They looked scary as hell.

And also sad. Ribs protruded from their sides. Each dog wore a black nylon collar attached to a silver chain that disappeared somewhere under the deck.

Shackled and abandoned.

"Poor things. There's no happy ending for these guys." Merry's voice was low.

"No. But I have to wonder—even if they wind up euthanized at the shelter, it can't be worse than living like this."

"I agree. Doesn't make me feel any better about making it happen."

"So what now?" Cara pulled back from the fence. The larger dog's unwavering gaze sent chills up and down her spine.

"I need to check for food and water. First, let's test their range on those chains." Merry gripped the gate and gave it a solid shake.

The dogs lunged forward, sounding as if they meant to rip her and Cara to shreds. They drew up short about four feet from the fence line.

Merry reached into her back pocket and produced a can of dog-repellant spray. She held it up like a weapon in front of her as she eased the gate open and peeked into the backyard.

Cara's heart thudded in her throat. "Jesus, Merry, be careful."

Merry glanced back with a smile. "Are you kidding? I just had my nails done. I'm not getting chewed on today."

She took a full inventory of the backyard as the dogs lunged at the ends of their chains, barking just feet from her face, their jaws making a horrendous crunching sound as they snapped shut. Finally, she stepped back and shut the gate. "So, I see one toppled water bowl, empty. No food but a few shredded remnants of the bag Trista heaved over the fence two nights ago."

"Okay." Cara frowned. It was Tuesday night. Five days since the Rogerses skipped town. That was a long time without regular access to food and water.

"I called animal control earlier. They're sending someone over in the morning, but they've got to post a notice to comply before they can do anything, to make sure no one's checking on the dogs. There's a whole process involved before they can seize them, depending if anyone responds to the notice."

Merry hurried back to the car, with Cara at her heels. "So let's get these guys something to eat and drink."

She pulled out a bag of dry dog food, a jug of water, and a large bowl.

Cara placed a hand on her shoulder. "If you get within reach, they'll bite you. They're chained up, defensive. This is a terrible idea."

"I don't have a choice. They might die of dehydration before animal control is able to do anything for them."

Cara thought of Matt. "Technically, this is breaking and entering."

"It's extenuating circumstances. If you go around the side of the house and distract them, I think I can sneak in and leave them food and water without them knowing I'm in their yard. That should buy them at least a day or so. I'm armed and not afraid to use it." Merry held up her can of canine pepper spray.

Cara rocked back on her heels. "Okay, I guess. But be careful, would you? I like you with all your fingers intact."

Merry clapped her on the back. "I told you, no one's messing up my new manicure. Now go around the other side and make some noise."

"All right." Cara didn't really like what they were about to do, but what choice did she have? She wasn't willing to let the dogs starve to death, either, and she didn't want to have to go to Matt for more advice. She'd barely seen him since they got home from Shelton.

She was trying to be a grown-up about it. After all, they'd agreed things would go back to normal once they got home. No ongoing romance. It was strictly a weekend deal. Except she'd thought normal would mean still seeing him around. Before their trip to Shelton, she'd bumped into him almost every time she stepped outside.

Too often to be a coincidence. Since their return yesterday morning, she'd seen him once. He'd been on his phone and given her a cursory wave as he hopped into his Jeep. And that stung, just a little. Okay, a lot.

So she was definitely not going to call him about this. Besides, she already knew what he'd say. Wait for animal control. Don't trespass. He was annoyingly "by the rules" that way.

Instead of calling Matt, Cara walked around the corner of the house by the street, away from Merry. She banged her fists against the fence and shouted. "Hey, who's a bad dog? Betcha can't bark louder than I can yell!"

Oh boy, could they ever. Five days without food and water didn't seem to have slowed them down much. They barked, snarled, and lunged at their chains, while Cara rattled the fence and hollered back at them.

"Okay." Merry called out, her voice nearly lost in the ruckus. "All done."

Cara jogged over to her, and they stood at the fence together, watching as the dogs dove into the bag of food Merry had ripped open and left in its entirety for them. They snarled and snapped at each other. The bigger dog lifted the bag in its mouth and shook it.

"They'll probably eat until they're sick," Cara said.

Merry nodded. "I know. I couldn't see a way around it. If they vomit, hopefully they'll just eat it back up when they get hungry again."

"Ew. But yeah."

"Well, enough trespassing for now, I guess." Merry led the way back to her CR-V. "Now it's our turn to eat."

"Good, I'm starving."

"How's Sadie?"

Cara felt the smile slide across her face. "She's great. Cough's almost gone. She'll be ready for surgery in another week or two."

"Once we raise funds. But I'm glad you got her. She's a lucky girl." Merry laid a hand on Cara's shoulder.

"For sure."

"Anybody say anything yet about you having a new dog?"

Cara shook her head. "No. I've mostly kept her in the backyard."

"And what are you going to do in two weeks when your thirty days is up?"

Desperation clawed inside her as she thought of the reminder shoved beneath her door just yesterday. That her time was almost up. That she had only days left to file an appeal. "I'll keep her until they throw me out, or you find a new foster home for her."

Merry sighed. "You know we're full."

"I'm working on a packet of information about the rescue and my foster dogs to drop off at the HOA office on Friday. It'll tug at their heartstrings, Merry. It has to. They can't make me live without dogs."

"And, for argument's sake, what if they do?"

"I'll put my place up for sale," she answered without hesitation. "But it'll take too long to sell, and I can't live without dogs, so I've *got* to pull this off. Wish me luck."

Merry looked at Cara, her eyes solemn. "You know how much I want this for you, but I think what you need right now is a viable backup plan."

* * *

Matt slammed the phone into its receiver. He felt like spitting nails. These past two days had been hell. Since he hadn't planned on spending the weekend in the mountains, he hadn't made any arrangements, and the work had been stacking up. He'd been up to his eyeballs sorting through paperwork, let alone the godforsaken Prentiss case.

Oh, how he wished Felicity had brought her business anywhere but his office that bitter December morning. Yesterday he'd driven all the way to Atlanta to try to retrieve any incriminating evidence. He'd talked with the hotel's front desk staff, bartenders, and housekeeping, all to no avail. No one remembered Ken Prentiss, or who he'd been with.

The drive to Atlanta and back had taken all damn day and hadn't yielded a single bit of useful information. He'd just have to wait until the bastard got horny again and hope it didn't take as long as it had the first time.

Matt, on the other hand, was going out of his mind thinking about Cara. He'd thrown himself into his work in an effort to get his head back on straight, but it was time to make nice with her before he totally pissed her off, if he hadn't already.

He glanced out his bedroom window. Her little blue Mazda was parked out front, not in its assigned spot next to his Grand Cherokee, but two spaces down in the visitors' spot. Yeah, he'd already pissed her off by not saying hi since they'd gotten home.

Okay, he was probably a jerk. Definitely a jerk.

Since she'd lost her job last week, Matt had noticed she often went for a mid-morning jog around this time. He could use some exercise, although the thought of watching Cara get all hot and sweaty in tight clothing had him breathing a little funny before he'd even left the house.

He changed into sweatpants and a long-sleeved tee, then stood inside his front door and did a few stretches while keeping an eye out for her. If she didn't head out soon, he'd man up and knock on her door. He missed her.

A lot.

His cell phone rang from the catchall table by the front door. If it was Felicity Prentiss, he just might hurl it through the wall. With a scowl, he lifted the phone and checked the screen. Relief unclenched his fingers when he saw his brother's name.

"Jason. What's up? Mom okay?"

He heard the muffled thump of Cara's front door and glanced out the window. She jogged down the front steps to the sidewalk, dressed in a long-sleeved pink shirt and gray jogging pants, her hair in a bouncy ponytail.

Matt's pulse jumped. He grabbed his keys and took a step toward the door to hail her down and ask her to wait for him.

"Matt —" Jason's voice sounded rough. "Mom's had a stroke."

# CHAPTER SEVENTEEN

The elevator door dinged, and Matt pushed past the couple beside him into the white-walled hall beyond. His long stride carried him quickly to a small waiting room with burgundy chairs and dull, gray carpet. Jason sat in a chair by the wall, head clasped in his hands.

"How is she?"

His brother looked up, a smile creasing the lines of worry on his face. "She's stable. They're going to be moving her out of ICU later this afternoon."

"Thank God." Matt rubbed his brow and let out a deep breath. The flight from North Carolina had been torturous as he'd worried that something would go wrong while he was thirty thousand feet in the air, unable to check his messages.

"I didn't tell her you were coming. Bet she yells at you for rushing up here like she's dying or something." Jason chuckled.

His younger brother looked a lot like him, with his dark, wavy hair and tall, sturdy frame. But unlike his brother, Jason had inherited their mother's clear gray eyes and her near-sightedness. His usual contacts had been forgone in favor of black-rimmed glasses today, evidence of the news that had jolted him out of bed.

"Bet she does." Matt clapped his brother on the back. "You okay?"

Jason nodded. "Scared as shit when I got the call this morning. She has some weakness on her right side. Doc says she'll need physical therapy, and all that jazz."

"But she's going to be okay?"

"Too soon to know for sure, but looks that way."

Matt drew another deep breath. His mom would be okay. Weakness on her right side. Physical therapy. Those were things he could manage. "Can I see her?"

"Yeah. Just one of us at a time while she's in ICU. I came out while the doc was in with her and to wait for you, but she's right back there in Triage Two."

"Thanks."

Matt headed down the hall, stopping in front of a gray door labeled Triage Two. He sucked in a breath and pushed the door open. Inside, he was immediately assailed by the antiseptic smell of medical equipment and the rhythmic beeping of machines. Before him was a row of beds divided by blue curtains.

His mother lay in the second bed from the left, wearing a blue hospital gown, a beige blanket pulled up and tucked beneath her arms. She rested with her eyes closed, an oxygen tube in her nose. Her short, brown hair jutted from her head in all directions, her pale face free of makeup. She'd have a fit if she could see herself in the mirror.

Tears clogged his throat. Matt walked to her bed and sat in the chair provided there. He took her hand in his. "Mom."

Her eyes opened, the right one drooping a bit. "Matthew."

"I'm here." He squeezed her hand.

"I told Jason not to bother you." Her words were slow and

deliberate, as if she tried not to slur them. The right side of her mouth drooped when she spoke.

Matt scowled at her. "That's insulting, Mom. You know there's nowhere else I'd be. I'm just so glad you're okay."

She huffed an indignant sigh. "Can't get rid of me that easy."

"Not trying to." Matt ran a hand over her cheek. She looked so frail, so old, all of a sudden. Things in North Carolina had lingered long enough. It was time to wrap up the loose ends and get to Boston.

"Thanks for coming." A tear snaked its way across her cheek.

Matt's chest shrank until he could barely breathe. "Anytime, Mom."

A pair of nurses pulled back the curtain offering his mother privacy from the man in the bed to her left and an elderly woman on her right. "Time to get you moved up to your room, Mrs. Dumont."

His mother nodded, then closed her eyes as they prepped her bed to wheel it into the hall. Matt fell into stride behind them, and Jason joined in as they passed the nurses' station.

"I talked to her doctor earlier," Jason said. "He said she'd probably been having these warning strokes, like mini-strokes, leading up to this one. That's why she was having some confusion over the last few weeks."

"And now?" Matt slowed his pace so that he and his brother walked a few strides behind, where they wouldn't be overheard.

"They're going to do that thing with the dye again, see if they need to do another bypass or anything. She's going to need a lot of physical therapy, and it's time to really crack down on her diet and exercise to keep this from happening again."

They rounded a corner and stopped a few feet away as their little convoy waited for the elevator to arrive.

"I agree. I'm going to wrap things up in Dogwood as quickly as I can to get back up here for good. She can't live alone in that house anymore."

Jason nodded. "I'll stay with her until you get here, unless she goes to one of those rehab places in the meantime."

"Is it that bad?"

"I don't know yet, bro. I just don't know."

*    *    *

Cara held out the bound packet of information she'd pains-takingly compiled in her defense. Inside, she'd filed the thirty-one signatures she'd collected, letters of recommen-dation, testimonials from adoptive families, before-and-after photos, and success stories from dogs she'd saved. It was a pretty impressive binder, and she was proud of her effort.

Phil Durgin placed it on his desk and thumbed through it, frowning through his bifocals. "Thank you very much, Miss Medlen. I can see you've put significant effort into this. We'll read it and discuss at our next meeting on February twelfth. You can keep your foster dog until then, unless he's adopted first."

Cara held in a whoop of triumph. That was a full ten days longer than she'd had this morning. She wasn't about to men-tion that the foster dog was a "she" now instead of a "he." Phil was reading Mojo's adoption story, looking at photos of the happy brindle mix frolicking with his new family. The picture of a loving family dog.

Phil smiled.

Tears of relief brimmed in her eyes. There was hope, a chance that this nightmare would end, that she could get back to fostering without guilt and focus her energy on find-ing a new job. Her severance pay from the Smythes would run out next Friday, and she really needed something new lined up by the time that happened.

"Thank you, Miss Medlen. We'll be in touch with our decision."

"I really appreciate it, and your willingness to reconsider. It means more to me than you could know."

She left the office walking on air. Matt's parking spot was empty, had been empty since Wednesday. Either he'd gone on an extended stakeout or he was avoiding her. That was disappointing. She hadn't pegged him as the type to avoid an awkward situation.

And she'd honestly hoped to continue their friendship. Right now, she really wanted to tell him about her victory with Phil Durgin. But she'd settle for calling Merry and gushing on the phone. Besides, it was probably better not to fling herself at Matt right now while she was all giddy and emotional. Who knew where that would lead.

Betty Albright shuffled by on her way to the mailboxes. Cara pretended not to notice as the older woman tightened her grip on her poodles' leashes. She glanced pointedly at Cara's empty hands, then relaxed her grip.

For the love of God. Her foster, Taz, growled at Princess *one time*, and she'd been acting like Cara was the devil incarnate ever since. "Hi, Betty. How are you today?"

"No complaints. Hip's still giving me some trouble, but I get by." Betty patted her right hip and sighed. Then she cocked her head and gave Cara a long look. "I thought I saw you with a brown dog the other day. Don't you have a white one right now? You didn't take in a new dog, did you?"

"What?" Cara drew back. *Dammit, Nosy Betty.* "No, of course not. Just one dog. I'm not trying to start any trouble, Betty. I just want to clear my name."

Betty's gray eyes softened. "It's not that we dislike you, dear. It's just that, frankly, you haven't been very sociable with the neighbors, and your dogs scare us. I'm too old to worry about being attacked by a half-tamed shelter dog on the way to my mailbox."

Cara pressed a hand to her chest. "I don't keep vicious dogs."

"I really am sorry." With an apologetic shrug, Betty continued on her way.

Her euphoria over the victory with Phil Durgin now completely dampened, Cara went inside and left Merry a long, rambling voice mail, then opened her laptop and spent a few hours applying for nanny jobs. She ate a quick lunch and debated taking Sadie for a drive, since she couldn't safely walk her around the neighborhood without fear of Nosy Betty seeing her and reporting her to the HOA board.

She held on to the hope that no one—other than Betty—would actually remember what her current foster dog looked like. If she could pretend Sadie had been here since the order was issued, she was still okay.

Her cell phone rang with a 910 area code. Cara frowned as she recognized the number. The Swansons, Casper's adoptive family.

"Hi, Cara, it's Tina Swanson." Tina sounded guarded and tense.

"Hey, Tina. Everything going well?"

"No."

Cara winced at the blunt answer. "Oh. Well, it takes some time for them to adjust to a new home, a new family. He's only been with you a week."

"And I don't think he will be much longer. Cara, he growled at my father-in-law."

Cara drew a breath, then exhaled slowly. "I'm sorry that happened. I told you he'd growled a few times when I had him; it's a fear response when he's feeling uncomfortable. He's never bitten anyone. I can recommend a good trainer—"

"My father-in-law says he won't come back to our house until Casper's gone. I can't put that kind of strain on our family over a dog. My husband is beside himself." Tina's voice was flat, emotionless.

Cara's fists clenched. "He's already been abandoned once—don't give up on him yet. He's a great dog. You can get through this with him."

"I'm sorry, but I can't. He's got to go back. I can't keep him."

Cara punched her fist into the couch. She couldn't take him back, couldn't risk being caught with two foster dogs when the homeowners' association knew she had only one. "Don't give up on him. Please, at least speak with a trainer. These kinds of issues can be worked through."

"I just can't. I need to return him, as soon as possible."

Cara bit back her rage. This woman didn't deserve Casper anyway. "Are you free this afternoon?"

"Yes, my shift doesn't start until five."

"Fine. I'll meet you at the McDonald's where you adopted him in an hour and a half."

What choice did she have? The rescue was full. Casper had nowhere else to go.

\* \* \*

The SUV pulled into the parking lot, and Casper's white face appeared in the window, ears back, eyes shuttered. No doubt he felt what Cara heard in Tina's voice over the phone. The lack of emotion, the failed bond.

The certainty that he was being abandoned. Again.

Cara stepped from her car. Their eyes locked, and Casper's ears jumped to attention. He leaped up and rammed into the window so hard that Tina, in the driver's seat, cringed.

Tina shut off the engine, climbed out of the front seat,

and opened the rear door. Casper hopped down and eyed Cara with a sort of forced aloofness, as if he held her responsible for this latest tragedy in his life. And rightfully so. The world-weary glaze over his eyes ripped right at the tender spot on Cara's heart.

"I'm sorry." Tina handed the leash to her.

"Me too." Cara bent and extended her arms to the sad, white dog. "So sorry it turned out this way. I missed you, dude."

Casper gave her one last, soulful look, then leaped into her arms. Cara held him tight as he bathed her in kisses. "You realize the adoption fee was nonrefundable."

Tina nodded. "I really am sorry, you know. But look...he loves you. He never acted like that at our house."

Cara rubbed the dog now upside down in her lap. "I'll have Merry get in touch with you, if you're still interested in finding a new dog."

"I think we'll take a little break, but yeah."

"Good luck."

Five minutes later, she was back in her blue Mazda, Casper sprawled across the backseat. So much the same, but so different, than the first time she'd brought him home.

He watched her with solemn eyes. He loved her. He trusted her, and she'd let him down. She had to make this right for him, to make sure his "happily ever after" stuck next time.

If only it were that easy. The fact that he'd been adopted so quickly the first time was nothing short of miraculous. Dogs like Casper, adult dogs with behavioral problems and less-than-photogenic faces, often took months to adopt out. The chances of him being adopted again before Cara's HOA deadline was up? Nil.

"Oh, Casper, what are we going to do with you?" she asked.

He just stared back, his expression unreadable.

When they got home, he and Sadie made hesitant

introductions. Sadie promptly bowed and gave him domi-
nant status, which helped set Casper at ease.

By bedtime, they were friends. In fact, the house felt full
and complete in a way it hadn't since Mojo was adopted.
She'd missed the sight of two dogs playing, the growls and
nips as they wrestled, the warmth of a dog on either side of
her as she drifted off to sleep.

It made her painfully aware of what she'd given up trying to appease the homeowners' association. She was more
determined than ever to win.

The next morning, she applied for a few more nanny
positions, then glanced out the window. North Carolina
was experiencing a burst of early spring, with temperatures
reaching the mid-fifties and bright sunshine beaming from
above. It was the perfect morning for a walk with her dogs.

She'd drive them to the parking lot of the apartment complex down the street so that no one from Crestwood Gardens would spot her out and about with two foster dogs. She
couldn't keep them cooped up any longer; Casper was too
high-strung not to go for daily walks, and Sadie could benefit from some light exercise too.

Cara collected their leashes and watched as they galloped
across the entrance hall, skidding over the hardwood floor.
Sadie bounced off Casper's rear and sprawled in a heap, her
little nub of a tail still wiggling.

He looked up, his mismatched eyes bright with life. The
brown one radiated warmth and love, while the blue one
always seemed to gleam with mischief. He was a different
dog from the one who'd growled at everyone the day she'd
brought him home from the shelter.

"To new beginnings," she said. She took his face in her
hands and planted a kiss between his eyes. He responded by
leaping up to kiss her back. Then Sadie was pushing her way
in, kissing Cara and Casper in a big love-fest.

"All right, all right. Let's go for a walk." Cara clipped on their leashes and led the way out the front door. She hustled them straight into her car.

Matt's parking spot was still empty. This was getting ridiculous. She hadn't spoken to him in four days. Besides the fact that she missed him like crazy, she really needed his advice about the Rogerses and their abandoned dogs. She and Merry had made one more food-delivery trip, but they couldn't keep it up. It was dangerous, and anyway the dogs needed proper care.

George Rogers had called animal control and claimed someone was taking care of them, but as far as Merry and Cara could tell, no one had been out there but them. Meanwhile, animal control had posted another notice and called it a day.

If Matt didn't show his face soon, she might have to suck it up and call him, because she and Merry were out of options and were desperately hoping he'd have an idea they hadn't thought of yet.

With a sigh, she tore her gaze from his empty parking spot and pulled onto Page Road. A little way down the road, she parked and let them out.

Both dogs bounced with excitement for their adventure. Cara inhaled a deep breath of fresh air. New beginnings. For Casper, for Sadie, and, hopefully, for Cara too. It was time for things to turn in her favor.

They settled into an easy stride, Sadie on her left, Casper on her right. The perfect balance. Peace flowed through her.

She and the dogs continued past the Four Oaks apartment complex until they reached the strip of green grass running beneath the power lines. Sadie and Casper scampered off to do their business, and Cara gazed up at the perfect sky. Blackbirds lined the wires above, chattering as they preened glossy feathers.

They turned left onto Dorman Street, walking on the grassy shoulder as they left the sidewalk behind. Grass crunched beneath her feet, brittle and browned by winter. Here and there a brave wildflower budded in response to the recent warm weather.

Across the street, Black Angus cows grazed around a pond. A red barn sagged on its foundation, overgrown with weeds sprouting from every opening. The farmhouse beyond wasn't in much better condition, with peeling white paint and a front porch that looked as though it might crumple under the weight of a visitor.

Cara, Sadie, and Casper walked on. This was Sadie's first official walk, a chance to sample some fresh air and get a feel for her new neighborhood. The dogs were relaxed, tongues hanging out as they loped along on either side of Cara.

Sadie glanced up, her under-bite causing one bottom tooth to catch over her cheek, giving her a goofy half grin that melted Cara's heart. Her fawn coat glistened red in the sun. Cara remembered the scrawny dog with dull, lifeless fur she'd taken from the shelter a week ago, now sleek and shiny with a little bit of loving care.

Shrieking children heralded their approach to the Victorious Praise Baptist Church. A chain-link fence contained the playground used for the church's preschool program. It was currently occupied by a group of exuberant kids yelling and whooping as they played tag. Sadie's ears pricked nervously, and she darted to Cara's right side, keeping her as a protective barrier between her and the noisy little people across the street.

They picked up the paved jogging path that ran around the outskirts of town and walked another half mile or so before Cara turned them around to head back toward her car. Casper looked up in surprise, wondering at their short journey. Sadie, on the other hand, looked euphoric about her excursion. It had been a perfect first walk.

"Maybe we'll sneak in a jog just the two of us later this afternoon," Cara told Casper. But this was enough for Sadie, until her lungs got stronger.

"Miss Medlen?"

Cara's head whipped up. Phil Durgin stood before them, his brow wrinkled. He wore a black sweatsuit and huffed for breath as if he'd just finished a jog.

He was staring at her dogs. Both of them. Her heart lurched into her throat. "Hi, Mr. Durgin. How are you? Enjoying the nice weather?"

"Very much." He watched as they walked closer. "What's going on here? Have you taken in a new dog?"

"Oh—" She was busted, so busted, and there wasn't a damn thing she could do about it. "Well, it was a last-minute thing, an emergency."

He frowned. "Aren't they all?"

She stopped walking a few feet away from him. Casper stared, ears pricked, his spine rigid. Sadie flattened her tail against her body and cowered behind Cara's legs. "Well, yes, a lot of them are. It's only temporary, until I can find someone else to take her."

"This is very alarming. It shows me you don't take our concerns seriously about keeping foster dogs in Crestwood Gardens."

"Oh, no, sir. Not at all." She felt sick to her stomach. "I do respect your concerns. That's why I brought over that binder of information yesterday morning to fight for my case."

"And if we decide to uphold our initial decision?" His voice had grown hard, cold. He was angry, and there was nothing she could say, because he was absolutely right. She had completely thumbed her nose at them by bringing Sadie home.

She raised her eyes to his. "Then I'll sell and move. I can't live without these dogs."

Sadie's little body pressed into the back of Cara's legs, trembling in fear. The poor thing had an innate distrust of men carried over from her former life, and Phil Durgin wasn't helping to change her opinion.

He took a step toward them, a finger outstretched in Cara's direction. "Listen—"

A low growl rumbled around them. Casper stepped between Cara and Phil, hackles raised, eyes fixed on the president of the homeowners' association. Casper growled again, louder.

Phil Durgin scrambled backward. "Is that dog vicious?"

Panic rose in Cara's throat. She tugged Casper's leash and tapped her fingers against his neck, breaking his concentration. "Easy, boy. It's okay."

He looked up at Cara, eyes wide with concern.

She stepped in front of him. "No, sir, he's not vicious. Just frightened."

"Betty Albright warned me about that dog. Say what you will, Miss Medlen, but several of the owners are frightened of your dogs, and you've just shown me that you have little respect for our concerns by taking in a new dog during your appeal process. I've made my decision. The ruling stands. You have until next weekend to remove all dogs from your property. The HOA covenants will be amended to prohibit keeping foster animals on Crestwood Gardens property."

Tears swam in Cara's eyes. Her knees shook. Behind her, Casper growled again. "Mr. Durgin, please—"

"I'm sorry, but my decision is final."

* * *

"I have a small confession."

Matt looked at his brother. "What's that?"

Jason studied his worn sneakers. "I saw this absolutely

phenomenal office space last week, and I put a deposit down."

Matt's fists clenched around his coffee. "What? Without even talking to me?"

"You were off in the mountains with that girl, and our Realtor said this space wasn't going to last long. I couldn't pass it up. I'll show it to you before I take you to the airport."

"Jason, we agreed we'd make these decisions together."

He scowled. "I know you don't trust me, big brother, but I called you three times to talk to you about it. You didn't answer, and you didn't call me back. So I made the decision myself."

Matt remembered the missed calls from his brother on Saturday. When he'd said Mom was fine but call when he got a chance, well, Matt had other things occupying his attention that weekend, and he'd forgotten. "It's not that I don't trust you."

"You don't trust anyone, Matt. I get it. It's not personal."

Matt leaned back in the stiff plastic chair in the waiting room where they sat, waiting for their mother to be discharged. Maybe he preferred to make his own decisions and live his own life. It didn't mean he didn't trust people. He trusted his mom—to cook for him, anyway. The woman was hopeless with any kind of financial decision. "I trust people."

"Right—" Jason looked up as the door behind them opened and a nurse motioned them into their mother's room.

"She's ready now," the nurse said.

Matt couldn't contain a smile at the sight of his mom, dressed in jeans and a floral sweater, arguing with the nurse about riding out in a wheelchair.

"I'm perfectly capable of walking on my own."

"Hospital policy, ma'am. Everyone rides out in a wheelchair."

His mom gave him an exasperated look, and his grin widened. Her right side still drooped, but she was holding her own and could complete physical therapy from the comfort of home. Jason would stay with her for a few days until Matt got things wrapped up in North Carolina and moved up to take over for him.

"Take the ride, Mom," he said. "No one's going to be pushing your lazy butt around in a wheelchair once you get home."

"Please, you and Jason are falling all over yourselves to treat me like an invalid. I won't have it. You can stay with me *until* you find a place of your own, Matthew Dumont. Not a moment longer."

"Yeah, yeah." She didn't know it yet, but he and Jason didn't intend to let her live alone again. Not after this. If her next-door neighbor hadn't been there when she'd had the stroke, if she'd been alone—well, he didn't want to think about it.

Jason went ahead to bring the car up front. Matt hung back and teased his mom as she was wheeled through the hospital and out the exit. They continued their good-natured jabs on the ride home, keeping the tone light.

But Matt saw the tears in her eyes as she crossed the threshold of the two-story Cape Cod where she'd lived for over thirty years. The house where she'd raised two children, loved and lost a husband, become a fearless, single, working mom.

Their home.

Matt followed her into the living room, choking on a painful tightening in his throat. The thought of her not being here, in this house...

He walked to the window overlooking the snow-covered backyard. There was the big oak tree where Jason had fallen and broken his arm when he was ten and the wooden fort their father had built for them. They'd spent countless hours holed up inside, plotting boyish schemes that had gotten them into worlds of trouble.

This house belonged to them, and Matt would do whatever he had to do to make sure his mother could live here for the rest of her life. She deserved that.

They shared a light lunch together, then left her watching soap operas and gossiping with her next-door neighbor, Kristin, as Jason prepared to show Matt the office space he'd chosen, then drive him to the airport.

"Wait 'til you see this, Matt." Jason looked like a schoolboy eager to please his teacher as they drove down the street.

Matt's thoughts were torn between wanting to stay and care for his mom and an overwhelming need to see Cara. To apologize for running off without telling her where he was going, to see what she'd been up to this week, how Sadie was doing.

He needed to see her. Now.

"The location alone is amazing," Jason was saying as they turned onto Main Street.

"Where is it, exactly?" Matt forced Cara from his brain and focused on his brother.

"Just down the street."

"Here, in Wilmington?"

"Yeah. Awesome storefront, lots of parking in back. Less than ten minutes to Mom's house."

"Won't that be a long commute for you?" Jason lived in a pricey condo in Charlestown, just outside Boston, with a killer view of the Charles River. He'd made a bundle over the years hacking into companies' online systems to show them breaches in their security. It'd been a lucrative business for him until he'd gotten a little too cocky and hacked into Back Bay Savings Bank.

He'd accidentally violated the privacy rights of thousands of Bostonians and had been lucky to escape without prison time. But he'd been forced to shut down his business. Now, Jason would be putting his cyber skills to good use once

again when Dumont Investigative Services opened its doors
next month.

"Not too bad. There's no traffic heading out of Boston in
the morning. Plus I can work from home a few days a week.
We both can."

Jason slowed in front of a white-clapboard office building with large, inviting windows framed by black shutters.
"Here we are." He pulled around back and parked.

Matt had to admit, so far he was impressed. He was even
more impressed when Jason let them inside and he saw the
space his brother had leased. There was a small entrance
area that could serve as a waiting room and two spacious
offices, both with views of the street below.

"So what do you think?" Jason leaned against the wall
and tapped his fingers.

"I think it's perfect. You did good."

He approved of the space, but the niggling annoyance
over being left out of the decision wouldn't dissipate. Was
Jason right? Did he have trouble trusting people?

Matt thought of the men he'd lost in Iraq, men who'd
trusted him with their lives and paid the ultimate price.

Perhaps it wasn't Jason's judgment he should be question-
ing as much as his own.

# CHAPTER EIGHTEEN

Cara watched as her Realtor's car turned left onto Page Road, then studied the For Sale sign freshly planted in her front yard. She gave it an extra shove into the hard red clay, then kicked it for good measure. Sadie leaned forward to sniff the new lawn ornament. Casper raised his leg and christened it.

"Good-bye, Crestwood Gardens." She turned around and headed for her front door, but her heels were rooted to the earth when she saw the man leaning in the doorway of the house next to hers, watching.

Matt.

Her heart fluttered, and her cheeks flushed. Hurt battled anger that he'd finally shown his face, after a full week of avoiding her like the plague.

Like a furry traitor, Sadie leaped toward him. The leash trailed through Cara's distracted fingers, and Sadie bounded all the way to Matt's doorstep, where she planted her front feet on him and attempted to kiss his face, if only she'd been tall enough.

Casper remained at Cara's side, ever her valiant protector.

Matt bent to greet Sadie, rubbing her neck as she bathed him in kisses, her nub a blur of excitement.

Well, at least someone was kissing him. Cara's face heated. Of all the men in the world, why did Matt have to be the one Sadie trusted?

He stood and faced her, then nodded toward the sign in her front yard. "Going somewhere?"

"Somewhere I can have dogs." She didn't even try to keep the bitterness from her tone.

"I take it things didn't go well with the board." His cocoa eyes fixed on hers again, steady and intent. Unsettling.

"Nope." Reluctantly, she closed the distance between them to pick up the end of Sadie's leash. Up close, she could smell his all-too-familiar scent: soap and sandalwood and man. Memories of their romp in the hot tub splashed unbidden through her mind. Bubbles and mind-blowing sex. Laughter as they spent the next hour mopping up the floor and removing bubbles from various nooks and crannies of the room. The most wonderful night of her life. And he hadn't spoken to her since. "Now if you'll excuse me…"

She turned and headed for her own door.

Matt stopped her with a hand on her shoulder. "Cara, wait."

"I'm actually really busy this morning. I have to—"

"I didn't mean to run out on you like that. My mom had a stroke. I just got back from Boston."

Cara stopped with her left foot dangling over the last step. "What? Oh, my God, is she okay?"

He nodded. "She will be, but she can't live alone anymore. I'm just here to wrap up loose ends."

*Wrap up loose ends.* She flinched. "Wow…well, I'm glad she's okay."

"Me too." He gave her one of those smiles that melted her from the inside out. "What's Casper doing here? I thought he was adopted."

"He was returned. He growled at his new owner's father-in-law."

"Aw, buddy, what'd you do that for?"

Casper looked up at him with those eyes that had seen so much—too much. He wiggled his tail and shoved his snout into Matt's hand, a gesture of love and trust.

What could she say? Her dogs had good taste in men. Unfortunately, they all shared the bad fortune to have fallen for a man who was moving on with his life. Without them.

Matt nodded toward Sadie. "And how is she?"

"Oh, she's great. A little skittish around men...except you, of course."

"Women have always found me irresistible. I can't help it." He stooped to rub Sadie again, and the little dog wiggled all over in excitement. "She looks amazing. Hard to believe this is the same dog we picked up last Friday."

"I know. They recover fast with a little TLC."

"You really are good at this." He looked up at her. "You have a way with these dogs. They blossom with you."

"Thanks."

Matt stood and locked those dark eyes on her again. "I missed you."

Her heart thumped painfully against her ribs. "Yeah, me too. Well, mostly I was pissed at you for avoiding me."

He chuckled. "I figured as much. I should have called."

"What's the point? A few more days and you'll be out of here for good."

His brow furrowed. "Wish it didn't have to be this way."

"It's okay, really. Before you leave, though, I need to pick your brain one last time about the Rogers thing. They've skipped town and left the dogs behind."

Matt scowled. "Can't animal control pick them up?"

"It's complicated."

"Come inside; let's talk."

* * *

Matt shoved his hands into his pockets and fought the urge to kiss her, to bury his face in her hair and inhale her scent.

Cara was eyeing the wall of boxes in his living room. "You've been busy."

"Planning to be out of here by the end of the week." He walked into the kitchen and busied himself preparing a pot of coffee to keep from standing there, watching her.

"What about your cheater?"

"If I haven't caught him by Friday, I'll pass the case along to a buddy of mine. I'm ready to be done with it and move on."

"Don't blame you." She twisted her hands and watched Sadie as she sniffed around his couch. Casper walked straight to the fireplace, curled up, and went to sleep.

Clearly, they had passed the casual conversation phase. If her thoughts were anywhere in line with his, right now she was thinking about a wild romp in his bed followed by a nice dinner, someplace fancy, with Cara wearing that sexy green dress she'd worn on New Year's Eve.

He'd really love a chance to take her out of that dress. Any dress, really.

Matt cleared his throat. "So, the Rogerses skipped town without the dogs."

She looked up. "Yep. No one's seen them since last Friday. Animal control posted a notice on their door, and George Rogers called in to say he's had someone coming over to feed them until he can come back to get them."

"But he hasn't."

She shook her head. "As far as we can tell, no one's been there but Merry and me. We've dumped food and filled their water twice, but I don't like it."

"I don't like it either. Besides the fact you're trespassing, and if the Rogerses ever caught you, they could have you arrested, I don't get a real friendly vibe from the dogs."

"Me neither. Merry's the one who's actually gone in and left the food. I just stand on the other side of the fence and jump around and yell to distract them."

He scraped a hand over his chin to hide a smile at the mental image she had just created. "And because Rogers called in to say someone's feeding them, animal control can't do anything."

"Pretty much."

"You've got to stop feeding them."

"They'll starve."

"For a couple days, then AC will get them. Right now, Rogers tells them someone's feeding them, they check in and see someone's been feeding them. They don't know it's you guys and not the dog sitter."

Cara bit her lip. "That makes sense. Merry's on the warpath about feeding them. I'll talk to her."

"Also, it wouldn't hurt to take it to the media."

"The media?"

"Small town. I bet some reporter would love to come over and make a video, tell the viewers all about the injustice being done to these dogs. You'd be amazed what kind of interest can be drummed up with a sentimental news segment. I bet you light a fire under animal control, and you might even find someone who wants the dogs."

Cara tapped a finger to her lips. "Hmmm. I never thought of that."

"Because even if you get them seized, they're going to be a big problem to adopt, right?"

"Yeah, probably. We won't know for sure until we have them evaluated."

"I can get you a few contacts to start with. Who knows, maybe you can even drum up some positive press for your rescue while you're at it."

Her eyes brightened. "That could work. Thank you."

He rested a hand on her shoulder. "Cara, promise me you won't do anything stupid. Those dogs aren't worth getting yourself on the wrong side of the law."

"I know. I figure it's a reasonable bet no one's going to bother us for feeding them, but I'll let AC handle the rest, I promise."

"Okay." Now that he was touching her, he couldn't seem to let her go. He tugged her closer, but she stiffened and stepped back.

"I should get going. Thanks again, Matt. I'll let you know how it goes." Cara grabbed the dogs' leashes and let herself out his front door before he could say a word.

He groaned and thumped a fist into the couch. As glad as he was that they were on speaking terms again, any time spent together now only made it harder to part ways at the end of the week.

His laptop beeped, a welcome distraction. Ken Prentiss was on the move.

Time to nail the fucker, once and for all.

* * *

Matt shoved the last shirt into a box, then sealed it with a layer of tape. He'd been packing for a solid three hours, and his limbs ached from being hunched over. He straightened. That finished his bedroom. Only a duffel bag of clothes to see him through the end of the week remained.

Yesterday, he'd tailed Ken Prentiss to the Country Suites in Wake Forest, where he had indeed rendezvoused with the blonde Matt had seen him with on several previous occasions. He'd gone straight up to her room, stayed two hours, exchanged a folder of paperwork and a handshake with her in the lobby. No kiss on the cheek, no clothing out of place from a quick romp in the bed.

Was she "L"? Or did he only visit "L" in Atlanta?

Matt had a nasty feeling his case was about to fly south faster than a goose in wintertime. He walked down the hall to his office, grabbed his laptop and camera bag, and headed out to the Jeep. He'd been meaning to pay Felicity Prentiss an unannounced visit for a while now, and there was no time like the present.

As the engine roared to life, Matt dialed the local PD and alerted them to his plans. Wouldn't want to be mistaken for a Peeping Tom.

If he couldn't get what he needed by following Ken, maybe he could get it from Felicity herself. Crazier things had been known to happen, and Matt was starting to get the crazy vibe about this case.

He drove across town to the two-story brick-front estate the Prentisses called home. With daylight obscuring any lights within the house, it was difficult to tell if anyone was home. But he was good at waiting.

Sitting in front of his computer all afternoon would have Matt ready to jump out of his skin, but he could sit surveillance all day. It gave him a sense of purpose, the scent of the hunt.

While he waited, he checked Ken's whereabouts on the GPS app loaded on his cell phone. His Lexus was parked in the lot behind the law office where he worked, just as it was supposed to be.

Matt pulled his binoculars from the glove compartment and trained them on the window of the eat-in kitchen. Nada. Window by window, he searched the front of the house. He caught glimpses of an oversized chandelier in a wine-colored dining room, a flowery sofa in the living room, and a four-poster bed in one of the upstairs bedrooms.

All familiar sights after weeks of staking out this house.

Movement caught his eye, and he focused on the last

window on the left, upstairs. The master bedroom. Matt could see the king-sized bed with its floral bedspread. A sliver of a woman's vanity. Felicity passed by the window and pulled open a drawer.

He lowered the binoculars. No need to spy on the woman in her own bedroom. But she was home, and that was good news. He'd really love it if she went for a drive and he could tail her around town, see what Felicity Prentiss was up to.

Why? He really couldn't say. It was a gut feeling, and he usually listened to his gut.

That night in Iraq, he hadn't.

He'd doubted his gut ever since.

Today he would listen. The Prentisses would not get a moment of privacy until Friday rolled around and Matt left town. If there was the slightest chance for him to clear up this case in that time frame, he meant to do so.

Cara's face flitted through his thoughts. What had happened with the homeowners' association? Obviously, she'd lost her appeal. Would she keep Sadie and Casper while she waited for the townhouse to sell?

Why did he care? So they had great chemistry. So his feelings for her went a bit past casual sex, maybe a lot past it. He was a grown man, a man with responsibilities, and a life waiting for him in Boston.

The garage door across the street began to open.

Matt snapped to attention. He cranked the ignition on the Grand Cherokee and trained his eyes on the gold Mercedes backing out of the garage.

He hoped he wasn't about to accompany Felicity to the grocery store.

He hung back and watched until she'd reached the end of the street, then pulled out just in time to keep her in sight. Most people on the right side of the law never paid attention to who might be following them, but in this case, since

Felicity had hired him to follow her husband, it was in his best interest to be invisible.

She'd be furious if she caught him. Like, fire-his-ass and not-pay-off-her-retainer kind of furious.

Matt wouldn't get caught. He lived for this stuff.

Felicity meandered through downtown. She stopped briefly at the Main Street Café, then continued down Highway 70 into Raleigh. Matt kept his distance, often riding in a different lane, always keeping several cars between them.

She turned onto Duraleigh Road, continued a few miles, then pulled into Covington Point, an upscale housing community. Matt drove past the entrance. It would be too conspicuous to follow her inside. There was a chance she'd seen his Jeep in the parking lot at his office when they'd met.

After driving around for a few minutes, he looped back and turned into Covington Point. He drove along, obeying the twenty-five-mile-an-hour speed limit, carefully looking for Felicity's Mercedes.

He took his time circling through the neighborhood, choosing streets that were not posted as dead ends, not wanting to make himself conspicuous by turning around in a bunch of cul-de-sacs. He got lucky on Amberleigh Street. Felicity's Mercedes sat in a driveway.

Matt tucked his Jeep around the corner behind a stand of heavy shrubbery, which all but hid the vehicle from view. With his high-powered binoculars, he might as well be on their front lawn. Again, he called Raleigh PD and gave his location.

Then he settled in to wait. The clock on his dashboard read one twenty-six. Approximately four hours until Ken was expected home from work. What the hell was Felicity doing across town at someone else's house? Visiting a girlfriend?

He scanned the house with his binoculars. From this angle, he had a nice view into the living room and backyard, but little else. A man passed by the large bay window in back. He held a glass of wine in each hand.

Matt's spidey sense went haywire. *Oh shit.*

Felicity took one of the glasses. They clinked them together. Then she leaned forward to plant a kiss right on his mouth.

Matt pounded a fist against the steering wheel. "Fuck. Fuck. Fuck."

Blood pounded in his ears. Anger soured his mouth and curdled his stomach.

Inside the house, Felicity and her mystery man sipped wine and sucked face. Matt clamped down on his composure, forcing the anger back. He reached into the camera bag beside him and snapped the 55-300mm telephoto lens onto his Nikon D5100.

He trained the high-powered lens through the living room window and snapped several photos of Felicity kissing this man who was not her husband. The very balls of this woman, to hire a private investigator on her husband, when she was no more faithful than he was.

Or was she? Had the entire case been a crock? Had she honestly suspected Ken of cheating or was she just trying to make a few bucks before she ended their marriage? Matt had followed Ken for weeks without collecting enough evidence to incriminate him. Had it been because there was nothing to find?

And if not, who the hell was "L" in Atlanta? It wasn't like the man would buy a diamond pendant for his accountant.

After the wine had been consumed, Felicity and her lover disappeared from sight, presumably doing the nasty in one of the upstairs bedrooms. Matt sat in his Jeep and fumed.

She'd taken advantage of him. He'd believed her tears, her anguish, when all along she'd been screwing around on her husband. Goddamn women and their cheating ways.

Holly's face sprang into his mind, welcome as a bucket of cold water dumped over his head. Her long blond hair, those blue eyes that had captured his heart before he'd even known what was happening. He'd thought he might spend the rest of his life with her.

And all along she'd been screwing around behind his back.

He'd thought after Holly, no woman would fool him again.

He'd thought wrong.

# CHAPTER NINETEEN

Oh, my God, Maddie, not again!" The harried young mother flung her hands out to stop eighteen-month-old Maddie from dumping her snack cup of raisins all over the carpet.

Thump. The cup hit the floor, and raisins rained across the carpet. Maddie shoved her sister, Grace, and took off toward a gate left unlatched at the bottom of the stairs. Skittles, the family terrier, lunged for the fallen snack, but Cara blocked him with her left arm.

"Sorry, Skittles." She scooped the raisins back into the cup.

"Oh, I usually let him clean up for me," Laura Fox explained as she hurried after her runaway daughter. Grace sat on the carpet and cried fat tears.

"Actually, raisins are toxic for dogs." Cara scooped Grace into her lap and soothed the offended toddler.

"Really?"

Cara nodded, then stood with Grace and walked into the kitchen to dump the dirty raisins in the trash. She felt a tug on her right pant leg and looked down to find Cody extending his little arms in her direction.

"Up!"

"Sure, buddy." Cara scooped him onto her other hip and walked with them to the play kitchen in the living room, where she plopped them down to play. Laura returned with Maddie and sat her with her brother and sister.

"Raisins can cause kidney failure in dogs," Cara said.

Laura's cheeks darkened. "Well, Skittles has eaten plenty of them. I guess I have something else to watch out for now."

"Random, isn't it? I was surprised when I found out." Cara sat with the triplets. Maddie handed her a pink tea cup. "Ooh, I love tea. Thank you so much."

The job interview was not going well. Or maybe it was, for Laura. But it was giving Cara a headache. The house was a disorganized mess, the triplets spent most of their time pushing each other, crying for attention, or further wrecking the house, and Laura looked like she might snap at any moment.

A far cry from her old job with the Smythes.

If she got the position, the money would be good, looking after three toddlers. The trick would be maintaining her sanity amid the chaos.

Laura sat beside her, and together they had a rather raucous tea party until the tiny trio had tired themselves out and settled on the couch to watch *Yo Gabba Gabba*.

"I'll be honest," Laura said as she perched on the end of the couch. "You're the first person I've interviewed who seems capable with the triplets. In fact, you seem to have a calming effect on them."

Cara sucked in her cheeks. A calming effect? If this was calm, she'd hate to see them when they were hyper. "Thank you."

"If your references check out, and I assume they will, I'd like to hire you."

"Oh, okay. Great."

"I'll be in touch in a day or two, and we can work out all the details, assuming you're interested, of course," Laura said. Beside her, three sets of eyes watched in rapt attention as DJ Lance Rock danced in his orange jumpsuit on the television.

"Yes, definitely."

"Great."

"Bye, Maddie. Bye, Grace. Bye, Cody. I enjoyed playing with you guys today."

They barely glanced in her direction. On the screen, Toodee was blowing bubbles.

"Bubbles!" Maddie exclaimed and clapped her hands.

Cara laughed. "Nothing compares with *Yo Gabba Gabba*, I guess. Okay, bye guys."

"Thanks again, Cara." Laura stood and walked her to the front door.

"You're welcome. Your kids are great. I look forward to talking to you in a few days."

Cara hurried to her car, eager to get home and take Sadie and Casper for a long walk. To think. To unwind.

This was a great opportunity. More responsibility and more chaotic than she had hoped for, but with the higher salary, she should be able to bank enough money for the telephoto lens she wanted, plus a more powerful laptop, before making photography her career.

Nannying for one child would be her choice. But so far, she'd been interviewed by two other families, neither of which had been a good match. One was really looking for an au pair—without having to pay for one. They'd expected Cara to clean the house while their daughter napped and grocery shop for the entire family. The other one was the most spoiled, bratty little boy she'd ever met. His parents never told him no and didn't want Cara to either.

So if nothing better came along by the end of the week, she would agree to work for the Foxes and their triplets.

It would be good exercise. Cara felt exhausted after just two hours in their house.

She sighed. Truth be told, she hated change. She missed the Smythes, and sweet Dylan. She liked her townhouse. It felt like home. At least as long as a couple of foster dogs waited for her in it, it did. She didn't want to move.

Didn't want Matt to move. She'd seen him twice over the weekend. Once they'd passed in their cars and waved politely. The other time, he'd come storming down his front steps while Cara was out with the dogs, his mood so dark even Sadie hadn't tried to say hello.

She hoped whatever had ruined his mood didn't have anything to do with his mother, but she suspected it might be that cheating-husband case instead. Matt had definitely looked angry, not grief-stricken.

Four days until he left town. She'd be okay. She refused to be heartbroken over a man who'd given her so much.

Cara pulled into the parking lot and parked next to his Grand Cherokee. His-and-hers For Sale signs decorated their front yards. But today, Matt's had a new addition. *Under Contract*, the yellow placard announced.

She sucked in a breath and waited for the ridiculous wave of hurt to pass. Because this was good news for him. And perfect timing with him moving at the end of the week.

Maybe she'd be next.

Her cell phone rang as she pulled open the front door.

"Hey, Mer." Cara headed for the kitchen, where Sadie bounced with excitement in her crate with Casper to the left, slightly more subdued but not by much.

"I'm going to be on the news tonight," Merry announced.

"Really?" Cara opened one crate, then the other, and crouched down to collect the excited dogs in her arms. She couldn't help it; her heart gave a little leap of joy to see them too.

"Yep. That contact Matt gave you for the woman at

Channel Two—she was all over it when I gave her the story. She interviewed me in front of their house, got some shots of the dogs through the fence, down that side street. They were barking and whining and rattling their chains."

"Wow, that's awesome. So you already filmed it?"

"Just got home. It'll be on at six. Check me out."

"Awesome. Will do."

"I'd call Matt and let him know too, but thought you might want to do the honors." Merry sounded smug. Cara hadn't told her what happened between them in Shelton, but her friend clearly had suspicions.

"Sure, I guess. I think I got a job today."

"Really? Awesome."

"Triplets. Hyper, crazy triplets." Cara stood and opened the back door. Sadie and Casper bounded out and took off at full speed across the backyard.

"Yikes. Sounds like a nightmare."

"Best offer I've had. And they're sweet. Crazed but sweet."

"Or you could just take a break and focus on your photography. I heard from Trista you turned someone down. Told them you were booked through February."

Cara heard the rebuke in her friend's voice. "I am. I only have so many slots available, between work and volunteering at the shelter."

"Then maybe you should be doing this full time."

"I can't, Merry. Not yet."

"Not until that doctor tells you the statistic you want to hear. And what then, Cara? In two years, if he gives you the all-clear, does that magically change things or will you still live your life like you're waiting to die?"

"That's unfair, Merry. I just want to be sure."

"There is no sure thing in life, sweetie. We're all going to die, and none of us knows when. Better grab on to life before it passes you by."

"Easier said than done."

"Okay. Well, I have some good news for you, then. I have another interested adopter for Casper."

"Really?" Cara sank into a chair. She hadn't expected another home so quickly, not with such a difficult dog to place. "A good one?"

"An awesome one. They'll be in touch soon. This one will stick, trust me. Casper just got lucky."

"Okay, well, great." But really, she didn't feel great. Since his return, she'd bonded tighter than ever with the quirky dog—growls, jowls, and all. She'd miss him.

But she'd be happy for him. She always was.

Even if she had to fake it, just this one time.

* * *

Matt stared at the computer screen, a sick sensation twisting in his gut. Felicity Anne Wornick Prentiss's Comprehensive Information Report was displayed on the screen.

Credit report, credit cards, vehicle registration, all the usual parts of the paper trail were present and accounted for, for the last three years. Before that, it was as if she hadn't existed. Which, Matt suspected, she hadn't.

*Goddammit.* He'd been played. By a woman.

Again.

His cell phone chimed from the back pocket of his jeans. He swiped it without looking at the display. "Hello."

"Hi, it's Cara." She sounded hesitant. Probably because he sounded disgruntled and pissed off.

Matt pinched the bridge of his nose and drew a deep breath. "Hey."

"I, um, I just wanted to let you know Merry's going to be on the six-o'clock news, Channel Two. They interviewed her this afternoon outside the Rogers house."

He squeezed his eyes shut and pushed the anger back. "That's great. I'll check it out."

"Okay. Just wanted to let you know, and to say thanks again for the referral. I'll talk to you later."

The line clicked, and she was gone.

Matt glared at his computer screen. *Who the hell are you, Felicity Prentiss?*

Or whatever the hell her name really was, because based on what he'd just seen, Felicity Anne Wornick was most likely an identity she'd assumed only three years ago, shortly before she married Ken Prentiss. So who had she been before? And what did she have to hide?

He shoved out of the chair, collected his things, and headed for the library. Halfway there, he realized he'd forgotten to set his DVR to record the six-o'clock news. Maybe they'd have the video posted online later tonight.

He wanted to be able to tell Cara he'd seen it. Why? No good answer. Not when he was leaving Dogwood—and Cara—behind in just four days.

At the library, he headed straight for the periodicals department. Ken and Felicity's marriage announcement graced the "Lifestyle & Celebrations" section of the *Dogwood Courier* from the June 16 edition, two years ago. The announcement listed Felicity as the daughter of Lisbeth and Paul Wornick of Winston-Salem.

And that was as good a place as any to start. Tomorrow, he'd make a day trip to Winston-Salem and see who Felicity Prentiss really was.

* * *

Cara pressed the doorbell and rocked back on her heels, a bottle of wine in one hand, chocolate cream pie in the other. Merry had called earlier with the awesome news that an animal sanctuary in southern Virginia had contacted her after seeing the segment on the news. They were willing to take the dogs once animal control got around to seizing them.

It was one of those nonprofit places that took in hard-to-place animals and gave them a place to live out their lives in peace. They'd have shelter, land to roam, and humans and dogs to interact with if their social skills allowed. And if they progressed enough, the possibility of adoption. A real home. A loving family.

It was the best possible outcome for them. And it deserved to be celebrated. Cara had been walking on clouds all afternoon, so insanely grateful that their efforts had paid off, that these two dogs who'd never known love or affection could now get that chance.

The door opened, and Merry stood there, curls disheveled and panting for breath. Ralph barked behind her, wiggling with enthusiasm. Piper and Felix, her current fosters, flanked him, one on each side.

"You caught us in the middle of a wrestling match." She gave her dog a loving pat, and he smiled up at her with wholehearted adoration.

The bond between Merry and Ralph gave Cara's heart a little pinch. She had plenty of dogs who loved her, even adored her, but they just as quickly bonded to their next owner when she passed them on to their forever home.

It would be nice to have that love, that devotion, for a lifetime.

Someday.

"I like the way you're thinking tonight." Merry snagged the pie and wine from Cara's hands and led her toward the kitchen. "But it seems our celebration may have been planned a little prematurely."

Cara frowned. "How so?"

"Animal control called a little while ago. It seems Terry Donalan from Second Chances isn't the only one who saw me on the news. George Rogers saw it too."

"Oh, no. What happened?"

"He called AC, said they're living in Florida now, outside Punta Gorda. They've just gotten settled into their new house. They'll be here on Thursday to pick up the dogs."

Cara smacked a palm to her forehead. "Shit."

"Yep. You ever been to Punta Gorda, Florida?"

"No."

"It's rural. Farms, open rolling land for miles. No one's going to be keeping an eye on a couple of dogs left outside without shelter down there."

Cara sat hard at the kitchen table. "Not to mention, it's even hotter and more humid."

"These dogs get down there, it's the end of the road for them."

"And AC won't pull them, not with the owners showing up day after tomorrow to pick them up."

Merry shook her head as she sliced two large pieces of pie. "Nope."

"What are we going to do?"

"Not much we can do. Legally, anyway." She looked at Cara with fire in her eyes. "But just imagine if Rogers showed up on Thursday and the dogs were gone?"

# CHAPTER TWENTY

$\mathcal{M}$att stepped inside the Winston-Salem Courthouse. Today, the anger had faded, leaving behind a burning resentment, a deep sense of betrayal. That he'd been fooled by Felicity. That he'd allowed her to fool him.

He crossed the yawning room to the birth and death records and settled in to find the answers to his questions. Felicity Prentiss listed her birth date as February 21, 1980. And, sure enough, Felicity Anne Wornick was born on that day.

Matt spent the next few hours unraveling the rest of the mystery. Felicity Wornick, a plain-looking little girl with brown hair and bangs, judging by the photo accompanying her obituary, died in 1985. She and her parents, Lisbeth and Paul, were killed in an automobile accident, leaving behind no survivors.

It was the oldest trick in the book. Find the record of a dead child of approximately the right age and the right gender, write to the courthouse to request a copy of the birth certificate, and—voila—you've got a new identity. The woman he knew as Felicity had done her homework, finding a child with no living immediate family who might notice someone going around using their dead child's identity.

Now that he knew who she wasn't, Matt needed to find out who she was, and why.

And what the hell he was going to do about it.

First, he needed to find out when the birth certificate was requested. Matt closed the heavy metal door of the filing cabinet and strolled up to the reception desk.

The woman sitting there had dusty blond hair and gray eyes shadowed behind horn-rimmed glasses. Her blue plaid blazer looked as old as the documents surrounding her.

He couldn't have conjured up a more stereotypical courthouse records secretary if he'd tried. "Excuse me, ma'am."

She fixed her watery gray eyes on him. "May I help you?"

"Yes, ma'am. I'm looking for any documentation requests on a Felicity Anne Wornick, born February 21, 1980, died May 11, 1985."

"Hmmm." Her lips pursed as she tapped the mouse and brought up the county's records on her computer. She tapped and clicked for several minutes, brow furrowed. "Yes, this is most unusual. I see that Felicity Wornick requested a copy of her birth certificate just three years ago."

"Do you have the address it was mailed to?"

More clicking. More pursing of lips. "Five twenty Mason Street in Greensboro."

"Thank you. You've been very helpful." Matt flashed a smile that made the older woman blush.

He spent the rest of the afternoon across town in the Greensboro Courthouse, familiarizing himself with the various occupants of 520 Mason Street, one Valerie Hightower in particular. Valerie's driver's-license photo showed a slightly younger version of the woman Matt knew as Felicity Prentiss.

Bingo.

Now on to the next phase of the investigation. As it was

already approaching five o'clock and state offices would be closing shortly, Matt decided to head home to Dogwood. He'd dig up whatever he could on Valerie Hightower from the comfort of his home office.

The hour-long drive took more than twice that thanks to a drizzly evening and loads of traffic. Frustration cramped in his veins and twinged between his eyes. Weather be damned, he was going for a nice long run later to relieve this tension before he exploded.

On the way, he stopped to drop off some paperwork to one of his corporate clients in Durham and to put gas in the Jeep. It was just past eight when he finally pulled into the parking lot at Crestwood Gardens. His stomach growled, and he sure hoped there was food left in his refrigerator.

He cut the engine and sat for a moment in the darkened Jeep until his fists unclenched themselves from the steering wheel.

Cara's front door opened, and she and Merry descended the front steps. Cara wore black pants and a black fleece jacket zipped to her neck, her hair in a sleek ponytail. Merry had on similar attire, her jaw set, eyes blazing.

The two of them were up to no good, and he didn't have the patience to deal with it.

Matt swung out of the Jeep, slammed the door behind him, and scowled at the two women now slinking across the parking lot toward Merry's silver Honda. "And what are you two Nancy Drews up to tonight?"

* * *

Cara gulped, certain that her face looked as guilty as a thief caught with his hand in the money bag. Matt stood next to his Jeep, arms crossed over his chest, a harsh frown creasing his face.

"Just off to check on the Keeney Street dogs," Merry said with a shrug. "You know, nightly food drop until animal control gets their head out of their ass and does something to help them."

Matt regarded her with those cold, dark eyes. "You always dress like supersleuths to bring food to those dogs?"

Cara stiffened. What the hell was the matter with him? Why was he so angry?

"Yeah, well, technically we're trespassing, or so I was told." Merry glared back at him, then continued toward her car.

"And yet you continue to do it." He swung his gaze over to Cara. "Cara?"

She resisted the urge to duck her head. "We don't have a choice, Matt."

"Sure you do. Stop feeding them, like I said. AC's not going to pick up a couple of plump dogs with full food bowls."

"They're hardly plump. And—" She cut herself off.

"And what?"

She felt the intensity of his stare despite the dim light of the parking lot. They were up to more than feeding the dogs tonight, and clearly he was wise to that fact.

"And nothing." She yanked herself free of his gaze and hurried to the passenger side of Merry's SUV. Merry clicked the locks, and they slid inside.

"What flew up his butt tonight?" Merry asked as she turned the key in the ignition. The engine rumbled to life.

"I don't know. He's looked pissed the last few days. I think his big case went sour."

"Or maybe he just needs to get laid."

Cara slapped Merry's arm. "I wouldn't know anything about that."

Merry turned and gave her a meaningful look. "Really?"

She considered that, then grinned. "It's been what, a week and a half since we got home from Shelton? So, yeah, he probably does."

Merry gaped at her. "You naughty thing, you really slept with that hunk of a man and haven't shared the details with me yet?"

Cara glanced over her shoulder, acutely aware they were still parked in the Crestwood Gardens lot, with the hunk of man in question potentially within hearing range. "I'll tell you all about it, I promise. Just, you know, after he's left town, and it's not all so fresh."

Merry rested a hand on Cara's shoulder. "Oh, sweetie. He didn't take advantage of you, did he? I'll kick his ass."

"Hardly. It's just weird, living next door to him in the meantime, that's all."

Merry finally shifted the CR-V into Reverse. "Okay, well, if he's a jerk, just let me know. Seriously, I'll put him in line for you."

"I appreciate the sentiment, but he hasn't been a jerk, I promise. He's just a super stickler for the rules, and clearly he suspects we're up to no good tonight. He'd have zero tolerance for what we're about to do."

"Good thing he doesn't know then, huh?" Merry glanced over her shoulder as they pulled out of the lot and turned onto Page Road. Her hazel eyes, normally so vibrant and carefree, were hard as flint tonight.

"Yeah, good thing."

Cara gulped a breath. Her chest felt too tight. Sweat dampened her palms.

"No second thoughts, lady. I see you starting to freak out over there."

"I know, I know."

But she *was* starting to freak out. They were about to break the law—big time—and despite the fact they were doing the best thing they could given the circumstances, it didn't stop her from feeling increasingly guilty and terrified the closer they got.

"You got the muzzles, right?"

Cara swiped her hands over her jeans. "Yep, they're in your trunk with the rest of the stuff."

"Just making sure." Merry gripped the steering wheel so hard her knuckles gleamed white in the dim light.

Unlike Cara, Merry was cool under pressure. So why was she on edge tonight?

With a shiver, Cara glanced over her shoulder at the two wire cages wedged precariously into the back of Merry's SUV. Had Matt seen them?

Of course he had. He saw everything. What difference did it make, though? He couldn't prove anything, and it no longer mattered what he thought of her.

Merry pulled down Keeney Street and circled around back, where Cara and Matt had parked that first night when they'd discovered the dogs were chained. The side street better concealed the CR-V, not that Cara was especially worried about anyone in the neighborhood reporting anything.

The neighbors all loathed the dogs and would thank any circumstance that led to their removal. Tomorrow, Merry would have Trista ask around to see what anyone might have seen or heard and tamp down any incriminating rumors before they started.

In the meantime . . .

Merry reached for the door handle. Shadows ringed her eyes, dark as the night outside.

Cara reached out and touched her arm. "You gonna tell me about it?"

She flinched. "What?"

"You lost one today, didn't you?"

Merry's nostrils flared. "Yeah, I did. And now is not the time, or the place, to talk about it."

Cara nodded, her chest heavy with sadness. She had no idea how her friend handled it. How she went back to work after one of her tiny patients lost their fight for life. How could you ever get over the loss of a child? "Oh, Mer, I'm so sorry."

Merry nodded. "It sucks, but that's life."

She tried to hide it, but each death took a toll. She mourned each child, held them in her heart in a place she refused to share, even with her best friend. Cara reached over and wrapped her in a hug, wishing there was more she could do, hoping Merry never had to add her to the list of people she mourned.

Merry pushed her away. "Like I said, not the time or the place."

She pushed her door open and left the car. Unfortunately, with Merry, the right time and place never came. By the time Cara caught up to her, she was already hauling the bag of dog food out of the back of the CR-V "Ready?"

Cara nodded. Together they slipped through the darkness enveloping the side of the house, so quiet that even the dogs didn't stir. When they reached the front gate closest to where the dogs slept, the rustling of the food bag gave them away.

Booming barks pierced the darkness, so close and so loud that Cara jumped about six inches into the air. Her heart felt like it might burst out of her chest. She was *so* not cut out for nighttime dog raids. Or daytime ones, for that matter.

Merry opened the gate and flung the tainted bag of food in their general direction. She eased it shut, any sound masked by the ongoing crescendo of barks. "Should take about ten minutes to kick in. Let's go."

Cara hurried after her around the side of the house toward

the car. A twig cracked beneath her right shoe, and again she jumped like a startled rabbit.

"Settle down," Merry whispered fiercely.

Back at the car, they rummaged through the trunk, removing the muzzles and two large black fleece blankets. Cara slung the blankets over her shoulder, while Merry clutched the muzzles. They approached the back gate and waited, still and silent in the darkness, for what seemed hours. Cara's heart thudded, and a sick feeling grew in the pit of her stomach.

What if the medication didn't work? What if it wore off halfway to the car? What if the dogs were too heavy for them to lift?

A dim greenish glow came from her left. Cara looked over to find Merry checking her Indiglo watch.

"Showtime." Her voice carried just louder than the breeze rippling around them. To be sure, Merry reached up and jiggled the gate, then kicked it several times with her boot.

Silence.

She pulled the gate open and slipped inside.

Cara followed. Her left shoulder brushed against something firm and warm, and she let out a startled squeak before realizing she'd bumped into Merry. Yeah, she made a terrible Nancy Drew. And an even worse burglar.

They stumbled through the darkened yard, tripping over unseen clumps of grass, sticks, rocks. Ahead of them, just visible in the moonlight, were the two sleeping heaps of fur. To be certain, Merry knelt and felt around on the ground, then chucked something at the closest dog.

No response.

Merry approached the first dog, crouching instead of sitting so that she could leap out of harm's way in an instant if necessary. She fastened a muzzle around the sleeping dog's snout, then quickly did the same to his brother.

"Phew." She breathed into the darkness.

Cara felt some of the tension drain from her shoulders. Jumpy as she was, in reality, no one was going to bother them tonight. If a neighbor saw anything, they'd probably look the other way. The biggest danger came from the dogs themselves, and their most dangerous asset had now been neutralized.

Still, they were breaking all kinds of rules tonight. No one knew they were here, not even other volunteers in the rescue. Merry never intended anyone to know what had become of the infamous dogs on Keeney Street. It went against rescue policy to steal a dog, even to accept a dog without proper paperwork.

They were lucky Terry Donalan at Second Chances was willing to be discreet. If anyone asked, he'd claim the dogs were left on his property anonymously during the night. But who would ever connect two mixed-breed dogs at a refuge in Virginia with the two abandoned dogs here in Dogwood?

Something silver glinted in the darkness, and Cara recognized the bolt cutter Merry now held. A solid crunch, and the chain fell to the ground. The dog was free. A second crunch, and both dogs were free.

Now for the hard part. Cara handed a blanket to Merry, then bent next to the nearest dog. She laid the blanket over him, then grabbed his feet and rolled him over until the blanket surrounded him. The dog twitched and let out a low growl.

Cara jerked back, then returned to grab the edges of the blanket. The plan was to drag them as far across the yard as they could, then carry them the rest of the way. She shifted her weight back and pulled with all her strength.

The dog bounced forward a few inches. She heard the

sound of fabric ripping, and another low-throated growl from the sleeping beast.

"Shit," Merry whispered nearby.

"This is harder than I thought." Cara bent and tugged, then heaved back against the blanket with little result.

They continued to strain for several long minutes, making mere feet of headway across the yard. Finally, Merry stopped. "This is taking too long. We don't know how much food they ate, how fast they'll wake up. We need to pick them up and get it done."

Cara looked across the moon-washed yard at the shadow of the CR-V some fifty feet away. A long way to carry this dog. It had to weigh eighty pounds.

She had the sudden distinct feeling of eyes watching her and jerked back from the dog at her feet. But when she looked down, his eyes were closed tight. She cast a wary glance through the penetrating darkness around them. A prickly feeling crept up her spine. Couldn't the moon do her a favor and be more than a freaking sliver tonight?

The total darkness was both a blessing and a curse. At that moment, she would have given almost anything for a flashlight to make sure she was the only prowler in the vicinity. She suppressed the urge to scream.

Merry had already hoisted her dog, slung it like a sack of potatoes over her shoulder, and was walking slow and steady toward the car. Panic jolted along Cara's nerves and tingled in her fingertips. No way was she getting left behind out here in the dark with this beast, muzzle or not.

She bent and slid her hands around the dog at her feet. Good God, he was heavy. She crouched down, hefted him into her arms, and stood on shaky legs.

Merry was just a shadow now, moving ever farther away. Cara began an awkward sideways crab shuffle. She staggered after Merry, arms straining under the dog's weight.

She made it maybe halfway across the yard, then the dog shifted dangerously in her arms so that his rear legs dangled just off the ground. Cara's shaking arms gave out, and she allowed him to slide onto the grass. The dog groaned and licked his lips.

His eyes were still tightly shut, although the sensation of being watched hadn't gone away. Cara shuddered, shook out her arms, and started again. This time she jogged, quickening her pace before her arms gave out completely.

She reached the back gate just as Merry was sliding the lock into place on the first dog crate. She walked to Cara and lifted the dog's hindquarters, taking half the weight for her. "As someone who lifts people for a living, you're doing this all wrong."

Cara gave a huff of indignation. "Apparently. Just help me get him into the crate."

The dog stirred in her arms again, and another growl rumbled through his body.

She and Merry rushed him into the crate and slammed the door behind him. Cara leaned against the car and exhaled. Her knees shook, and her heart slammed into her ribs.

"Phew." Merry slapped her a high five and climbed into the driver's seat.

Cara hustled around the back of the SUV toward the passenger door. She would not be adding dog stealing to her resume. She wasn't sure her nerves would ever recover.

She peeked through the rear window at the sleeping canines. They had a two-hour drive ahead of them now to the Second Chances Ranch in Blackstone, Virginia. But that was the easy part. Maybe the long drive would even give Merry a chance to talk to her about the tiny patient she'd lost today. It was a long shot, but Cara was prepared to be persuasive.

She tugged her ponytail loose, her heart rate finally

approaching normal. A cold breeze rustled the night around her. She threw one last glance toward the Rogerses' back-yard, making sure they'd closed the gate behind them, then hurried toward the passenger door.

A hand clamped over her right bicep, stopping her short. Her scream was swallowed by the darkened night.

# CHAPTER TWENTY-ONE

Cara shrieked in horror. She whirled and smacked into a big, masculine chest. Fear blossomed to panic. Before she could scream again, his familiar scent enveloped her.

Relief punched the air out of her lungs, and she sagged against him, gasping for breath. "Jesus, Matt, you scared the crap out of me! What the hell are you doing here?"

His eyes glittered in the darkness. "Isn't it obvious?"

Yeah, now that her brain had had a chance to catch up it was. Her pulse fired back up, not from fear this time, but in anger. "You followed us. Were you watching the whole time?"

"Yeah, and, believe me, I wish I'd stayed home."

Cara gulped air. Too much oxygen had given her knees the consistency of rubber.

The front door of the CR-V clicked open, the interior light illuminating Merry in its faint glow. "Cara? What the hell are you doing out there?"

"Answering to me." Matt's voice rumbled from the darkness.

"Matt?" Merry sounded confused.

"Yeah."

"Oh, shit." Merry's voice rose.

"That's right."

Merry came up beside them. "Listen, I hate to break this up, but we've got a long drive, and they're not going to sleep forever, so . . ."

His hand tightened on Cara's arm. "She's not going anywhere."

*Wait a minute.* She pushed at his hand in annoyance.

Merry hissed out a sound of pure rage. She pointed a finger at Cara. "You trust him?"

"What? Of course, but—"

"Fine, I don't have time to argue. You stay and deal with him. I've got to get these dogs delivered."

"What? Wait . . ." She yanked unsuccessfully against Matt's iron grip. "Will you stop it? I'm going with her. We can talk about this tomorrow."

But Matt was already hauling her through the darkness, presumably toward wherever he'd parked the Jeep. Behind her, Cara heard Merry start the CR-V and drive off.

Now she was alone with Matt. Her heart pounded. "Stop it!"

He released her, and she stumbled through the darkness. Her outstretched palms collided with the cold, smooth rear bumper of the Jeep.

He stepped around her and yanked open the passenger door. No light greeted them from the interior. Dammit, he was so much better at this stealthy stuff than she and Merry were. "Get in. We'll talk about this at home."

"You're damn right we will." Because she was really, *really* ready to get the hell off Keeney Street, and her only remaining option was to ride home with Matt. She swung into the passenger seat and slammed the door behind her.

Matt slid into the driver's seat and cranked the engine. It was too dark to see his expression, but she felt the anger radiating off him. It bounced off her, agitating her already taut nerves and elevating her own temper.

She glared into the darkness and bit her tongue as he guided them down Keeney Street. Neither of them spoke a word during the five-minute drive home. She was seriously pissed that he'd held her back, that Merry had to make the long drive by herself, alone with those dogs.

That Matt had seen what she'd done.

As soon as he'd parked, she pushed the door open and leaped out. She stomped toward her front door with Matt hot at her heels.

"What the hell—you're a thief now?"

She kept her back to him. "You should have minded your own business tonight."

"Trespassing. Larceny. You could go to jail." The anger in his voice was offset by something else. Disappointment.

Cara's stomach twisted into a knot as she turned to face him. "L-larceny?"

"Theft. Dogs are considered personal property. As long as they're valued at under a thousand dollars, you're only looking at a misdemeanor. Still carries jail time."

Jail time? Cara felt nauseous. She believed in what they'd done, was glad for the dogs to get this chance. But, okay, she'd never really thought she might go to jail for it. She stepped back against her front door and rested her head against the cold wood.

Matt stepped closer, his thick shape blotting out the glow of the streetlight behind him. "Why, Cara? Why would you do something like this?"

"I could explain it to you, but I shouldn't have to. Don't you trust me?"

He met her eyes. "I thought I did."

She blew out a breath. Damned if that didn't sting. More like an arrow to the heart. "Good to know."

"You promised me, Cara."

Her stomach dropped. Oh God, she had. That afternoon in his townhouse, she'd promised not to do more than feed them, to let animal control handle the rest. She'd broken her word, broken the rules, punched him right where it would hurt the most.

Her heart throbbed painfully. "I did, and I'm sorry."

He stared at her, his expression cloaked in shadows.

"I'm not your responsibility, Matt," she whispered. *Not like the men you lost that night in Iraq.* "I gave life to two creatures facing certain death, and I stand by what I did, one hundred percent."

Because sometimes rules had to be broken, and if he couldn't see the difference between pissing on a corpse and saving a dog from abuse and neglect . . .

"They'd have been fine if you'd just backed off and given AC a chance to do their jobs."

She shook her head. "The situation changed since the last time I talked to you, but it doesn't matter. What's done is done." And she shouldn't have to explain herself to him.

He squeezed his eyes shut and rested his right hand against the door behind her. "This is a hell of a shitty position to put me in."

His heat washed over her, sending her nerves haywire. It was all she could do to keep from reaching out and running her fingers over the stubble on his jaw, yanking him closer to press her lips to his. She did neither. "You put yourself in it when you decided to follow me."

"Doesn't change things now, does it?" He opened his eyes, and the night around them grew heavy, thick with lust and emotion.

She lifted her chin. "Are you going to turn me in?"

His lips lingered over hers, so close she could almost taste the heat of his mouth, the passion waiting to explode at that first touch. "No. But don't take that to mean I'm even the tiniest bit okay with what you did."

He lurched backward and was down her steps and through his own front door before she could draw enough breath to speak.

Which was better anyway, because now he wasn't there to see the tears brimming in her eyes.

* * *

Matt couldn't recall a time he'd ever felt so angry. He suspected Cara and Merry had noble intentions, but it didn't change what they'd done, what he'd unintentionally made himself a witness to.

He'd observed a crime. He hadn't reported it, nor did he intend to.

It went against everything he knew, everything he'd been raised to be. What he'd felt when he'd watched Cara and Merry snap those chains and haul those dogs across the yard and into the back of Merry's SUV—it alternated between rage and a sickening sense of betrayal.

Cara had gone back on her word, done the very thing she'd promised not to do.

Worse, she'd broken the law.

It was too late now to go for that run. And he was long past needing supper. He reached into his fridge for a cold Sam Adams and a leftover burrito that did nothing to feed the gaping emptiness inside him.

He ate quickly, without tasting much, which was probably for the best since the burrito hadn't been great last night and probably tasted worse tonight. He choked it down, then went upstairs to his office to begin piecing together Valerie Hightower, also known as Felicity Prentiss.

* * *

Bright sunshine bored through Cara's eyelids. She squinted and rolled to her side, her left arm finding and embracing Sadie's warm shape next to her in bed. Sadie wiggled closer and let out a sigh of contentment.

Yeah, Cara enjoyed waking up next to her too. Casper joined in the party, rolling belly-up on her other side, feet in the air, jowls spread in a silly, upside-down smile. He'd be going home soon. Again. Merry had told her to expect a call from his new adoptive family today. She didn't feel her usual excitement over his impending departure.

Okay, truthfully she didn't want him to go. But she would be happy for him if it killed her. And in the meantime, she was going to grill the hell out of his potential family to make sure this one stuck. No one was going to give up on this dog again.

If she had any reservations about the adoption, even the tiniest doubt, then he just wasn't going. That was all there was to it.

Today was Thursday; three days until she'd been ordered to go dog free. Merry as yet hadn't found a replacement foster home for Sadie, and Cara honestly didn't want her to. Sadie wasn't scheduled for surgery for her tumor until the middle of next week, and Cara really wanted to be with her through that.

She'd be bringing in a decent salary in a few weeks when she started working for the Foxes and their triplets. Enough that she might be able to afford a small apartment while she waited for her townhouse to sell. It was a foolish thought, but one she'd been entertaining in the back of her mind as a way to keep Sadie with her for a little while longer.

Cara stretched and grimaced. Her body felt tired, achy, sort of hungover, except she hadn't had a drink in days.

Actually, she felt like she was coming down with something, and that sucked. She had enough on her plate this week without having to deal with being sick.

She reached up to brush her fingers over her aching throat and froze. Needles of fear stabbed viciously along her spine. Cara lurched upright in bed and ran her fingers along the side of her neck again. Her lymph node protruded hard and hot beneath her fingers.

Oh, no. *No, no, no.*

Nausea rose in her throat.

Beside her, Sadie watched in wide-cyed concern, then snuggled closer against Cara's right leg, offering silent support. Casper abandoned his upside-down clown pose to press against her other leg.

It could be nothing. An infection, an impending virus. Or it could be the very thing she'd lived in fear of for the last eight years.

Relapse.

Dots swam in front of her eyes. Her head spun. She was breathing way too fast. Cara sank back into the warm sheets and clutched Sadie in her arms, holding on to her like a sturdy tree in hurricane-strength winds.

Not now. She was about to start a new job, selling her townhouse, maybe moving into an apartment. Her photography career was just starting to take off. She couldn't nanny triplets while undergoing chemo. It wouldn't be possible.

And Matt. Not that there was anything left between them, especially after the scene last night. He'd looked so angry, so disappointed. The disappointment still stung. The very reason she'd held him at bay was now coming to fruition.

She ran her fingers again over the swollen lymph node below her jaw.

*Cancer.* The word lodged in her throat.

Cara sat back up as the initial wave of panic wore off.

She'd beaten cancer once; she could beat it again. She looked down at Sadie, whose face now rested on Cara's thigh, those warm, brown eyes gazing up at her with unwavering loyalty and support.

"You and me, huh? Did I find you so I'd have someone to go through this with?"

Sadie slid her front paws into Cara's lap and nuzzled her neck. She sniffed the swollen lymph node, perhaps alerted to the heat and inflammation there, then licked it gingerly and replaced her head on Cara's lap.

Well, then.

"That's that, I guess." Cara stroked her soft head. "I'll help you through yours, then you help me through mine. Deal?"

Sadie wagged her tail in agreement.

Heart still beating double-time, Cara slid out of bed and walked downstairs to let the dogs out. She flipped on the coffeemaker, then tapped her fingers against the counter top as she waited for Sadie and Casper to finish up in the backyard.

No sense putting it off. She walked to the catch-all below her telephone and thumbed through it until she found Dr. Rosen's card. Her oncologist.

She dialed his office and made an appointment for first thing tomorrow morning. Then she took a deep breath and got on with her day.

Merry called just before ten. "You have no idea the night I've had."

"Why, what happened?"

"They woke up about the time I crossed the Virginia border and started thrashing around in their crates so bad I thought they were going to break free."

"Oh, my God, Merry. But they didn't?"

"No. I was sweating it for a bit, but they're safely delivered. The ranch isn't really all that, but it's better than what we pulled them out of. They'll have their own space until they're ready to integrate into a larger pack of dogs. Terry seemed hopeful."

"Good. I'm glad for them. I hope it's the start of a much better life."

"Me too. So what the hell happened with Matt?"

Cara huffed out a breath. "He followed us. He was there watching the whole time."

"He *watched*?"

"Yep."

Merry laughed. "Well, he could have at least helped. Damn, those dogs were heavy."

"He's pretty furious about it. Said we committed larceny. We could go to jail."

"Larceny?"

Cara smiled at her friend's incredulous tone. "That's what I said. We stole personal property."

"He's not going to turn us in, is he?"

"He says no. But talking to him made me feel like maybe we did a stupid thing. I didn't really think about maybe going to jail; I was just thinking about saving the dogs."

"Me too." Merry sounded subdued. "Okay, no more dog stealing. And if it goes down, I'll leave your name out, since it was my idea. But I don't think the Rogerses would press charges, even if they knew. They wanted those dogs gone. They just didn't have the balls to do anything about it."

"I agree." She rubbed her neck and winced.

"So do you have a dress?"

"What?" Cara's mind filled with an image of herself dressed in white, walking down the aisle toward Matt. She shook it away. "What dress?"

"For Saturday night? The shelter ball thing?"

"Crap." She'd forgotten all about it, and it was the last thing she wanted to do Saturday night, but she couldn't very well skip, since Marilyn was honoring her contributions at the shelter. "I haven't even looked, but . . . no."

"Me neither. Wanna go shopping tonight? I get off at seven. Maybe we could hit the mall, grab dinner after."

"Yeah, sure." If she had to dress shop, Merry could make it bearable. Besides, while she sounded like herself again today, Cara still wanted to check on her, see if she wanted to talk about yesterday's loss.

"Cool, I'll pick you up about seven thirty."

Cara hung up, bouncing with nervous energy. She headed upstairs and dressed for a jog, glad to have Casper back as a running partner. Sadie's lungs weren't strong enough yet for anything but a casual walk, so he would be her only companion this morning.

She swallowed a couple of Advil to dull the ache in her neck, then headed out into the cool morning air with Casper at her side. She lost steam about a mile in and looped back toward home, winded and furious with her body for being so weak.

The message light on her answering machine was blinking when she went inside. She pressed the button and filled a tall glass of water.

"Hi Cara, it's Laura Fox. Just calling to let you know your references all checked out—although you knew that—but anyway, the job's yours if you want it. Please give me a call when you get a chance so that we can finalize the details or, if you've found something else, just let me know so that we can keep looking. Thanks, and I hope to hear from you soon."

Cara pressed her forehead against the cool glass. A drop of condensation ran down her cheek. Nannying triplets. Ooh, boy.

She had to know what was going on with her body, whether the cancer had returned. Thank goodness she'd been able to get an appointment tomorrow morning.

Even a day felt too long to wait.

The doorbell pealed, and Cara jumped, sloshing water down the front of her shirt. Casper skidded across the entranceway like it was a sheet of ice, barking to wake the dead. Sadie hung back, crouched in trepidation.

If she'd been just a little smaller, Cara would have been tempted to scoop her into her arms. What had happened to make Sadie so fearful?

Anger burned through her that these two dogs, and so many others, had been so badly damaged by the people who were supposed to love them. People sucked. Really and truly.

On that thought, she hooked a finger through Casper's collar and yanked the door open to find out what lousy member of the human species had decided to intrude on her pity party.

Matt stood there in jeans and a blue knit pullover, sporting a day of stubble and looking so handsome her heart forgot to beat for several long seconds.

"You gonna invite me in?" he asked with a wry smile after they'd stared at each other in silence several beats too long. His gaze slid to her chest and lingered there.

Cara glanced down and cringed at the outline of her sports bra clinging to the wet front of her T-shirt. She clutched the shirt in her fist. "You're not here to arrest me, are you?"

"Honey, I'm a PI, not a cop. I can't arrest people." He stepped past her into the foyer, where both dogs assaulted him with slobbery greetings. "But actually, I'm here about a dog. This dog, in fact."

His hand rested on Casper's head.

Cara gasped. Well, *shit*. She hadn't seen this coming. "You're kidding me."

She pressed a hand to her forehead. She was going to kill Merry for leaving her in the dark about this. She'd strangle her later tonight, after her fashionable friend had helped her find the right dress to wear to the shelter gala.

"Well, you know, I'd been thinking about getting a dog after I moved back home, and you were the one who insisted I rescue." His dark eyes were steady on Cara's. "So I was thinking, I'm pretty fond of this guy right here, seems like he's fond of me too. He can growl at me all he likes; I don't scare easy. I work long hours, but my mom's going to be home a lot. I can count on Casper to watch out for her while I'm gone, don't you think?"

She swallowed over the lump in her throat. *Oh, Casper.* It might rip out a piece of her heart to let him go, but he'd be living with the man who held the other piece. "Oh, yeah."

"Merry tells me you guys don't usually adopt to folks out of state, but that she'd make an exception for me, just this one time." He winked.

"I'm going to kill her later," she whispered.

His eyes narrowed. "You don't approve?"

"Oh, I do. I really do." So much her knees wobbled with it. "But she could have given me a heads-up."

"Somehow I think she was enjoying stringing you along."

Cara ran a hand across her brow. "Somehow I think you both were."

Casper sat at Matt's side, shoulder against his right leg, as if he already knew. He'd be happy, so happy, with Matt and his mom. It was the kind of perfect match that made her go all warm and gooey inside.

"Anyway, I leave tomorrow, and I'm going to be flat-out crazy from now until then. It's probably better if I just pick him up before I leave, if that's okay with you."

She nodded. "Yeah, I think that sounds best."

"Okay, then."

"Matt..." She stared at him helplessly, too choked up on all the things she wanted to say to get anything out.

His eyes darkened. "I'm sorry I got so angry. You caught me at a bad time."

She pressed a hand to her chest, wishing she could slow her heart, because it felt like she was about to go into cardiac arrest. "But..."

He took a step forward and rested a hand on her shoulder. "You were right. You don't answer to me. Let's just forget about it."

"I can't—"

He pressed a finger to her lips. She shook with the effort to hold herself together because it was almost too much, loving him, losing him, and dealing with his condemnation of her actions all at the same time.

But apparently he didn't want to talk about that.

So, fine. She'd just fall apart later, then.

She took a step back and wrapped her arms around herself.

"I'll be in touch." Matt chucked his new dog under the chin, and Casper gazed up at him with rapt devotion. Cara's wounded heart clenched.

He closed her front door behind him, and Cara sank to the floor. Both dogs piled into her lap, and she held them tight. She was happy for Casper. So, so happy for him. In fact, she'd never felt so good about an adoption, which was ironic, because all she really wanted to do was curl up in the fetal position and sob.

* * *

Matt strolled up the weed-choked walkway toward a ramshackle cottage that had seen better days. The sandy lot and crushed-shell driveway were the only indications that the Atlantic Ocean roared just five miles to the east. Here, there were only pine trees and crabgrass, hallmarks of any part of North Carolina.

He pushed the doorbell and rocked back on his heels. Today he would put this godforsaken case behind him once and for all. Valerie Hightower of Greensboro turned out to be another deceased child, but her last known address had been used during the same time period by one Heather Haile of Wilmington, who still lived and bore a striking childhood resemblance to the woman he knew as Felicity Prentiss.

One thing Heather, Valerie, and Felicity all had in common: they'd all married wealthy men, claimed infidelity, and taken them for all they had in the divorce. This woman was cold and calculating. She got what she wanted from a man, cleaned out his bank account, then assumed a new identity and started all over again.

With each reincarnation of herself, she moved up the social chain. Her tastes became more refined, her husband richer, the divorce settlement containing another zero at the end.

She was the physical embodiment of everything Matt despised in a woman.

The front door swung open, and a woman in her sixties peered out, dressed in an orange plaid housedress and yellow slippers, her gray hair molded in short curls around her face.

Matt extended his hand. "Good morning. I'm looking for Beverly Haile. Have I come to the right address?"

The woman pursed her lips and nodded. "That's me. And who are you?"

"Phil Lancaster with the National Lottery Clearing House." Matt watched her eyes widen at the mention of a lottery. "I'm actually trying to locate your daughter, Heather. It's come to our attention that Heather was the recipient of some unclaimed funds back in 2005. We need to locate a current address so that the money can be properly allocated to her."

"I don't keep in touch with Heather—haven't heard from her in ten years or so."

"Not even a card? It's a lot of money, Mrs. Haile. If we can't locate Heather in the next thirty days, it will just go back into the lottery fund for the next winner."

Beverly's eyes narrowed. "How much money?"

"Two million dollars."

Her hands fluttered to her mouth. "Come inside, Mr.— uh, what did you say your name was?

"Lancaster. Phil Lancaster." If he'd told her his name was Tooth Fairy, she probably wouldn't have questioned it. It was amazing the things people would believe when he showed up on their doorstep with a semi-credible reason for getting in touch with a loved one, especially if he dangled the promise of something enticing like two million dollars.

"Two million, huh?"

Matt followed her into a living room with seashell wallpaper and a tired beige couch. It smelled of stale cigarettes and beer. "That's right."

"You know, I think Heather did send us a card at Christmastime. She's living over in Raleigh now, or thereabouts. Married to a fancy lawyer."

Bingo. "That so?"

"Yeah." Beverly stood in the doorway to the kitchen. "You want some sweet tea? I'll go look for that card."

"Sweet tea would be great, thank you." Matt pushed his hands into the pockets of his khaki pants and walked to the mantel over the fireplace. Not many pictures. One of a much younger Beverly with her arm around a balding man in a wifebeater and jeans. One of a little brown dog with a pink bow in its hair. And one of teenaged Heather in a tank top and jean cut-offs, grinning into the camera.

No question this was the home Felicity Prentiss had grown up in.

"Here you go." Beverly reappeared with a tall glass of iced tea in her hand, the dog from the photo at her heels.

Matt accepted the glass with a smile. "Thank you."

"That's Heather there." She pointed to the photo. "Let me go find you that address."

"Appreciate it." Matt took a sip of the tea and made a sound of approval. Beverly smiled and headed down the hall.

He wasn't faking, either; it was damn good tea. He'd miss sweet tea. There were a lot of things he'd miss about North Carolina.

He sat on the couch and drank tea until Beverly returned about five minutes later, a small piece of paper clutched in her right hand.

"This is where she's living now, best I know." She handed it to Matt.

He examined it, then nodded. His heart beat faster. Oh yeah, he knew this address, all right, had spent many a night parked outside the sprawling brick estate house there. *Gotcha.* "Thank you so much, Mrs. Haile, for your time and your hospitality."

He drained the last swallow of tea from the glass and stood.

"You're welcome."

"I'll be sure to let Heather know how helpful you were. Hopefully you'll get more than a card this year for Christmas." He winked.

Beverly blushed, and her eyes gleamed. Matt felt a twinge of guilt for leading the woman to believe she'd get a cut of the imaginary money. She seemed nice enough; maybe it wasn't her fault her daughter was a heartless criminal.

On the two-hour drive home, Matt called his friend Mike Rankin in the Dogwood PD and let him know he'd be stopping by with a decade-long identity-theft case all wrapped up on a silver platter. He still didn't understand why Felicity had gone to the trouble of changing her identity after each divorce, but with any luck, she would be spending the night in jail.

That left one final detail for Matt to wrap up: the identity of "L" in Atlanta.

# CHAPTER TWENTY-TWO

Cara lay perfectly still as Dr. Rosen moved the ultrasound wand over her neck. It pressed against her inflamed tissue, sliding through the cold gel the doctor had spread across her skin.

She tensed, fingers clutched onto the crinkly white paper beneath her.

"Just a few minutes more, Cara. You're doing great."

She pressed her eyelids together rather than stare at the images on the screen. It all looked foreign and scary to her, mysterious shadows and lumps that all seemed to scream *cancer*.

"All done." Dr. Rosen removed the wand, then wiped the gel from her neck. He extended a hand, and she scooted upright. "I didn't see anything terribly alarming in the ultrasound. Once your blood work comes back, I should have a much clearer picture of what's going on."

"Okay. Can you give me an educated guess? Odds? Anything?"

He patted her knee. "From your physical exam, we know that you have enlarged lymph nodes throughout your body.

This one in your neck seems to be ground zero for whatever's going on. I won't lie to you, Cara. There's a definite chance it's cancerous, especially given your medical history."

She sucked in a breath and nodded.

"There's also a good chance your body's fighting some other kind of infection. I'm going to start you on a broad spectrum antibiotic as a precaution. Even if it's cancer, if the lymphoma has returned, we'll fight it. You've beat it once; you can beat it again. We've likely caught it earlier this time than you did eight years ago."

She nodded again. "Thank you for being honest."

"You're welcome. Now go home and take it easy. I'll call as soon as I have results."

Cara walked to her car in a daze. Gina's face lingered behind her eyelids. Alive, vibrant, glowing with life. Cold and pale in death. Her husband, Jeremy's, tortured expression at her funeral. Little Ben's confused sobs.

*Not me. This is not happening to me.*

Merry called on her way home. "How did it go?"

"It went. We won't know anything for sure until the blood work comes back."

"Oh, Cara. Sweetie, if you need anything..."

"I know, thanks."

"Are you still going to the ball tomorrow?"

She groaned. "I wish I didn't have to, but I do. You still planning to come over around six and ride together?"

"Yep. And I have some exciting news too."

"What's that?"

"I had a foster home open up for Sadie."

Cara's foot lurched on the accelerator. "Oh, my God. Really?"

"Yep, they're brand-new to the rescue. She'll be their first foster. You'll like them—a really nice family, two kids. Lost their boxer at age thirteen last year."

"Okay, well, that's great." Cara swallowed over the lump in her throat.

Merry cleared her throat. "Or you could keep her."

"No, I can't. I've gotta go, Merry. I'll see you tomorrow." She hung up the phone and tossed it into her purse.

Tears burned, and she forced them back. This was for the best. It really was. She could stay in her townhouse until it sold, with no one to take care of but herself when and if she had to undergo chemo. Once she was better, she'd get a new house and fill it with as many foster dogs as she wanted.

Or she could screw it all and keep Sadie. Find an apartment this weekend. Move there and start over with the dog who'd already wormed her way into Cara's heart.

Sadie. Matt. Hell, even Casper. Cara's heart was getting pretty full these days. Just what she'd tried to avoid, for this very reason. Keep things simple until she had a clean bill of health.

But it was too late for that now.

She pulled into the parking lot, parked, and hurried inside. Sadie greeted her with excited squeals from the kitchen while Casper banged his crate against the wall. Cara let them out and shooed them into the backyard. Then they went upstairs and took a nap together.

After lunch, Cara opened her laptop and browsed apartment listings. Maybe she could find one in the same building as her friend Olivia. That would be fun.

She Googled Olivia's apartment complex. It was affordable and allowed a dog of Sadie's size. On a whim, she dialed the office and found out they had a one-bedroom available February fifth, just one building over from Olivia's.

She told the office manager she'd be over later to fill out an application.

What was the harm? Let the new foster family save another dog from the shelter. One more life saved. Cara could see Sadie through her surgery and recovery, keep her until she was adopted. And then, maybe—maybe she'd stay in the apartment and get a new foster dog.

Take that, Crestwood Gardens.

She looked over at Sadie, sleeping beside her. "What do you think, hon? You want to move into an apartment with me? It's kind of lame, downsizing to a one-bedroom. Totally selfish of me when there's a big, happy family wanting to take you. But I was thinking, maybe we should stick together for a little while."

*Or forever.*

Sadie wiggled her nub and snuggled closer.

Guess that settled that.

She sent a quick text to her friend, and Olivia replied right back with a photo of a lap full of squeezably cute boxer puppies. *Want a couple? They're perfect for apartment dwelling!*

Cara laughed in spite of herself.

A dull throb had settled in her neck. She stood and went into the kitchen for Advil, then walked to the bathroom and surveyed herself in the mirror. To her eyes, the lymph node was a bulging monstrosity, but she doubted anyone not looking for it would notice.

She hoped not, anyway, because Matt would be here any minute to pick up Casper, and she had no intention of him finding out before he left town. Earlier, she'd watched the moving truck load up and drive off with all his belongings. Now all he had to do was pick up his dog and be on his way home.

God, this was going to suck. In so many ways. Really, it might go down as the worst day of her life.

After he left, she planned to take a sleeping pill and do her best to hurry the hell into tomorrow. Because tomorrow was a new day.

Tomorrow would be better.

With a sigh, she turned away from the mirror and trudged into the kitchen. She put the dogs out back so that she could prepare a bag to send with Casper without alerting him ahead of time.

She bagged several days' worth of food, some treats, and all his paperwork. Her heart felt heavier with each passing second. Oh, please let her make it through this without crying in front of Matt. She'd always been emotional and never made apologies for it.

But she needed to get through this good-bye with her dignity intact.

Right on time, the doorbell rang. Not wanting to face him alone, she went to the back door first and let the dogs in. They raced laps around her, blissfully ignorant.

She pulled the door open and stared at Matt's chest, not trusting herself to meet his eyes. He wore a burgundy sweater that clung to his strong frame.

"Cara."

"Hey." She flicked her eyes up to his, then stepped back to invite him in. As usual, the dogs mauled him with kisses. Casper glanced around, ears pricked, aware something out of the ordinary was going on.

"I'm not any happier about this than you are," Matt said.

"Why not? It's not like there was any future for us anyway." She seized her temper and clamped onto it, grateful for an alternative to tears.

He stared her down, annoyingly calm. "Don't."

"No, tell me. If things were different, if you weren't leaving town, would you be able to get past what you saw the other night?"

A muscle in his jaw ticked. "I don't know."

"Lucky for you you don't have to make that decision, right? You get to keep your moral high ground and walk away."

"Cara, don't do this. I don't want to fight with you."

She lifted her chin. "For the record, I don't regret saving those dogs. I'd do it again."

He came at her then, eyes blazing. He slid one hand behind her head and drew her up against him. She pressed her hands against his chest, intending to push back but instead gripping his sweater as he lowered his mouth to hers.

"Stop it," he whispered against her lips. Her heart throbbed, and her body arched against his involuntarily, seeking his heat, his strength. And then he kissed her.

His lips brushed hers, once, twice, and the spark between them ignited into all-consuming flames. Matt's fingers clenched in her hair as he crushed her against him, kissing her like his life depended on it. She whimpered, lost to him, trembling with need, pulsing with it. Her heart pounded until her head swam.

Matt lifted his head and gazed at her with eyes so hot they scorched her. "That's better."

She swiped at the tears wetting her cheeks, straining to catch her breath. "If you say so."

His mouth hitched in a smile. "I'd rather kiss you than fight you any damn day."

Lucky for him, her body seemed to agree. She turned away and walked into the kitchen, taking a moment to regain her composure. She flattened her palms against the kitchen counter and breathed. Matt's hands settled on her shoulders.

She picked up the bag she'd put together for Casper and stepped out of his grasp. "So, here's his stuff. I just need you to sign the contract."

"Okay." He flipped through the papers she'd left on the counter, initialing each one and signing at the end. He reached into his back pocket, produced his wallet, and slid a check for the adoption fee on top of the signed contract.

"Congratulations." Her throat constricted painfully. "You've got a dog."

Matt looked at her, his eyes heavy with things that remained unspoken. Regret? Sadness? Disappointment?

She'd never know.

"He's a hell of a dog," he said finally.

"Yeah, he is." Cara turned to the dog in question, who sat at their feet, watching intently.

Matt reached down and stroked his chin. Casper wagged his tail, his eyes locked on Matt's in loyal devotion.

So it came down to this. Cara's heart melted and broke at the same time as she watched Matt and Casper cement their new role in each other's lives.

"Take good care of him for me, will you?" She spoke to the dog. He smiled up at her.

"We'll get by." Matt's voice was gruff.

"Okay, well, you guys should probably get going, then. Are you making the whole drive today?" She walked them to the door.

"I think we'll leave first thing in the morning and drive straight through."

"Be safe." She wrapped her arms around herself.

Matt clipped on Casper's leash and stood beside him. They filled her doorway, the strong man and his loyal dog.

Sadie pressed against Cara's left leg and whined. She would miss the boys. So would Cara.

"Bye, Cara."

"Good-bye." She knelt and kissed the top of Casper's head.

Matt tugged her up, pulled her in. Kissed her until her lungs ached and her body burned.

Then he took her dog and left.

* * *

Matt had just loaded the last bag in the Jeep when his cell phone rang. He smiled to see his mother's name displayed on the screen. "Hi, Mom. Jason driving you crazy yet?"

She laughed. "No more so than you plan to, Matthew."

"I plan no such thing."

"So when will you be home?"

"Jeep's loaded, but today got away from me so I'm going to leave at daybreak tomorrow. Should be home by supper. Oh, and I got a dog." Matt glanced down at Casper, sitting at his feet. The dog hadn't left his side since he adopted him, no doubt wondering why they didn't just go next door and get Cara and Sadie and have a big smoochfest. Matt was wondering the same damn thing.

His mother laughed. "A dog?"

"Yeah. You'll like him."

"I'm sure I will. How's that last case coming? If you need extra time in Dogwood to finish it..." She trailed off, and Matt's instincts jumped to attention.

"Wrapped up this morning. Why do you ask? Did something happen?"

"Nothing important. I'll talk to you about it once you get home."

Matt's grip on the phone tightened. "Talk to me now, Mom."

She sighed. "Oh Matthew, you're such a worrier. It's just, well, I've decided to move into an assisted-living community. Sunrise Place. My friend Mary's lived there for two years, and a spot just opened up."

"What? You don't need assisted living, Mom. I'll be there tomorrow, and—"

"It's not a nursing home. I'll have my own apartment. I'll still be living independently. There are just some really nice amenities available, like an indoor pool, buses to shopping, and other services if I need them in the future. I don't want you taking care of me, Matthew. You're a young man. You haven't even started your own family yet. I won't be a burden to you."

"You're not a burden. I want to do this."

"I know you do, because I raised you to be honorable and do what's right. But this is the right thing for me now. It's going to be wonderful. Mary's got a whole list of activities for us to sign up for together."

"What about the house?" Matt's head was spinning.

"I'll have to put it up for sale. Actually, I was hoping you might buy it. I know how much you love that house, and it would mean a lot for it to stay in the family."

"Christ, Mom."

"I know I've dumped a lot of information on you. Take your time to think about it. We'll talk when you get here. Speaking of family, what about this girl Cara who Jason said you were seeing?"

"It didn't work out."

"Why, because you had to rush up here to take care of me?"

Yeah, partly. "It wouldn't have worked out anyway. We're too different."

She chuckled. "Your father and I were as much alike as oil and vinegar, you know. Keeps things interesting. There's no spark between people who're too much alike, I say."

"Mom..." He grimaced. There was no way he was talking about sparks with his mother.

Sparks, hell. He and Cara set off fireworks together, the kind that still raced hot and fierce through his blood whenever he thought of her.

"Jason says she works with dogs."

"Yeah, she's in animal rescue."

"I don't suppose she had anything to do with the one you're bringing home?"

He glanced down at Casper, still Velcroed to his left leg. "He was her foster dog. I guess I got pretty fond of him this past month."

"And maybe his foster mom too. You know, Matthew, it

hasn't escaped my attention that you've had some trust issues since you and Holly broke up. I'm guessing that's her fault, but don't let it keep you from finding happiness, okay?"

"I don't have trust issues."

"Why are you upset with Cara?"

His spine stiffened. "She broke the law."

"To what end?"

And just like that, his resolve softened again. "To save a couple of dogs that were being neglected."

"Do you trust her judgment?"

"Yes, but not on this."

"Because she broke the law." His mother spoke softly. "If you trust her, then trust that she made the best decision she could."

"Okay, maybe I was a little hard on her. Doesn't change the fact I'm coming home tomorrow."

"Sure it does. If you love her, it changes everything."

"Love?" he sputtered. Who said anything about love?

"Matthew, tell me how you feel when you think about her."

"Like I can't think straight. Like…like the air's been sucked out of the room when she leaves." He heaved a sigh and rested his head in his palms.

"Oh, yes," his mother exclaimed in delight. "That's love. Now go make up with her, and don't you dare come home until you do."

\* \* \*

Cara's plan with the sleeping pill failed. She tossed and turned her way through the night, filled with regret, sadness, fear, too many emotions to name. As the sky brightened with dawn, she watched Matt load Casper into the Jeep and drive away. Sadie kissed away her tears.

Around noon, her mom called, wanting to meet for lunch.

Cara declined, claiming a sore throat. No way was she getting into any of the rest of it with Jean until she knew for sure what she was dealing with. Her mom raved about her new mattress and how it had totally cured her back pain. At least one of them was cured.

Cara hung up the phone and took a nap. She was groggy, emotional, and sore, and the last thing she wanted to do was get dressed up and go out.

But like it or not, she was going to the Starry Paws Gala, and she was going to look her best too. No one needed to know she felt like crap, or that her heart was broken.

First things first. She stepped into a long hot shower, then blow-dried her hair. She blew it straight for a different look, with a little flip at the bottom. She slipped out of her robe and reached for the dress she and Merry had picked out for her to wear tonight.

It was a pale aquamarine, like the sun glinting off the glassy surface of an iceberg. A strapless satin bodice was secured by a snug band of white ribbon, then flowed in chiffon folds to her knees. Merry had gone nuts when Cara tried it on, and she had to admit that it was a pretty dress.

She walked to her closet and pulled out the silver Vera Wang pumps she'd worn on New Year's Eve. They glittered under the fluorescent bulb in the closet.

A heavy sigh escaped her lips as she slipped them on. They reminded her of sticky gum, spilled beer, and Matt. His very fine ass as he bent over the pool table. His dark, intense eyes as he crowded her against the wall and sent her hormones into overdrive.

Stupid hormones. She'd known better than to let any of this happen. She'd let herself fall for him, and now here she was, sick and alone in ridiculously overpriced shoes.

"Pfft." She blew out her frustration. No sense throwing a pity party for herself.

She fastened a thin silver chain around her neck and grabbed the matching aqua wrap to keep herself from becoming a Popsicle during the gala. She was halfway down the stairs when she heard Merry knocking on the front door.

"Coming." She hurried down the remaining steps and tugged the door open.

Matt stood on her doorstep, dressed in a black tux and with a warm smile, looking mouthwateringly handsome.

She inhaled sharply, and her knees wavered. "What in the world?"

His grin widened. "Change of plans. I'm your date tonight."

# CHAPTER TWENTY-THREE

Cara gulped and stared at him. "Come again?"

Sadie burst past her like a fawn-colored bat out of hell and catapulted into Matt's chest. He bent to her level for a quick pat, then straightened. "Easy, there, Sadie; no slobber on the penguin suit." He turned to Cara and held out a bouquet of multicolored gerbera daisies. "These are for you."

"Um, thanks. They're my favorite. What the hell is going on?" Her eyes were locked on this vision of Matt in her doorway, in a tux. His dark hair was groomed back and neat, his cheeks freshly shaven and still smelling of aftershave.

Matt. Here, in her house. Not in Boston.

Her heart stumbled over itself, beating so hard her chest ached.

"My God, Cara, you look beautiful. Stunning." His eyes traveled over her, leaving heat everywhere they touched. By the time his gaze reached her shoes, her cheeks were burning and Matt's expression had glazed over with lust.

"What's going on? Where's Merry?"

"Well." He met her eyes, but it looked like it took significant effort. "I called her earlier, and we had a nice chat. She was happy to back out tonight so that I could have the chance to take you myself. Here." He pressed the flowers into her arms and stepped inside.

Cara followed him into her living room. She lifted the flowers to her face and drank in the sight of them. She loved daisies. They were so bright, cheerful, fun. Clearly, Merry had clued him in on that detail too. "Thank you for the flowers. Aren't you supposed to be in Boston right about now? And where's Casper?"

"He's hanging out in my bedroom next door. I don't have a crate yet, but the place is empty, so hopefully he won't get into too much trouble. And, yeah, I left for Boston this morning."

Cara managed not to snort with laughter at the thought of how very much trouble Casper could get into, even in an empty room. She tilted her head, holding the flowers as a buffer between them. "Then why are you here and not there?"

"Because of you. I made it as far as D.C., then I turned around and drove back." Matt stepped closer. He lifted the flowers from her arms and tossed them on the couch. Then he gripped her elbows and brought his mouth to hers.

His lips were hot and demanding, and she yielded like putty in his arms. His hands pressed into her back, holding her against the firm wall of his chest, and something inside her bloomed as warm and bright as the discarded daisies on the couch.

She flattened her palms against his chest, felt his heart pounding wildly through the heavy fabric of his tux. Her lips parted, and she surrendered to his kiss. He tasted like coffee and sex as his tongue swept into her mouth.

A groan escaped her lips. Matt's arms tightened around her. He kissed her until her head spun and her knees wobbled.

Then he lifted his head and stared at her with those rich chocolate eyes. "I missed this . . . you . . . us."

"Me too." Her voice sounded all raspy and breathless, totally unlike herself.

"I have some things to talk about with you tonight, but first, I hear there's this ball where you're being honored." He gave her a crooked smile.

She narrowed her eyes. "There is."

"Better get going, then."

"No." She twisted free of his grasp and took a much-needed step back.

Matt turned. "I just spent the better part of the day driving back here to take you to this dance, and you're turning me down?"

"Why would you come back just to take me to this stupid gala? Go home, Matt."

He was watching her with that unsettling X-ray vision of his. She crossed her arms over her chest, as if it might block his access to her poor, broken heart.

"Well, I want more than just to take you to the dance, but since it starts in half an hour, I thought we should do that first."

"Stop it. Just stop it." She raked a hand through her carefully styled hair. "This isn't fair. We already said good-bye."

"Cara." He tugged her up against him again, and her traitorous body melted right into him. "Stop thinking so hard. Just come with me."

She shoved at him, but he didn't let her go. "I can't do this." Her voice was a pathetic whisper.

He brushed another kiss against her lips. "Come with me, and I'll explain everything. I promise."

She drew a shaky breath. He wasn't going to take no for an answer, and she couldn't miss the gala. *Dammit.* He might have noble intentions, but nothing could come of tonight but more heartbreak. Even if he'd somehow found a way to stay in Dogwood, she couldn't have him.

Not now. Not with her health in jeopardy. And not with him still standing in judgment of her actions to save the Rogerses' dogs.

She swept her gaze over him one more time. She'd get plenty of stares tonight because her date was going to be the most handsome man in the room, by far.

And he was hers—sort of. Just for tonight.

* * *

Matt folded his hands in his lap and drank her in. Cara stood at the podium, her cheeks flushed pink as she fumbled her way through an impromptu speech after the shelter director recognized her as Volunteer of the Year.

She ran her hands over the flowing skirt of her dress. That dress. Oh hell, she was gorgeous. It clung to her breasts, showing off just a hint of cleavage, then swirled to her knees. And the color... like the Caribbean on a sunny day. It set off the blue of her eyes and complemented her strawberry-blond hair.

He liked it straight. Okay, he loved her curls, but this was nice too. Sexy. Sophisticated. He'd pretty much be willing to sell one of his organs to take her out of that dress tonight. And if he had his way, he meant to make her his every night.

Cara looked out over the crowd. "So, um, thanks so much. It's been my pleasure helping at the shelter and photographing the animals. I hope this year is even more successful."

She stepped down amid a flurry of applause and scurried back to her seat. He slid his right hand into hers and felt her trembling.

"You did great," he whispered.

The shelter director took the microphone. "Thanks again

to our Volunteer of the Year, Cara Medlen. The SPCA funds for our new clinic will be a tremendous lifesaver for our animals this year. And now, I'll turn things over to DJ Chris. Don't forget to place your bids on our silent-auction items in the back. Bidding runs for another two hours."

A slow country song began to play. Here and there, couples made their way to the dance floor.

Matt stood and extended a hand to Cara. "May I have this dance?"

She gave him a smile so sweet it turned his heart into a big gooey mess inside his chest. He led her to a corner of the dance floor, which was a feat in itself, as they were interrupted four times on the way by shelter patrons thanking Cara for her efforts and congratulating her on her recognition as Volunteer of the Year.

He slid his hands around her waist and pulled her against him for what was left of the song. She rested her head on his shoulder and swayed to the twang of the guitar.

"You okay?"

She nodded. "Just tired. It's been a long day, a long couple of days."

"Sure has."

She raised her head. "I still don't understand why you're here."

He laughed dryly. "I'm not sure I do either."

Cara buried her face against his shoulder. "This is such a bad idea, Matt."

He tugged at her chin. "That's the thing—"

"No 'thing.'" She shook her head, throwing his words in Shelton back at him. "The same rules still apply. For all intents and purposes, you're already gone."

"I'm standing right here, and I'm trying to tell you something, dammit."

She looked up then, her eyes wide.

"I don't want this to be the end for us, Cara. When I was in the Jeep this morning, headed north, all I could think about was how wrong it felt to be driving away from you."

A tear splashed over her cheek, and she dashed it away. "That sounds romantic and all, but what about your feelings about what I did Wednesday night?"

"I don't approve, but you're an adult, and you did what you thought was right. You probably saved those dogs' lives. I just wish you wouldn't have risked what you did to accomplish it."

She sucked in a breath. "That's a pretty significant attitude adjustment."

"Yeah, it is. I've done a lot of thinking." So much thinking his brain hurt from it. And he meant every word he'd said. Cara Medlen was one of the most amazing, honorable, and selfless people he'd ever met. Who was he to stand in judgment of her actions?

The song ended, and his arms tightened around her. He wasn't ready to let her go. Apparently the DJ was on the same wavelength, because another slow song began to play. Matt sent up a silent thank-you as they moved together to the music.

Cara settled closer against his chest. He pressed his hands into the small of her back, loving everything about the feel of her in his arms. By the end of the song, he was so turned on he had to bite his lip to keep from suggesting they find a dark corner and explore what Cara had on underneath that blue dress.

Her hips brushed against his, and she looked up with a surprised grin. "Geez, Matt. That's not very gentlemanly."

"I don't recall promising to be a gentleman, not tonight anyway. You just have this effect on me. It's out of my control."

She bent her head closer and whispered against his cheek. "Just so you know, you have the same effect on me."

He swallowed over the sudden dryness in his throat. "Good to know."

They danced, they ate, they bid on a few items in the silent auction. By ten o'clock, Cara looked flushed. He'd noticed her rubbing her neck, as if she wasn't feeling well.

He slipped a hand around her waist. "Why don't we go outside and get some air?"

She grabbed her shawl from the back of her chair and followed him to the patio. It was a beautiful evening, cold and crisp, with a sky full of stars twinkling from above. Portable heaters blew warmth around them, taking the bite out of the winter air.

"You okay?" He rubbed a finger over her cheek.

"Yeah. Tired. I think Marilyn probably wouldn't notice if I left before they read out the winners of the auction."

"I'm sure it would be fine." He pulled her close and kissed her.

She tasted so good, so sweet. He couldn't imagine another day without her in it. "Cara, I've done a lot of thinking. I told you in Shelton I was crazy about you, and that's not exactly true."

Her eyes widened, and she stiffened in his arms.

"The thing is, I'm crazy in love with you."

She let out a squeak. "You're *what*?"

"I'm in love with you. Forget logistics. Let's make this work."

Cara just stared. Not exactly the reaction he was hoping for, but what the hell. No going back now.

"My mom's moving into assisted living, and I'm going to buy her house. It's a beautiful house, two acres of land. Room for as many dogs as you want. Maybe a couple of kids too."

Her mouth popped open, and she pressed a hand over it.

He chuckled. "This would be a good time for you to tell me you love me too."

She backpedaled from his arms and turned away. "I...I can't do that right now, Matt."

"Right now, or ever?"

"I don't know," she whispered.

He reached out and touched her arm. "That's okay. Maybe you could come for a visit, see what happens."

Gently, he tugged her around to face him. Tears glistened on her cheeks. He bent his head and kissed them away. His mouth found hers again, and he took what she offered, kissing her until they were both breathless.

He understood her hesitation, the reason she held back, and he'd work his way through her protective shell. If she'd just give him a chance, he'd prove to her that his love could weather whatever life threw their way.

He nibbled his way over her jaw and down her neck.

Cara cried out in pain. She whirled from his arms, one hand pressed to her neck. Her breath heaved in uneven gasps.

Unease twisted in his gut. "What's going on tonight, Cara? Is something wrong? Are you sick?"

He peeled her hand away and touched the spot that caused her pain. He felt the heat, the inflammation, the hard knot beneath her skin. *Fuck.*

She pulled free and clasped her arms around her waist. "It's back.... I mean, maybe. I don't have the test results yet."

Oh, Christ. He raked a hand through his hair and saw another tear slide down Cara's cheek. His ribs tightened over his heart.

He reached out and pulled her into his arms. "Oh, honey. I'm so sorry. Why didn't you tell me?"

She shook her head against his chest.

Right. Because she didn't want anyone to worry about her, no commitments until she had a clean bill of health. Well, too damn bad.

He pressed her hand against his heart, which was about to

knock its way right out of his chest. "Feel that? The thought of you being sick, that terrifies me. I can hardly breathe right now."

Her nostrils flared. "See, this is exactly—"

"It's exactly what everyone goes through some time or another with the person they love. I want to be with you, Cara, in sickness and in health."

She blinked and sniffled.

"Is this about your friend that died? Do you think her husband regrets marrying her? Loving her? Do you think he wishes their son didn't exist? "

"That's not—"

"I've never met the man, but I can guarantee you that he doesn't regret a minute of their time together. He loved her, and I love you, Cara. If you'll come with me to Boston, I'll find you the best doctors in the city. If you want to stay here, I'll stay with you. I'm not leaving you."

She shook her head again. "I can't—I just can't talk about this. Not until I know for sure."

"Life doesn't come with a guarantee. I love you. I'm hoping you love me too, although you're really making me squirm here, you know that?" He squeezed her, and she pulled away.

"I'm sorry, Matt. I think I just need to go home."

Disappointment mixed with fear to sour his stomach. He nodded. "Okay, let's go."

\* \* \*

Cara stared straight ahead. She drummed her fingers in her lap and feigned interest in the darkened landscape outside the window as Matt drove. Silence hung heavy in the air between them.

*He loves me.*

In a million years, she had not expected those words from him tonight. Or ever, really.

What in the world was she going to do? There was no way she could even think about a relationship with him until she knew what she was facing.

*Why not?* a little voice in her head wondered, but she didn't have an answer. She only knew that it terrified her to the point of total paralysis even to think about.

She looked over at Matt. He stared out the windshield, lips set in a firm line, so handsome he made her heart go pitter-pat without even glancing in her direction.

She'd hurt his feelings. He might be tough, but no guy wanted to profess his love for a woman and not have the feeling reciprocated.

She leaned into the seat and closed her eyes. She was so tired, so ready for today to be over. What a nightmare.

Matt steered the Jeep into the Crestwood Gardens parking lot and shut off the engine. He turned to her in the dim light, his eyes dark and intense. "I'm not finished with you yet. Stay put."

He stepped out and came around the front of the car to open her door for her. That was Matt: always a gentleman.

What would happen now that they were home? Was he planning to come in? Did he want to stay the night? Did he plan to just screw her brains out until she said she loved him too?

Oh, God. It might even work.

He stopped in front of the Jeep, staring off into the shadows of the parking lot. Then he turned and started to walk away.

Well, if he'd changed his mind, she was perfectly capable of getting out by herself. She unclipped her seat belt and reached for the door handle. That was when she saw the woman standing a few cars down. Long blond hair, heavy makeup, designer clothes. She looked spitting mad too.

"What the hell is going on?" the woman demanded.

Matt hooked his thumbs into his pockets. "You know damn well."

"You're wrong. There's obviously been some kind of mis-understanding. Now I need you to fix it."

Cara leaned forward to hear them better. What in the world? If she didn't know him better, she would swear she'd just stumbled into a lovers' spat.

"Can't do that."

"Come on, Matt. Just tell them you were wrong. You can't do this to me!" She clasped her hands in a desperate plea.

"But I'm not wrong, *Heather*. Face it: the gig's up." Matt took another step away from the Jeep. He reminded Cara somehow of a cat, muscles bunched and ready to pounce on its unsuspecting victim.

The woman lunged forward, fists flailing. "Goddammit, how dare you! This is completely ludicrous. I hired you to nail my husband, you jackass, not take out an arrest warrant on me." Anger rolled off her tongue so heavy and thick that Cara recoiled, even from within the relative safety of the Jeep.

"Dogwood PD issued a warrant for your arrest, not me."

She shrugged. "Semantics."

Cara's mind finally clicked up to speed. This was the wife in the cheating-spouse case that had caused him so much trouble. Whatever had gone down, she looked half crazy, and there was a warrant out for her arrest. A tingle of fear crawled up Cara's spine.

Should she call someone? Notify the police? This woman couldn't weigh more than a hundred pounds. Surely Matt could take her down if necessary.

Cara reached for her cell phone and clutched it in her sweat-dampened palm.

"I still don't understand," Matt said, edging farther into

the parking lot, away from the Jeep. "Why did you change your identity? It's not illegal to divorce and remarry. Hell, everybody does it these days."

The blonde scoffed at him. "Did you meet my first husband? He sold cars, for crying out loud, and he called *me* white trash? Heather Haile never could have married Ken Prentiss. I had to leave her behind."

"So this was all about social status?" Matt sounded incredulous.

"I've just improved myself." She patted her perfectly coifed hair. "It's the American way."

He shook his head. "Why did you hire me if Ken wasn't actually cheating? What did you expect me to find?"

"Oh, don't fool yourself. He's as guilty as I am." She laughed bitterly.

"You really don't know, do you?" He had narrowed the distance between them from yards to feet. Cara was beginning to think he really did mean to tackle the crazy woman to the ground.

She leaned forward in her seat. This could be entertaining. Marine versus trophy wife. Cara's money was on the marine.

"Know what?" the blonde asked.

"Your husband bought that pendant for Leah Kelly, his sixteen-year-old daughter."

"His *what*?"

"The blonde I saw him with a few times? That's Sara Kelly, Ken's high-school girlfriend. She recently got in touch to let him know he was Leah's father. He's been driving to Atlanta to get to know his daughter. He never cheated on you."

"Are you fucking kidding me?" She flung her hands in the air. "Why didn't he tell me he had a fucking daughter!"

*Probably because you're psycho, lady.* Cara tightened her grip on the phone.

He nodded. "Ironic, isn't it? He was faithful, when you weren't."

"The police froze my bank accounts. Ken called them when I tried to come home and pack a bag this afternoon. I've got nothing left." Hysteria edged into her tone.

Matt extended his hands palms-up. "Listen, what you need to do is go down to Dogwood PD, turn yourself in. You'll be out on bail in no time."

"Hell, no!" she shrieked. "They're not locking me up. You did this; now you fix it for me. Either make the charges go away or find me a new identity so I can get out of town."

"I can't do that."

"The hell you can't." Something metallic glinted in her right hand.

A gun. Oh, God. She had a gun.

Matt froze, then slowly raised his palms in the air. "Calm down, now. Let's talk this through and figure out—"

"Don't tell me to fucking calm down. Now be a good boy and let's go inside. I know you know people who can do this for me."

Cara fumbled her cell phone with fingers gone terrifyingly numb. *Gun.* Pointed right at Matt's head. *Oh, God.*

"No." Matt's voice was chillingly calm.

Cara pressed nine, then one . . .

"You know what, fuck you!"

He lunged. The crazy woman screamed.

A loud bang shattered the night air.

Matt ricocheted backward, then crumpled onto the pavement.

# CHAPTER TWENTY-FOUR

Cara tumbled out of the Jeep. She raced toward the woman holding the gun, brandishing her cell phone in her right hand and screaming at the top of her lungs. "I dialed nine-one-one! The police are on their way."

The crazy woman gaped at her, then turned and bolted in the opposite direction.

Cara spun. Matt lay flat on his back on the asphalt, a dark stain spreading across the white expanse of his shirt.

*No, no, no. This is not happening.*

She dropped to her knees. "Matt! Oh, my God, Matt..."

Her heart slammed into her ribs, making it difficult to breathe. She pressed her hands against his chest, feeling for the wound, desperate to staunch the flow of blood. "Can you hear me?"

He didn't move. He'd lost so much blood. Oh, God, was he breathing? She was shaking so hard she couldn't tell. Tears poured over her cheeks. "I love you, Matt. Stay with me."

Somewhere in the back of her consciousness she heard a car engine roar to life and tires squealing against pavement. The crazy lady had made her escape.

She gripped his shirt and gave him a little shake. "Matt," she sobbed. "Wake up. I love you. Please don't leave me."

He groaned. His eyes opened enough to squint up at her. "What did you just say?"

She gasped. Okay, not dead. *Matt's alive.* More tears swirled across her vision and splashed onto his bloodstained shirt. "She shot you. Oh, my God, Matt."

"Got me in the shoulder. Hit my head pretty hard when I went down, though; think I blacked out a minute."

She choked on a laugh. "You *think*?"

He braced his right arm beneath him and pushed himself into a sitting position with a grunt of pain. She helped him scoot backward against the rear bumper of the Jeep.

He closed his eyes and grimaced, his skin ashen. "Not that I mind seeing three of you, but..."

"Oh, God." She grabbed at his jacket as he slid to the side. He probably had a concussion. And he'd lost so much blood.

He squinted up at her. "Did you dial nine-one-one?"

"No, I—uh..." She held up the phone still clutched in her fist. Oh, God, she was an idiot. She hadn't even called for help! Matt could bleed to death in the meantime.

He managed a thin smile. "Give me that."

"We should try to stop the bleeding."

"Okay, you do that while I call it in." He fished the phone out of her hand with his good arm, pressed the final "1," and hit Send.

As he gave their information to the dispatcher, Cara eased the jacket of his tux from his left shoulder. The white shirt beneath glistened with his blood, inky black in the pale light of the street lamp. She ran her fingers over it until she located the hole in the fabric, then pressed her palm against his torn flesh.

Matt grunted in pain. "No, the suspect fled in her vehicle. The area is safe for paramedics." He spoke into the phone for another minute, then set it on the ground beside him. Sirens wailed in the distance. He looked at Cara. "Tell me again what you said when you thought I was dead on the pavement."

She gulped a breath. Matt's blood trickled over her fingers, hot and sticky. It slicked her skin and stained her new dress. He'd nearly died tonight. Cara had nearly died tonight, running at a woman with a gun, armed with nothing but a cell phone.

Maybe love trumped death on the scale of importance.

Maybe she should grab hold of this man who loved her, who she loved with all her heart, and never let him go. Maybe they'd live a long and happy life together, maybe not. Who the hell knew? Like he said, life didn't make guarantees.

It was time to start living her life, to hell with the consequences.

"I love you." She leaned forward and pressed her lips to his. "Please don't leave me."

His right arm came around her and pulled her into his lap. "Oh, honey, I'm not."

Two police cars screeched into the parking lot, followed by an ambulance, casting the night around them in an eerie kaleidoscope of flashing red and blue lights. In moments, the place was crawling with men and women in uniform.

She held tight to his right hand as paramedics loaded him onto a stretcher and bandaged his left shoulder. They answered seemingly endless questions from the police, then rode together to the hospital in the back of the ambulance, and answered them all again after Matt had been stitched back up. Luckily, the bullet had passed through his shoulder without causing any major damage.

"They're checking for inconsistencies in our story," he told her as police approached the bed for round three.

But as they were telling the truth, there were no

inconsistencies, and Felicity Prentiss, or whatever her real name was, was picked up less than an hour later on the interstate headed toward Florida with the smoking gun still in her purse.

Finally, they had the little curtained-off cubicle to themselves. Matt scooted to the left and patted the empty side of the bed. "Hell of a night."

She slid in beside him and rested her head on his good shoulder. Fatigue tumbled over her. She clung to him as the emotion of the day caught up with her. "I almost lost you before I got the chance to tell you I love you."

"Next time don't wait so long." His voice was gruff.

She looked up at him and saw the love reflected in his eyes. "I'm really going to hate winters in Boston, aren't I?"

A smile creased the lines of pain on his face. "If it gets too cold, we can always camp in the Jeep."

She wrapped her arms around him and rested her head against his chest. "Nah, I'd rather take a bubble bath."

# CHAPTER TWENTY-FIVE

Cara stood on the back deck, hands shoved deep into the pockets of her winter coat. While an early spring bloomed in North Carolina, Massachusetts remained deep in the heart of winter. Here and there, pockets of snow coated the yard.

Sadie streaked across the yellowed grass and leaped into the nearest snow pile, skidding through it and out the other end. Then she rounded the corner and headed for the next. Apparently, her dog liked snow. Who knew?

Her dog, her house, her man walking out the back door, phone in hand.

She liked these new additions to her life, things to call her own. Especially that last one.

Her townhouse in Dogwood hadn't yet sold, and Merry sure as hell hadn't forgiven her for leaving town, but, already, this felt like home.

Matt leaned in for a quick kiss. "It's for you."

He passed the phone to her, then jogged down the steps to romp with Sadie.

"Be careful!" she called after him. It had only been a

week since the shooting, and he still had stitches, though he tended to act like he was fine. Stubborn man.

She walked inside and closed the door behind her. Casper stood by the fireplace, tail wagging, waiting stoically for his family to come inside. No playing in the snow for him. He preferred the warmth and comfort of home.

She'd given him up twice, and he just kept bouncing back. It hadn't taken him nearly as long as it had taken her to realize that he had already found his forever home.

Cara bent to kiss his head, then brought the phone to her ear. "Hello?"

"Cara, hi. It's Dr. Rosen. My apologies that it's taken so long, but I'm calling with the results of your blood work. I was surprised to hear that you've moved to Massachusetts since we last spoke."

A mix-up at the lab had delayed her blood work, but with everything else going on, she had barely noticed. The results seemed somehow less important now than they had a week ago. Whatever it was, she would face it, with Matt at her side. "Yeah, lots of changes. For the better."

"That's great. Well, I have some more good news for you. Your white-blood-cell count showed an elevated level of neutrophils, indicative of an infection. With lymphoma, I would expect to see a preponderance of basophils and eosynophils, as well as anemia, but your red-blood-cell count was normal."

Her breath left in a whoosh. "No cancer?"

"That's right. No cancer. Just an infection, which the antibiotics should have cleared up."

"Wow, that's great. Really great." She had the odd sensation of floating up off the floor, like she'd just come untethered from the last of the fear that had been weighing her down. Casper cocked his head, then trotted over to nuzzle her free hand.

"It is. I'd like to have you follow up with a doctor in Boston, as a precaution. I'll have my office get in touch with a few recommendations."

"That would be wonderful. Thanks so much."

She walked into the kitchen and slid the phone into its cradle.

*No cancer.*

Her knees wobbled in relief.

Jewel, the little tabby cat who'd bonded with Cara that afternoon at the Dogwood Shelter, hopped from the kitchen counter with a guilty look on her face. But Cara was in too good a mood to chastise her.

Charlie, the black-and-white cat from the cage below Jewel's, napped in a patch of sunshine by the window.

The back door opened and closed, then Matt's right arm slid around her. Sadie burst past them to chase Jewel across the linoleum. The cat hissed, gone bushy as if she'd been plugged into an outlet, then streaked toward the stairs. Their relationship was still a work in progress.

"Test results?" His lips brushed her cheek.

She nodded.

"Before you tell me, I have a question for you."

She leaned into him. "Okay. But—"

"Shh." He pressed a finger against her lips, then led her through the living room and up the stairs. Down the hall toward the master bedroom.

*What in the world?*

"Go on." He gave her a gentle push, propelling her through the doorway.

The bedroom was filled with flowers. Roses and daisies of every color in the rainbow.

And pictures. The walls and dressers were covered with them. Photos of Cara, of Matt, a portrait of them together taken by the photographer at the Starry Paws Gala. There was one of Cara and Sadie, walking together behind Barbara's Bed & Breakfast.

Her hand flew to her mouth. "Oh, my God."

"You're not the only one who owns a fancy camera, you know."

"Matt..." She looked at a beautiful close-up of Casper, head tilted, mismatched eyes bright with adoration. And not the only one with photographic talent either.

He pressed a kiss to her cheek and pulled her against him. "Photos are forever, right? I want to fill the whole house with them."

Tears welled in her eyes. Of course he'd noticed that she didn't take photos of herself, that she kept only photos of her dogs. Of course—because he *knew* her, really knew her. He understood her, and he had even managed to outsmart her fears.

So, yeah, he could fill the house with photos if he wanted.

He nibbled on her earlobe. "Take a peek in the bathroom."

She peered through the doorway into the bathroom. The tub overflowed with rose-scented bubbles. Candles flickered on the windowsill.

"Oh! When did you...what..."

"While you were outside with Sadie. Cara," He dropped to one knee and pulled a small blue box from the front pocket of his jeans.

Her heart performed a series of back flips in her chest. *Oh, my God.*

He flipped the box open. A diamond ring sat inside, the center stone flanked by a small sapphire on either side. It was gorgeous, unique. Perfect.

"Will you marry me?" He looked up at her with such unabashed love on his face that her heart swelled until her chest hurt to contain it.

Everything came unleashed inside her. So much love, so

much joy, there wasn't room for anything else. No more hesitation, no more fear.

Tears streamed down her cheeks as she fell into his arms. "Oh, yes."

Sadie chose that moment to chase Jewel through the bathroom. Matt tripped over the terrified cat, and they tumbled into the bathtub. Scented bubbles splashed onto the floor.

Cara wiped them from her face and kissed her future husband. "I love you, Matt Dumont, as long as we both shall live."

Return to Dogwood, as Merry
Atwater opens her heart to a stray
dog—and a rugged cowboy . . .

Please see the next page
for a preview of

*For Keeps*

# $\mathscr{C}$HAPTER ONE

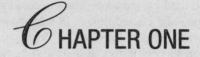

$\mathscr{M}$erry Atwater was about to do something she hadn't done in almost a decade. She closed her eyes, clasped her hands together, and prayed. As in, to God. She had little faith the Big Guy was listening, but she was desperate.

When she opened her eyes, the numbers on the screen hadn't changed. Not that she expected God to alter Triangle Boxer Rescue's account balance, but He did perform miracles from time to time, didn't He? The truth was, the animal rescue she had poured her heart and soul into for the last six years was flat broke.

"What am I going to do?" She steepled her fingers and pressed them to her mouth.

Ralph, her six-year-old boxer, scooted closer on the couch. He plopped his head into her lap and gazed up at her with adoring brown eyes. Behind him, her foster puppies Chip and Salsa lay piled on top of one another. Collectively, they took up nearly the whole couch, but Merry didn't mind. She enjoyed having a couch full of happy dogs, especially knowing she had saved each one from an uncertain future at the shelter, guaranteeing them a happy ending through Triangle Boxer Rescue.

She'd founded TBR as a twenty-two-year-old fresh out of nursing school, eager to do more to help the dogs she'd come to love and depend on. Since then, she'd devoted as much of her time and hard-earned money as she could spare to saving abandoned and abused boxers in and around the small town of Dogwood, North Carolina.

She'd been successful too, at least at first. Several years ago, she'd begun receiving an anonymous donation of one thousand dollars a month from an unknown benefactor. She'd tried and failed to find out who was behind the mysterious donations, but at some point, she'd come to depend on them. Then, six months ago, the donations had stopped. Now the rescue's bank account was drained, and she'd nearly maxed out her personal credit card trying to cover the difference.

She traced her fingers over the zigzag pattern on her pajama pants. It was nearly nine o'clock, and she was ready to call it a night. She had a twelve-hour shift ahead of her tomorrow and needed a good night's sleep.

A quiet knock sounded at her front door. Ralph lifted his head and let out a sleepy bark, while Chip and Salsa tumbled onto the floor in a tangle of puppy legs.

Merry sucked in a breath. Had God heard her prayer after all? Had someone arrived to miraculously bail Triangle Boxer Rescue out of financial ruin?

Not likely, but she'd always considered herself a glass-half-full kind of girl.

"Just a minute," she called as she herded the puppies behind the gate in the kitchen then walked to the front door with Ralph at her side. She pressed her eye to the peephole, hesitant to open the door to an unexpected guest in her pajamas.

A woman stood outside, dressed in a pink tank top and jean shorts. Wet tendrils of brown hair stuck to the sides of her face from the rain pouring beyond the safe shelter of Merry's porch. She looked vaguely familiar. A neighbor, maybe?

Merry pulled the door open. Ralph let out a powerful bark, eyes fixed on the bedraggled dog at the woman's side. It appeared to be some sort of Lab mix, with soggy amber fur and the kind of glazed eyes that Merry had seen too many times.

She gave Ralph a quick hand signal to keep him from greeting the unknown dog. He sat, tail wiggling against the hardwood floor.

"Hi," the woman said, extending a rain-drenched hand. "I'm Kelly Pointer. I live down the street." Kelly looked to the left, toward the cul-de-sac at the other end of the road.

Right. Merry had seen her before when she was out walking her dogs. She took Kelly's hand and shook. "Sure. Hi, Kelly. What can I do for you?"

"Well, I heard you rescue dogs." Kelly gestured to the dog at her feet. It stood, hunched, looking pathetic and miserable, and a heavy feeling settled in Merry's gut.

God hadn't sent an answer to her prayers. Instead, He'd added to her burden.

"Yes," she answered carefully. "I'm the director of Triangle Boxer Rescue."

She glanced pointedly at Ralph, still sitting politely at her side. He cocked his chestnut head, gazing up at their visitor with warm chocolate eyes that had melted many a heart.

"Well," Kelly said, "I found this stray. She's been wandering the neighborhood, and I was afraid she'd get hit by a car. I was hoping you could take her."

Merry looked at the stray. The rain-soaked Lab mix avoided her gaze, looking like she'd dart off into the watery darkness if given half a chance. "Have you called the Dogwood Shelter to see if anyone's looking for her?"

"Uh, no. I just brought her to you. I was hoping you could take her." Her neighbor extended a thin piece of white rope that had been fashioned into a makeshift collar and leash.

"Well, I don't exactly—" Merry gripped the rope, looking down at the pathetic dog on her front porch. This wasn't the first time someone had brought her a random dog, expecting her to take it because she worked in animal rescue, and it wouldn't be the last.

She'd always felt it a bit rude and presumptuous. It wasn't as if Kelly didn't have a home of her own where the dog could stay, warm and dry. Merry would have been happy to help her find the stray a home. But nope, she was apparently the designated receptacle for all unwanted dogs in the area, like it or not.

"Good luck with her. She seems sweet." Kelly tucked her hands into her pockets and turned to go.

"Thanks, but I'll probably have to bring her to the shelter in the morning."

Kelly's eyes rounded. "What? I thought maybe you could keep her, or something."

"I run a rescue—for boxers. This is not a boxer. I already have two fosters and a dog of my own. I really can't keep her." Merry said the words. She meant them too. Then she glanced down at the dog huddled on her front porch, and she knew she'd never follow through.

Kelly shrugged. "Well, that sucks. I hope she finds a home."

And with that, she walked off into the rainy night.

Merry looked at the dog, who, for tonight at least, was hers. "So you're spending the night with us, huh?" The soggy Lab mix stared at the floor of Merry's porch, tail tucked between her legs. She reeked like wet, dirty dog.

Merry looped the rope around the railing. "Just a minute. I'll be right back, okay?"

She stepped inside and put Ralph behind the gate in the kitchen with her two nosy foster puppies. She couldn't introduce the new dog tonight, knowing nothing about her, and, besides, she wasn't keeping her long enough for it to matter.

She'd have her scanned for a microchip, call the local shelters, and, if all else failed, she'd look for another rescue to take her, because Merry couldn't keep her. She never kept more than three.

And in case God had forgotten, Merry was broke. She'd learned a long time ago that she couldn't save them all. It was a bitter lesson to swallow, but true, and important to remember, lest she drown in guilt over the ones who couldn't be saved.

She returned to the porch with a towel and gently rubbed as much rainwater as she could from the soggy stray. "Ready to come inside?"

The dog planted her feet, unwilling to enter the house. Merry shrugged, unfazed. She sat on the top step, staring out into the rainy June night, still warm and muggy despite the hour.

"Life's been pretty crappy to you lately, huh?" she said softly. "I know what that feels like. It's going to get better, though. At least you have a dry bed waiting for you tonight, right?"

She kept talking, watching the rain fall beyond the protection of her front porch. Finally, the stray took a hesitant step toward her.

Merry reached out and stroked her chest, telling her what a good girl she was, patiently earning her trust. After a while, she stood and gave the rope a gentle tug. The dog followed her into the house.

The boxers in the kitchen barked and pranced, eager to make acquaintance with their visitor. Not yet. The dog at her side was tense, defensive. Terrified.

Merry led her to the crate she kept in the den for new dogs just getting settled.

It would do. For tonight.

* * *

T. J. Jameson leaned a hip against the counter and watched the pretty brunette's frown deepen. From the looks of it, his buddy David Johnson had just declined her credit card. David owned Dogwood Animal Hospital. T.J., on his way home after checking on a colicky horse out in Creedmoor, had stopped by to see if his friend might have a recommendation to replace the dog trainer who'd just bailed on him.

The brunette tossed back a curly lock of hair and rummaged inside her purse. She was dressed for suburbia in fitted jean shorts, a purple blouse, and sparkly flip-flops, with a brown dog at her feet. T.J. pictured her in Wranglers and cowboy boots, and he liked that image a whole lot better. Dressed like that, he'd really have a hard time taking his eyes off her.

She glanced over, and their eyes met. Hers were a bottomless hazel that sparkled with trouble.

She turned back to David. "Try this one," she said, handing over a blue credit card.

David swiped it through his card reader. "You've been paying for a lot of foster dogs with your personal card lately."

She shrugged. "This one's not technically a foster. I'm just keeping her for a day or two, to see if anyone shows up to claim her."

Behind him, the door chimed. T.J. glanced over his shoulder to see a teenager in baggy jeans and a T-shirt emblazoned with "#AWESOME" enter the waiting room, busily texting on his cell phone. A brown-and-white dog walked at his side, some kind of mixed breed. It lunged toward the one the brunette held, barking and snarling, straining against the end of its leash.

"Knock it off," the teenager said, pulling the dog toward the other end of the waiting room.

T.J.'s skin prickled. Clearly that animal was not a suitable pet. It was only a matter of time before it bit someone. He ran a hand over his throat, feeling for the scars that had long faded.

He looked back at the brunette. She'd moved her dog out of sight behind the reception desk and was signing her receipt.

"Thanks, Dr. Johnson. I'll see you next week for the puppies' next round of vaccinations." She started for the door with the brown dog at her heel.

The teenager's mutt lunged again, and this time its leash pulled free. It bounded across the lobby toward the brunette and her dog.

Vicious barking shattered the air, setting T.J.'s adrenaline pumping. The brunette froze, and the dog behind her cowered against her legs. Easy bait.

His stomach soured at the thought of her at the dog's mercy, her blood staining that pretty purple blouse as she tried to defend herself. No. No way.

"Hey!" T.J. lunged in front of the runaway dog.

It stopped and snarled at him, teeth bared. T.J. felt the hair on his arms stand on end. He raised his arms as if he were corralling a wayward calf and took a step toward the animal.

The dog pinned its ears and growled.

"Brutus, no!" The teenager grabbed the end of the leash and hauled the dog, still growling, into an open exam room.

T.J.'s heart thumped against his ribs. The scars on his neck stung, a vicious memory of the night he'd almost gotten his throat ripped out. He still heard the snarling barks, felt the teeth crushing his throat and his own warm blood flowing over his skin.

"Holy shit."

He turned his head to see the brunette staring at him, her hazel eyes wide. His hand was on her shoulder before he knew what he was doing. "Are you okay?"

She nodded. "You are *so* lucky you didn't get bit just now."

Yeah, he knew that; knew it better than most. He pulled back, tucking his thumbs through his belt loops. "Better me than you."

"He wasn't really after me; he was after my dog. But I was ready for him." She opened her right hand to reveal a small, black spray canister.

T.J.'s eyebrows lifted. "Mace?"

"Citronella spray. It's kind of like Mace for dogs, except it doesn't hurt them." She slid the can into her purse. "FYI, next time you might not want to wave your arms around in an aggressive dog's face. It's asking for trouble, but... thanks. Most people wouldn't bother to try. You're our hero."

She gave him a sweet smile, then strode out the front door, brown dog trotting along at her side.

T.J. stared, then snapped his mouth shut, feeling more confused than heroic. He turned to David, who still stood behind the reception desk, flipping through paperwork. "Who was that?"

David waggled his bushy eyebrows with a smile. "Merry Atwater. She's a nurse, so at least she could have patched you up if you'd needed it."

T.J. grunted. Good to know. "That kid with the vicious dog is a client of yours?"

"His father is, but he's out of town. Brutus isn't all bad, but the family refuses to have him neutered, and he gets a little territorial around female dogs."

"Brutus? The dog's name is Brutus? That should be a

warning right there." T.J. had never had a dog, never planned on getting one, but if he did, he'd find a reputable breeder, choose one with champion bloodlines and a solid temperament. He'd never understood why people took in dogs like that one, dogs of unknown heritage, with obvious behavioral problems.

He'd seen what happened when dogs like that got loose. He'd seen livestock attacked by prowling dogs. Hell, he'd come within an inch of losing his own life to a couple of stray mutts. Dogs like Brutus were a serious problem.

David nodded. "Brutus might need to be muzzled in the lobby area. I'll have a talk with them about it. So what brings you out my way?"

"Hoping you might be able to help me out."

David headed for the back room, motioning for T.J. to follow. "Oh yeah, how's that?"

"That dog trainer I hired for the summer camp bailed on me." He was seriously pissed about it too. He'd spent months getting everything in place, and now, with only a week to go, he was back at square one.

"So just put the kids to work in the barn," his friend said with a shrug.

"I plan to, but dogs are an important part of the camp—for Noah especially." And the whole point of the camp was to help his nephew. Noah had been diagnosed a few years ago as a child with high-functioning autism. He was a smart kid, bright as a hundred-watt bulb, but he struggled to communicate with his peers, which had led to problems at school.

T.J.'s sister Amy was a single mom fighting to make ends meet. She wouldn't accept money from him, no matter how hard he tried to help. Instead, he'd decided to establish a summer camp on his farm to help kids like his nephew, using his horses for equine therapy and incorporating a local dog trainer who'd bring several trained therapy dogs to work with the kids.

Noah communicated with dogs on a level he struggled to achieve with members of his own species. The camp absolutely couldn't happen without dogs.

"Well, here's an idea." David reached into a wire crate to check the IV port on a chocolate-colored cocker spaniel. "Merry Atwater, the lady who just left? She runs a boxer rescue, and I happen to remember one of her dogs is a certified therapy dog. Maybe she could help you out."

"Really?" T.J. thought back to the pretty brunette. He couldn't quite picture her getting her perfectly manicured hands dirty out on his farm.

David nodded. "She's good people. And between you and me, her rescue's in some financial trouble right now. If you offered her a donation in return for her help, I'm sure she'd be more than happy to be part of your camp."

"I don't know. She didn't really look like the farm type to me." The last thing he needed was some girly-girl running around on his farm, complaining about getting her expensive shoes dirty or breaking a fingernail.

But camp started next week, and, at the moment, he had no other leads.

"She's tougher than she looks." David led the way back to the waiting room, where he pulled a business card from a pile in a drawer behind the reception desk. "Give her a call. See what she says."

\* \* \*

Merry pursed her lips and tried to ignore the dog sulking in the crate at the far end of the kitchen. She'd called every shelter in the area to report her found, but so far, no owner had come forward. From the looks of her, the mutt probably hadn't had an owner in some time. Her fur was matted with burs and mud, her nails untrimmed, ribs protruding beneath her heavy coat.

Merry couldn't bring herself to take her to the shelter, but she couldn't keep her, either. She wasn't a boxer, for one thing. Not to mention, her tiny house was already at capacity with Ralph, Chip, and Salsa. And she was broke.

Couldn't forget that part.

Which led her back to the email on her screen. A woman named Tracy Jameson had contacted her, said she'd gotten Merry's name from her vet, David Johnson. She was looking for someone to help out with canine-assisted therapy at a summer camp she was running for local kids. In exchange, she'd write a check for a thousand dollars to Triangle Boxer Rescue.

Tempting. Very tempting.

Ralph was a therapy dog. Merry took him in once a week to visit the kids on the pediatric floor of Dogwood Hospital. He'd be great for the summer camp.

In fact, he'd love it a lot more than she would. To Merry, summer camp sounded dirty, sweaty, and exhausting. And while she did have some vacation time saved up at the hospital, she'd planned to spend it fund-raising for Triangle Boxer Rescue, not wilting in the summer heat on this woman's farm.

Still, a thousand dollars sounded pretty irresistible right now.

First things first. She had to figure out what to do with the stray dog in her kitchen. Merry approached the crate and eyed the nameless, hopeless dog. "So, I was thinking about putting up some flyers around the neighborhood. Want to come with me?"

The dog looked up, her brown eyes so sad, so empty, that Merry's heart broke. No matter what, this dog couldn't go to the shelter. She wouldn't last a week.

Merry opened the crate and coaxed the frightened dog out. She reached into the cabinet and pulled out a bag of training treats, then sat on the floor and praised and rewarded her for every shy wag of her tail.

Once No-Name had received a much-needed boost to her self-esteem, Merry clipped a leash onto her collar. She grabbed the pile of flyers she'd printed earlier, along with a stapler, and she was ready to go.

"You need a name," Merry told her. She named new fosters all the time, and yet she couldn't bring herself to name this one.

The dog stood patiently beside her while she stapled flyers to lampposts up and down her street and around the neighborhood. It wasn't likely, but it was possible there was a family out there somewhere looking for her and wanting her back.

No-Name stared straight ahead as they walked, making no eye contact with Merry, showing no emotion at all. Her tail hung limply behind her, which was a step up from tucked between her legs, but no amount of sweet talk from Merry could get it to wag again.

A high-pitched shriek was their only warning before a toddler barreled onto the sidewalk, arms outstretched. "Doggy! Doggy!"

Merry tightened her grip on No-Name's leash and tried to put herself between the dog and the runaway child, but it was too late. The little girl flung her arms around No-Name's neck with a squeal of glee.

"Violet!" A woman ran down the driveway after the wayward child. "Oh, my gosh."

Merry tensed, ready to intervene if necessary, but No-Name's tail wagged steadily. She looked calm. Happy even.

"Thank goodness your dog likes kids," the girl's mother said.

That was an understatement. Merry wouldn't have intentionally introduced such a new dog to anyone's child just yet, but now that it had happened, No-Name did indeed seem thrilled.

The little girl patted her roughly on the head then ran off toward a pink tricycle outside the garage. Her mom waved and followed her up the driveway. No-Name gazed after the toddler, tail still wagging.

Merry hustled her home. As they walked in the front door, her cell phone rang. She glanced at the display. "Hey, Liv."

"Hi," Olivia said. "I got your message, and no, I can't take another dog right now. I nearly got evicted from my apartment when I was fostering those damn puppies."

"Oh, come on, please? This one's full grown. She's housebroken, and I haven't even heard her bark. She'd be easy."

"Nope, sorry." Olivia Bennett had never formally agreed to foster for Triangle Boxer Rescue. She was a friend of Cara Medlen, who'd moved to Massachusetts a few months ago, leaving Merry short a good foster home, and a best friend, both of which roles Olivia had temporarily stepped in to fill.

"Know anyone looking for a dog? She's some kind of Lab mix, very shy, but well behaved."

"I'll ask around, but offhand...no."

"Okay, well, thanks anyway." Merry led the dog back into her kitchen. This morning she'd allowed her to make introductions with Ralph, and it had gone well. No-Name had tucked her tail and bowed her head submissively when Ralph greeted her. It was a good start, but she wasn't ready to throw her somewhat less predictable foster puppies into the mix just yet.

Currently, they were asleep upstairs in her bedroom. If No-Name stayed much longer, she'd think about introducing them all, but she hoped she'd be passing her along before that became necessary.

She opened her laptop to see if any of the Lab or all-breed rescues had responded. They hadn't, but the email from Tracy Jameson still waited in her inbox.

She didn't want to get involved in a summer camp, but maybe...

Maybe she could make it work to her advantage. She sent Tracy a quick reply, asking to meet with her to discuss things further, then closed her laptop to start preparing dinner for herself and the dogs.

The next day, she worked her usual twelve-hour shift at Dogwood Hospital. Exhausted, she grabbed a Cajun Filet Biscuit from the Bojangles' drive-through and headed for Tracy's farm.

Like many towns in the area, Dogwood had experienced a burst of growth in the past decade due to its proximity to the Research Triangle Park, where many large pharmaceutical and other high-tech companies were located. Modern neighborhoods gradually gave way to rolling country roads that hadn't changed in generations.

She drove down one of these country roads, past the rusted-out shell of a barn, a cornfield, and several miles of open farmland. Merry rolled down her window and breathed in the fresh air. She loved to drive through the country, see the horses and cows, smell the wheat and fresh earth. Actually rolling up her sleeves and getting dirty didn't sound as appealing, but if it would help the rescue, she'd take one for the team.

Tracy's farm was at the end of the street, a modest two-story, brick-front ranch house. Tracy had texted her a few minutes ago to say she was running late, so Merry pulled past the house and parked by the barn to finish her chicken biscuit. It melted in her mouth in buttery perfection. She washed it down with sweet tea and a sigh of contentment.

Behind the barn, two horses grazed in a lush green field, while a third lounged nearby beneath a shade tree. Merry's knowledge of horses was pretty much confined to the pages of *Black Beauty* (which had earned her a childhood nickname of Merrylegs), but these were obviously well cared for and absolutely gorgeous. Their brown coats glistened in the sun over sleek, well-muscled haunches.

She leaned back in her seat and settled in to watch them. The larger horse, a male, swooshed his tail to and fro, fly-swatting for himself and the female beside him. Equine chivalry. Aww.

A few minutes later, a black Ford F-350 pickup truck pulled into the driveway with a roar of its diesel engine and parked next to Merry's CR-V. She looked up, impressed. That was a badass truck for a chick.

She stepped out of her SUV, making sure she wasn't wearing any crumbs on her scrubs, and rounded the rear bumper just as the driver's door opened on the truck.

She saw the cowboy boots first, brown-stitched leather at least a man's size twelve. Her gaze traveled up a pair of jeans filled out by very muscular, very masculine legs. The man wearing them swung out of the cab and tipped his cowboy hat at her.

Well, well. It was her would-be hero from Dr. Johnson's office. What in the world was he doing here?

She'd never been a big fan of cowboys, but this guy was seriously sexy. His dark hair was mostly hidden by the hat, which shadowed his face, hiding the exact shade of the brown eyes currently locked on hers. He wore a crisp, blue T-shirt tucked into his jeans, filled to perfection by strong, muscled man.

His face was rugged, a bit too rough to grace the cover of a catalog for western wear, but good God, he was gorgeous. And clearly not Tracy Jameson.

"Merry Atwater?" His voice matched his image perfectly, deep and smooth.

"That's me. And you are?"

He extended a hand. "T. J. Jameson. Thanks for driving all the way out here. I figured you'd like to see the place before you made up your mind."

She took his hand and shook. "Uh, where's Tracy?"

His lips curved in amusement. "Tracy Allan Jameson III, in the flesh. My granddaddy was Tracy, Dad calls himself Trace, I go by T.J."

She almost swallowed her tongue. "You're Tracy."

"Yes, ma'am, but please call me T.J."

Merry sucked in a breath. So Tracy Jameson was a guy. And not just any guy, but a strappingly handsome cowboy oozing testosterone from every pore.

Summer camp had just gotten much hotter, in a completely new way.

## *Fall in Love with Forever Romance*

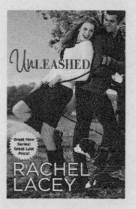

### UNLEASHED
### by Rachel Lacey

Cara has one rule: Don't get attached. It's served her well with the dogs she's fostered and the children she's nannied. But one smile from her sexy neighbor has her thinking some rules are made to be broken. Fans of Jill Shalvis will fall in love with this sassy, sexy debut!

### MADE FOR YOU
### by Lauren Layne

She's met her match... she just doesn't know it yet. Fans of Jennifer Probst and Rachel Van Dyken will fall head over heels for the second book in the Best Mistake series.

## Fall in Love with Forever Romance

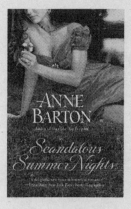

**SCANDALOUS SUMMER NIGHTS**
**by Anne Barton**

Fans of Tessa Dare, Julia Quinn, and Sarah MacLean will love this charming and wickedly witty new book in the Honeycote series about the passion—and peril—of falling in love with your brother's best friend.

**HE'S NO PRINCE CHARMING**
**by Elle Daniels**

A delightful retelling of the classic tale of *Beauty and the Beast* with a wonderful, sensual, and playful twist that fans of Elizabeth Hoyt won't want to miss!

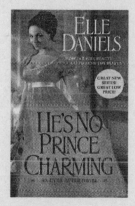

## *Fall in Love with Forever Romance*

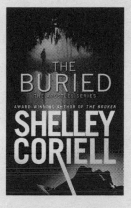

### THE BURIED
### by Shelley Coriell

"It's cold. And dark. I can't breathe."

Grace and "Hatch" thought they'd buried the past, but a killer on a grisly crime spree is about to unearth their deepest fears. Don't miss the next gripping thriller in the Apostles series.

### SHOOTING SCARS
### by Karina Halle

Ellie Watt has been kidnapped by her thuggish ex-boyfriend, leaving her current lover, Camden McQueen, to save the day. And there's nothing he won't do to rescue Ellie from this criminal and his entourage of killers in this fast-paced, sexy *USA Today* bestseller!

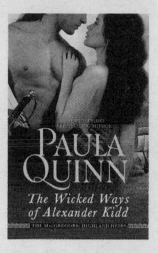

## THE WICKED WAYS OF ALEXANDER KIDD
### by Paula Quinn

The newest sinfully sexy Scottish romance in *New York Times* bestselling author Paula Quinn's Highland Heirs series, about the niece of a Highland chief who stows away on a pirate ship, desperate for adventure, and the pirate captain whose wicked ways inflame an irresistible desire...